Ian H. James was born in 1948 in the town of Cheshunt in Hertfordshire, England. He met and married Béatrice, a French student spending a year in England as an *au pair*. They settled down to married life in Shrewsbury and had two daughters, Chloé and Lucie. Ian became a teacher of science and mathematics at several schools in Shropshire before retiring and moving to France where he now resides.

Ian H. James

DESTINY

AUSTIN MACAULEY PUBLISHERS™

LONDON • CAMBRIDGE • NEW YORK • SHARJAH

A CIP catalogue record for this title is available from the British Library.

ISBN 9781528984232 (Paperback)
ISBN 9781528984249 (ePub e-book)

www.austinmacauley.com

First Published (2020)
Austin Macauley Publishers Ltd
25 Canada Square
Canary Wharf
London
E14 5LQ

The paranormal encounters mentioned in this book are those experienced by the author during his younger years.

Despite Man's many failings, it is his acts of selfless sacrifice that put him amongst the realm of the gods.

Chapter 1

Stanton Moor—the sign pointed the way. Though I'd walked this track many times before, tonight—this Halloween night—it felt different. The sky was mesmerising, high above the town. The stars in all their magnificence, together with a faint rising moon, gave sufficient light for me to make my way along the same path that I had walked but merely two days ago. Then, it had been light; then, it hadn't been a special night; then, I hadn't been afraid. I felt the yielding moorland grass give beneath my feet. Soft like a sponge, it sprang back as I walked on as though I had never been there. On both sides of the path, bracken, heather and moss—easy to be lost in if one was to miss the path.

I paused and inhaled the crisp air. Here, amongst the ragged and mystic peaks of Derbyshire, I could absorb the splendour of the Universe. No soul, no person, no being was with me tonight; I was alone. I held out my arms as though I could embrace the cosmos before me. I encapsulated those stars and galaxies that had eluded man for so long. Closing my eyes, I could hear the chant of the spirits of the moorland calling, beckoning—enticing me to dance and sway with them in the ripples of the breeze; momentarily, then the breeze had gone.

A sound from the bracken! A rabbit darted along the path and then into some gorse. I moved on, but my heart and my senses told me to turn around. I knew this track and I knew where it ended, but the darkness pulled at my imagination and told me to go onwards. Within the next gust of wind, the sprites of the undergrowth called to me again, in harmony. Their callings were louder now as if they were nearer than before. Wisps of mist blew across the moorland and covered the moon…but the light had not diminished. Then I saw it! By the woodland, within those few trees that survived this harsh land, I saw the unmistakeable sign of light. Not natural light, but light created by man. Sporadic and idiosyncratic shadows cast their forms onto those trunks and branches. I froze.

"Go! Go now!"

But the voice in my head was overruled by my instinctive curiosity. I knew that I should go. I knew that below, where the luminescent lights of the town shone, lay safety. But here…here lay the excitement, the enigmatic and the unknown. Within the copse ahead was the stone circle. I had been to it before and run my hands around those weathered forms of granite in my search for the unknown, the unexplained and the supernatural. Here, over the millennia, warlocks and druids had chanted…and sacrificed; I knew why. Within this bounteous display of nature, the human mind searched for answers, firmly believing that forces beyond their understanding were controlling their fortunes…or their fates. It was to these forces that Man turned for an understanding of this great beyond.

The copse was now no more than 50 metres away and, crouching and walking stealthily, I crept nearer.

As I espied the moving figures, I crawled through the undergrowth and, with pounding heart, slithered like a serpent within the boundaries of the coven. This was no druid gathering; these were witches and sorcerers—and on the altar, the human sacrifice! The chanting grew in crescendo as I looked on, transfixed by the scene before me. Was it a coincidence? Was it a chance encounter? Was it the sentinels of this gathering? The High Priest glared at me. My eyes had reflected in the flickering lights, like a cat on the prowl. Pointing at me, he called out with a venomous cry, "Infiltrator!"

I leapt from my hiding place and raced from the throng; raced like I had never raced before; raced for my life. "Infiltrator!"

I heard the cry again as footfalls followed closely behind me. The moon had returned and I made an easy silhouette for the predators chasing me. Did they know the path as well as I? I stumbled but kept my balance as I sped on the moorland path. Behind me, I could hear the laboured panting of those pursuing their goal. But laboured or not, they were after their prey and not conceding. Suddenly, the ghostly path disappeared from view as more mist swirled around the moor and enveloped the moon. My chance! I hurdled from the path, dived into the heather and lay panting in the undergrowth. My pursuers ran on but stumbled themselves in the darkness. Nearby, I heard the cry of pain as the thud of a body fell onto the bracken. An anguished shout beckoned to the others, as I lay breathless and frightened. Torches scoured the area as they searched for their comrade—and their victim. But camouflaged amongst the moss and heather, I was invisible to any searchlight as my attackers slowly made their way back to complete their ceremony. A serenity took over me as I heard the chanting continue in the distance and I knew I was safe. But laying, gazing up at the multitude of pinpricks of light, staring into the infinite, a feeling of resolution pacified my thoughts. "That…that is my destiny," I heard myself say.

"Ten minutes to lift-off."

My heart was pounding like a drum as the memory faded. That one long night had directed me to this very moment. A night, an instant in my distant past that had set me on the course that was before me now. I tried to remain calm as we had done in all the rehearsals; but those were just make believe, they were not absolute. They did not pose a life-threatening situation. If anything went wrong, we got out, analysed and repeated the whole exercise again until we got it right. This time, there was no going back; this was the finality, the reason we had committed ourselves, our time, our resources and our lives. After all, I was not an astronaut; I was a scientist on a mission—a serious mission. My hands were sweating and the perspiration on my forehead, luckily, was removed by the cool current of air on my visor. At least I could sweat as much as I liked without obscuring my vision. Jamie beside me was an experienced astronaut. This was

10

his fifth trip and I was truly impressed with the way he remained calm. He was a very sociable and funny guy; always performing pranks and taking the edge off awkward situations, usually with a culmination of salacious comments.

"Five minutes to lift-off."

The intercom gave the announcement for the final countdown. I started to hyperventilate.

"Easy, Michael. Remember, deep breaths, slowly, slowly. Take your time—let your mind relax."

These were the words that Jamie had said to me when I had been practicing underwater exercises at the start of the programme. I had panicked and just wanted to swim to the surface as fast as possible. He held my arm, looked into my eyes and with the up and down motion of his free hand, had said these words through my headset. He knew how I was feeling; perhaps he, too, had felt like this during his first underwater exercise? Or was it just that he was a natural pioneer, an adventurer, a thrill seeker, prepared to put his life on the line just to see if he could do it? We were so very different. I could only see the consequences of the worst scenario, but Jamie got his high from the chance that that scenario would not happen, albeit that it still could. Not a risk taker in the normal sense of the word, but someone who, if the odds were stacked against them, believed in fortune, not fate.

Jamie and I had been introduced by the Operations Director at NASA after the selection of the crew had been made. Having presented my case to the committee, rather forcibly, a year before, the decision had been made to go. A combined mission but, for my part, one which I was not allowed to divulge. Jamie and the other members of the team were bound for *Proxima b*. They were unaware that I had been briefed on another mission, using the *Proxima b* venture as a means of concealing my reasons for being there. I had been introduced to all the team members as an exceptional astrophysicist with designated assignments that I had to perform on the approach to the planet rotating around its parent sun, *Proxima Centauri*. Secrecy was paramount as any notion of what my undertaking was really for and the project would have not been funded; even the President—especially the President—would have ensured that the task be terminated. Luckily, I had presented my case to men who truly believed in the beauty of the human mind; the belief that truth and goodness outweighed any of the negative sides of human nature and that mankind could not be allowed to self-destruct.

I had decided to contact NASA after watching another disturbing news flash:

'... *North Korea, supported by China, has detonated a neutron bomb in the Pacific Ocean. The blast was recorded as equivalent to one hundred times the power of the Hiroshima bomb and created a tsunami that hit the east coast of Japan. There are no reported casualties, but many offshore homes have been damaged by the tidal wave that hit the east coast. North Korea reported the news on state television this afternoon. The Japanese government ...'*

11

I was invited to Florida and after being given a comfortable hotel some distance away from the Kennedy Space Center, was taken by limousine to the offices of NASA. Most of the officials were sceptical and one or two aghast that I should have been invited at all with such a flimsy hypothesis. But, with a well-earned reputation behind me as an exceptional and innovative astrophysicist, I had managed to change several minds regarding my ideas. The persuading factor in the end was that it was better to try something, rather than nothing at all. But, in addition, the information and data that I could relay as I approached a black hole would be invaluable in reassessing our understanding of the mathematics involved with such an awesome, unknown object. I couldn't help, despite the eventual, almost unanimous, acceptance of the project, but remain suspicious of the American-German laser section leader, Karl Guttenberg. Throughout the entire meeting, he had been adamant that the project was a hopeless cause and had no foundation whatsoever. I had refrained from reminding him that his fellow countrymen—Hitler, Eichmann and Himmler—had resorted to astrology and the occult when deciding the fate of Germany and the whole human race many generations ago. It would have served no purpose, other than to antagonise a fellow scientist and one that I needed to keep on-board, to drag up old history. It may have well started racist arguments that we did not need at this, or any other, time.

After the meeting had concluded and the decision made to go ahead, Karl came up to me.

"Well, young man, you have won a decisive vote. But I for one—and I know several others who, though agreeing to your proposal—do not fully support you or your scatter-brained ideas. How could you, as a member of the scientific community, possibly suggest such an outrageous idea that we use the paranormal to change the course of history? It is absurd, as I told you and everyone else at the meeting, and if you had not had such an impressive qualification and reputation, I would have doubted your credibility as a scientist."

"Mr Guttenberg, I understand fully your scepticism but the personal experiences that I have encountered lead me to believe that there is a possibility that time travel can, and does, exist. As scientists, we are programmed to believe in facts and what we can replicate, time and again, under stringent, scientific conditions. But science can also be blind to those things it cannot explain—better to dismiss than to acknowledge the plausibility that something intangible can be part of the universe. It alters the very fabric of the physics and mathematics that we know and have used for countless generations.

"I trust, now that a vote has been taken and a decision made, that I can count on your full support and cooperation?"

"I will endeavour to assist as I have been trained to do, but I hold out very little hope."

"I also hold out very little hope, Mr Guttenberg, but hope is all we have."

"Sixty seconds."

Jamie and his co-pilot, Christian, sat flicking switches, looking at dials, checking lights and screens in the way they had been trained to do. I guess for them, being so involved with the controls, they had little time for the nerves that the rest of us felt. We all knew that there would be very little chance of returning to Earth—they were the pioneers of a new and exciting adventure: to try to colonise another planet around another star. All were true professionals and had said their goodbyes to families and friends the night before. Unlike them, though, I *knew* that I would not be returning; mine was a one-way trip with no return ticket—and I would not be colonising anything.

I had been briefed by NASA to talk in confidence to Jamie—who was in command of the entire mission—once we had left the solar system. I was to explain to him the purpose of my role in this journey. He was a trusted and reliable commander, with a wicked sense of humour. I had wanted to take him into my confidence earlier and nearly let slip on more than one occasion my real motive for being part of this venture. He was both a trained and skilled pilot and an engineer. He had a masters in aeronautical engineering from Harvard and had decided to approach the US Air Force after qualifying. His engineering skills were immediately apparent, but his wish to take to the sky left the commanders at the base under no illusions that they had a first-rate pilot and engineer.

I turned my head to the right. Jamie remained still. All flicking and tweaking seemed to have come to an end; he just kept glancing from one screen to the next, seemingly satisfied that he had completed all that was necessary for a successful launch. He turned his head to the left, looked at me and smiled. I realised that no longer was he just a fellow colleague and friend, he was the controller of our calling; our lives depended upon this one man. His skills, his knowledge, his very character would determine whether our lives would be short-lived and whether the destiny of Man would be doomed; perhaps forever.

I tried to smile back but I could tell that my facial expression demonstrated fear, not joy. He stretched up an arm and raised his thumb. "Easy, Michael. Remember, deep breaths; slowly, slowly. Take your time, let your mind relax."

As though he had rehearsed this phrase many times, he said the same words to me again as he had done during my first dive and followed it with: "It will be fine, Michael; trust me."

Then looking straight ahead, he said quietly but firmly: "Good to go, NASA, let's get this baby born!"

"Ten…nine…eight…seven…"

Unlike in the past, this time, plasma was being used as a rocket propellant. The old chemical fuels that had been used since the first rocket launches were now deemed too inefficient and incapable of getting us to the speeds necessary for such a journey as we faced. Several unmanned launches had been attempted using the new plasma engines. Of the five prototypes so far attempted, four had been successful, and only one, the first one, had ended in disaster. This represented an eighty per cent chance of success—and survival. Jamie had spent months talking to the engineers and designers and, I believe, had even made his own suggestions and modifications to the version that was now going to propel us to the stars—literally.

The plasma had been slowly generating the power required for lift-off several minutes before and the rocket was filled with a vibrant hum as the plasma now reached the critical level needed to force us from the Earth's gravity. I saw a hint of hesitation in Jamie's reaction as he reached for the switch to turn the electromagnetic field on and send the plasma soaring out of the base of the rocket.

"Six…five…four…three…"

Jamie now looked tense. I could see even Mr Joe Cool was sweating as I noticed glistening in his visor. His forehead appeared to be a mass of perspiration. Unlike me, Jamie had all the responsibility of the success of the launch resting on his shoulders. He had acted with bravado but I knew that he now was as nervous as the rest of us—perhaps more so with such an accountable role. I felt honoured to be captained by such a brave and charismatic man. Until this point, he had shown no fear whatever and I truly admired his ability to keep his exact feelings hidden from the rest of us. This was a man I could follow and trust; a man who would not yield even under such duress. His typical gung-ho approach to every situation was now at breaking point but he did not show it.

"Two…one…ignition."

Jamie flicked the electromagnets into their maximum position. The gentle hum became a roar as the plasma exuded from the base of the rocket. Despite being enclosed in a spacesuit designed to withstand the extremes of space, the noise was deafening. Nothing seemed to be happening apart from the intense roar of the plasma and a rocket that was vibrating as though every nut, bolt and frame would be shaken from their holdings. The forces acting on us as the rocket began to leave the safety of Earth were not too apparent at first, but then as we were propelled faster, the unpleasant feeling of defying the laws of gravity came into play. The missile, our missile, began to accelerate at an alarming rate as the planet beneath us became more distant. The aspirations, dreams and hopes of mankind were encapsulated in this vessel that was sending us ever faster towards our goal, towards the stars, towards our destiny, but those forces that we were overcoming—that held on to us as they had always done, keeping us prisoners in our own domain—were being challenged at a cost. The pressure was becoming unbearable. I tried to look at Jamie but my head would not turn; it was forced into the headrest behind me.

"You're looking good, Proxima."

I could just make out movement from Jamie before I passed out.

Chapter 2

I awoke and could sense the sun shining down. The autumnal afternoon displayed the gold and orange over the landscape that had captivated so many artists of the past. Movement seemed easy and I lifted my head to take in the view before me. I was resting by a large oak tree, the frontier that separated the open scene before me and the woodland behind. The leaves of all the trees in that wood played out in harmony to the music of the wind but I felt no breeze.

"Ah! There you are!"

Before me was an old man, staff in his hand and cloak around his shoulders. How he had arrived unseen was a mystery. His face had the markings of a man well into the twilight of his life but his gait and mannerism displayed a person of a younger demeanour.

"You were expecting me?" I asked.

"Why yes! You sent for me but I wasn't sure where to find you. The tree! The tree! The old oak! Of course! And so, I made haste; you couldn't be anywhere else!"

"But…but I never sent for you; I don't even know who you are…"

"You do not know me? Yet you have searched for me for so long; it is I, the one whom you become."

"Become?"

"Yes, become. Have you not searched for me since time immemorial?"

"Have I?"

"Yes indeed, my friend…though why is something only you can discover. Find me or you will be forever lost."

A loud crack distracted me and I turned to see that a branch of the oak tree had fallen but a short distance away.

"Look, I am at a bit of a loss…"

But the old man had disappeared. The fields before me glistened as before, but there was no sign…no evidence that anyone had stood before me a few seconds ago.

What! Where am I? I thought. *Where is this place?*

Yet try as I might, nothing made sense. I searched for my name, my meaning—myself, but I could recall nothing. I felt somewhat perturbed but at the same time, I also felt enervated. Lying back down, my mind began to race. Was this a dream? Was I living in a fantasy? I stretched my arm forward. If this was a dream, then another scene would take over and send me spiralling into an inexplicable situation where I would be the central actor and intangible events would seek out my innermost inhibitions, whilst I gazed on. Yet, my arm stayed stretched out in front of me. It did not waver; it remained where I had set it and the fields still glistened in the sun.

First things first! I thought. *Take this slowly, logically. What is my name?*

I had no idea. I also had no idea where I was or even where I came from. Some part of me did not seem to care, but another part was curious. I felt no hunger, no pain. But then I felt no joy either, just a wish to wander.

Below the fields in the distance, I could see a walled-up town. Despite this feeling of lethargy, I forced myself up and started the gentle descent towards this place. I was sorely tempted to turn towards the corn-filled meadows to my right. I wanted to run through the fields and feel the swish of the corn as I raced onwards but I felt obligated to continue towards the town. Suddenly, I stopped. I turned around and could see the oak tree that I had left. This was not a dream! If this was a dream, then there would be no place that I had left and could return to. Another episode would be taking place, transporting me into an additional realm of fantasy that I would be powerless to control. So, if this was real, who was that old man? But was he real or had I imagined him from the start? Lost in a myriad of thoughts as I continued forwards with no conception of time, I found myself outside the town gates. The only entrance into this place was through this archway. Two large solid wooden doors stood open behind two armed sentries. One guard had dark eyes and flowing auburn hair whilst the other had a short-bobbed cut and blue eyes, like mine.

Eyes like mine—blue! How did I know that! My name! What's my name?

"HALT!"

The dark-eyed guard lowered his fauchard into a threatening position.

"What's your business here?"

I did not know my business, not even why I felt so desperate to enter those gates.

"Speak up! What is your business?"

"A peddler, my good man. I seek only to bargain within these walls with yonder good townsfolk."

"I've not seen you before in these parts."

"I come not from this region. Three days I have been travelling on foot and am weary. I wish only to venture into this town, seek shelter, food and lodging and make an honest living as my skills permit."

"What are your skills?" said the guard, lowering his weapon.

"Blacksmith by trade."

"Blacksmith, hmm?" said the bobbed-cut guard.

"Yes…and a bit of carpentry too."

"Why you peddling then?"

"Luck ran out. Squire wanted the cottage and bade me leave. 'Already had one blacksmith', he said, 'and didn't see the need for two—couldn't afford it', he said. I tell you this; he could have afforded to keep me on and twenty more besides. Mean old screw."

"Hmm, blacksmiths needed here—and carpenters. Report in at t' gatehouse just inside. Methinks they'll be looking for such as you."

The guards raised their weapons and we walked through the arched gate, the peddler pulling a small cart behind him. I could not believe my luck—a peddler arriving exactly as I approached the gate. As relieved as I was, one thing bothered me though—they did not broach me. Probably thought that we were together.

As we walked through the arch, we became aware of the town we had entered. People were dressed mainly in clothes that served only to maintain their modesty and keep them warm. Fashion was not apparent and their attire was of a similar colour, grey and brown. I did notice one woman who seemed to be more elegant than those around her. She wore a flowing cloak of blue and moved with an air of confidence, unlike the shuffling of the other townsfolk. Her face was not that of a beauty, but her smile gave her an attractive demeanour. She walked with purpose, but not in a manly way, only as one who needed to keep to a rendezvous without seeming too anxious.

The buildings were made mostly of plaster and stone with timber frames to keep everything in place. Some seemed to have dried mud exteriors in place of the plaster. A few of the dwellings were bowed, probably brought on by the winds and rains of winters past. Dried mud and animal excrement were everywhere on the ground, though less obvious in the streets where cobblestones had not been laid. A beggar approached us and held out his palm, mumbling a few incoherent words to the peddler, but the peddler continued on without acknowledging the man's plea. Ahead of us, I could see a rectangular-shaped building with a roof resting upon ten sturdy oak beams, though I couldn't, from this distance, make out the layout of the interior. It appeared to be some kind of market hall and inside, I thought I could see stall holders in the process of going about their business.

"Oi, turn left here. That's it."

Dark eyes was behind us, still with his foreboding weapon. We walked into a wooden shack. There was little in the way of comfort—a wooden bench, an old oak table, a few spears resting by a fireplace, with logs ready for the cold of winter.

"Ye gods! What a stink!" the peddler whispered.

Beside him was an open window where I could see another soldier outside, urinating against the granite wall, his spear leaning beside him. The wind was blowing into the room judging by the sackcloth curtain billowing towards us, but I felt no breeze. A ruffled soldier sat at the table, a tankard by his side. His form was difficult to decipher as he was stooped over the table in a manner suggesting that he was reading or engaged in some intimate task. "Captain!"

The man looked up. I could see from the scars on his face that he had seen some activity on the battlefield. I guessed that he was unaware of his appearance and looking at his tousled face, was unlikely to have cared anyway. He was probably somewhere in the region of forty years old but could easily have passed for seventy. Almost, as though it were painful, he slowly rose, scraping the wooden chair behind him. He was taller than I had imagined and had a torso that suggested he was not a man easily beaten in combat. He gazed out of the small window, letting the sackcloth gently brush his face, then slowly walked to the front of the oak table and equally slowly, sat on the edge. The table creaked under his weight. With no courtesy to the subordinate before him, he gave a one-syllable reply: "What?"

"This man claims to be a peddler looking to pursue his trade in our town."

"So, what's that to do with me; why bring him here?"

"He says he has skill as a blacksmith, Captain."

"Oh? That right, then?" he said, turning to the peddler.

"Yes, that's right and a bit of carpentry too, just like I told this soldier."

"Maybe he's a spy, sir. Just says that he's selling so that he can get into town and snoop around. You know, seek out our defences and military strength?"

"He might also be telling the truth. If that is the case, he would be of much use here. We have need of armoury and weapons. This roof is leaking, to say the least, and the need to improve our defences is of paramount importance in view of the recent turn of events around Avignon."

Avignon? I had a recollection of such a name. But the details were beyond me. Why could I not remember my name?

The captain turned his gaze to the peddler.

"Why are you really here, then? Is it as this soldier has said?"

"Well, if it was, I'm hardly likely to say, 'Why, yes, I'm a spy.' Am I? In truth, I came to make a living in whatever way I could. Peddling seemed to be the easiest option."

"What's in your sack on that cart of yours?"

"Pots and pans, some forks, knives and the tools of my trade."

The captain stood up and walked slowly outside the shack. He tipped the sack upside down into the peddler's cart and the contents spilled out. He took one of the pans, scratched it with his fingernail and then hit it against the side of the cart. It rang with a dull thud and appeared to be almost as sturdy as the cart itself.

"You make this?" he said, turning towards the peddler.

"I did. Everything in that sack I made, except for the tools; they were what I used to make them with."

"These are good, solid and not unattractive. This axe—you made this?"

"Yes, that too."

"Needs carpentry skill as well as Smithying," said the captain, as he ran his hand around the axe's handle. "If you made these, and I'll need proof, then there could be work for you here."

"That's what I seek, sir. Payment will be included?"

"First, I need proof. Tonight, you can have shelter and food. Tomorrow, my man here will take you to the forge and you can make one spear; that needs carpentry as well as Smithying. If that looks good, I will then need a well-balanced sword—one that can reach my enemy before he can reach me and can slice bread without tearing at the loaf."

"Sounds reasonable, sir…and payment?"

"Payment is my patience. Prove yourself, and then we may discuss details."

The captain then turned to go back into the gatehouse.

"Take him to the guardhouse. Give him food, water and bedding. When dawn strikes, take him to the smithy. Give him what he needs for his work, and then bring him back here. I want to see for myself what this 'peddler' is capable of."

We walked out together. The sun was waning fast and shadows had taken hold of the town. *Dark eyes* no longer held his weapon in a threatening manner but led us through narrow, cobbled streets where houses were so close that neighbours could almost reach out and shake hands. I felt a bit uncomfortable; something did not seem quite right.

"But what about me? He must think I'm your apprentice or something; never asked me a single question."

The peddler did not answer.

Chapter 3

Slowly, the landscape became darker, even though the sky was cloudless. Then, a distant hum and crackle, with a feeling as though static were everywhere. I looked up and there, coming menacingly towards me was an object so large, so totally dark and devoid of form, so fearsome, that I trembled where I stood. The force of the wind was barely perceptible at first, but then grew in strength until the earth was being wrenched from beneath my feet. I held onto the trunk of the oak tree beside me, but the force that preyed on me was gaining in ferocity. My feet left the ground; that beautiful safety of Earth was no longer my footstool. I was being dragged inexorably towards that void ahead by a force unseen. My face was being slapped and beaten by the branches of the oak tree that I held onto. I was powerless and I screamed.

"Michael, wake up! Wake up!"

The voice in my head would not go.

"Michael! Michael! WAKE UP!"

"All is looking good, Proxima. Perfect lift-off. You are now in orbit."

I opened my eyes. Where was I? Proxima? Oh, yes! Then I remembered.

"Michael! Are you alright?"

It was Jamie.

"Jamie, Jamie...thank God, it's you. That was the second time that I have had this nightmare."

"Tell me about it later. We have got to dock up with the main ship and she is coming into view now.

"Mission Control, approaching mothership. Payload ready for docking. Permission to dock."

"Go ahead, Proxima."

Through the transparent screen, I could see the mother ship ahead. She glistened in the sunlight like a dazzling star. She only appeared as a very bright, shiny, saucer-shaped piece of metal. I guessed we were about twenty kilometres away.

"How far to the main ship, Jamie?"

"Two hundred kilometres."

"Two hundred kilometres! But, she's huge then?"

"Oh, yes. She's a big bird. Four hundred metres wide, nine hundred metres long and two hundred and fifty metres high."

"Wow! How did you get a thing that size up here?"

"She was built in stages. Three hundred and thirty-five launches give or take a few, over the past fourteen years. Many of the crew have been on her now for over three years. As to be expected, lots of teething problems, but they all seem to have been sorted now."

I looked below and could see the Earth turning slowly around, or was it us speeding above the atmosphere? Within less than a minute, we had approached her outer shell. I looked up and could just make out Orion as the constellation disappeared beneath her overhanging upper deck. This was a superb piece of engineering, but its scale just left me in awe. I guessed Jamie must have read my thoughts as he briefly glanced in my direction.

"A beauty, isn't she!"

"Magnificent. Absolutely magnificent!"

"Approaching docking port, Mission Control."

We flew quite rapidly towards the large opening on the main ship.

"Applying retro-jets."

It was almost like docking a boat, we approached at a speed that looked to be much too fast and then rapidly slowed down to what appeared to be almost a standstill. Twenty large metal clamps extended from the back of the main ship and made a skeletal tunnel. Jamie allowed our ship to glide evenly between these locking devices and held our rocket steady as the clamps closed around the frame. I felt a slight judder as the first clamp took hold and then the others rapidly followed, giving metallic clunks as they did so.

"Docking complete, Mission Control."

"Good, Proxima. You are free to enter the mother ship."

"Will everyone unfasten their safety belts and make their way to the grappling holds at the end of the rows?"

The crew all unfastened their safety harnesses and, following Jamie's instructions, floated towards the ends of the rows, keeping themselves secure by the grappling holds. They awaited Jamie's arrival. Jamie pressed a button by the airlock door and waited for a response.

"Captain James Fraser requesting permission to come aboard, Proxima."

"Please await pressurisation."

There was a faint hissing and clunking of locks.

"Airlock safety catch released. You are free to enter. Welcome aboard, Captain."

With that, the door slid to one side and we all floated along a small tunnel using the holds to project us towards the main vessel. At the other end, another door remained closed. Jamie pressed the large red button and this door slid open as effortlessly as the one from which we had just passed through. After a few handshakes, lots of smiles and hugs, the airlock door slid closed and with a clunk, we were now secure in the main ship.

I looked around and was surprised at how normal everything appeared to be inside. As we approached her, she had seemed massive but inside, it was just like large, normal rooms. Again, Jamie sensed my reaction.

"Impressed or disappointed, Michael?"

"I don't know what to make of it, Jamie. Outside, it looked like we were about to enter inside the gizzards of some monster; but inside—well, it's just like normal."

"Over two thousand different rooms, though. That normal?"

"Two thousand! Yup, that's big."

"Well, when you think about it, we are not coming back, are we?"

"So, you have a room for every contingency, then!"

"Just about, I guess. We are in the process of populating another world—well, at least another planet. So, we have, hopefully, everything that will set us off to a promising start. Technicians, doctors, dentists, nurses, botanists, mechanics, farmers…"

"Jamie, I don't need a blow-by-blow account; how many in total are currently on board?"

"Fifteen hundred, give or take a few."

"Fifteen hundred!"

"Yeah well, as I said, 'give or take a few'. Michael, I need to have a good, long talk with you, but right now, I have to get this beastie star bound. If you go with Anna here, she'll take you and the others to your quarters. Ask her nicely and she may even give you a tour; though that could take several days."

"OK, Jamie. I need to have a long talk with you as well."

"Yeah, I know, that's what I wanted to talk to you about."

"See you in a bit, then?"

"Yeah, see you in a bit, as you Brits say."

It was Anna's turn: "OK, first, before I show you to your rooms, we ought to have a quick briefing. Please follow me to the lower-bay conference room."

We all floated, following Anna as she moved swiftly through a few corridors before arriving at a room marked 'Conference Room 4'. We followed her into a large, oval-shaped room with tiered seats that resembled the lecture theatres that I had attended as a student.

"Please, rest against the walls and use the harnesses beside you to stop you floating aimlessly around.

"Now, on the main screen, you will see a plan of the ship. It will take you several weeks to familiarise yourself with most of the locations, but as we will be together on-board for the next four years, I'm sure you will be fully conversant with her before we get to our destination!

"Captain Fraser will be taking us out of the Earth's orbit at twenty hundred hours. Our initial destination will be the moon and then a return to Earth as we project ourselves to our main goal: warp-drive factor zero-point-five. We then shall use the gas giants and hope to increase our speed even further. As explained in your Earth briefing yesterday, because of the complexity and hazardous nature of leaving the solar system, you will all reside in the dormitory and remain insentient until it is safe to return to normal wake-mode."

I already knew what was required, having studied the depths of space for several years. The idea of reaching for the stars had always been a myth, one of which so many stories had been told. This was the first time that that myth was going to be put to the test. As a theoretician, I knew that mathematically, the entire universe was achievable; as an engineer, I knew nothing. This was where Jamie and his skills came into their own. My specialities, and ones over which I was passionate, were black holes and time. It was that theoretical knowledge and my own personal experiences that had set me on this quest, one where there would be no turning back.

Luckily, for me, I had no immediate family. Both my parents were dead and with a couple of failed relationships behind me, I had no ties to keep me on the planet that had been my birthplace. Yes, I still had siblings, but with them being so involved with their own families, I was merely a name, a relation, for whom a loss would have been no more than a sad affair. In fact, I guess I was the ideal candidate for such a mission. Too many other scientists—seriously good scientists—had emotional ties that would have made it nigh impossible for them to leave our dear Earth and the lives that they were leading.

I would have liked to have had a partner, someone to share my passions with, but my own career and interests, together with the lack of certainty of having a place to really call *home*, had been the main stumbling block in a permanent, secure and loving rapport. However, despite all this, I still longed to have a special someone to be with, someone to hold hands with, someone to share my desires with, someone to whisper to at night, someone with whom I could share both my joys and those times when I wanted to weep, someone to hold when the world became a burden. How I longed just to gaze into my lover's eyes as sleep took us to another dimension of life, and I knew I was a lonely man.

"OK, please synchronise all time-pieces. It is now eleven hundred hours. I will show you to your rooms. As you have no luggage, you will need no time to unpack! I suggest that you all try to rest until thirteen hundred hours and you will be called into the canteen for your first 'weightless' lunch and a chance to meet with some of the other colonists who have already arrived. Every room has a speaker and microphone, so you will be able to contact the main control room, as they will you. Please wear the safety harnesses whenever you are likely to rest; we don't want you to go aimlessly floating around!

"Right! All to your rooms; follow me and don't forget to use the grappling holds!"

Anna directed us through a series of further corridors until we came to what, apparently, was the cabin section. Each person was given a room, though nine couples shared. I noticed, for the first time, that there was a family with us—a couple with their two small children, a boy and girl. Both were no older than ten and then I realised that in order to populate a planet, one needed not only adults, astronauts, engineers and technicians, etc, one also needed everyday folk, like this family here.

I entered my room and was surprised how much space there was inside. Unlike a conventional house on Earth, every item needed was in this one room: a bed, a lounge area with television, a small kitchen and the necessary shower and toilet. Within the bedding area, there was a small wardrobe. I opened the wardrobe and inside were items of personal clothing, such as undergarments, some smarter clothes, such that one would wear for an evening out, toiletry items and bedding. Nothing else was needed and it appeared that the logistics team at NASA had planned for every eventuality. I was far too excited to sleep, I just wanted to roam and explore, but even more, I wanted to be up front with Jamie and watch our journey to the moon. However, as we were not due to leave for another nine hours, I endeavoured to calm down and relax on the bed. Without realising just how tiring an exciting journey like this could be, I lost consciousness.

Chapter 4

The peddler and I were shown into a large room, which appeared to be both a dining room and dormitory. The guard showed us a space on the floor with straw for bedding. The peddler settled himself down and was soon snoring. I sat down in a small corner, but I didn't feel in the least tired. I was neither hungry, tired, happy, sad nor—capable it seemed, of any emotion or sensation other than curiosity. I had questions and I needed answers, not the least being, 'where was I…and who was I'?

The desire to wander became too great and I decided that I needed to explore. The guard on duty was steadily falling asleep and his other two comrades were busily occupied in drinking and playing some game on a barrel that required a lot of laughing and raucous behaviour. I got up carefully and quietly as the guard dropped his head, started snoring and slowly made my way outside. There was a smell of cooking in the air and the sky was dark. Not as dark as I had known somewhere in my past, but dark enough to easily lose oneself.

As I left the guardhouse, I could just make out the outlines of the houses against the starlit sky. I wandered towards some buildings where I could see flickering light, but suddenly felt an overwhelming urge to turn to my right. In the darkness, I could sense the absence of buildings. The hoot of an owl and the darting of a small bat were suddenly apparent, despite the absence of light. There was a large tree in the middle of this space and I guessed that I was standing in the town's main square. I became aware of a gradual light permeating in a ghostly form through the buildings some way across the square and I noticed the rising of the moon behind a steeple in the distance to my left. The tree formed a silhouette and its shadow spread across the open expanse. On the ground, I could make out fallen leaves, suggesting the impending seasonal change that was in the air. I heard a creaking and looked up. A shutter had been opened and by the flickering candlelight within the room, I could see a form urinating onto the street below. A satisfied grunt and the shutter swung to and the candlelight was gone.

I still felt the urge to move on and crossed the square. As I did so, a macabre sight came into view in that ashen light—a gallows. Its occupant swung with a slight groaning of the wood as the breeze blew the corpse like it was a pendulum, keeping time to the rhythm of the wind. The agony of that distorted face, with the tongue lopped, made me shudder. How barbaric. I thought I heard voices calling or was it the wind blowing through the streets.

The moon had risen enough and gave sufficient light so that I could easily see along the very narrow streets, cobbled and uneven. But though the ground was rough, I felt no discomfort from the terrain. After some time and having turned yet again into another narrow passageway, I knew that I was now lost, or at least, would not be able to retrace my steps to the guardhouse. But that was of little consequence to me; more important was to find out exactly who and where I was. Was there anyone who could help me somewhere in this dark, forbidding town? Without any fatigue whatever, I meandered on.

As dawn struck, the town started to come into life. I could smell the baking of fresh bread and soon found my way to a small building with a glowing oven inside. I could see the baker at his trade as the first batch of loaves were removed from the oven and placed on some trays to cool. Apprehensively, I braced myself for my first human contact. Aside from the peddler and soldiers, I had had no communication with any other person and that contact had left me uneasy. Was I now a wanted criminal? Was there a price on my head for leaving the guardhouse? Would I face the same fate as that human pendulum in the square? Though I felt the urge to turn away and keep myself concealed, I knew that I had a purpose and that purpose would not be fulfilled without help; and that help was perhaps here before me now.

"Excuse me, sir."

The decision had been made and I had made myself known. There was no going back now. The baker continued with his work and loaded into the oven fresh dough for the next batch of loaves. He obviously had not heard me from the noise of the wood crackling in the oven. He stacked another few small logs into the back of the oven and turned to face me. He walked towards me without showing any concern or surprise at this stranger in his midst.

"I'm sorry to disturb you, I can see you are busy, but I am a stranger here and totally lost."

But the baker not only ignored me—he walked through me!

"WHAT!"

I stood trembling for a few seconds, then an awful truth dawned upon me— I was dead! Within a matter of several seconds, my mind raced uncontrollably. Rooted to the spot, I reflected upon everything that had happened in the past twelve hours or so. It now started to make sense why the guards did not question me; they could not see me—a phantom. Yet I was so truly alive, but without a physical form! Or perhaps I did have a physical form that was transparent. The peddler! He had ignored every comment that I had made and the captain did not ask *me* why I was there; he could not see me either. I remembered that I had felt no breeze even though the wind had been blowing into that gatehouse and by the oak tree as the leaves had rustled in the wind. The oak tree! Where I awoke; where I had become aware! But the old man! Had there been an old man? Had it been just a hallucination, a figment of my imagination? But he had spoken to me…well, if he had been real, that is. What had he said…'Ah, there you are'? He had been expecting me to be there? Dead! Would I awake to find this all a dream…? I hoped so. But if this was a dream, it was none like I'd ever had before. Scenes, actions, happenings all seemed to be following in a sequential order…like they did in life…not like they did in dreams…! So, there were two options: either this was a dream—a very bad dream, or it was real and I was truly beyond mortal form and into the next dimension of life…or death! So, with the two options, I had two choices: wake up…eventually, or seek out the only person who knew of my existence…if he did?

I HAD TO find him. I HAD TO. But I was now presented with the dilemma of who to ask; no one could see me! As I started to recover from the shock of my death, I also began to realise something else, something so fundamental it had escaped my attention in those past few hectic moments…I was conscious! I had awareness; I had the ability to think, reason, sense. I had intelligence. I then became quite euphoric; I had emotion! As I reflected upon this traumatic situation, in which I was the principle, nay, the ONLY actor, I now had to resolve my future. There could be no doubt at all that I needed to find the old man. He was the only person that was able to know that I existed at all. He was my only salvation.

I decided that I had to search each and every household. I did not need food, shelter or even sleep. I could simply search slowly until I found what I was after. Then another thought occurred to me—walking. I remembered that I had not felt the difficulty of the terrain, despite it being uneven and rough. I looked down; sure, there were my legs, but were they needed? If I really had no physical form, then I had no legs and yet I had moved here. Perhaps I had moved here by thought, not by movement? I turned to my right and decided that I would watch myself move as I journeyed to the far end of this narrow street. Yes, the legs moved as they should, and yes, the end of the street was nearer than before. But surely, they were not needed? I continued in this fashion until I reached the end of the lane. At the junction, I found myself once again in the main square. I could see the tree in the middle and everywhere around; people were bustling to and fro. I saw a crow on the ground pecking at some morsels of food, or was it sinews; the gallows were nearby and scavengers were pecking and clawing at the corpse. Disturbed, the crow flapped its wings and flew up into the tree. As it did so, my thoughts were of that crow. It flew. If I was truly not of this world and had no physical form, could I not also fly like that bird? I stood rigidly by the opening to the square, stared at the tree and willed myself to join that crow; willed myself to the treetop; willed myself to fly. I rose as though being blown in the breeze and, like those reptiles of the air; I arrived at the treetop. I could fly!

Chapter 5

I hovered on the branch. As with the realisation that I was now immortal, the act of being able to fly filled me again with euphoria; I was ecstatic!

I looked down at the ground and leapt from the tree. Diving down, I imagined a swoop and, lo and behold, I swooped! The sensation was amazing. I soared up to the top of the tree and darted down again. Time meant nothing to me…time? What was this? What was time? What *was* time? One thing was for sure, I would no longer have to carry my body, or whatever it was, around as I had done previously. I could flit from one place to another in a fraction of…time? Is this what time was, how long it took to move from one place to another? Why, of course; that was how I could determine when something was happening, whether, or when, it would end. But how could I measure time? What was the importance of time? I felt somehow that that was not significant right now. I just had to be content that I could feel if something was quicker or slower. That was all I needed to know…for the moment. And contentment was something I really felt right now.

I imagined the town from up above and instantly I was above the rooftops gazing down. I wanted to swoop again; it had been such a good sensation. I saw a narrow street ahead and forcing my mind to swoop, I fell to the earth as a bird in flight, but in a balanced, gliding fashion. People were coming towards me from every angle. Actually, no—that was wrong; it was me; I was the one coming towards the people. Nobody blinked, budged, ducked or changed their course of direction as I darted through the street. Nobody was aware of me! I was invisible, not surprisingly after all, I was dead, dead but immortal! As I flew from one street to the next, I caught sight of the guardhouse and flew down to observe my fellow companion, the peddler. I wanted to know whether he had made the spear and sword the captain had demanded. Instantly, I was standing in the very same room that we had been directed to when we had arrived. The captain was in the process of wielding a sword, first this way then that, then balancing the very hilt on the palm of his hand. The peddler looked on apprehensively but the captain stopped and smiled.

"Very good, my friend. But can it slice bread without tearing the loaf? SERGEANT!"

An equally scruffy-looking soldier ran in.

"Captain?"

"Fetch me a loaf—today's; one that is soft when squeezed but hard as rock on the outside—now."

"Sir."

And with that, the Sergeant disappeared from the gatehouse and returned five minutes later with the loaf of bread demanded.

"Today's?"

"Aye, sir, today's."

The captain placed the loaf on the table, lifted the sword and gently placed its edge on the bread. Without using any force, he held the hilt and allowed the sword to do what the peddler had intended; it sank through the bread like a hot knife through butter.

"My friend, you have work! Tell the sergeant what you need and get yourself breakfast…here, take this loaf, you have earned it."

"Payment, good Captain?"

"Food, shelter and the same pay as the soldiers here, the ones keeping our town safe. Apprentice needed or you OK on your own?"

"Apprentice would be a good thing, Captain."

"Apprentice doesn't get payment; just food and lodgings—understood?"

I had seen enough and moved on. The desperation that I had felt earlier to find the old man had somewhat dissipated. With my newfound means of transport, the urgency felt less pressing. However, it was still important to find him; if nothing else, to find out who and where I was. At least I had now the pleasurable experience of flying and being unseen, I could flit wherever I liked, with nobody the wiser.

I made my way back to the square and there, stalls were spread around as various tradespeople sold their wares in the town's market. I studied the items and try as I did, I could not pick them up. The physical world—the world of these people—and my world—the world of the unseen—co-existed but only in terms of awareness; interchanging from one to the other did not seem possible. I heard music and turned to see a street musician. He was playing a small whistle that created a sound strange to my ears. My ears! How could I hear? Again, how could I see! Of course, I couldn't, I sensed!

Suddenly, I saw a small boy run out from a side street, followed by two rather rough-looking men.

"Come here, you little toe rag!"

Being bigger and stronger, they quickly caught up with the lad who I guessed couldn't have been more than five, or six, at best. They whacked him about the head and took the bread that he had been holding. It was not even a full loaf, just the end piece. They dragged him off, crying and screaming towards the gallows.

"No, no please don't, please! We were hungry, me and me mam. Just a crust, that's all."

"Thieving toe rag. No quarter for you, me lad. You'll get what you deserve for thieving."

They pulled the lad to the gallows, disturbing the crows and rats pecking at the corpse. Dragging him up the steps, I saw one of them gag.

"What a stink! Can't someone cut him down?"

"Leave him here 'till the birds and rats are done. That keeps the folks wary…keep them to the law, it will."

Up onto the scaffold, they tied the boy's hands behind his back. Looking to the crowd gathering around, they raised the pillory and clamped the lad's head in the humiliating device. After whacking the boy again about his head, then kicking him in the legs, the two men descended from the scaffold, leaving the weeping lad in the stocks. The men crossed the square and disappeared up the side street from where I had seen them chasing the boy. I felt sorry for the lad and went up to him. His sobbing was pitiful and though I knew that stealing was wrong, this child *was* hungry and had been forced to desperate measures. Those two brutes deserved castigation for the way they had treated this boy. A gesture of kindness wouldn't have gone amiss; they could have chased and caught him, then after verbal chastisement, given the lad the morsel of bread. That would have had far more reaching consequences rather than trying to put the fear of God in him. But this was the way of life here. It seemed strange to me, foreign even, but I was unable to recall my own life when I had a physical body. Questions immediately again started to arise and the thirst for knowledge drove me again to find answers. I needed to find the old man! The one person who could see and communicate with me.

Chapter 6

With the clonking of shoes, the mistress descended the stairs and turned into the room at the bottom. The room was cluttered with shelves containing old leather-bound books and phials. At the only table, an old man sat gazing into a roaring fire. His eyes stared intently into the flames that danced, almost in unison, to unheard music.

"Ah…you are off again, Anne."

"Yes, off to the apothecary to collect the arsenic, laudanum, ground nutmeg and belladonna that I had ordered."

"Don't forget the mandrake."

"Ah, yes, nearly forgot. Agnès?"

As before, the sound of wooden shoes descending the stairwell brought the young maid into the room.

"Yes, madame?"

"Would you fetch me my blue robe—the one I wore yesterday, please. Then, collect your cloak and the large raffia basket. We are off to town."

"Yes, madame."

With a curtsey, the maid left the room to collect the items her mistress had asked for.

Despite the years of married life behind them, Anne, his wife, was kept from his darker secrets. She knew that he had a wonderful gift as a physician and healer but was oblivious to his true passion and capabilities. The verses and Almanacs he composed were very popular amongst the gentry of the land and had earned him an enviable reputation as a poet of some mystical means. They had started with easily understood meanings but had now become quite cryptic. Some had started to question his sanity but as far as the townsfolk were concerned, he was an interesting and valuable member of their community.

Anne left together with her maid and skirted around the side streets until she came to the main square. She passed the gallows and saw the poor lad in the pillory. No one had cast any rotting food his way or abused him. The general feeling seemed to be more prone to sympathy than anger, many people being in a similar situation. The plague had seriously left its mark throughout the town and though it was still current, some of those not infected believed that they had been spared because of living virtuous lives; it certainly encouraged fresh enthusiasm for the faith. This had not gone unnoticed by the Catholic Church either, profiteering from such abject fear. Certainly, the power of the church increased significantly as the priests and bishops decried those infected as having been sinful in the eyes of God. Anne, herself a devout Catholic, did not hold the common belief that it was the wrath of God that had brought about this pestilence. Being with her skilful and revered husband, she had adopted a more scientific way of thinking and believed, as Michel had shown her, that it was more likely due to infestation—Besides, she believed in a God of love, not of vengeance.

"Madame?"

"I ordered some medicines and herbs yesterday. Your wife said that they would be ready for today."

"Ah yes. She told me that you would be collecting. Let me see, where did she put them all? Hmm…not here; perhaps on the top shelf… No. I'll just give her a call, if you'll excuse me, please?"

With that, the plump old man popped into a back room. Anne could just hear the two talking.

"Angeline, that package you prepared yesterday, where is it? Yes, the one for Madame Nos…"

The door opened and Anne's concentration was directed to the new customer entering the shop.

"Good day to you, madame."

"Good day to you, good sir."

"A fine day, is it not? Good to be alive."

"Indeed, for those of us not affected by the pestilence."

"Ah, yes! The black death! A plague on us all. May we be spared this wrath of God. Heaven knows why He sent this to us. Too much sin in the world; we have drifted from the path of righteousness and…"

"I do not hold with such thinking, good sir. I believe that this pandemic has been brought about not by some divine intervention, but through natural causes."

"As you wish, madame. I merely felt, after bishop Franc…"

"Your package, madame."

The interruption of the shopkeeper was a blessed relief. Anne had felt the conversation was bordering on a dispute—one that could have had more serious implications if the church got to hear of it.

"Why, thank you. You will send the bill to my husband as usual? I don't deal with the finances in our household."

The shopkeeper looked hesitant.

"Excuse me, madame, I'll just check with my wife."

He disappeared into the back and returned just before the man could continue his conversation.

"That's fine, madame. I shall send my son this afternoon."

He handed over the basket of potions and medicines to the lady's maid and the two left.

I left the square and decided to retrace my steps since my encounter at this level of consciousness. Within an instant, I was facing the oak tree with the depth of the woodland behind. Turning around, I surveyed the magnificent golds and greens of the meadows laid out towards the horizon. The sun was now behind me and cast long shadows from the hills that stood sentinel over the valleys in the distance. With no shadow cast before me, I meandered back down the path that I had taken a short while ago towards the town. The overwhelming urge to run through the sheaves of corn again took hold! Why? The longing to drift above those fields and brush my hands through those sheaves was almost uncontrollable but, though I could skirt above the land, I was still drawn onwards to the town below. I approached the city gates and, as expected, passed straight through without being challenged by the sentries. As I walked through the arch, there before me was the same woman in blue that I had noticed yesterday. Was this a replay? Was this really a dream after all? Would I keep returning to this same spot as the actions repeated themselves over and over again? But this was different; this time the woman in blue was with another woman, a servant girl, it seemed. This was real. I decided to follow her.

Chapter 7

I awoke some hours later. I looked at the time; it was 18.34. In my drowsy state, I tried to reflect where I was and what I should be doing. Ye gods! I remembered that I should have gone for lunch at 13.00 but had slept through. I tried to arise as quickly as my body would let me but I was groggy. This was my debut of sleeping in a weightless environment and I found that I could not get out of my bed. I immediately remembered that I had strapped myself down and leaping out of bed wasn't really an option. I smiled as I released the harness that prevented me and my bedding from resting in the middle of the room. I saw a grappling hold and grabbed it as I pulled myself over to the intercom and pressed the red button for communication.

"Hello, Michael?"

It was Anna.

"Anna, it's Michael here."

"Yes, I just said, 'Hello Michael'."

"Oh, yes, so you did. Oh, so you know who you are talking to, then?"

"Yes. Every person is logged onto the main screen and we know who is contacting us."

"Anna, I'm so sorry that I missed lunch. I know that you said thirteen hundred but I lay down and fell asleep. The next thing that I am aware of is now!"

"No worries, Michael, so did most of the group! It is not unexpected after leaving Earth. Everyone, without realising it, finds it very tiring. We never make a point of waking people up. If they sleep through, it is because they need to."

"Thanks for being so understanding, Anna. I was just wondering whether Jamie was around?"

"He's here in the main control room with me and a few of the other officers…engineers, communications, logistics…"

"Oh, so he's busy, then?"

"Michael, Jamie is always busy…"

"Hi, Michael, it's Jamie… Sorry, Anna, didn't mean to interrupt. We were just going through final preparations before moon launch, but we have just finished. What is it?"

"Nothing serious, Jamie. Just woke up feeling bored and excited and was hoping to be involved, from an observer's point of view, that is, in this transit to the moon. But if you are involved in a meeting, then forget it."

"Michael, it is not a problem. Come on up, I always love this part—the launch."

"Yes, thanks Jamie, I'll be up straight away."

I went into the bathroom and looked around again before making my way to the door. I then realised that I had no notion of where the main control room was. I went back to the intercom and pressed the red button. A male voice answered with a strong French accent: "'Allo, François 'ere."

"Hi, it's Michael here…oh yes, you already know! Damn! I'm sorry, I just spoke to Jamie. He invited me up to the main control room but I haven't the foggiest where it is."

"It is foggy?"

"No, no, sorry; that's just an expression we Brits use when we don't know something. What I mean is that I don't know how to get to the main control room."

There was a knock on the door.

"Michael?"

"Excuse me, I'm sorry; there is someone knocking on my door."

"Yes, it will be Anna. She came down to show you 'ow to get 'ere; we realised that you wouldn't 'ave—'ow do you say—'ze foggiest'."

"Ha, ha, yes. Good one, well done. I didn't think the French had a sense of humour."

"We 'ave our moments."

"Michael!"

"Yes, coming Anna…sorry."

I pulled on the grappling holds and sped towards the door. With a swish, it opened as I approached and I realised that it was sensor controlled. Anna was outside.

"Sorry, Anna. I was on the intercom and…"

"Yes, I gathered that. Take hold of the grappling holds and follow me."

I attempted to memorise the route that we took as we zipped along the corridor but even though the journey took less than sixty seconds, there were too many twists and turns to make my way back without help. I hauled myself up into the main control room and saw Jamie seated and strapped into his chair. Anna floated to her seat next to Jamie and strapped herself in. Next to Anna was another female officer similarly tanned but with features that suggested that the two women were not from the same hemisphere. Wearing a baseball cap pulled tightly down on her head, there was no evidence of hair length or colour. On the other side of the control panels, I could just make out three other people, judging by movement and hair.

"Michael! Take a seat and strap yourself in. We are in the final stages of countdown before moon launch. All systems are looking good, the logistics have been agreed and at the moment, there don't appear to be any spanners in the works to prevent a smooth take-off."

"Jamie, why are we going to the moon?"

"There has been some revolutionary and innovative engineering going on over the past twenty years. And I mean really revolutionary. Twenty-five years ago, this mission would not have been possible. But at the concept of all this research, NASA decided that if the engineers and designers could accomplish what they said they could achieve—and they were totally confident that they could—then this mission would go ahead. Billions of dollars have been invested in this project, including the small prototype that was despatched seven years ago."

"A prototype?"

"Yes, sent away when you were still in short trousers!"

"Jamie, you are not much older than me. What were you wearing then!"

"Short trousers, just like you. Ha ha."

"OK. Explain then, prototype…and moon launch?"

"In order to reach for the stars, we needed a radically new approach to the engineering required. Believe it or not, it was part of my research thesis for my doctorate."

"You PhD then?"

"Nah, damn it, I never finished; spotted and snapped up by the Air Force. They were happy with my masters and I was itching to get into some serious, real engineering rather than this hypothetical post-grad stuff. But then once in, I couldn't wait to get into the air! The world was…and still is my oyster! Hell, I'd never known such a thrill once behind the controls of the Air Force's top strikers. But I also missed the engineering and the research. I guess NASA was contemplating this venture back then and the Air Force suggested that I was the best man for the job. Envisage that—the first captain to take a starship to another habitable world, revolving around another sun—albeit a red dwarf, not like our own sun—imagine that! We are the forerunners of an exciting adventure."

"Yeah, I am fully conversant with *Proxima Centauri*. Now the prototype, Jamie?"

"Ah, yes, sorry. Got carried away there. The prototype used an engine that we constructed that is propelled by means of plasma instead of conventional rocket fuel, kerosene or liquid hydrogen. We generated this plasma, then directed it through a magnetic field. In its focused form, we got temperatures of over six million degrees…and that is Celsius! That is hot, even hotter than the surface of that solar masterpiece out there!"

"How beneficial is it, then, over conventional rocket fuels?"

"Factor twenty-plus! We're talking three hundred thousand kilometres per hour! At full throttle on plasma, we can make the moon in just over the hour."

"Pretty fast! NASA gurus briefed me a few days ago. At that speed, we should make Mars in thirty-nine days!"

"Yes, but as you know, that is still not fast enough. If we stay at that speed, we will all be long dead before we can reach our goal, *Proxima b*. So we are going to use planetary gravities to accelerate us even faster, but wait for the hot-boy; just as we leave Earth's influence, NASA will send a command to a set of lasers—ten kilometres wide and one kilometre long—from the desert in Salt Lake Springs. The laser beams will be focused onto our 'sails'. These receptors will send this beauty to one half the speed of light!!! Now *that* is fast!"

"Yeah, in the briefing the other day, they mentioned that too, but not the moon launch. Jamie, did the prototype survive all this; is it still en route to *Proxima b*?"

"Yup! We tracked it throughout its journey and it's still speeding towards *Proxima Centauri*."

"… And it's still…functioning…correctly?"

"As from yesterday, when I received my last update, it was."

"Just how big was this prototype, Jamie?"

"Ten cubic metres."

"Ten cubic metres! You've got to be kidding me! Do you mean that this whole venture is based on the success of one probe, sent without life support, a communication delay of months…even years and no means of determining if the stress of the forces imposed created any lasting, permanent damage? I mean, even a minute rupture of the shell, though perhaps not creating any hazards for the probe, will be cataclysmic for us!"

"Not strictly true about life support; we did send a dozen experimental mice."

"And?"

"We believe that they didn't survive the laser beam blast."

"JAMIE!"

"But we are confident that we know why and that has been addressed with the construction of this starship, and also, the launch procedures that are in place…hence the need for destination, the moon."

I remained silent, looking ahead at the cosmos before us. I wished I hadn't asked; in fact, I wished I had stayed asleep until after the ship had been destroyed from the laser beam discharges. At least I would have remained unconscious and sublimely oblivious to our impending doom. I could feel that Jamie's enthusiasm had gotten the better of him and he had probably told me more than I should have known. My incredulity was probably felt by Jamie and Anna too, who was nearby. It was Anna who broke the silence.

"Michael, you must understand that Earth is no longer the safe haven of the past. Two hundred years ago, man started on his venture to destroy his birthplace. As the decades proceeded, innovations in technology took us to where we are now—on the brink of Armageddon. It is not the fault of our inventions that is destroying us, it is those malign *daimonians* who use these very creations for their own greed, their own gain. Even now, East fights West, and not just in a war of words but actions, too. Even the American president is battle-ready, too trigger-happy, despite the international protests for diplomacy. It may be that we leave this beautiful…and it is so beautiful…planet behind us for the last time. We no longer have time on our hands. We are the new generation; we are the vestiges of mankind compelled to continue our existence in the universe under the control of another star world.

"There are many different nationalities on-board. It is not just an American venture; it is a global venture that we are undertaking. That is why there are children and families travelling together. We must keep man alive and these

37

people—all volunteers I may add—are willing to risk everything for the continued existence of our species and, perhaps, just to stay alive."

Anna had put it so eloquently, so in context, that I began to regret feeling bad towards Jamie and this irresponsible adventure. Yes, I remembered all the hype and verbal outbursts one country vented against another and why I came to be part of this journey in the first place. There *was* no time. Another ten years! Why, another ten minutes could see our homeland destroyed before our eyes. We were not the brave ones; the brave ones were those who stayed behind and directed us to this New World whilst they remained to face the consequences of demonic tyrants prepared to destroy everything if their ways were not met. And Anna was right, even the president was not without blame.

"Fifteen hundred…hell, that's a lot of people to be responsible for, Jamie. Sorry, I should not have prejudged."

Jamie smiled, probably relieved that I had been spoken honestly to by not only him in his rumbustious way, but Anna.

"Well, at least you are now aware and we can travel with our eyes wide open! It helps knowing that I can confide in and discuss things with you…no secrets."

"Does that make me your number two then, Jamie!"

"After Anna, Petra, Charlie and Simon, it does!"

"Charlie… Simon…?"

"Simon, say hello to Michael. Simon is our chief engineer and is responsible for maintenance and any engineering and technical issues."

I looked over the other side of the console where we were sitting and saw a sporty-looking young man somewhere in his late twenties. Next to him was a rather solid-looking man, one who would possibly have been mistaken for Rock Hudson, had he still been alive.

"Charlie is responsible for all logistics—keeps an eye on me and the stock, should any whiskey remain unaccounted for!"

Both smiled and waved a 'Hi' sign to me.

"Which one is which, Jamie?"

"Charlie is the Rock Hudson lookalike."

Sheesh…either Jamie was a mind reader or Charlie really did resemble Rock Hudson.

"Petra is next to Anna. Oh, and there's François. He's responsible for personnel welfare, medical staff—"

"Proxima, ten minutes to moon launch."

"OK, Mission Control. All good here. What's it like with you?"

"Cloudy for once, Jamie. President is going to give an address to the people tonight. Don't hold out a lot of hope, with that monkey in charge."

"Fingers crossed, Mission Control. Keep us briefed, even when we are star-born."

"Will do. Nine minutes to launch."

Jamie spent a few minutes rechecking his console, then held a small conversation with his number two and Petra. They seemed to be in full agreement with the planned schedule and when he looked calm again, I decided to continue with my enquiries.

"So, what's the purpose of going to the moon then, Jamie?"

"Surely, you should know that, Mr Astrophysicist of the Year!"

"Jamie, I am an astrophysicist…a theoretician. I perform mathematical hypotheses on the weird and wonderful—negative matter, dark energy, black holes, time…"

"Joke, Michael, relax. I was only…how do you Brits say—'taking a piss'?"

"*The* piss, Jamie; it's 'THE piss'."

"There's a difference, then?"

"Oh, yes. A big difference."

"God, no wonder you relied on us to help you out with Herr Hitler, you can't even take a piss without making a debate about it! Ha ha ha."

"Ha ha ha… Jamie, I didn't know Americans could make a joke without background hysterics, telling us when we should laugh!"

"Ha ha ha…!"

I looked over and even Anna and Petra were smiling.

"OK, moon launch is the first stage to increase our speed. As I mentioned, this is one of the reasons that we believe the mice didn't make it; their organs could not take such a force exerted at one go. We will do this in stages—"

"Five minutes to moon launch."

That notification from Mission Control reduced the levity somewhat. But we needed light relief with the serious nature of our two missions at hand and every opportunity to lighten the strain with a joke or a bit of clowning around was a necessity if we were going to survive this journey with our sanity intact.

"At least we have the full support of Mission Control; they will pull out every stop to make this undertaking a success."

"Full support, Jamie?"

"Yeah, of course… Why, do you think someone's out to sabotage… Ha ha…?"

Jamie's laugh was not convincing. I sensed a hesitancy in his reply.

"Problem, Michael?"

"Well, I'm sure that he will endeavour to remain professional but I can't help feeling that Karl Guttenberg is not altogether sold on this project."

"Karl, yeah? I don't know the man too well, but he is very—how do you say it?—Germanic. You know, strict, disciplined, authoritative, no sense of humour. Why, do you feel uncomfortable with him then?"

"Well, Jamie, like yourself, I don't know the man at all but if there was a weak link in this mission, I just feel… Well, can he be trusted?"

"Every person involved with this enterprise has been vetted. All credentials checked, background, family history. I mean, this is the most thoroughly scrutinised undertaking ever. But, Karl… Karl is something of an enigma. His family came to the US from somewhere over in the Far East—Laos, I think. They became naturalised US citizens when Karl was about seven. After Princetown, Karl went on to Harvard and got his doctorate in physics, specialising in laser

39

physics. But apart from that, I know very little about him; he tends to keep to himself and never socialises outside of work. But you can't hold that against him; a solitary figure doesn't make the man a menace."

"No, I guess."

"One minute to launch."

"Anna, would you, please?"

Anna leaned over to the intercom, looking at me and Jamie as she pressed the central button.

"Will all personnel please secure themselves wherever they are? Use harnesses if you are near one or if not, please grasp onto a grappling hold. We do not expect any force to be exerted; this is for your security and safety only. I repeat, this is for security and safety only."

Anna leant back, looked ahead, then turned to Jamie and smiled. She raised her thumb to me in a reassuring way, giving me that same warming, consoling smile. The sort that my dentist used to give just before a tooth filling.

'This won't hurt…much!'

"Ten…nine…eight…seven…"

Just as with the lift-off from Earth a mere twelve hours earlier, my heart was thumping like a drum. I wondered if anyone else could hear it. It felt as though my chest would burst but, as with the earlier lift-off, I had to trust Jamie; I had to believe that every engineer, designer, astronaut…even every laser physicist…was behind the success of this assignment.

"Three…two…one… Ignition."

Chapter 8

I thought that I felt a surge but then it may have been just apprehension. There was just a vibrancy as the plasma burst into life and we sped onwards. I could see the moon through the canopy—a brilliant, dazzling ball. Jamie continued to pull the electromagnets into focus and though I felt no force acting on me, I could see from the concentration on his face that we were accelerating at an incredible rate. Finally, he released the lever and sat back, quite relaxed. He looked over to Anna: "OK, Anna, let them relax for a while."

Anna leaned forward to the intercom.

"All personnel, you may continue with whatever you were doing. Security is not required for a while. Please be prepared for a full security alert in just over an hour's time, that is, at twenty-one hundred. Please be near full harnessing equipment for twenty-one hundred."

Jamie looked over to me.

"A beauty, eh? I've never had the controls of such a magnificent piece of engineering in my life. I thought the Strikers were amazing, but this, *this*... I'm just lost for words."

"Lost for words—that's a first, Jamie!"

"Ha, ha, ha! You know, with you lot and the adventure ahead, I think this is going to be one hell of a trip, if you ask me!"

"Yeah, I've got a feeling you're right; one hell of a trip!"

"Jamie be back soon. Got some people to help out."

"OK, Anna. Make it for twenty fifty-five so that we can get everyone secured."

And with that, Anna pushed herself towards some grappling holds and hauled herself out of the main control room. I turned to Jamie and could see from the smile on his face that he was enjoying this moment—this historical time—a time when future historians would praise his name, along with that of the crew. These pioneers—taking mankind beyond their home planet and star for the first time.

"Anna, she's an attractive girl, Jamie."

"Sure is, Michael, but I'm afraid she's spoken for, if you've got any romantic ideas going on in that clever little British head of yours."

"Oh...by who?"

"By half the male crew on-board."

Jamie and I both screeched with laughter. Yes, this was going to be 'one hell of a good trip'.

"And you included?"

"Oh yes, me included!"

"Good God! That's the moon in front! A minute ago, it was like a football and now it occupies half the canopy!"

"Yup, this baby is travelling at one heck of a speed."

"How fast is 'one heck of a speed' at the moment, then?"

"Two hundred and fifty thousand kilometres per hour; that fast enough?"

"Yup, that's fast! You confident with this moon slingshot?"

"Yeah. The main problem is what G-force we will be subjected to, not whether the slingshot will work…that's already been proved. Boffins back at base calculated that we could reach up to a fifty per cent speed increase, depending how steep we approach Silver Cloud in front."

"So that's…three hundred and seventy-five thousand kilometres per hour."

"Yeah, give or take a few ten thousand. Let's say, four hundred thousand tops?"

"OK. I can live with four hundred thousand."

"Right. We will fly into its gravitational pull and be forced around its circumference, all the time being accelerated—first, by the initial pull, then second, as we gently descend towards the surface. I will be using the retro rockets at the side of this baby to stop us flying off into space and stop us crashing onto the moon itself. At its closest, we will probably be about thirty kilometres from the surface. As the Earth comes into view on the other side, I will fire the plasma boosters and send us back to Earth. This journey back will take less than fifty minutes."

I looked at Jamie, who had a big smile on his face. He was really enjoying this moment; probably like he did the first time he broke the sound barrier in his Striker. But then, I just wanted to gaze ahead and watch the moon become ever increasingly bigger by the second.

"What's the time, Michael?"

"Twenty thirty-eight."

"Right, well, we have approximately eighteen minutes until I'm needed again. One for the road, Michael?"

Jamie proffered me a small flask with a plastic straw, which clearly had marked on it 'Finest Single Malt Hooch. Made in Kentucky'.

"Jamie, you can't be serious! You're driving!"

He laughed his addictive laugh and I realised that he really was clowning around.

"Not until we get out of the solar system…then I'm going to let my hair down! But not until then, I promise!"

Anna returned and strapped herself into her seat beside Jamie.

"One for the road, Anna?"

"Thanks, Jamie, I think I will."

I looked on a bit aghast as Anna relieved some of the contents of the flask through the small straw. She looked across to me and saw my look of incredulity.

"Juice, Michael, just juice!"

She raised her eyebrows in a 'want some?' manner and smiled.

"Yeah, OK, thanks."

With a gentle nudge, the *Hooch* flask drifted past Jamie and I took hold. I'm not sure whether I would have agreed if Jamie had just sucked on the end of the straw but as it had been Anna, I took the end piece in my mouth. I imagined Anna's lips curled around the same end of the straw that I now used. Was I falling for this very attractive West Indian girl? But then, as Jamie had said, so had half the male crew!

"Anna, I'm going to close my eyes for ten minutes; need my concentration for the slingshot ahead. Please keep alert and prod me in ten, thanks."

"OK, Jamie, will do."

Without hesitation, Anna took over the controls of Proxima. Short of realising it, I had stereotyped her. It was only when I witnessed her in control that I appreciated that, in my mind, I had given her a subordinate role. She was obviously a highly skilled member of the crew. I sat for a few minutes just absorbing the rapidly approaching scene in front, before talking to Anna again.

"What is your position here, Anna?"

"I am responsible, after Jamie, for this mission. If, for whatever reason he becomes indisposed, then I have to assume full command."

"Quite a responsibility, then. What did you do before to get selected for this project?"

"I was a fighter Ace, like Jamie."

"A fighter Ace! Gee, I had no idea."

"Thought that I typed letters and filed correspondence, Michael?"

"N…n…no, no, not at all. Well…I have to be honest, Anna; I mean you are such an attractive girl; I had placed you in a role that involved elegance, perhaps a little less militaristic, certainly glamour. Basically, I hadn't given it any thought at all; I just saw you and thought, 'wow'. There!"

"Keep talking like that, Michael, and this journey is going to be real fun."

She then giggled in a way that I expected the stereotype I had pictured, would. It was the sort of laugh that sent ripples down my spine. As she did so, she looked across at me and smiled that big, beautiful, West Indian smile.

Yes, Anna, I thought, *this could be real fun.*

"Jamie, ten."

Though not fully asleep, Jamie had had the luxury of a few minutes of allowing his mind to relax and prepare him for his next challenge."

"Thanks, Anna. OK, alert the crew."

"All personnel. All personnel. It is twenty fifty-five. Please secure yourselves into the harness nearest to you. Parents confirm that your children cannot undo the device. Those women with babies, please ensure that the baby is strapped to you. In four minutes, you will start to feel the effects of gravity again as we approach the moon. The sensation will be slightly different to what you experienced on Earth as we skim through the moon's gravitational field. It will feel more like the lift-off you experienced twelve hours ago. The duration of this will be about one hundred seconds. Captain Fraser will notify you as we approach."

Again, I saw Jamie change from his sociable, happy-go-lucky character into the professional that he was. His eyes were glued to the dials and controls before him. Even though it was becoming a tense and crucial moment, I somehow trusted this man who I had known but a few short weeks. Trusted him not only with my life, but the lives of the other fifteen hundred people on board. Somehow, even if it had been Anna in control, I would have felt safe.

"All personnel, three…two…one…hold tight!"

The moon was almost directly in front of us. I could just make out the black of space beyond the horizon of this celestial body that we were about to encounter. It was 20.59 and to the second, the pull of the moon was being felt as we entered its gravitational field. Perhaps even Jamie had underestimated what effect the body was going to have on us—the size that we were, travelling at the speed that we were. There was no buffeting; the sensation was smooth but I felt as though I could not speak. Had I done so, my voice would have come out deep and in slow motion. In fact, Jamie's actions seemed to be in slow motion as he guided the spacecraft around the circumference of the moon. I turned my head to the right and saw, beyond Jamie, Anna's pretty face distorted by the forces exerted upon us. Jamie was now using the controls beside him on his seat, as he too was now unable to move. I saw his finger move and heard a hiss as one of the plasma engines burst into life. I tried to raise my eyelids and could just see the surface of the moon below us race by. It was as though I had been watching a film that had been sped up one hundred times. I looked at the red dial in front of Jamie; we had been racing above the moon's surface now for fifteen seconds. I struggled hard against these Newtonian forces acting upon us and looked ahead through the canopy. The surface was nearer than when I had first looked and I remembered Jamie saying that we would descend towards the surface in order to increase our speed even more. In slow motion thought, I calculated that we were probably doing somewhere in the region of three hundred and seventy-five thousand that Jamie had mentioned earlier. The force of the lift-off had been dramatic enough, but this was incredibly more painful. How would the children be coping? Luckily, I wasn't there to find out but perhaps they had been spared the discomfort by losing consciousness. I, personally, had always been a theme park addict and loved the thrill of feeling the forces of nature acting on the roller coaster; but this was a different league totally. It was probably all those years of drops and *loop de loops* that had helped prepare me for what I was experiencing now. Fifty seconds, and the moon's surface appeared almost close enough to touch out and reach.

I turned my head slowly and painfully towards Jamie and Anna. Her face was now distorted beyond recognition and Jamie looked as though he was wearing a mask. His eyes were tightly closed and his head lolled to one side. My mind worked slowly as I realised that Jamie had passed out! He was unconscious and in charge of everyone's life on board—lives that we were about to lose! I tried to call out but all I could hear was 'Ja…mmm…ie', deep and bass. I had started to lose consciousness also but brought myself to with the dread of what was about to happen. The moon's surface seemed a few metres away and we were now doomed to crash. The last thing I could see was the red dial registering ninety seconds. I…could…not…pass…out and called out again, 'Ja…mmm…ie'. I saw Jamie's wrist twitch and suddenly, his eyes opened, sluggishly but they opened. 'Ja…mmm…'. As I lost consciousness, I heard, in my imagination, a hiss.

Chapter 9

The mistress and her maid manipulated their way into the main square and looked towards the far end where the boy stood in the pillory, next to the corpse swinging in the gallows. She stopped, as did her servant, and gave the impression of assessing the situation as though she had a decision to make and was not sure what to do.

"Agnès, do you have that small dirk with you?"

"Yes, madame."

"Let us hasten, then."

The pair made straight for the gallows, climbed the scaffold and with a swift swipe of her knife, cut the rope binding the lad's hands. Then removing the wooden peg, lifted up the pillory and eased the boy from the wooden mount. By this time, the child was weak, both from hunger and having been left in this position for several hours. She searched in her basket, but only had herbs, medicines and potions. Smiling kindly at the boy, she spoke softly, "Come with me, young man."

"Where are we going?"

"To buy you some bread!"

The three took off to the end of the square, turned left into a small alley and there before them was a small *boulangerie*. The mistress went inside and was back out again immediately with a long baguette.

"Here, take this home and help your mother prepare some broth. That should keep you from starving for a day or two."

The boy looked up to this elegant woman, then bowed his head in shame and humility.

"Thank you, miss."

Before she could reply, the lad had gone, running up the street with his loaf to give to his mother.

"Come, Agnès, we must hurry away ourselves."

The two then stealthily retraced their steps from where they had come with me alongside.

"Agnès?"

"Yes, madame?"

"Do you get the feeling that we are not alone?"

"Why, no madame."

"Strange. It feels like someone is watching our movements as we make our way home."

"No, madame. I don't have that impression at all. There are other people in the street, that's all that I feel."

She looked behind her, then suddenly turned in my direction, looking straight at me walking beside her. I concentrated as hard as I could to get her attention but she merely shook her head, sighed and continued her way home. I could feel an excitement within me. If only she could see me, sense me…but then, she did have an awareness of me…didn't she? She had 'felt' a presence, *my* existence! I tapped her on the shoulder but she merely looked ahead and paid no heed to my attempted contact.

The houses started to take on an air of more splendour, more grandeur, as we turned from the wretched poverty behind us in the small alleyways. The streets became somewhat wider and the buildings appeared to be built of stone, rather than mud, wood and thatch, as I had noticed earlier. The mistress and her maid strode up a cobbled path and opened a large oak door but I did not follow them in. Though I was able to transport myself by means of thought and could sense the world of mortals, I knew that I did not have the ability to have contact with the solid world. I could not touch or hold. The door before me would remain firmly closed unless someone opened it or I could will myself through. I looked at the oak door and tried to envision the other side. I tried to picture a corridor with adjoining rooms. I tried to visualise the two women sorting out the contents of the basket on the kitchen table. I used every fibre in my wraithlike being to transport myself into this house, but nothing worked. Either I was doomed to await the opening of the door to gain entrance, like a vampire awaiting his invitation, or I had other means of which I was not totally familiar. I had no choice. I strode up to the door, closed my eyes and stretched out my arm. I felt a vibration as my arm made contact with this other dimension of existence. I opened my eyes, projected my right arm forward and could see it penetrating through the wood. However, I could not see beyond the door; I could not see my hand. With my left hand, I pushed on the door and as before, I felt a faint tingling as it, too, disappeared through the wood. With a pounding sensation, I closed my eyes, clenched my fists and walked forward. My phantom form juddered slightly and then became normal. Hesitatingly, I opened my eyes. I was in a long corridor. I turned around and there behind me was the oak door. I had done it! It had worked! And I now knew that I could do it again and again, wherever and whenever I wanted. But now I had to find the woman in blue.

I turned at the first room on the right. The room was large and appeared to be in the form of a drawing room. Three comfortable sofas were scattered around, in what appeared to be a haphazard way. Some cushioned chairs with tall backs were placed underneath a large sash window. Towards the middle of the room was a large solid walnut table and to one side was a smaller table with a green felt covering. The main striking item was a beautiful large open fire, with a huge oak lintel supporting the chimney's weight above. The fire had been prepared but was not yet lit. To the side of the mantelpiece were a stack of logs ready for the onset of winter. Above the fireplace was a painting, depicting a seer at his work. A dog lay curled in front of a roaring fire and small bottles and potions were littered around some shelves on the wall. The seer was sat at a small rough table, scrying, using his crystal ball. By the far door, a woman, not unlike the mistress of this house, was standing apprehensively. The background and her form were much darker and more difficult to see as though the painter had intended to create an atmosphere of malevolence. The seer had a quill in his hand and looked as though he was about to write something on a scrap of paper resting on the table beside him. Behind the woman, I could just make out a phantom form peering over her with two amber eyes. Beside the seer, kneeling on the floor was an older woman, looking towards him with her hands held in a praying, pleading manner. Her face depicted an expression of anguish.

As mesmerised as I was by this painting, I needed to move on and find the mysterious woman in blue. I turned around, went through the door that I had just entered and continued down the corridor. In front of me, at the end, was a closed door. This time, with far less apprehension, I marched boldly on and through the door into what I realised was a child's playroom. There, at the far end was a rocking horse and beside this, a group of wooden soldiers, laid out in battle formation. The combatants were coloured in blue and one held an insignia, the meaning of which I did not understand. Beside this group of soldiers were also some rag dolls, suggesting that perhaps more than one gender had used this as a playroom? I heard voices, both female, and assumed this was what I had been searching for. Even though I had made my way through the door, I realised I could just as easily have passed through the wall. However, to avoid getting lost, I needed to follow recognised paths. There was a second door, almost opposite the first that I had been into and, though it was closed, I knew that this no longer presented me with any problems. I could hear the women talking and stepped through a rather plain-looking door with a latch into a scullery. There was an array of pots, pans and cooking utensils hanging on hooks on the walls. I was surprised at the lack of cupboards, though a large solid-looking pine dresser was at the end of the room by an open door where I caught a glimpse of the maid's skirt in the room beyond.

"Agnès, you need to prepare the soup. Your Master will be wanting his meal soon. I shall take these potions into the library."

"Yes, madame. Will you also be requiring soup?"

"Yes. Oh, and please add more garlic; the season's not been good and the vegetables have lost their flavour."

"Yes, madame."

The mistress, now without her blue cloak, made her way out from the kitchen and into a room yonder. Though the kitchen had been light, this room was far more sombre. With only one small, high window, a lamp had already been lit and was standing on a small table by the far wall to give the room some degree of brightness. The walls were of a dark wood with panelling, which considerably hindered the late afternoon light penetrating the room. I heard the swishing of her skirt and the noise of her shoes on the wooden floor in the room beyond and saw her disappear down a flight of stairs to my left. I paced across the room and descended the stairs as well. Unlike the flooring, the steps were made of stone and the staircase was in the form of a spiral. At the bottom, she knocked on the gnarled door and without waiting for a reply went straight in.

"Michel, I have the next batch of potions, herbs and medicines. Where shall I leave…"

But there was no reply; the room was empty. She made her way over to the crooked table and placed her basket on top. There were some candles burning above the mantelpiece, one on either end and one candle on the table. I recognised this scene straightaway as the painting that I had seen upstairs. On the table, there were open half-empty bottles, some small glass vessels as one would have used to mix potions together, two rather large books, each opened upon a certain page, and a crystal ball. In this room, one would have needed candles even at the height of the day as there were no windows. She turned her gaze to one of the open books, looked, then turned the page and studied the contents furtively. My gaze was now directed to her. She had a captivating countenance and with her smile that I had seen earlier, I felt that this was a woman—had I been in her dimension—that I would have wanted to get to know better. I wanted to touch her hand to see if she could feel my presence. I stretched my hand forwards and gently stroked the back of her hand as she followed the words on the page of that book. She shuddered slightly and withdrew her hand straightaway and, turning her head towards me, she again looked directly into my eyes. As though she could see me, she allowed me to continue to gaze into her deep green eyes. My excitement again increased whilst I studied these two living emeralds that seemed to infuse sincerity, passion and emotions beyond my comprehension. With the back of her gentle hand, she brushed some strands of her fair hair across her forehead and turned her face back to the book. Once more, her hand rested on the book as her forefinger traced out the words on the open page. Delicately, I rested my hand on hers; this time, there was no tentativeness and, though she paused momentarily, she continued as though I had not been there.

"Ah, Anne, my dear."

"Michel! I called out but you were not here."

It was the old man of my dreams! Well, not dreams if he was real…is real! Was this perhaps the very person who could answer all my questions? The very person, perhaps the only person, who could see me, communicate with me! Ashamed, I immediately removed my hand from his wife's. Had I realised, I would not have been so bold and thoughtless.

"Did you bring the mandrake?"

"Yes, it's underneath the witch hazel."

She continued to finger the words on the open page.

"Are you still trying to defeat this pestilence?"

"I know the mandrake will prove itself, mixed with the rose pills, and they have saved many already. But I will need the moon to be new before I can start. That will be tomorrow night. What do you think; does what I have written make sense?"

"Yes, yes, it does. You have already proved your potion to several now."

49

Michel walked over to the righthand side of the mantelpiece. There was a sturdy bookcase and he thumbed through several volumes before pulling out a book wrapped in leather binding. The book was large and heavy and the wizard needed both hands to carry it. He laid it on the table with a thud next to the candle as dust flew across the room. On the cover, I could see the design of a complete man standing with arms extended and legs drawn apart. He was enclosed in a circle with diagonal lines drawn through the body. Michel opened the book and thumbed through the pages.

"Ha, ha, here it is:

By the light of the torch in the sky,
When darkened at its newest revelation;
The screaming root with the flower of the garden
Will multiply thrice over the power of Death.

"You see, I need the mandrake to complete the potion. The rose pill will be far more effective with the blessing of the new moon."

Then I realised…he could not see me! He had no notion of my presence! How had he been able to see me before and speak to me and now he could not? Now I became really worried. I was totally at a loss as to what I could do. He and his wife, Anne, continued to discuss the potions as I stood aghast; however, at least it appeared that they were more concerned with how to improve and maintain life rather than how to dispense with it. I continued to look on, realising that neither of them knew that there were three of us in that room.

"Michel?"

"Hmm, hmm?"

"You do realise that our practices here may well be deemed heretic; does that not concern you?"

"I am a devout Catholic in the eyes of the people. But I believe in the mercy of God and He knows that our work is for the good of the people."

"Yes…but there may well be other, less holy people, that would deem what you are doing to be against the teaching of the Holy Church."

"Anne, anyone decrying what I do to be the work of the Devil will have not only me, but the Monarch to contend with."

"Queen Catherine does not hold the authority that her husband, Henri, does, so be careful. You have ruffled many feathers and there are countless who would rather see you on top of a stake than warming yourself by one."

"Ha, ha, that is true, my dear. But I feel committed to pursuing my experiments. If those that have gone onto another plane of existence wish to contact me, then who am I to deny them that opportunity? The Holy Book, Chapter four, verse one, John said, 'test your spirits'. He wished us to explore and use this contact, of that I am convinced. Was he not speaking the word of God?

"Think of all those who have left their loved one's grieving. Who can deny them the comfort of knowing that they live on? Who can deny them that chance of contact again? And these spirits, these phantoms of the night, bring messages and warnings; these can be invaluable to those recipients, if only they were to believe."

"Michel, I agree, totally, I agree; but just, please be careful, that's all."

"But what about me?" I shouted, "What about ME!"

I sped from the room and within an instant was back by the tree where it had all started. I did not know whether this is where I wanted to be, but perhaps my inner self wished for me to be alone, away from the city, away from people, away from hope. I sat melancholic, distraught and in despair. Despondent, I gazed around and felt so alone. In this world of isolation and hopelessness, was I doomed to face eternity on my own? Was I but a murmur from those around me, unable to make my presence known? I wanted to weep, but no tears could come; how could they, I was dead!

"Hello?"

I turned and there behind the tree was a young girl. Her age was deceptive, but I surmised her to be about seventeen. Her skin was like that of an olive and glistened in the fading sun. Her hair was as black as coal and her voice was soft, like water flowing gently from a stream, but most of all, her eyes—dark as ebony, they sparkled with a vibrancy and desire. She smiled and with that smile, I became entranced with this perfect thing of beauty before me.

"Hello? You can see me?" I replied.

"Why yes, perfectly. Why should I not see you?"

"Because...because I am not of this dimension."

"Oh?"

"But *you* can see me!"

"Why yes, as clear as day. But, then again, I can also see *others* who are not of this world."

"Really! So, you must be a wizard then?"

"No, I'm just an ordinary girl...perhaps with a special gift, but otherwise, I'm nothing special."

"But you are not ordinary...you are, dare I say it...beautiful!"

"Truly! You think so? But, you, you...your form...your features are, are...quite stunning!"

"Me! No, no, no. Why, I am small, quite plain, with features that do not appeal to girls. I am no Adonis, believe me."

Suddenly, I realised that I was describing myself; how I looked, how I was just a plain man with nothing that was in the least attractive to girls. How did I know this? I could not remember my name but I remembered that my eyes were blue. There was something markedly strange but I could not place my finger on it. And here was this perfect young woman before me, saying that I was, in her eyes, attractive...stunning!

"But, if you are not of this world, as you say, then I must be able to see you...the real you, the true spiritual you, and that is why you are...more than stunning...beautiful, yes...beautiful."

I began to feel very humble. How was it that I, of all people, should become aware of this angel before me? I held out my hand to her and without comprehending that it was happening at the same time, she held her hand out to me. My hand and hers met, but at that moment of meeting, of touching, there was nothing but a glow of warmth. She trembled.

"Oh! You indeed are not of this world."

We gazed at one another without speaking. I explored her countenance and with elation, wondered again whether this was just a dream. Was this merely a façade in my existence to overcome the grief of being totally lost and without hope? Was this purgatory, where hope was given one moment, only to be dashed the next, then to be given hope again? Was I going to have to experience eternity going from one intense emotion to another? I started to become angry—angry with whatever force it was that was toying with me, like I was some kind of plaything being dangled on the end of a string. I was suddenly brought out from my reverie when she spoke: "No! Stop! Stop!"

There was fear in her eyes as she backed behind the tree.

My anger abated at the sound of her voice.

"Your form was changing! Well, not so much your form as the aura that I could sense. It was becoming…malevolent."

The frightened look in her eyes and her frown lessened.

"Really! Oh? I just started to feel bad thoughts. I began to ask myself whether all this…whether *you*…were real. Or whether this was a dream, another disappointment."

She stepped towards me again, letting go of the oak tree beside her.

"No, this is real. I am real and you are real, real to me, that is. Why are you here?"

"I have no idea!"

"Are you a troubled spirit, seeking revenge, here to haunt and taunt?"

"I really wish I knew but I am at a total loss as to why I am here, or where I will go."

"Well, perhaps you will stay, then?"

"I have nowhere else to go—no home, no hope, no purpose."

"Well, then…will you stay?"

"Yes…yes, I will stay; I really *have* nowhere else to go."

I felt at peace with her question. Perhaps I needed her more than the old man. She could see and communicate with me and I needed that, very much.

"What is your name?"

"I don't know. I have been searching for my name for a while now, but I cannot remember. I know that my eyes are blue, though, I can remember that, but I don't know how…"

"But your eyes are not blue! I can see a colour, but it is not a colour that I know."

She gazed into my eyes and I felt an exhilaration build up inside me. Those beautiful ebony eyes peered into my very existence.

"They are not blue. They are like…well, they are like a warmth, mixed with reflections on rippling water…they really are quite wonderful and mesmerising."

"Not blue, then?"

"No, they are simply…fascinating!"

We both continued gazing into each other's eyes. It was as though we were exploring each other's soul, searching for that spirit within. She smiled and with that smile, I felt a sweet contentment take control and I smiled back.

"When you smile, your whole form shimmers—like your eyes. A golden fire, warm, not one that burns. You should smile all the time, it feels nice!"

"Well, I must say that this is the first time that I have felt like smiling; you have made me smile! Tell me, what is your name?"

"My name is Mai."

"Mai? That is a name I do not recognise. The old man I saw, he is called Michel and his wife, Anne; these are names that I do feel familiar with. But I do not feel familiar with Mai."

"I do not come from this region, this country, and our names are not the same as others here."

"Where do you come from then?"

"Far away. Father sometimes talks about our old home. 'Indochina', I think he calls it. My family were brought here when I was a child. We were brought here as slaves but my father proved his value as a healer. He practices the Arts and gained his freedom because of his value to the people. He also can see the *others*, but not as I can."

"Indochina? Yes, I know this name. What did I call it? I cannot recall."

"Where did you come from?"

"Oh, how I wish I knew! I have no…well, not strictly true; I have very little that I can recall. I became *aware*, if that is the best word to use, the other day, just here by this tree. An old man appeared and talked to me as though he were expecting me. Then told me to seek him out or I would be forever lost. I found him a short while ago and he couldn't see me! Yet, he saw me and talked to me. I am confused and a bit frightened for I do not know why I am here nor what to do."

"Oh, I see. It is getting dark and I must get back while there is still some light. Will you walk with me?"

"Yes, of course. What is the name of this town before us?"

"Aix-en-Provence."

The sun had dropped below the horizon and we slowly made our way down the hill towards the town.

"What country is this, then?"

"Why, this is France!"

"France! I recall this name but not the name of the town before us."

The woods and the tree were now almost obscured in the fading light but in the open, there was just enough to see the path ahead.

"What do you do…do you go to school?"

53

"School! Why no! Girls don't go to school. School is for boys…rich boys. I help my mother in washing clothes, which keeps us in food and shelter. My father, he gets paid for his healing work. He has helped many with the pestilence, but I worry that one day, we will get it too; he is often near those with this illness. The local people in the town believe that it has been brought here by God as a punishment but we are not of their religion and my father believes that there is some other cause."

We continued talking, getting to know one another as we made our way into the town. At the entrance, the guards raised their fauchards without hesitation. They obviously recognised Mai and could not see me. As we passed through the arch, I noticed that torches had been lit and were leaning on the walls, lighting our way through the arched gate. Once inside, however, it was dark, though I could sense the streets and houses around. There was not much hustle and bustle; most people seemed to have gone into their houses. Mai led us through a series of streets until we came to a small house made of mud, wood and thatch.

"I live here with just my father and mother. My brother was taken from us by this black plague a while ago. That is why my father uses the Arts to help others…and protect us."

"What are these *Arts*, then?"

"Before we were taken from our homeland, I was told that my father and other people in our village could contact our dead family and relatives. They could bring us comfort and healing when we were sick. They could warn us of dangers and advise us what we should do. But in this country, such practices are forbidden. The people of this country serve another God and what my father does is considered evil. If he were discovered performing his Arts, he would be burned and decreed a sorcerer."

"Didn't your dead family warn you of being caught as slaves, then?"

"Yes. They told the people in our village that fair-skinned warriors would be coming and that we were to leave the village and hide in the hills. But we were discovered after they had burned our village down. I was too young to understand, but I do remember being very frightened. There was shouting and angry men beating my father with sticks. I was crying and so scared, when suddenly, all became calm. I saw an old woman who told me that she was my grandmother. She said, 'Don't be afraid child, we will protect you from all harm. We will guide you. You and your family will be safe and all will be well.' That was the first time that I realised that I could see the spirit people. At times, when I saw them, they appeared more real than the people of this world."

"But they didn't save your brother?"

"They couldn't save him. My father had stopped practicing the Arts after we were taken from our homeland and village. But they warned me that he was going to die. I told my father, but he did not believe me. It was then that I realised that he needed to perform his rituals to contact those not of this world. Yet, I needed no such practice; I could see and contact just by being still and allowing my body to float into the world of dreams. That is why I go to that tree; it is so peaceful and beautiful there and I can listen to my spirit people. I was drawn there tonight and you came!"

"So, your father will not be able to see me, then?"

"Unless he practices his skills, he will not know of your presence. Our people believe that nature is our God, that everything around us has power and consciousness and is precious. We call upon nature to guide us, but we can only do this by performing special rituals. These ceremonies require calling the spirits…and the chanting can be heard! So, he must be very careful that he is not heard when he performs these rites. But it is this very practice that has given us our freedom because he can heal sick people."

"You keep talking about 'your people' yet, if there is only your family here, then 'your people' do not exist here. So how do you know these things?"

"My mother told me as I was growing up. I wanted to know so much. She said all the things that I have just told you. She sang to me as I was sleeping and I could hear her voice in my dreams. I told her that I could see 'people' not of this world when I was older but she told me not to tell anyone. She said she would be scared for my life if it became known. But I do believe that she can *see* at times."

"So, your mother may be able to see me then?"

"Perhaps; I am not sure."

She turned towards me as we continued to study each other's countenances.

"May I see you tomorrow, then?"

"Of course. I don't want to lose you now that I have found you."

I tried to kiss her on the cheek—goodnight—but again, there was just a feeling of warmth on my lips. I felt elated. I wanted to be with Mai but I needed to allow her the freedom of being alone. If she wanted me, she needed only to ask. But the excitement of our meeting had had a drowsy effect and she needed to lay down and sleep. I was restless and decided to explore the town again and flew off into the night.

Chapter 10

I couldn't wait for the morning to arrive and see Mai again. I had flitted aimlessly throughout the night but with vibrancy and hope. Hope that, at last, I had found a mortal with whom I could communicate. But more than that, it was as though nothing now was more important than us being together and talking again. There was an aching within me, but not an aching of pain; an aching of longing, yearning…even desire. How much had changed in the short time I had been in this city. Yesterday, I had experienced the emotions of anger and frustration; today, it was the emotion of affection and yen. Knowing that I was dead had been but a momentary concern. Realising that I was immortal had set me on a path of discovery, a path of adventure, a path of awareness.

I arrived at Mai's house and stood outside her front door. I looked up and tried to picture which was her bedroom and how the house was laid out. In my mind, I could see her upstairs lying under covers of white cotton with a soft pillow puffed up around her jet-black hair. I smiled to myself and walked through the door. The scene that greeted me was totally alien to the one I had imagined a few seconds ago. The room that I had entered had mud walls, which in places had become loose. The floor was wooden, but uneven, with gaps and some broken boards. In the middle of this small room was a rough wooden table with four home-made wooden chairs. To my right was a small fireplace with ashes from a recently lit fire. Just through the wall opposite, I could see the kitchen. I went through and saw a woman scrubbing clothes and linen in a small tub. Beside her, I could see a pile waiting to be done. I guessed her to be Mai's mother and stealthily moved up beside her to examine her features. Slim, like Mai, she had a kindly face with the same slightly slanting eyes that Mai had. She appeared to be about forty years old, though the lifestyle that she must have endured may have made her look older than she really was. I was slightly concerned, from what Mai had told me, that she may be able to see or at least sense me. So, I made sure that I did not attract her attention.

I heard a rustling in the main room and turned around. It was Mai. She was kneeling down by the fire and raking out the old ashes. She had a bundle of twigs and was setting in motion the preparation of a new fire. I crept behind her, leaned forward and kissed her on the forehead. The sensation was warm, a wonderful glowing feeling. She smiled and stroked herself where I had just kissed her.

"Hello," she whispered.

"Hello, my beautiful, mortal girl."

I wanted to hold her, caress her, and just gaze into those magnetic eyes. But this was not the right moment. She was not the girl of my imagination before I had entered the house. She was not able to lie in bed under soft cotton sheets and idle away the daylight hours waiting for her lover to arrive. She was a working girl who had to suffer the hardships of these times just to survive.

"When will you finish?"

Quietly, she arose from the floor and held her hand towards my cheek. I reached out to take her hand and hold it. With my other hand, I stroked her cheek as she stroked mine. There was no contact but the sensation was electrifying!

"I don't know. I must help my mother until she has finished. I need to fetch water from the well outside. Then I will wash clothes with her; we have a lot today. My father has gone to help a sick child who has the black death. When he returns, I will help him prepare for his ceremony. We have some people from the town coming here with their sick children and all needs to be ready."

"How will you help your father?"

"I need to pick and fetch the flower petals, herbs and medicines that he uses during his ceremonies. I also must prepare some candles, both for the rituals and also for us when it gets dark."

"Where do you buy your candles; perhaps I could go with you?"

"We don't buy them, I make them from the fat of animals that have been slaughtered; but we can go later to the tree where we met?"

"Of course. Think of me and I will try to sense you calling. If that works, then you will only have to put me in your thoughts and I will be by your side."

I kissed her on the cheek, though I desperately wanted to kiss those adorable, tender lips. The kiss was pleasing even though there was no interaction. Mai too tried to embrace me, but only held on to air.

I pretended to leave her and went through the wall to the street outside. I returned immediately and watched her settle down to prepare the fire. She snapped the twigs and laid them deftly one on top of another in the form of a pyramid. Pyramid! How did I recognise that shape and name? I was sensing that I was beginning to comprehend a little more of my life, as it was. Though I was still unable to recall my previous existence when I had a mortal body, snippets of information were continuously making me more and more aware of whom I used to be.

Mai began to hum as she worked. I started to sense her as a person and her physical prettiness was but a mere splash in the ocean to that lovely spirit I saw before me. I could feel that here was a girl who had a beauty beyond those of the physical senses, here was a girl that I wanted to be with constantly, here was a girl who, if I had a corporeal body, I would have laid it down gladly to see her happy. I had felt anger, frustration, fear and hopelessness, and now I was feeling a new emotion…and this was the most powerful of all; it was a good emotion.

Reluctantly, I left Mai as she rose and went into the kitchen to her mother. I now felt an urgency to return to the old man. After the anger of yesterday, I was surprised to have this feeling of wanting to see him again. After all, he could not see me or sense my presence when we were last together, so why the wish now?

I did realise, though, that he had been able to see me once and had given me a warning regarding not being able to find him. The problem now was Mai. She had changed my priorities. Yet, as much as I wished to stay, I knew that I had to go. With that, I was in the room before him. He was in the library, gazing into his crystal ball. Without turning around, he said: "So, you have come at last!"

I looked towards the door but there was no one else there or in the room. Hesitatingly, I replied: "You can see me?"

"Oh, yes. I am relieved that you are here. Yesterday, I sensed you too but I did not want to worry Anne. She has been very concerned about my 'dabbling', as she calls it. Talking to the dead…well, let's face it, that would have convinced her that I am in league with the Devil!

"I have used my crystal here to communicate with you. It took a while but my crystal showed me that you were here, in the town. I could see a young pretty girl also, but it made no sense why I should see her. Perhaps, she is part of the reason that you are here? What I do need to know is why you have contacted me."

"Me! It was you who contacted me…by the tree. You told me to find you!"

"The tree was the location that my mind was sent to; my spirits told me to go. They said that you wanted me; they said that the future of mankind would be decided by your contact with me. I know no more than that. So why have you come?"

"I have absolutely no idea!"

"No idea? But surely you must know why you are here…and why you so desperately needed to contact me?"

"None at all. Suddenly, I was there, aware and conscious, but how and why I came to be there is an enigma; as is why I should need and want to contact you…you, whoever you are. But you told me to find you or I would be forever lost! I need to know what you meant."

"It is what my spirits told me: 'if he does not find you, he will be forever lost…and mankind, too.' They are the ones who foretold of your coming. But I assumed that you would know why you are here, that you would know your purpose."

"This remains a mystery; obviously, I had at one time a body and I was mortal like you but I cannot recall my physical earthly life. Why should that be?"

"Perhaps without your body, you have no memory, no recollection of how you lived your life, good or bad."

"But then you said, 'You are to become what I am'. What did you mean by that?"

"I really don't know! As my crystal became hazy, I was inspired to say it, something inside prompted me. I had not planned to say it; I just heard the words issue from my mouth!"

"Maybe your spirits…your ghosts…"

"Ghosts! Nay! Ghosts only perform aimless hauntings. They knock on doors, walk the walk of the dead, scream in the dark of night. They terrorise the living, scare the cats, curdle the milk, all for what?"

"But you contact these ghosts?"

"I contact no ghosts. My spirits appear to me in my dreams, in my crystal, but I seek out no ghosts."

"But aren't spirits and ghosts the same thing?"

"Not at all. Ghosts are the phantoms of the night that serve no purpose, no purpose at all. There is no good ghost; ghosts are malign and cruel. Ghosts are the soldiers of the Devil himself—harbingers of doom, meaning only to destroy all that is good—portents of the very hell from which they were sent to roam restlessly on this earth."

"Then, how can *you* help me? How can your spirits help me if I know not my purpose in being here? I am really lost!"

"Sit with me. Let us use my crystal. Let me see what is to be, or what may be. Come sit, but tell me, what is your name so that I may ask of my crystal on your behalf?"

"I don't know my name! I know my eyes are blue or at least I thought they were blue, and that a pyramid has the shape it does. Sometimes, I find I understand a little bit more than I did and this information stays with me as an experience. Yes, once I have experienced something, then it stays with me, but unless I have witnessed it, I cannot recall, *remember*, as you say."

"Let us see what my guides bring me."

With that, the wizard waved his hands over the crystal ball. He peered intently into it and spoke to it as though it were a human being.

"Ah, ha, something misty is appearing. Wait! Oh, it is becoming clearer."

As though he could wipe the misty screen clear, he rubbed the surface with his hand.

"I can see a young man here…oh, it has gone!"

"I am young then?"

"Well, not young as a child but younger than me. Perhaps, you have seen thirty-five summers?"

"What is your name?"

"My name is Michel. Michel Nostredame but I am also known in Latin as Nostradamus… Nostradamus the seer."

"Nostradamus! Yes! Yes! Yes! You are the one I was meant to see…but why?"

"Perhaps you wish to know the future, your future?"

"No! I *am* the future!"

"The future!"

"Yes, yes, oh yes, the *future*."

"Then tell me, why do you think that you have been sent to me?"

"If I am from the future, then perhaps I am here to tell you of the future, to warn you?"

"Ha, ha. I have prepared many almanacs for those rich enough to squander their money. Even the King of France himself, Henri…well, perhaps his Queen, Catherine, has sought my advice. Yes, the young prince, Charles, he too has been given my prophecy at the behest of his mother, Queen Catherine."

"So, you can see the future, then?"

"Not me, no! It is my spirits who tell me, my crystal tells me, but it is not always clear. The words, the meanings, they get jumbled and confusing and I am not always sure that I have got it right."

"So, why tell people about the future if you are not certain that it is correct?"

"I started prophesying many years ago. Then, I was inspired; I felt an urgency to tell people what I could 'see'. It was as though I was on fire, it burned and had to be released. It was unbearable to keep it inside. In those days, I had no need of my crystal.

"It all started when I was young, younger than you are now. I was sitting by the oak, where I first saw you. It was a most magnificent evening and my mind was meandering when suddenly a voice spoke to me.

"*Hello?*" I answered and turned around. But there was no one.

"Thinking that I had imagined it, I closed my eyes and felt the sun's warmth on my face. I was drifting in that peace and calm, when again, I heard someone calling my name: "*Michel; awake!*"

"I was startled, frightened, even. But the voice, I realised, was in my head. Though it was as clear and solid as any mortal speaking, I could feel it was coming from within.

"*Yes? I am listening.*"
"*Michel, the room will burn. The fire is near. Go quickly and warn.*"
"*Which room? Where?*"
"*The garrison. The evening torch is blowing in the wind. Go now!*"

"I got up and made haste, running into town…and in those days, I could run! The guards at the entrance stopped me and asked what was wrong and I told them. They laughed.

"*You've been drinking too much young wine!*"
"*Smell my breath, I have not had a drop. No! No! It is happening. Inside, quick!*"

"Such was the craving inside me and they could see that I was not drunk, that one of the guards came with me. We arrived at the garrison. There were about twenty or so soldiers inside. But there was no fire. I felt stupid and the guard started to chastise me. The other soldiers started to laugh, throwing wine at me and mocking me. Humbly, I walked outside and as I did so, the guard, who was slightly ahead of me, turned around to abuse me again. As he did, I saw his face turn from one of anger to one of fear.

"*Fire! Fire! Get out! Get out!*"

"The wind had blown the flames of the evening torch and had lit the thatch on the roof. The soldiers ran out but the barracks could not be saved, such was the ferocity of that fire.

"Needless to say, there was much talking about how I had saved their lives. I had become a hero and yet, but a short while earlier, I had been the villain. They praised me and took me to their captain, saying how I had saved their lives. But then questions started to be asked: 'How did I know this? How was it possible? Had I gone in league with Beelzebub himself?' It took a time for the accusations to drop, but then it was realised that I had saved lives, not attempted to injure them.

"Sometime later, my neighbour's daughter had been betrothed to a much older man in town. In fact, he was an official of the council with some fiscal means. Whether this man was a suitable match for the young woman or not was irrelevant. Unknowingly, he had the pox and would have infected her if the marriage had been consummated. I warned my neighbour, much to his consternation as he would have received a comfortable dowry for the marriage. Not so much him, but the daughter, who was not too keen on this union, delayed the wedding. Shortly before it was to go ahead, the groom-to-be came out in spots and ached and pus started issuing from his private region. His maid, who knew the wife of my neighbour, found out when she had to wash his clothes and linen and discovered this disgusting foulness and told her. The daughter was relieved, to say the least, and my neighbour, far from being displeased, was grateful for saving his beloved daughter from the wretched infection that this marriage would have brought.

"Rumours spread and before long, people were coming to me and asking for guidance—could I forewarn them of impending dangers, could I bring them wealth, could I foretell their futures? Then, because of this pestilence, could I heal their loved ones from the plague? I had already found that I had the gift of touch and could heal many of the sick of whatever they were sick with. I wasn't sure whether this was due to my *touch* or the herbs and medicines that I had found to be beneficial, but I did find that I had an uncanny knack of healing sick people. By word of mouth, the rich, the aristocrats—dukes, barons, nobles…and even the monarchy—came to me for help. Everyone wanted to know more. Everyone was out to benefit from my gift. I was offered positions of great wealth to reside with them.

"The main problem was that I was being harried into clairvoyance on demand and this is not how it worked. It was my spirits within my crystal or dreams that came to me, not the other way around. The pressure to satisfy their demands became overwhelming and though I didn't categorically fabricate information, I started to use more obscure responses—answers that would be enough to satisfy their insatiable appetite for the unknown. It appears that man has a voracious ability to believe what he wants to believe. So, the elucidations became of their doing, not what I told them. However, the healing…well, that does seem to be genuine enough."

"So, you believe what you tell them, then?"

"More importantly, they believe what I tell them."

"Well, can you help me or not?"

"Let me try again; after all, it is they who contacted me and told me of your coming."

With that, Michel again rubbed his crystal and peered intently into it. We waited for a few moments and then there appeared to be movement within his orbuculum. I detected a mist in the interior of the crystal and what seemed to be like covered figures. Michel was far more conversant and soon he was making notes and talking into this glass sphere. He grew increasingly agitated and finally leapt up from the table and strode over to the fire. He gazed intently into the burning logs and gave the impression of mulling over what to do.

"Well?" I asked.

"What they told me is highly seditious. You can change the course of history and mankind. It is within your means...and mine. But what you must do is beyond my capabilities."

"But your capabilities are to predict and foretell the future."

Nostradamus leaned on the fireplace and turned towards me.

"Yes, when my guides want me to. But their future is the immediate future, the here and now, things that will happen within the lifetime of the generations living today. What *you* can do is tell *exactly* the future of the happenings in between now and your lifetime, whenever that may be."

"OK, so what good will that do?"

"People will listen. People will take heed. People will act! I can give all kinds of double meanings or vague predictions, just as I have been doing. But to tell them the future precisely, with dates and names that cannot be misinterpreted, then the populace will credit me with the ability to prophesy—and I would be called a prophet. Man would listen to every word that I say and follow my guidance. I would be unchallenged. Those evil men and women who, for reasons of avarice wish to seek dominance over the world, would be challenged...and defeated. The world would become a haven—a safe place. Do you not realise the awesome power that you hold in your possession?"

"Yes! Yes, I see that. But how do I give you this information? I cannot even remember my own name! You, you have your name, Michel Nostredame, whether it be in French or Latin or whatever other language you wish."

"It is Michael in English, Michel in..."

"MICHAEL! My name is MICHAEL! My name is Michael; my eyes are blue and I have found the purpose for which I came—to find *you*!"

"Oh, that is good! Good! Now, Michael, what can you now remember? What will happen, in say, twenty years from now? Who will be King of France, of England, of the world?"

"Why, I still do not know any more. My memory still fails me. I still do not know which century I lived in and I cannot foretell all the things that can change the course of history. It is fruitless!"

Nostradamus turned back towards the fire and gazed at the leaping flames. He spoke quietly and firmly: "Then what my guides have told me *must* happen...if we are to succeed."

"Which is what?"

"You must take possession of a body. Once you are mortal again, all your experiences will be converted into memories and you will be able to function as you did when you were living."

"So that's what you meant when you said, 'you are to become what I am'!"

"That is what my spirits told me. But I have never been possessed and do not know how. I understand that it is truly dangerous. Once possessed, there is no guarantee that the process can be reversed. Even the Bible tells us that it takes a God—Jesus himself—to drive the evil possessions out of a man. I cannot do it."

"But we must try if that is the reason why I am here."

"I know of only one other who possibly could be possessed."

"Then let us go!"

"But he is malevolent...the Devil incarnate."

"Really, that evil?"

"He is a necromancer."

Chapter 11

"Everyone OK? I repeat, everyone OK?"

I looked up. This time there was no pain, no pressure, no pull.

"Am I dead?"

"Ha, ha, it'll take more than that to kill you, you little runt."

Jamie was back to his flamboyant boisterous self. I looked ahead and through the canopy could see Earth looming, blue, bright and frighteningly large.

"Jamie?"

"All right, my little British friend?"

"Yeah, I guess. A little nauseous, but otherwise OK. Please confirm, what happened back there? You had passed out. I saw your head lean towards Anna…and your eyes were closed. The last thing I remember was your wrist twitching as you opened your eyes."

"Michael, you hallucinated, most likely caused by lack of oxygen as the pressure increased. Both Anna and I were fully alert, though movement was virtually impossible. We have been trained for this. All controls were within our reach. However, we did have auto-pilot backup in case of any unforeseen problems."

"God, Jamie! That was the most scared I've ever been in all my life. I may have to change my trousers and NASA hasn't been that generous with clothing."

"Michael, I knew what to expect, you didn't."

"How long have I…?"

"Twenty minutes."

I looked over towards Anna. Like Jamie, she seemed to be in full control of her faculties and was busy making calculations on the computer in front of her.

"It's alright, Michael; Jamie and I have been trained to do this. Don't feel that you should have recovered as we have done…even if I *am* only a typist and filing clerk!"

Jamie smiled and turned to Anna.

"What's this? You didn't tell me you did filing! Oh, while you're at it, go get me a cup of coffee."

"It's OK, Jamie, I overstepped the mark and Anna is making me feel bad."

"Michael! How could *you* overstep the mark?"

"Anna, leave the sarcasm to the Brits; it's their second nature, you know!"

At that moment, I felt closer to Jamie and Anna than I had done since meeting them. I loved them both but in a friendly and professional way; though I think I could have loved Anna in a more personal way, given time.

"Michael, I just love British humour, it really is the best in the world. But sarcasm, well…we are pretty good at it too."

"OK, Jamie. I see our planet ahead; come on brief me…speed?"

"Petra! Mr Astro here wants an estimate of our speed. Can you oblige, please?"

"Five hundred and twenty thousand, fast enough?"

"Fast, but no, not fast enough! What's next, because at this speed, we should reach *Proxima b* in…eight thousand and eight hundred years."

"We are going to perform our next slingshot in twenty minutes using Earth's gravitational field."

"As bad as just now?"

"Perhaps, but there's still Mars, Jupiter and Saturn; we could, hopefully, also end up with both Uranus and Neptune if our calculations are correct, just to complete…well, almost complete our trajectory."

"So what's the next objective, Jamie, please?"

"We will enter the upper layer of Earth's atmosphere and be slung around towards Mars. The acceleration will double our current speed and bring us up to one million kilometres per hour. As we slip away from the pull of Earth and there is no gravitational pull, Anna will deploy fifty acceleration sails. The calculations have all been based on the position of Salt Lake Springs being directly behind us as we hurl towards Mars. On my command, NASA will fire all ten square kilometres of laser beams onto our sails and, should we outlive the mice, we will reach one half the speed of light, with no casualties."

"Jamie, why should we be any different to the mortality of the mice?"

"Well, first, because we didn't bring the speed up to what it is now. We beamed them from their speed of one hundred and fifty thousand kilometres per hour. Second, the sails will be deployed sequentially before all being extended together. So, our speed will be increased in stages rather than all at one go."

"Right."

"OK Anna, send them down."

Anna leaned towards the intercom as she had done earlier.

"Will all personnel please return to the Pod corridor at your level and climb into your allocated pods? Each pod has your name on it, but there will be a crew member to direct you. Strap yourselves securely in and close the lid. You will lose consciousness as the gas is introduced. Parents with young children, please ensure that your child is securely fastened in, the lid closed and they are asleep before entering your own. If you wish to view Earth one last time, please go immediately to the observation points. You have two minutes, then you must go to your pods. May God's love be with us all."

"What's it to be, Michael…you staying here or are you going to the Pod area?"

"You don't expect me to leave my two best friends to fend for themselves, do you!"

"Best friends now, is it!"

Earth was now immediately in front—big, blue, perfect. I gazed on in awe.

"That's the saddest thing in the world to see—my home, my memories, my friends, all to be but distant experiences of my life."

"Hey, I thought we were your best friends…well, at least we were a minute ago! Second thoughts now; how shallow!"

"Jamie…?"

"Michael, I feel exactly the same."

I thought I caught a glimmer of a tear in Anna's eye. She wiped her cheek with her hand and with her wrist wiped underneath her nose. A little sniff suggested emotions were running high between us.

"OK, Anna?"

"Just a mild cold, Michael…nothing serious."

"Yeah, I think I've caught it too. Damn viruses."

I looked at Jamie.

"Well, if we make it through, the first thing I'm going to do is get totally bladdered with a pretty West Indian girl."

"What? After me?"

"Hey, guys, I'll decide who my drinking pals are!"

"Who mentioned you, Anna? We just said a pretty West Indian girl…you think too much of yourself!"

Jamie and I sniggered. We really did share a common sense of humour. I noticed Anna blush slightly but she treated the comments in the good fun they were meant to be. She leaned forward towards the intercom, probably unnecessarily, I thought, perhaps to hide a shade of embarrassment.

"All personnel in pods, now, please."

"Shame that place in front isn't where we are headed…looks pretty good to me."

"Detour, Michael?"

"Nah… Probably boring; let's go to our planned destination. Tally-ho!"

Chapter 12

"Mission Control to Proxima."

"Go ahead, Mission Control."

"Jamie, it is Karl here."

"Hi Karl. Five minutes to Earth slingshot."

"Yes, we've got you clearly in sight. Jamie, the laser bank has been powered up and we will give you a pulsed blast every ten milliseconds. For your calculations, each pulse will be ten to the power three kilowatts per antennae."

"Got that, Karl, thanks."

"We have determined that you will have enough power to reach warp-drive factor zero-point-five. You need to wait until Salt Lake Springs is directly behind you. Our calculations have worked that out to be twenty-two zero three; please confirm your time now."

"Twenty-one fifty-three."

"We have twenty-one fifty-three also—good; there has been no time change since your return from the moon.

"Not even two-tenths?"

"Well, maybe two-tenths, but insignificant for the next procedure. There will be radio and communication silence from the moment you enter Earth's mesosphere. Once you have reached full power from the laser bank, communication will become increasingly unreliable, until you are beyond Uranus. At that point, all communication will cease and you will be on your own; we will be unable to assist."

"Registered."

"I shall hand you over now to Operations, good luck."

With that Karl Guttenberg left the Operations room and went down the corridor to his office. He shut the door as the telephone rang. It was the Chinese Ambassador to America.

"Karl, how are you?"

"Good, Kim, you?"

"Yes, good. How is the mission going; any mishaps?"

"Not as yet, all seems to be in order."

"Good. We all want to see the success of this mission and learn from it. The People's Republic of China has been working on the second generation of starships and we will be ready to launch ahead of schedule.

"The little delicate matter that we discussed at our last meeting in Beijing— everything is as arranged?"

"Yes, but personally, I do not think he can possibly succeed and I have told him. I categorically do not believe in all this airy-fairy stuff."

"Nor do we, but we can take no chances. He must not succeed; the consequences would be disastrous for us…and for you. Explain again to confirm; after all, we need to be in full agreement."

"Two hours after Proxima has reached Saturn, I will fire the laser signals that will destroy all electronics and communications in the module *Venture*. Proxima will remain unaffected as the module would have been released from the mothership and be on its trajectory to the centre of the tertiary star system, without guidance or control."

"Excellent. Do you see any reason why this will not work?"

"None; provided all systems are functioning at the time of laser contact, destruction of his mission will be total. Our little British pioneer will be heading for oblivion."

"The People's Republic of China is most grateful. Do you want to speak with your wife and son now?"

"Yes; put them on, please."

Back on Proxima, tensions were high. All the personnel, apart from the six of us, had slipped into their pods and were now asleep.

"You sure you don't want to join the others having a rest, Michael?"

"Jamie, how the hell could I! I am as high as a kite. I want to witness all of this, every last second."

"Bad word, Michael."

"What was?"

"*Last*, bad word."

I saw Jamie smiling and knew, despite the ordeal he now faced, he was in total control. With over four hundred thousand tons of spaceship in his hands and fifteen hundred personnel, the last thing anybody wanted was a nervous commander. Anna and Petra seemed to be relaxed but I could tell, by the unnecessary rechecking of calculations, that they were feeling the strain.

"See the mesosphere ahead?"

"Hmm, hmm?"

"Beautiful, isn't it?"

"Sure is."

"You know, if we missed our angle of approach and went too steep, this honey would destroy everything beneath us, every living thing, that is. It would be just like the dinosaur asteroid again. If we went too shallow, we would never reach the speeds necessary to get us to *Proxima b* in time for lunch! You hungry?"

"You bet, Jamie, I could eat a horse. Hit those lasers and get us home for dinner!"

"Mission Control from Proxima."

"Go ahead, Proxima."

"Speed now reading one million kilometres per hour and accelerating. Entering mesosphere in sixty seconds. Final contact…over."

"Jamie, I speak for everyone here. Mission Control wishes you total success. We will plot your progress as you leave the solar system but we may well be unable to assist as your speed could outrun our communication signals. Keep us briefed daily on progress."

"Will do."

"Thirty seconds to blackout."

"Finally, as pioneers, who have sacrificed every comfort and security for the benefit of mankind, we hold each one of you dear to our hearts. Your bravery and courage are an example to us all here. Take the knowledge of Homo Sapiens wherever you go and use it wisely and with compassion. Use the positive and good side of our species for the benefit of all in your new world, embrace love, not hate in this ultimate venture. God bless you all."

"And you, Mission Control."

"Ten seconds."

Jamie turned to me: "Michael, it won't be as bad as the moon approach, but there will be a slight gravitational affect and you may feel a little pull on the lower regions, like..."

"SHEESH!"

"Yes, like that!"

Observers from the Space Lab watched as Proxima hit the outer regions of Earth and like a skimming stone, hurled around the outer boundaries of the atmosphere and off into space.

"OK, everyone?"

We all acknowledged positively.

"Jamie, speed is now one and a half million kilometres per hour and steady."

"Thanks, Petra."

"Laser beam activation in seven seconds. Anna, deploy sails one, three, seven, fifteen, seventeen, twenty-five and forty-nine."

"Sails deploying...and in place."

"Four...three...two...one..."

On Earth, light as bright as the sun pulsed towards the stars. Even at the angle it was at, Space Lab saw the planet glow white from the region of Salt Lake Springs down below. On board Proxima, there seemed to be a mild surge as though someone had got outside and given the spaceship a gentle push.

"Yes, yes, yes!"

"Careful, Anna. Still a long way to go...a long, long way!"

"Jamie, speed ten million kilometres per hour and accelerating!"

If there had been tension before, the air inside the cabin was electric with both fear and anticipation. Charlie, Simon and even Petra had downed tools and looked on hopelessly and helplessly as, between the two of them, Jamie and Anna held all our lives in their hands.

"Anna, deploy sails fifty, forty-eight, forty-six, thirty-six, thirty-two and twenty."

Anna switched open the sails and I saw a look of triumph and desire in her eyes.

The feeling of fear was now slowly being replaced with hope. The thoughts of following those mice into a frizzled termination still remained, but there was an expectancy, a belief, that this time, the ingenuity of man would overcome that original disaster.

"Speed, fifty million kilometres per hour and accelerating."

"Deploy all even sails."

This time, as though there were going to be no hitches, Anna went through the manoeuvre without hesitation.

"Changing units, speed two-point-five million kilometres per minute and accelerating."

"Anna, I want a full check on all electronic systems. Petra, check hull and frame stresses and communication systems. Report in five seconds."

"All good."

"All good."

"Anna…deploy all sails."

As a routine now, Anna completed the exposure of all the photoreceptors to the onslaught of the laser beams directed at Proxima.

"Speed eight-point-three-five million kilometres per minute and accelerating…eight-point-six-five million kilometres per minute and accelerating… Warp-drive factor zero-point-five…and steady!"

"Yes, yes, yes!"

"That went quite easy, didn't it?"

"For us inside, yes. I don't yet know what effect that will have had on our little home… Petra?"

"Checking now, Jamie. All pressures are holding, so no leaks or structural weaknesses. Communications and electronics…yup, all have survived."

"OK, folks. Mars in six minutes and forty-three seconds. Be ready to encounter mild pull as before."

"Well, Jamie, so far it has gone like written in a textbook."

"I didn't really have any qualms that it wouldn't, Michael. We know the mice got frizzled but that's how we learned, from our mistakes. It'll be interesting when we reach warp-drive factor one, though!"

"Warp-drive factor *one*! Are you *serious*?"

"Do you remember back in the forties, the 1940s, that is, just after the end of the war, that Chuck Yeager broke the sound barrier?"

"Yeah, I remember."

"He was one of my heroes. Looked up to him, great courage—a good leader. In fact, he was one of the reasons that I joined the Air Force; I was inspired with the likes of him and those other mavericks of the age. Well, at the time, there was wild speculation that breaking the sound barrier would have disastrous consequences, creating sound waves that would have monumental effects on the air and subsequently on the environment, not to mention the structural damage that such an undertaking would cause."

"I didn't go into the philosophical sides of the event so no, I was unaware."

"Well, Michael, we are very much like Chuck—we are entering into the realm of the unknown. There has been a great deal of speculation, mainly by sci-fi writers but egged on by the tabloids, about what the effect of a body with mass will have when it reaches the speed of light. Some have written that is impossible to reach that goal...the great man himself stipulated in his *theory of relativity* that nothing with mass could achieve this. Others say that at that moment, space will distort into some kind of new web and we will travel back in time like a time-machine; even those who think that the whole fabric of our physical world—in other words, us and what we are—will simply disappear into pure energy. Well, young hypothesiser, I suggest we find out. Personally, I believe that we will continue just as we are and just as Chuck Yeager did, back in...1947, I think, and discover that nothing has changed. He just achieved another technological breakthrough, just as we will."

"Yeah, as you say, we will find out. Mathematically impossible! A bit exciting, though, isn't it?"

"Exciting isn't exactly the word that I had in mind, more like terrifying."

"You scared then, Jamie?"

"A bit, I guess...no, not scared; when I said *terrifying*, it wasn't in the scared sense, it was more like...worried, worried that all this that we've dreamed of, hoped for and worked towards, will just disappear into energy."

"Jamie, when I was involved in discussions with NASA eighteen months ago, there was no mention of attempting to disprove Einstein's theory and travel at the speed of light. Who has been involved with this? Who knows about this?"

"After the success with the prototype—except for the dead mice, that is—a few of the engineers back at base felt that the planet slingshots may get us close to, or even reach, the speed of light, if that was hypothetically possible. There had been some theoretical physicists who postulated that this was conceivable, using modifications to the mathematics used by the great *Albert*. I was called in by the Operations director and, together with Anna and Petra, was briefed by these theoreticians. Because of the sensitive nature of these hypotheses, we were sworn to absolute secrecy. As far as the populace knows, we will be flying at one half the speed of light and we have reached that already!"

"Out of curiosity, was Karl Guttenberg included in these discussions?"

"Yeah, he was included... Hey, don't worry; I'm sure he is one of the 'good guys'!"

"Jamie, I have a slight blip in the computer, bytes of information are fading out."

"Virus?"

"No, not virus. I wonder if the laser blasts have had a detrimental effect on the computer's memory chips?"

"Repairable?"

"I believe so but I need to strip down and check out."

Both Jamie and I looked at one another and burst out laughing.

"OK Anna, you strip down but not now, Michael here is excited enough and that may be too much...he has a weak heart, you know."

Anna realised the double meaning of what she had just said and smiled.

"In your dreams, Mr Astrophysicist, in your dreams!"

It was Petra's turn: "Mars ahead, Jamie. God, that planet looks stunning! Just red and brown and…just beautiful."

"OK, everyone. One hundred seconds to Mars contact. Anna?"

"I think the memory chips have definitely been damaged and will need replacing. We will need to revert to emergency backup until I can replace the damaged chips. I will turn off the main computer and call on the reserve."

"Does it have to be done now?"

"The longer it is left, the more unreliable it will become, and perhaps the more erroneous, possibly even corrupted, the information it will give, especially on planet coordinates and calculations."

"How long, Anna?"

"Perhaps a couple of hours."

"Right! Mars encounter first…no buts! Then, priority has to be sorting out the main computer; otherwise, we will be running blind and that will be a recipe for disaster. Can we survive on this encounter, Anna?"

"I think so, Jamie. I have only just noticed so there can't be too much corruption at the moment, but the sooner the better."

"After Mars, we will have one hour and thirty-six minutes to the Jupiter encounter; Anna, that's your timescale. Can you do it?"

"I think so."

"Good…sorted. Mars in ten seconds…hold tight."

The red planet grew from a small red globe to covering our whole canopy in the space of five seconds. I could see the faint red-pink Martian atmosphere on the horizon in front of us and only realised that we had entered it by the pull on our bodies. The effect was different to that which we had experienced with the Earth slingshot. Even though the gravitational pull of the planet and its atmosphere were far lower than Earth, the incredible speed we were now travelling at meant that the forces acting upon us were exacerbated. Even though we had traversed only one quarter of the planet and the duration of this discomfort was less than one-twentieth of a second, the effect on our internal organs was intense, to the point of getting severe leg and stomach cramps.

"Everyone OK? Anna, Petra, Michael?"

"Wow, that hurt."

"Sorry, Anna. Look, I think we are going to have to modify the schedule somewhat. First, Petra, what is our current speed?"

"Warp-drive factor zero-point six."

"OK, an increase of twenty per cent. But we cannot endure that with the gas giants. Those big sugar balloons will destroy our internal organs, no mistake. I propose that we direct ourselves at higher planet altitudes than originally planned. This will reduce the acceleration but if we manage to include Uranus and Neptune to bring us up to speed, we should be on target. Everyone agreed on that?"

"Yeah, makes sense. We can't go through that again; after all, Jupiter alone will be nearly two seconds at upper atmosphere altitude and the gravitational pull will be in the order of six times that of Mars and I, for one, can only see us travelling to the stars as blobs with an encounter like that. Proxima will probably suffer structural damage as well even if we did survive. No, I say go with the proposed modified plan."

"Don't ask me, Jamie, I'm not an engineer, only an astrophysicist. I'll leave that decision-making to you guys."

"Anna?"

"Yeah, I'm for it too. As Petra said, we would not survive the planetary pull at this speed. I shall notify Mission Control… Oh, hold it, they are just coming through; we haven't reached non-communication point yet. Oh, forget it, they want to know our location and how the Earth slingshot went."

"Anna, tell them of our change of plans and our new trajectory once Petra has completed the new calculations. Petra?"

"I suggest we go for the orbit of Metis. She will be on the other side of Jupiter, so no possibility of collision. The gravitational pull will be less than what we have just experienced and I estimate that the duration will be two-point-one seconds and our speed will increase by another…thirty-five per cent, giving us warp-drive factor of…zero-point-eight."

"That's good; Anna, agreed?"

"Yes, Jamie, I'm on board with this one."

"Right, Anna. Transfer to emergency computer backup. Then, priority must be given to the repair of the memory chips of the computer. Transfer all data to storage in case of any hiccups. We are all stressed and tired and I want to avoid any mistakes because of fatigue, so, Anna, hit the gas for twenty minutes, then work on the computer repair.

"Petra, please take over command. Inform NASA of our current status, though it is unlikely that they will be able to take any corrective action or give us corrective procedures before the encounter with that Big Boy up ahead. After that, it will be nigh on impossible for Mission Control to effect anything as we may be beyond the reach of their transmissions. I'm going to hit the gas for forty minutes as I won't be needed until we get closer to Jupiter. Petra, please take twenty minutes after Anna recovers."

"OK, Jamie, sweet dreams."

Anna was asleep immediately and Jamie not far behind. Petra busied herself with final corrections for the new coordinates, taking us to the orbit of Metis, Jupiter's nearest moon. She was in the process of contacting NASA, giving our current status and path modifications.

"Michael, I know that you are not needed for the next four years, but if you want to join the others so that you don't miss the next bit of excitement, then perhaps you should hit the sack as well?"

"Oh OK, Petra. You sure that you are going to be alright on your own?"

"How can you help me, Michael, if I do run into problems?"

I saw Petra smile as she nodded towards the other two asleep. With the visor over my head, I joined Jamie and Anna in the land of dreams.

Chapter 13

I looked on horrified.

"Necromancer! I'm not sure I feel comfortable with that!"

"No, nor am I, but I see no alternative. Body possession is serious—it is dangerous, it can be irreversible—it can sometimes lead to death, even oblivion! The necromancer contacts the deceased, he raises them from their rest, possibly, perhaps, against their wishes. The possessor has to be guarded or trusted— totally. But even the mortal, he may be as malicious as the spirit raised; while the spirit of that person long gone will have the power of mortality again, the necromancer may not wish to return to his earthly form."

"Well, surely the reluctant spirit doesn't have to possess the necromancer?"

"The force of the necromancer is strong. Sometimes too strong for the dead to resist. The will of the necromancer in a trance is almost overpowering. It is he who is in control, not the elevated spirit."

"But what if it is the reverse? What if the spirit is stronger than the necromancer?"

"Then a battle ensues. The force of the Underworld comes into play. The outcome could be calamitous. Should Lucifer become aware, then he may seek out the mortal's body and use it for his own means. A human body possessed by Satan himself…why, the consequences are beyond imagination."

"So, trust is total?"

"Indeed!"

"How much do you trust this man, then?"

"I don't. I am a man who believes in God, a practising Catholic; though I do not believe in the practices of the church."

"Aren't they the same? I mean, if you are a practising Catholic, surely you are a believer in the church itself?"

"Man has twisted the church to his own means. These 'Holy' men are anything but what they pretend to be. The word of God is as written in the Holy Book. This is what I believe; this is what I have faith in. But I must follow the teachings of the church if I am to remain unharmed. The Inquisition is strong; it is violent; it is unjust. It is the herald of evil and fear and superstition. It denounces those that question, just because they too believe that the church is wrong. They have a voice and the church tries to keep that voice silent. But that voice is strong and will rise up again and against this corrupted hierarchy.

"Martin Luther comprehended the corruption being created of His word by the church. A brave man indeed, to stand up to such a mighty force. Yet he was

75

bold enough to suggest: 'You are the evil ones, who pretend to speak in His name. You use the Church and create your own Doctrines for your purposes-not His'. Luther's followers are many and will increase. Indeed, Lutheranism practices more the real faith than the Orthodox Church; but I know my place and that of my family. It is for their sake I do not rise up against these slanderers of His word.

"But this man, this necromancer, he really is the personification of evil itself. He believes that intercourse with the Underworld—the world of ghosts, demons and goblins—will bring him the power and adoration that he seeks. Yes, that is what he seeks—adoration."

"Then, we cannot even contemplate using him. If he is as bad as you say, then the odds are stacked highly against us, against me."

"We have one advantage, my spirit friend."

"And that is?"

"His vanity, his seeking of adoration and his voracity. If I can convince him that I can enhance his power and his wealth, then he could be a most willing advocate."

"How do we do that?"

"You are a spirit from the future; he does not know that, nor must he. He will believe that he has raised you, like the others, from the dead and that it is he, and he alone, who has the controlling power."

"OK. Then what?"

"Once you have used him for your means, then revert to the real you. I shall record everything and we shall be as we were, or as we were meant to be."

"There is one other problem, though…"

"Which is what?"

"I do not know who the real me is or why I am here now or what my purpose is meant to be."

"That, my friend, is a problem but a problem only you can face and solve. My spirit guides told me of your coming, so they may be able and willing to help you, for they may know your true purpose."

"I am desperate to know who I am and why I am here. I now know my name—Michael. I have snippets of information and perhaps, with time…*time*! That is something also I now know. Time, Michael, Nostradamus… If only I could recall the rest! Yes, let's go for it!"

"I will make contact and tell him I need to raise a recently deceased spirit. When he asks why, as he almost certainly will, I will tell him that the deceased has left a sum of money to me and failed to tell me where it was before he passed on. I know that he will demand a share of my 'inheritance' in exchange for his services, to which I shall reluctantly agree after we have haggled over how much I will pay him."

"But once you get your 'inheritance', you could leave and not pay a penny!"

"True, but he will threaten me with retribution from his phantom army."

"But where will you find this 'inheritance'? You will have to pay him."

"Hmm… Can you search and find any 'loose change'? The Inquisition has been very successful at extortion, condemning those unfortunate enough to believe in their false promises, then sending them to the stake. I'm sure that money won't be too difficult to find…probably in the coffers of the church. Need to keep these *holy* men in the manner to which they are accustomed!"

"If your spirit friends can help, I'm sure we'll find something of interest!"

"OK. Go now and I will summon you when I am ready. Read my thoughts as I call you."

I left Nostradamus, though I didn't feel too confident in the task that he had set me. I found myself by the same tree and reflected back on what had taken place. I had to steal from the church money that they had stolen themselves with false promises to those desperate people, who they had falsely accused of witchcraft or blasphemy or any other untrue and meaningless reason. Condemning them to an unbearable death, all in the name of greed and self-righteousness. Morally, I had no problem taking the money from these supercilious and hypocritical men of the cloth. But physically, well, that was a different kettle of fish.

"Hello, my beautiful spirit."

"Mai! You knew that I was here?"

"I felt compelled to come here. Father told me that my work was finished and he needed to be alone with those he was trying to heal. The candles had been prepared and the flower petals had been arranged. The spices and herbs had been laid out and all was ready. Perhaps one day, I too will be a healer."

"Mai, I have known you only one day, but I feel as though I want to spend all my time…even eternity with you. Come and sit with me by the tree."

Mai knelt down, brushing her skirt underneath her. Her delicate manner of arranging her skirt as she rested on the ground was entrancing. I wanted to place my hand on hers, kiss those beautiful eyes, caress her face and stroke her pretty, raven-black hair.

"I have never felt like this, either. I see you…sense you, but cannot touch or feel your embrace, and I want to…so much. Am I destined to be the widow of a phantom?"

"Widow? No, we can be together…why, just like this…"

"Just like this is not enough; I want to be with you, the real you, the mortal you."

"Mai, that is impossible—I have passed beyond the mortal level. I am spirit now, but immortal."

"In old times, you would have been deemed to be a god…immortal."

"I am no god, Mai. I have some purpose; of that I am certain now. Perhaps it was just to meet you…be with you? But I feel that is not the reason. I feel that our meeting was a chance encounter. And I thank the spirits, whoever they may be, for this opportunity to meet and feel this emotion. My feelings are of joy, excitement and, dare I say, perhaps even…love."

"Feel love!"

"Yes, feel love. That is the passion that I feel for you…love."

"Oh, if that were true! But I also feel this excitement. Does this mean I also feel love for you! But how can I love something that I cannot have?"

"Mai, hold me."

"How!"

"Can you see me?"

"Of course."

"Then lay your head on my chest and feel my heart beating out your name. Take my hand and let our fingers entwine. Do not speak, but feel my thoughts, thoughts of affection…and love."

Mai rested her head on the ground where my ethereal heart raced, beating out the passion of a person in love for the first time. I embraced this mortal goddess as though, if I were mortal, she would break. I stroked that head resting on my waiflike heart. I took the strands of delicate hair and twisted them through my ghostly fingers. I kissed her gentle forehead.

"Hmm…that's nice," she said with eyes closed.

"Can you feel this?"

"I can feel gentleness, warmth, desire… I can sense your feelings for me, and these feelings are profound and sincere. What can you feel?"

"I feel your thoughts and these thoughts, like you, are pure and innocent. Mai, I am not going to let you go…I am not going to lose you. When my mission is done—MISSION! That's it; that is my reason for my being here!"

"I do not understand! Why have you suddenly become preoccupied and serious? A moment ago, you were speaking words of tenderness and now you talk of *mission* as though it were the most important thing in the world…more even than me?"

"Mai, YOU are the most important thing to me, believe me. I want to spend every single moment with you, and I mean every single moment. But before that can happen, let me explain as much as I understand and know."

Mai sat up, her beautiful dark eyes looking troubled and questioning.

"Mai, I love you, of that I am sure. There is nothing else in the world that I want more than to walk with you, stay with you, be with you…lay with you."

Mai looked a little taken aback at this bold statement.

"That is not permitted…not until we are married—and that can never be! Though my heart tells me that I want nothing more than to feel your presence join with mine…completely."

"Mai, my name is Michael. I discovered that earlier today, after I left you. I discovered a few more things. I have no memory, or at least, I have little recollection of my past. But, a bit at a time, small thoughts return to me. I am here for a purpose; that purpose is my *mission*. I also learned today that I am from the future, not the past."

"The future!"

"Yes, Mai, the future."

"Then, what does the future hold for us?"

"Mai, I do not know what the future holds for us. I do not know the future—yet. My first state of awareness was a few days ago. I was here, at this very spot.

When I became conscious, I saw before me an old man…I now know him to be a wizard. He told me to find him and disappeared. I did not know I was dead and could remember nothing at all: my name, where I was, why I was here, my past. I had no recollection of family, friends—even my country. After travelling around the town, I discovered that I had passed this realm of existence and that no one could see me, except for the wizard. I needed to find him, for as he left me on this hillside, he set me a riddle. He told me that I would be forever lost if I did not find him and that I was to become him. I found the wizard eventually and slowly, together, we have started to unravel my reason for being here; we even began to discover who I was, though there is still a long way to go."

"What is this wizard's name?"

"Michel Nostredame."

"Michel Nostredame? Ah yes, I have heard the name; I believe he is known as… Nos—"

"Nostradamus. Yes, that's right."

"I have heard that he is a powerful wizard and can foretell the future. People are wary of him and the church is frightened of him; I think that they seek to persecute him and prove that he is a sorcerer. So, that is why you have been drawn to him so he can foretell the future…your future?

"My future, no; that has already been written. I need him to draw out my memories so that I can determine my reason for being here and that is my *mission*. Mai, *this* is not the reason that I have found you, but now that I have—and I thank the spirits who sent you to me—now, I need your help."

"My help?"

"Yes. You see, I need to materialise into a living human; without this, I will have no recollection of my true purpose for being here."

"Materialise! Living human! Why?"

"Once I can take control of a human body, I think that all my past experiences will then become memories in the form that I possess. With these memories, I will at last discover the true me, who I was, where I am from, why I am here. I will be able to tell you the real future, the future of my time."

"And this wizard—Nostradamus—he has agreed to perform this materialisation?"

"No, he cannot. He has never been possessed before and says that he cannot do this, but he does know someone who can."

"Who is this other person then?"

"I do not know his name, Michel referred to him as the *necromancer*."

"Necromancer! No, no, no! That is evil; that is calling upon the Fiend himself to assist you. Michael, NO!"

"Mai, I am dead, gone from the world of the living. This necromancer cannot harm me; I am not living the sleep of the dead; I am alive in spirit form. These corpses decaying in purgatory, awaiting their judgment, these are the ones who should be afraid. The necromancer does not know and will not know that I am a conscious being. He will believe that it is he who is in control, that it is he who has awakened me! No, Mai, I will be the one in control; it is the necromancer who should dread me! His fear should be real for if I do not wish to return to the 'grave', then it will be him who will be subjected to hell and damnation! But there is no grave for me, no tombstone to return to. I am alive…and in love! So fear not."

"You say that you need my help and now you also tell me that you need to possess a necromancer's body. I'm not sure that I feel comfortable with this but tell me, what is it that you want me to do exactly?"

"Mai, I want you to steal."

"Steal! Am I to become a burglar?"

"Yes, steal…from the church."

"Michael! I trusted you!"

"Listen, Mai. The wizard and I have hatched a plan to entice the necromancer to help us. He will demand reward for his work."

"So, I will have to steal like a thief in the night!"

"Mai, have I yet given you cause to doubt me and my intentions?"

"No…no, you haven't, but stealing!"

"Mai, are you Catholic?"

"In the eyes of the people, yes. We attend Mass every Sunday, but in my heart, no."

"In my eyes and, I believe, in the eyes of others, the church is the sinful one. They control the people in the fear of damnation should they not conform to *their* teachings. They have wrongfully and wickedly sent people to their deaths in the name of the church, not in the name of God. Many people have tried to save themselves by paying the church and its overseers…pay those who judge and sentence innocent people it deems heretic, just because it suits their cause. It is this money—this *blood money*—that they have extorted from the guiltless, that I wish to take back. It is not theirs to keep."

"Oh, I see! Yes, I guess, putting it like that, perhaps it doesn't make me feel like I'm stealing, but nevertheless…"

"Mai, will you help me, please?"

"Yes, yes, I will."

Chapter 14

I stayed with Mai as she walked back home. I told her of my plan and though what was asked was alien to her nature, she knew that she had to help if we were to succeed. I still needed to know so much more about myself but that was insignificant, and unjustifiable, to be the reason to involve Mai with such an undertaking. It was to know of my purpose and how that would be of benefit to mankind. I was now convinced that this was the reason that I was here.

I left Mai at her house and asked her if I could stay with her for the night after I had completed my surveillance.

"I have the small room next to my father and mother. I would like to know that you are near me...it would bring me much comfort."

"Mai, I will be at your side as soon as my task is done."

"May God speed you on your way and keep you safe."

With our farewells made, I kissed my phantom kiss on those beautiful soft lips. If only Mai could feel my embrace...if only I could feel hers. Somehow, though, I felt that she sensed that warmth that she had mentioned before. She smiled, looked at me and, with a brush of her hand on my cheek, she went inside her home.

I now needed to find a church. I remembered my first night as I meandered through the square; as the moon had risen, I had seen a steeple silhouetted against the twilight sky. I was instantly in the square. The corpse had now turned putrid, flesh dangling from once solid legs and arms was being torn from exposed bones by hungry rats. I rose up above the square and could now see that, as I had suspected, the steeple belonged to a church. I flew straight to the belfry and noticed the solid bronze bells, three in a row. I descended to the ground and faced the large wooden door barring access to all corporal beings. I walked through and felt an atmosphere totally different to the atmosphere I had just left. The outside had a feeling of pain, suffering, cold, hunger and fear. Here, inside this magnificent Gothic building, there was a sense of peace, calm and longing. I wished to study this more closely so I passed very slowly through. Having arrived at the nave, I meandered to the aisle on my right and along this wall—adorned with sculptures and paintings of martyrs and saints—were the stopping points on the road to Calvary.

Each figurine seemed to be depicting his, or her, own martyrdom and the way to eternal life. I wanted to take the extended hands and hold them in my own and ask for guidance, but I knew that these were simply effigies of mortals who had gone to meet their Maker. I arrived at the transept and looked back from where I had come, then gazed upwards at the ornate ceiling showing more saints and archangels praising their deity. If I needed a belief in God, then this place would surely sway me.

Suddenly, I heard voices harmonising and realised that I was now witnessing Evensong. I watched from where I was as the throng shuffled towards the altar. In hooded gowns and bowed heads, the monks then knelt in prayer, whilst the priest, in his fine array, gave each one his blessing as he gave them Mass. Unlike his subordinates, dressed in ragged cowls and simple cords of flax tied around their waists, the Holy Father was finely dressed, like a brazen peacock. Here was the injustice, here was the wealth that had been stolen from the multitudes who, in ignorance and innocence, had bequeathed their paltry sums each week in the search of the hereafter, believing that those in power knew the road to salvation and had the forgiveness of sins at their command.

I waited until the Mass had ended and each of the monks had left for vespers and then followed the priest to his sacristy. He removed his mitre and placed it in a cupboard opposite the door. His magnificent robe, encrusted with gold, he placed on a hook on the wall. He went to the table in the middle of the room and poured himself a large glass of red wine. Without batting an eyelid, he swigged the entire contents down without pausing for breath. As he poured out another glass, he went to the cupboard where he had placed his mitre and removed a bunch of three keys that were hanging nearby. With the keys in his hand, he moved out of the room and returned to the altar. After making the sign of the cross, he made his way to the tabernacle, located slightly to the right of the altar. With a deft turning of a key, the door opened. He removed the gold cross that he had placed inside—moments before after the Eucharist, and behind this, another locked door was opened with a second key. He removed a heavy, small, solid chest and placed it on the altar beside him. With the third key, he unlocked this, opened the lid and exposed an array of coins, gems, gold and trinkets.

The people's wealth, I thought. *Your blood money!*

"This is what you have stolen! This, you have no right to! Paid for by the citizens that you have had butchered in the name of your God. Have you no shame, no moral scruples! In your egotistical and ecclesiastical belief, did you really think that you have saved souls in the name of the church? You, you are the one who should be feeling the flames of pain!"

But he could not hear me.

He removed a handful of coins and returned the chest to the tabernacle. Placing everything back in order, he made his way back to the sacristy to enjoy another glass of wine, probably paid for with the stolen coins in his secret booty.

I now knew where Mai had to come to collect the necromancer's payment. Though infiltration was merely a thought's move for me, to get a mortal in, such as Mai, was not going to be so straightforward. But I now had an idea to get her in! In the space of a thought, I was by her side in her room. Awake, she looked beautiful…but asleep—asleep, she looked exquisite! Her soft lips gently turned into a pout as she breathed softly in a slumberous manner. Her raven-black hair, fallen over her closed eyes, whilst her hands and delicate fingers protruded from the cover of her bed. I could tell from the shape lying before me that she was curled in the way a baby would cling to its mother. I saw a Madonna before me! Yet, try as I may, I could not enter into her dream state; I could not wander into that land of real and false and run with her in the breeze of her imagination. It was a shutter to me and I was surprised and troubled. I had started to believe that dreams were the separation of the body from the soul and that once her soul was free from mortality, we would be together in our own world…and touch.

As dawn broke, so too did Mai's slumber. There was a noise behind, which startled me. It was her mother. She looked towards me but showed no recognition of my presence. She pulled back the rag curtain and shook Mai. Mai drowsily opened her eyes and saw me. She stretched out her hand to me and smiled.

"Mai?"

"Oh, sorry, Mother! I was dreaming."

"Hmm… Well, you'd better get yourself out and working, dreaming or no dreaming. We've got more laundry today and I will need water as soon as you are up. Please get Father's breakfast afterwards and get yourself something too; you'll need all your strength today, my girl, make no mistake."

Mai's mother turned and looked directly at me. She paused for a moment and tightened up her eyes into a squint. I was starting to worry that she could see me; I certainly had a feeling that she could sense something. She turned to Mai.

"Are you alright in here?"

"Why, Mother, yes. Why shouldn't I be?"

I could tell from Mai's answer that she felt apprehensive just as I did.

"I am not sure… I can feel something…strange… Something not of this world…not malicious, just something unfamiliar."

"Mother! Have you been drinking Father's wine? There is nothing strange here."

"Hmm… Perhaps you are right. Well, you'd better get up, young lady."

With that, Mai's mother left the room but as she did so, she turned and looked at me again. I was worried that should she be able to see me, or at least sense me, it could put my visiting Mai in jeopardy and the thought of that was unbearable. As her mother went to the stairs to go down, Mai got out of her bed, came up to me and slightly trembling, held her face to mine. She whispered into my ear, "Mother can see you."

"Are you sure?"

"Yes, I know her and she can see you. I have inherited her gift of 'sight' but mine is more acute than hers. She will ask me later, I am certain."

"So, must I leave you now, then?"

"Yes, but I will find you later."

"Just think of me and I will be there."

With that, Mai began to take off her night garments and as she did so, I stood and stared. Her slender body was as stunning as her face. She looked at me and hesitated, then with her adorable smile, she removed the remainder of her nightclothes, letting them drop to the floor, and stood naked before me. I felt a passion build up in me as I could not recall before. I wanted desperately to hold

83

her so tight and not let her go. The thoughts that invaded my being overwhelmed me and I, losing all manner of reason, reached out to that naked, young, olive body, only to find I held nothing but the air in her room.

"My God… But…but you are beautiful… Truly, truly beautiful."

"As are you! But go…go, this is breaking my heart!"

Reluctantly, I left Mai but could not let go of the picture that stayed before me—her naked form in such perfection. Instantly, I was by the tree but could think of nothing…nothing but this human goddess. I closed my eyes to shut out the world, but again saw nothing before me but this young girl. I had a mission but this had started to take on a lower priority now that I had met Mai. A few days ago, all I could think about was my reason for being here; now it was as though I had found Mai to be my real reason for being here yet I knew that this was not the case. My true reason had to be greater than my love for another in this different dimension of cognisance.

As I rested by the tree in total perplexity, I heard the crunching of leaves underfoot. It was Michel.

"I thought I would find you here."

Was this Michel as before using his crystal or was this really Michel in physical form?

"You sensed it or felt obliged to come?"

"I am not sure. I was talking to Anne and suddenly felt this strong urge to go to the library. At the foot of the stairs, I saw a glow within the room. I went in and my crystal was ablaze. There was a luminescence that I had never observed previously. I slowly and tentatively moved to the table, sat down and gazed into my orb. The light was blinding. As I sat there, I heard a voice in my head speak out:

'In golden form, the Spirit trembles;
It knows not its resolve, nor its direction.
For passion too, speaks its mind;
The bough will break under coercion.'

"I knew that I had to come here and not delay; though did I 'sense' it—no, I think I felt compelled."

"Michel, I am in love, totally, unashamedly and insanely in love."

"Ah, ha, you have recalled another memory. That is good."

"No, Michel… It is not good. I am in love with a mortal in this dimension, in this time zone. A love that surely cannot survive."

"Ah! The girl!"

"What girl?"

"The girl that I have been shown. I did not understand why I was shown her—a very pretty young thing—but now it makes sense. She is part of you and your mission."

"My mission! Michel, my mind…my whole being is besotted with her. I can think of nothing else. Every waking second, she is in my thoughts and as I don't sleep, that makes it a frustratingly long time."

"Ah, Cupid has misfired! Michael, love is utterly blind, oblivious to the real world around the person it controls. But overcome it you must. Of all the emotions that man experiences, it is love, not fear that is the greatest. It knows no bounds and has an energy that, were it tangible, could lift off the roof of the world and throw it into the heavens. Michael, you have but one goal—to seek your destiny, and that of Man."

"Hell, Michel!"

"Hell, indeed."

"Michel, I…I just cannot, cannot…"

"Michael, I now know why I was despatched here and with such haste; you are at a crossroads and are suffering from a dilemma that needs guidance. I am old and do not feel the passions of the young, so I am more suited to steering you along the path that you must follow. This girl…what is her name?"

"Mai."

"This girl, Mai, she *is* part of your reason for being here. She is innocent and does not realise that she has been included in this design for Man's future. She may be more than a pawn in this grand game of chess and, God willing, will not be merely discarded once her services have been fulfilled."

"Michel, once this 'grand game of chess' has met its conclusion, I will find every which way I can to be with Mai…for eternity."

"Ah, yes, that is love talking indeed."

"Michel, I need to borrow your cloak and I will need a hood. I have a plan for how to get the payment for the necromancer, and believe it or not, Mai is a major player in this 'grand game of chess'."

"A cloak with a hood? I do not have one but I know someone who has— Anne."

"I have seen hers, blue, I think?"

"You have been watching Anne?"

"Before I met you, I saw her and followed her; it was her who led me to you. Perhaps the spirits are truly on our side; somehow, events all seem to have fallen into place one at a time. On reflection, it is as if a well-laid plan has gradually come to fruition, then finally, the whole purpose will be clearly laid before us. You know, I am becoming more confident that a hand bigger than yours or mine is guiding us along an irrevocable path, the consequences of which will be determined by the characters it has chosen, as actors, to play. Michel, I need a cloak and a hood of sackcloth, a flax cord and sandals of leather—can you provide?"

"Yes, come by my house tonight and I will have them ready."

"Also, your orb, we may need assistance with this."

"That I cannot command. We will sit at its circumference; what will be, will be."

I contemplated what Nostradamus had said and knew that he was right. If I had been mortal, my passion for Mai could have been seen as a testing time for me, but as I had already passed beyond redemption, I felt that this was not the case. I was immortal, in love…and in France. That, apart from an unknown purpose, was all that I really knew. I tried not to think of Mai as I planned my strategy for obtaining payment for the necromancer. This was proving difficult as I kept being drawn to her; I guessed that she was thinking of me and this feeling was making me want to go to her side. I resisted; God, it was hard. If I had been a believer in the faith, I would have got down on my knees and prayed. But I was an entity that knew no divine being and had to resolve my issues alone.

I returned to the church as I wanted to observe the priest in his daily chores. If my plan was to succeed, then I had to be confident in him not discovering Mai and had to determine his routine. Morning Matins were irrelevant; I needed to watch him after Evensong, but also knowing how he went about his day would be beneficial. I found him in his sacristy; he was drinking again. As a celibate, perhaps this was his only solace? Even so, it appeared to me that as an example to others, he should have been resolutely living the life of a pure man with no vices.

There was a knock at the door and he immediately got up and placed his unfinished glass of wine in the cupboard.

"Yes?"

"Excuse me, Father, there has been a rumour that Michel Nostredame has been at his practices again. I have heard that he is summoning the undead for his occult ceremonies."

"Is he, indeed? We need to catch him first-hand. He has too many contacts in high places to be easily taken to the Inquisition. The last time that was tried, my predecessor was sent to the Emerald Isle as a lowly monk by way of a penance for his false accusations. Find out what you can and bring me word."

With that, the friar left the room and the priest returned to the cupboard to finish his liquid refreshment. So, they were going to set a trap for my friend! Not if I could help it! With dusk approaching, I heard the harmonies of Evensong again and the line of monks made their way to the altar. I decided that I had seen all that I needed and left for Mai's house. She was in the small room at the back where she and her mother had previously been washing the laundry. Creeping up behind her, I placed my transparent fingers over her eyes and kissed her neck. I thought that I could almost feel her raven-black hair that traipsed down her back brush my cheek.

"Mai."

She was sobbing.

"Mai?"

Unabated, she continued, her head now lowered towards the bowl where a few hours previously, she had been working with her mother.

"Mai, what's wrong?"

"Michael, it's Mother…she *has* seen you."

"Oh! Well, at least that is out in the open. No more hiding."

"Oh, no…worse; now it's even more hiding."

"Why?"

"She does not recognise you and thinks that you may be haunting this house and mean me harm."

"Mai, what did you say to her when she confronted you?"

"She asked me who was in my room and I said 'no one'. She then asked me if I could not see the ghost before us. And I said 'no'! Michael, I lied to my mother! I lied!"

As hard as I tried, Mai was inconsolable. A mortal would be able to bring more comfort by simply having a physical body with which to embrace someone distraught, but all I could do was look on. Finally, after several minutes, Mai looked up at me and in her eyes I saw not love, but anger mixed with sorrow.

"Michael, since I met you, I have known love, passion and grief. I have even lied and agreed to be a thief. What person are you to make me do such things! Are you what you appear to be or are you a fiend?"

"Mai, I am no fiend. Believe me. But I did not—and do not—want you to lie, not to anyone and certainly not your mother. The lie was decided by you—"

"I lied because I was afraid—am afraid—of losing you. I have never known such contentment as when I am with you. I am frightened, so terribly, terribly frightened. Frightened that my world, my happiness, my meaning will be destroyed…and that is something I cannot endure."

"Mai, I love you; that is the only meaning that I am certain about. Nothing else matters as much to me as you do. Even though I am spirit, I could not face eternity if you were not beside me; I would rather die…but that is impossible. Without you, Mai, I would face perpetuity in purgatory.

"I mean to find out and complete whatever I came here to do. For this, I need you and I need the wizard. If what we are doing is right, for the good of man and the spirits are consoling, they will help us and, God willing, when all is done, they will bind us as one. Dear God, if there is any justice in the world, then eternity will be ours…together."

I looked into Mai's eyes filled with tears, tears that I desperately wanted to kiss away. I raised my arm and with my hand, brushed her brow. She closed her eyes and a tear squeezed out, running down her cheek.

"I felt that…I really felt that…"

"What did you feel?"

"I felt your hand brush my brow. I can also feel your compassion and your devotion to me and I know that they are true…your feelings for me. I know that you are no fiend; my anger and fear are waning and I feel comfort again, all because you are near me."

"Mai, would you like to fly?"

"Fly! Fly? Why, who wouldn't? Yes, of course, I would love to fly!"

"Then, close your eyes. Tightly, close your eyes. Now think of me and see me with your eyes closed."

"Yes, I can see you."

"Can you see my hand stretching out to you?"

"Yes! Yes, I can see that!"

"Take my hand; take my hand and hold it firmly in yours as though you will never let it go."

Mai stretched out her hand as her mother looked on.

"Here we go, Mai!"

With that, I took Mai above the roof of her house where she could gaze all around at the city below us. In the distance, I saw the steeple and took her rapidly along, skimming over the rooftops. We perched by the belfry, gazing around in the twilight with the last rays of the sun on the horizon. I put my arm around Mai's slender waist as she did likewise with mine.

"Hold on, Mai!"

She held me tight. I then took Mai up into the evening sky where we could see even more of the setting sun. The clouds on the horizon made a spectacular display of pinks and reds, even a contrast of grey, as the sun dipped below the surface of our land.

"Michael! This is…this is entrancing! Oh, to fly like a bird! I have never dreamed that this would be possible—oh, this is wonderful!"

"But Mai, this is my favourite…"

With that, I took Mai and zoomed down to the ground, then curved up just before we reached the bottom and soared towards the tree in the square. Mai squealed with delight as we rested at the top. She looked at me and threw her arms around my neck—we could actually touch. Our mouths met and the kiss was the sweetest moment I could ever recall—

"AHH…!"

"Mai, what's wrong? Mai! Mai!"

"Mai! Mai! Wake up, girl! What's the matter? Mai? Mai! Mai!"

Mai was back again in the kitchen with her mother shaking her.

"Mother?"

"Mai, what is going on?"

"Going on?"

"The truth now, girl—the truth!"

Mai looked at me and her mother turned around.

"Begone, fiend! Begone!"

"Mother! No! No! He is no fiend!"

Turning around, she glared at Mai and with a finger pointing directly at me, shouted: "You see him, Mai, and you saw him too, in your room! You lied to me!"

Then, turning back to me, I could see fear and hate in her eyes as she shouted:

"May the Devil take you back from where you came!"

"I mean you no harm, please listen!"

"Go! Son of Satan, GO!"

"Mother! He is talking to you, listen to him!"

"I cannot hear him; I can see him, shimmering in the dark, but I cannot hear."

"Mother, he is saying, 'I mean you no harm, please listen'."

"You can hear him too?"

"Yes, Mother."

"You have possessed my daughter!"

"She was not possessed, she joined with me in thought form; she was free to go at any time if she had wanted."

I could see the fear in her eyes abate, somewhat, as she realised that I was a thinking entity, but I could still see anger.

"Then why are you here? What do you want of us? What do you want of Mai? Is this house haunted…possessed?"

"This house and the people living within its walls are not haunted; there are no evil spirits here."

"Then what are you, ghoul?"

"Although I am not of this dimension, I am no ghoul, no spectre, no undead. I am here with a purpose, which I do not yet know. I am not from your time…I am from the future."

Mai's mother seemed rather taken aback at this statement. The furrows on her forehead had also diminished and I could feel her anger decline. She was still distressed, though more prepared to listen than a few minutes ago. The main thing had been her fear—fear of the unknown, fear of the incorporeal.

"If you mean us no harm, then what do you want with my daughter?"

"There is a plan afoot to discover my purpose. Mai is needed to help me uncover my reason for being here."

"Why Mai?"

"Mai can see me and more importantly, she can 'hear' my thoughts. It is for this reason, and this reason alone, that I have chosen Mai."

I could not, and deemed that it would be highly inappropriate, mention that I had fallen in love with her daughter; that would have been tantamount to spectral suicide.

"I need Mai…more than you can understand. She needs to come with me to help me with my mission. There are risks and there may be danger, that I cannot deny, but without your beautiful daughter…and her beauty is the Chi that I see within her—without your beautiful daughter and the courage of her spirit, not only I, but perhaps the future of mankind, is in jeopardy."

"Danger! What danger?"

I could see that Mai's mother had selected one word that I had used, rather than the meaning of everything that I had said.

"Do you wish to see Man destroyed—everything around you devastated and void? Do you wish to see the discontinuation of life as you know it? Do you want the future of all those you know and love, including Mai, sent to oblivion?"

"No…no, I do not."

"Then you must trust me, as Mai has trusted me."

"Hmm…"

"I will protect your daughter with everything in my power. I will strive to keep her safe. I believe that the spirits of good are here, with us, guiding us towards our destiny. Indeed, they sent Mai to me…not I to her, and that surely shows that Mai was intended for this momentous task before us. Without Mai…well, I feel this task may well be doomed."

"Mai?"

"Mother, I am willing to help. Michael has already explained all of this to me."

"Michael! You know his name?"

"Yes, Mother. He needs time and help to reveal his commitment for being here. He has no memory but occasionally something returns to him and one of those things was his name."

"What is it that you are asking Mai to do?"

"She must come with me this evening to the wizard's house. We will collect what we need and practice our strategy for the next stage of the ruse."

"The *wizard's* house? Which *wizard's* house?"

"Michel Nostredame."

"That's Nostradamus! He is a good man, I believe. He has cured many of the plague. I've also heard that he can see the future…that's why you need him!"

"He is a major player in this strategy—as is Mai. But we need to go now to meet with him. Will you permit Mai to go, please?"

I sensed that I knew her answer before she spoke but wanted to hear it first-hand. I was certain that it was the mention of Michel's name that had persuaded Mai's mother to allow her to go. Whether it was because of the contact with such a distinguished citizen of the town or because she felt more secure about Mai's safety with him involved, I was not sure; but she agreed to let her daughter help me.

"Make sure she remains unharmed."

"I will—and thank you."

I could not take Mai flying to Michel's house unlike when I had in her thoughts when her mind had been clear. Her body was not in my control, only her awareness.

"Be safe, Mai."

"I will, Mother. I will be back before the bell strikes one."

She put on her cloak, bade goodnight to her mother and closed the door.

Though hesitant at the task ahead of us, I was euphoric with Mai by my side. As I had done just a short while earlier, I placed my hand in hers but there was nothing that I could hold, just a tingling in my fingers. Mai responded by clasping her fingers through mine until they were interlocked in a lover's hold.

"Mai, how old are you?"

"Eighteen...nearly nineteen next month."

"How could you love an old man like me?"

"Michael, you are not old, I do not see 'old'. I see your spirit and in that I see beauty, courage, strength and youth. I cannot explain but 'old' to me is frail and weak and wrinkled, and you have none of these makings."

"But Mai, what if I was old, what if I possessed all these attributes of an old man?"

"I would love you as much as I do now. Irrespective of the physical definitions of age, I see before me a man prepared to face destiny with tenacity and determination...that is the man that I love and no stigma, no social barrier, will ever change that."

"You have a head on your shoulders, my young Indochinese queen, make no mistake. You have youth, yet you also have the maturity of a person who has lived through hardship, who has tasted the bitter pangs of sorrow and yet is empathetic with those around you, with life, even."

"We had a difficult life as slaves. Father was beaten with sticks and with whips, but he did not yield to them. He did his work without complaint. Mother had to cook, wash laundry, keep the house in order and look after the children. I had to clean fires, clean rooms, chop wood—even clean chimneys by climbing up inside. The working days were long and I was still a child!"

"How did all this change then?

"The Master's only son became ill. The doctors here could not help him, they bled him and gave him medicines that did not work. The boy became worse and the doctors told him that he would die and they could do no more. Father's spirits visited him and told him that they could heal the boy and they told him what he should do. Father risked everything to be free; he told the Master that he could heal his son, but to do so, he demanded that he should be made a free man with his family. At first, the Master dismissed him with a beating but the boy became

91

so bad with pain, crying out to his father, that the Master agreed to my father's conditions. Father cured the boy but the Master did not keep his word. He did not want to lose a man who had the gift of healing and chained him in the cellar. So, Father put a curse on the Master and his house. The spirits worked well; they made such carnage and fear in the house that the Master had to let us go. He pleaded with him to be gone and was too afraid to risk taking Father's life lest my father's spirit returned to avenge his death.

"We were turned out of the house but had no shelter. Father built a hut from the trees outside the wall of the town…and we were free! This freedom tasted so good; we worked as hard as we did when we were slaves, but the work was for us. After this, word got around that Father could heal the sick and people came to us for healing. Mother was offered laundry work, while Father was paid as a healer. We were able to buy this house within the town walls and no longer had fear of the wolves and villains."

"Wow, Mai, that is sad; what a terrible young life you have had."

"Wow! What is 'wow'?"

"I have no idea! It was just something that came into my thoughts."

Mai giggled. It was the sort of sound I just wanted to hold onto in my sentience, a sound so full of vitality and comfort, I did not want to let it go.

All too soon, we arrived at Michel's house. I wanted our perambulation to continue forever, as did Mai, but we had a task ahead of us and this had to be faced. Michel was waiting for us as we knocked on the door. It was opened by the maid.

"Yes?"

Without thinking, I started to explain that we had come to see Nostradamus. Mai listened on but the maid was taken aback by this young girl at the door, not answering her question.

"Yes, what do you want?"

Mai realised instantly why the maid had ignored me.

"We—I have come to see Michel Nostredame."

"It is late. He is not expecting anyone."

"Please tell him that Mai… Michael is here; Michel Nostredame is expecting him…her."

The maid looked at Mai with suspicion and curiosity. She did not afford Mai a curtsy but said that she would check. With that, she closed the door.

"Mai, I cannot believe that I just spoke to someone without realising that I cannot be seen or heard except by you—and of course, the wizard. We have been together so long that I forgot I was not of this dimension."

"And I forgot too. You are so clear to me, and even though you speak to my mind, it is just as though you have a voice."

The door opened and the maid returned.

"The Master will see you now. I will take you to him in the library."

Mai followed the maid, but without thinking, I just found myself in the library, facing Nostradamus.

"Ah, ha, you have arrived. Where is the girl?"

At that point, the thud of footsteps on the spiral staircase could be heard as the two girls descended. The maid stood in front of Michel and did a curtsy.

"Miss Michael, sir."

"Thank you, Agnès."

"Ah, more beautiful than even in my crystal. No wonder that the spirits themselves find you so captivating."

"Michel, this is Mai."

"Yes, I thought that it was."

"Good evening to you, sir."

"Mademoiselle, please take a seat. I shall fetch your cloak, hood and cord."

"Michael, why do I need a cloak, hood and cord?"

"I shall explain, Mai."

Chapter 15

I awoke. Both Jamie and Anna were working. Jamie was in conference with Petra regarding the new trajectory, whilst Anna had removed the casing of the ship's computer and was removing old data storage and memory chips.

I wanted to return to sleep; the excitement of the past twenty or so hours had taken its toll and I was weary. I closed my eyes again but could hear the others in the background. I forced myself to come to.

"Welcome, Mr Rip Van Winkle!"

"Hi, Jamie. What time is it?"

"It's fifteen minutes to Jupiter encounter. How's it going, Anna?"

"Struggling a bit here; I have identified five memory chips that have been corrupted, almost certainly from the laser blast. If nothing else has been affected, then I should be able to remove and replace them within the next forty minutes. However, there is an indication that this may not be the only damage incurred during that contact time."

"Keep at it and keep me informed. Petra?"

"Good, Jamie. Metis orbit calculated and sorted. Just checking on laser pulses."

This was the first time that I'd honed in to Petra. I had always found it hard to differentiate between a South African and New Zealand accent.

"You're not, by any chance, from Pretoria, are you?"

"Good guess; just a whisker away—Auckland."

With that, she pushed out her tongue and made the well-defined Kiwi face used by the All Blacks and laughed:

"Auckland, why, that's…erm…why, that's…?"

"Yeah, only fourteen thousand kilometres; in fact, we're almost neighbours!"

"Oh, I guess I'm not as good on accents as I thought I was."

"This your Brit chat-up line, Michael?"

"No…no…why, I erm…was merely…hmm…"

Petra was amused by my mild embarrassment and judging by the twinkle in her eye, it may have held a little attraction for her.

"What about Anna, then? I bet you've been itching for the chance to find out where she is from?"

Anna looked up and both women laughed.

"Well, I guessed that she was from the West Indies, judging by previous conversations?"

"West Indies! Michael, Anna's from Madagascar."

"Oh! I really got that wrong…"

Both women screeched with laughter as I started to crumble under even more embarrassment. Jamie joined in too.

"Come on, girls, give the little lad a break. Hey, Simon, where's Anna from?"

"Oh, I heard that she's from some little island just off the coast of some big place. You know, big, big place… Begins with 'A'…"

"Africa, pal, Africa."

"Ah, yes, that's it, Africa."

There was a furore going on in the main control room as all four of Jamie's team joined in with the good-natured banter. I turned to Anna:

"You really from Madagascar then?"

"No, Michael. A small island in the Caribbean but it's a terrible chat-up line!"

And with that, the entire main control room was filled with laughter—myself included. Yes, this was going to be a good trip.

"Oh! There she is, folks—stunning, big and dangerous—Anna?"

"Jamie, memory chips can be replaced and put in order but something's still not right. Do you think that you can do the Metis orbit on backup?"

"All stored data programmed in?"

"Can do that now; should take about twelve minutes."

"Leaving us three minutes to Metis orbit. Yeah, that's fine."

Though somewhat tense, I settled back in my seat as best as I could. Petra continued to scan the path ahead whilst Anna began data download onto the back-up computer system. I looked ahead and saw, with unaided eyes, that magnificent giant in the distance. Although over one hundred and sixty million kilometres away, she represented the brightest 'star' in the sky and with every second, this gas giant became slightly larger, brighter and more defined. I was mesmerised with this planet ahead. As a theoretician, my intimate knowledge of the planets, and indeed the solar system, was confined to textbooks, calculations and mathematical hypotheses. I had always loved the night sky even as a child, but I had never been a true astronomer in the real sense of the word. Constellations were more than mere names, but I was by no means an expert or even an amateur expert when it came to identifying the celestial bodies above our planet. I was just getting lulled into a false sense of security when Petra called out: "JAMIE! Bandit ahead!"

"Bandit? Where?"

"Two-seven-zero degrees of flight path."

"Identify bandit."

"Rogue asteroid, mass, trajectory, speed unknown."

"How come we cannot have this information?"

"Computer's down, Jamie," Anna answered.

"Do we have visual?"

"Afraid not. Laser sensor only."

"Distance?"

"Forty-three million seven hundred and fifty thousand kilometres, contact time four minutes and five seconds. Evasive action, Jamie?"

"Petra, prime torpedo one on laser pulse trajectory."

"Torpedo one, primed and on target."

"Without full information on trajectory, mass and speed, it will be a hit and miss avoiding a disaster if it is in our flight path."

"Let's hope it won't be a 'hit', Jamie," I chirped in.

"Hey, I heard that you Brits had a strange sense of humour, especially in times of danger."

"Jamie, what size torpedo do you plan on despatching, if you despatch?"

"One megaton."

"Do you have a massive armoury on board?"

"Adequate, but not massive. Why?"

"Did NASA take into account Proxima's speed when arming this ship?"

"Actually, it was the Air Force, but why do you ask?"

"Well, Jamie, at this speed, if we were to bump into a small planet for instance, with our mass, we would annihilate that planet."

"OK...?"

"So, at this speed, any projectile would severely damage the trajectory of, or even destroy, an object itself."

"Meaning?"

"You don't have to waste heavily armed or nuclear missiles to effect a drastic alteration of the threatening projectile. Even a pebble from a catapult at this speed could pass through any material, creating enough energy to totally ionise the pebble and have a devastating effect on the object it hit."

"So, I don't need a nuclear device?"

"Jamie, you don't even need an explosive device. Just fling out your shoes, socks...underpants; it'll have a destructive effect."

"Conventional, then?"

"Yeah, conventional."

"45 kg sufficient?"

"More than sufficient."

"That's good news—we've got stacks of those. Arm a 114 Hellfire, Petra."

"Arming now, Jamie."

"Say, for an astrophysicist, you sure do know a lot more than just space."

"It's all theories and mathematics, Jamie; but I do know a lot about energy, mass, speed and time."

"Update on bandit, Petra?"

"Without computer backup, I'm going on laser sensor readings; graphical extrapolation suggests that bandit will cross our flight path four seconds before Proxima arrival."

"Confidence level...ten being guaranteed?"

"Nine."

"Four seconds? That's just over seven hundred thousand kilometres."

"Put like that, it looks like it's not even close."

"But four seconds is four seconds, no matter what distance we are talking about."

"Jamie, with that degree of confidence, do you think it would be wise to attack the asteroid with a ballistic missile? If you got a direct hit, the trajectory would change, the bandit probably annihilated, BUT there would be rogue debris flying off in all directions and we could fly into all that with consequential damage. It would be like flying through the rings of Saturn!"

"Michael, I'm glad you came along for the ride! What would you propose then?"

"Laser sensors are very accurate. Petra is a top-notch engineer and I would trust her calculations to the millisecond. My advice—though I hold no authority here—my advice would be to do nothing but let Proxima run its course."

Petra's beaming smile hit me directly.

"Now *that's* what I call a good chat-up line!"

"Hey, Pinkie, don't get too cocky now. Michael said to the 'millisecond'; nothing better, you know!"

"Pinkie?"

"Hey, Petra, take off your cap."

Petra removed her cap to reveal a short crop of intense luminescent pink hair.

"Hmm…nice…very nice. What's your real colour, Petra?"

"Mousey…boring mousey."

"Oh, mousey's not boring…it's…yes, I guess you're right…boring."

"That's it, Michael; give her both barrels! OK, I'm going with Mr Astro here on my left… Petra?"

"I'm good with that."

"Anna?"

"Yeah, me too."

"How long, Petra?"

"Thirty-eight seconds…but visual will be impossible without screen magnification and the Main is down until Anna has finished. Bandit will be too small and far away and we will have to rely on laser sensor probes. I'll transfer readings to your screen, Jamie."

"OK…yeah, got it. Oh, man, look, we're not even going to notice this small fry. One for the road, anyone?"

"Nah, I'm good, thanks."

"Screen tracking… Look at that. Here she comes. Five…four…three…two…one…bye, bye, bandit. Petra, you were—"

"JAMIE! SHIT! Visual…second bandit!"

As with the moon sensation, the whole scenario seemed to play out in slow motion. We were totally powerless as the second asteroid glinted in the distant sunlight. It was directly in line with our flight path and grew from nothing to the size of a football in the space of two seconds. It was Petra who I thought I heard first, though it could have been anybody as all voices seemed to be stretched out in a very low bass frequency.

"It…must…have…been…hidden…by…the…first…bandit!"

Slowly, though it must have been instantaneous, Jamie depressed the plasma burner switch and I heard the hiss and felt the reverberation as the plasma engines burst into life. The football was now the size of a house and we were directly headed for the front door. Anna held up her hands to her face as if to cover the horror unfolding before her. I saw Simon sluggishly turn his head to the canopy in front of us and open his mouth at the approaching apocalypse: "Holy cow…"

I was frozen! Not a muscle, sinew or fibre moved within my body as we were now directly in front of a mountain. The potholes, score marks and cavernous depressions of millennia of confrontations with other extra-terrestrial bodies were directly in front of us. I felt a slight judder as the mountain passed instantaneously to our right…and was gone! It was Jamie who spoke first: "Did you say *underpants* just now, Michael? Well, the state they're in, if I had hurled them at that, I think it would have obliterated every object in the Universe!"

I was trembling. I noticed Petra, Anna, Simon and Charlie were all unable to speak or function; the shock of what had just passed had created jabbering wrecks of all of us. None of us moved; we were spellbound by the scenario of the previous five seconds. I slowly took on board what Jamie had just said and realised that in the face of death, he was the only one who had remained in control throughout. As a fighter ace herself, if Anna had been at the controls, perhaps it would have been her, not Jamie, who would have remained as cool as a cucumber; after all, it was what they had been trained for.

"Nobody speaking to me?"

"J…J… Jamie…"

"Yeah, I know my name…don't wear it out. Now who said that? Oh yeah, it was from that film long-gone, some blonde singer and a dancer?"

"Jamie…that was incredible. I'm still trembling, and here's you talking about some long-gone film and cool, calm and—"

"Collected?"

"Yeah, collected."

"Well, someone has to! I mean, who's gonna make my 'sunny side up' breakfast if we all dither at the slightest glitch!"

With the professionalism that they had been trained, everyone continued with the tasks that they had been allocated. Charlie, in charge of logistics, which included weaponry, and Simon, for the running and maintenance of the plasma engines and all flying craft, seemed to be working as normal. Whether they were still shaken or not, they did not show it, but I, for one, had not properly recovered. I looked in front and there was Jupiter in all its colour and glory. The most spectacular and magnificent of all the planets in our solar system.

"Jamie?"

"Yes, Petra?"

"You tweaked the plasma burners just now?"

"Sure. Automatic reaction to avoid meeting my Maker before the predetermined date."

"Yes, well, I'm afraid that has created a bit of a problem with the Jupiter encounter."

"How so?"

"You've altered our flight path."

"NO! No! No! No! What does backup show?"

"You are still on track for Metis orbit, but we are going in the wrong direction; we are going clockwise instead of anti-clockwise. Jamie, we are going to meet and strike Metis!"

"Anna?"

"Sorry, Jamie, backup only. Main is still presenting me with problems."

"And that means…?"

"Yup, no auto-pilot without Main!"

"Petra, how long to Metis orbit?"

"Two minutes and twenty-five seconds."

"I am going to have to dip inside Metis…closer to that giant in front than I wanted. This means more gravitational strain on us and Proxima. The ship should be OK but I fear a bit for us; after all, we are entering unchartered territory. I guess that's what pioneering is all about. Petra, contact Mission Control and send bandit encounter and Jupiter reprogrammed information."

"Now, Jamie? I'm setting trajectory coordinates for Metis orbit."

"Oh, sorry, yeah, complete that first; otherwise, it may be the last data transmission we send."

"Metis orbit, clockwise…programmed, Jamie. What shall I despatch to NASA?"

"Give them bandit encounter and corrective action taken. Tell them we will enforce personnel and electronic safety with anti-radiation shield."

"Jamie, that means we will not be able to use any external programmes—no laser pulses, no radio communication, no microwave transmission. Jamie, we will be flying blind!"

"I'm aware of that, Petra. But we will be visual…just like Anna and I have flown many times before."

"That was on Earth, in an environment you knew!"

"OK, this is all new. But I am worried that the radiation from that Bad Boy will obliterate all our electronics, never mind what it will do to us! Don't want to travel for the remainder of eternity riddled with every type of organ cancer known to man. Besides, if that radiation does penetrate the ship, we can kiss this mission goodbye, once and for all."

"Point taken, Jamie."

"How long?"

"Twenty seconds."

"Metis location?"

"Zero four-five degrees of flight path."

"Current speed?"

"Warp-drive factor zero-point-six."

"Estimated Metis contact time?"

"Fourteen seconds."

I looked up in front at this most wonderful, yet frightening, coloured giant. This hobgoblin of our solar system—would it eat us up or let us pass by unhindered? Would we be too insignificant to stimulate its interest? What are you going to do, my monstrous beauty?

"Picking up radiation from radio transmissions."

"Transmit all data, Petra."

"Done."

"OK, all electronic systems…shut down. Anti-radiation shield, activate. Oxygen masks on, set to forty-five per cent. I have full manual control…now!"

Unlike the asteroid' encounter, we all were fully aware and functioning logically as Jamie took control of the ship. We had had time to prepare and our minds were normal. This time, there was no dreamlike state, no psychological protection from the traumatic experience before us. Everyone stopped their work and stared ahead through the canopy. Jupiter had covered the whole of the screen in front for over ten seconds and the only sense of distance was the clarity of the storm clouds before us. That great red spot was now stationary; Jupiter, despite its swirling atmosphere, did not rotate. It was as though it wanted to watch our transit. We were travelling at sixty per cent of the speed of light alongside the king of planets, aided by the protection of modern technology, trusting only in the skill of man and the help of God.

"There she is…dipping in…now!"

Jamie turned on the plasma engines and directed us towards the troll on our right. I thought I caught a glimpse of Metis on my left, but the moment was transitory—just a shimmer against the blackness of space. Though we were protected from the radiation, the goblin was drawing us in. With no auto-pilot support, Jamie had to survive the king's invitation to dine with him on his own. Just like the moon encounter, all movement was impossible. Jamie held onto the plasma switches and again, I heard the hiss and felt Proxima vibrate as we all passed out…

Chapter 16

I waited by the altar until I could hear the chant of Evensong. The melodious harmonies, though droning in a somewhat tuneless chant, were exquisite. If ever I should take an interest in music, I thought, it would be the magic of harmonics that I would encompass and develop. Even sombre music, such as the monks were now singing, rang forth like a herald on Judgment Day as the faultless harmonies combined together. A few seconds later, the file of friars entered the church and with conventional humble gait, they made their way with bowed heads towards where I was resting.

From out of his sacristy came the priest, preparing for evening Mass. He went to the tabernacle and removed the golden cross, placing it with pomp on the altar before him. Bowing low in accordance with traditional reverence, he turned back to the tabernacle and withdrew the paten and chalice. Again, I noticed that both were made of rare and precious metals—the paten of highly polished silver whilst the chalice was made of gold. I could feel anger welling inside of me—*more blood money*, I thought.

The Mass started and though I felt nothing but contempt for this little gathering, I felt that it was not the throng that were evil, only those capable of the atrocities performed in the name of the church. I was interested in gazing upon the faces of the featureless friars and left where I had been residing and went down amongst them. I knew that as they were to be given the bread and wine, they would be forced to raise their heads and I would use this opportunity to gaze into their souls—whether they were truly devout or merely in need of refuge from the revulsions outside.

Though the Mass was spoken in Latin, I understood every word. Irrespective of whether they spoke in French or Latin, I was tuned into their communication—their thoughts—and because of that, language was an unnecessary means of conveyance. However, I felt that it was said without conviction, without the depth of feeling that seemed to be portrayed to the congregation when on public display. After the bread, the priest took the golden chalice and held it high before the altar in front of the golden cross. Having sipped himself, he then turned to the brothers before him and offered each one in turn their opportunity of eternal life through the blood of their saviour—everlasting life in the kingdom of glory.

The first monk raised his head to sip from the goblet and I noticed the withered lines of a man in the twilight of his life. His heart, his soul, they were genuine. Here was a truly devout man who believed the lies told by the ornately arrayed man in front of him. The second friar equally had the goodness and purity one would have expected from the likes of these people before me. As he handed the chalice to the third brother, the man kneeling before me suddenly hesitated and trembled…and looked at me directly in the eye. He could see me! I moved quickly to one side, watching his eyes all the time, and they followed my movement. This was not what I had expected. The friar held the goblet with a shaking hand.

"What ails you, my son?"

"F… Father… I see an apparition before me."

"Where is this apparition?"

"There, Father, beside you!"

The priest turned, looking all around him. As he did so, I flew immediately out of sight of the group and remained looking down at the group from the arches above.

"Father! The fiend…the—"

"There is no apparition! This is the house of God! No apparition, demon or sprite would dare make his presence here. The power of the Lord is too strong. Come sip, you have hallucinated, *the blood of Christ*."

With that, the monk, still trembling, sipped from the cup and the priest then moved onto the friar next to him. He was sworn to obedience and dared not raise his head, though I could feel in his spirit that he so desperately wanted to. As the priest moved along the line of celibate men before him, the 'sensitive' monk made to pick his paternoster from the floor and as he did so, turned his head around searching for the phantasm that he had unquestionably seen. However, he did not think to look up to the architraves where I had stationed myself.

I remained out of sight until the Mass had finished and the monks arose to make their way to their dormitories. I saw the priest returning his precious 'booty' back in the tabernacle. As he turned his back towards the nave, the last monk turned and deftly made his way back to the third set of pews and ducked out of sight behind one of the benches. Was this my 'psychic' monk, I thought, come to confirm that his vision was real and that he had not 'hallucinated', as the priest had implied? I felt that I needed validation that neither this friar nor the priest were able to see me so I returned to the altar. With his set of keys, the ecclesiastic locked the tabernacle and returned to his sacristy. The wary monk, though, was hidden from view, despite me surveying quickly around. I went into the sacristy and watched the priest disrobe. As he hung the keys in the cupboard, he withdrew another bottle of wine and poured himself a generous glass. It struck me that both times that I had been here, this 'Man of God' was satisfying his obviously insatiable appetite for wine and may well be dependent on this drink. As I stood there, he continued unabated, sipping from the glass and I felt confident that I was transparent to him. He finally blew out the candle and left the room, holding onto the bottle that was by now only one-third full.

I returned to the main part of the cathedral and in the darkness of the nave, I distinctly heard movement. I could sense a heart thumping fast, as of one in panic, and started to investigate the source. As I passed by the third set of pews,

I saw him, cowering beneath the bench. In the gloom, with confidence rising, the monk slowly rose and pushed his hooded head above the top of the bench. As he did so, glancing around, he saw me.

"Aaaahhh!"

"Calm yourself!"

"Michael? It's me, Mai!"

"Mai? Why did you scream?"

"I was startled when I turned around and saw you before me."

"Well, you can relax, Mai…it really is me; I thought you may have been the monk who witnessed my presence during Mass."

"I was worried, too. I heard him talk to the Holy Father and I knew he could see you as I could."

"But Mai, you were supposed to wait under the table in the sacristy? I looked for you but you were nowhere to be seen!"

"I panicked, Michael. I saw the Holy Father at the tabernacle with his face towards the wall and I just became flustered and ran to hide under the pew here, where you found me…at least the cloak, hood and flax seem to have duped everyone."

"Yes, that's good; I thought it looked most authentic. How do you feel now?"

"Shaken…shaking. See, my hands are trembling."

I put out my hand to Mai's and though I did not expect to be able to clasp her hand, the gliding of my fingers through hers seemed to have a soothing effect. I wanted to embrace my little heroine so badly, this brave, brave girl who was risking punishment for being here, for the sake of love.

"Right, Mai, are you ready; do you think that you can carry on?"

"Yes, Michael…let's do this."

"I shall stay with you throughout. I shall be your lookout; listen to my calling."

"I'm ready."

We surreptitiously made our way through the aisle to the altar. Some light shone through the stained-glass windows, helping Mai see her way. We turned to the left and walked towards the sacristy. At the door, I motioned to Mai to open it and go inside. As we went in, Mai started to fumble as she could not see even her hand in front of her face—it was pitch black.

"Mai, just follow me…slowly. Stay right behind me and I shall ensure that you do not bump into anything. OK?"

I sensed where everything was but had to make sure that I did not pass through them as, even though I was able, Mai was not. I knew where the cupboard was and though closed, I could feel the keys hanging on the hook inside.

"Mai, table to your right… We have reached the end…now…turn right, good. Walk slowly ahead…stop. Now, turn to your left…a bit more…stop. Walk ahead about five paces…one, two, three, four, five…no, one more…stop. OK, the cupboard is directly in front of you. Stretch out your arm, slowly…a bit more—"

"OK, Michael, I can feel it."

"Good, now there's a latch on the right…lift it up…"

"Got it…"

"Right, pull on the latch and the cupboard door will open."

There was a creaking that I had not noticed when the priest had opened the door earlier. Initially, I was worried that the noise would be heard, but then I remembered that we were totally alone. Even so, the noise did seem to reverberate in this sparsely furnished room.

"Mai, in front of everything, you will feel the priest's mitre, take it out and place it on the table behind you. I will guide you backwards."

"Yes, I can feel it, Michael. I think it is on a hook…but it seems to be stuck."

"Don't wrench at it, Mai. Try lifting it gently upwards."

"Yes, it is coming up; it is free."

"Don't turn around. Walk backwards six paces… one… two… three… four… five… six… stop."

"I can feel the table behind me; my cloak is brushing it."

"Good, without turning around, place the mitre on the table…good. OK, let's go back to the cupboard…one…two…three…four…five…six…stop."

Mai stretched out her arm as before until she felt the cupboard again.

"OK…the keys are hanging slightly to your right…higher…"

"Yes, I can feel them…"

"Right…gently lift them… Mai! I can hear someone coming! Leave the keys…make your way backwards as before and hide under the table."

I could feel Mai becoming anxious; I could feel her little heart beating so fast…so very fast.

"Mai! Slow down, don't panic…slowly now, let me count you backwards…one…two…three…four…five…six…"

"I feel the table, Michael."

"Get on your knees…crawl underneath…no, a bit to the left…a bit more…stop; quiet! Don't make a sound!"

I saw the undulating flicker of light becoming brighter, then a pause. A male voice spoke and I knew it was the priest who had returned.

"What the heavens! I shut this door, I'm certain!"

He walked in, placing the candle on the table and stood with his mouth agape. There, before him, was his mitre on the table. He looked up and saw the cupboard door open.

"St Peter above!"

He grabbed the candle from the table and marched over to the cupboard. The keys were hanging there and other items seemed to be in place. He went to the corner and dragged a chair towards the table. Taking the candle with him, he went back to the cupboard, removed the keys and strode out into the church. I followed and saw him go straight to the tabernacle. I returned to the sacristy.

"Mai! He's coming back. Move towards me away from the chair; with the shadows, he will not see you but he may feel your presence under the table with his feet."

Mai moved closer to the edge that I was at and remained kneeling on the floor. I could hear her breathe as she panted in fear.

"Mai! Shh... You must calm down. He will hear your breathing; try and relax...slower, slower, I am here with you."

"Michael," Mai whispered, "I am scared, really scared!"

"Look at me, Mai...look at me."

Mai lifted up her head and gazed into my eyes. I stretched out my hand to her cheek and she tilted her head towards my clasp. I lay beside her under the table and enclosed her in my arms as she settled down.

"You bold, daring girl... I love you... Now, shh..."

The priest returned and the room became brighter again. I heard a thump as he lay something solid and heavy on the table above us. *Your gore treasure*, I thought. Mai was much calmer and I motioned to her that I was going to rise and observe the priest. She nodded approval and lay like a foetus on the floor.

As I arose, I saw this mercenary man of God before me. I was filled with loathing for such a hypocritical and despicable human being. Like a tax-collector, he removed the top pile of coins and trinkets to uncover another layer of treasure underneath. He didn't count but just surveyed this immense wealth before him. Satisfied that his worldly goods were safe, he shut the chest and locked it with one of the three keys on the table.

"Too much wine, Pierre!" he said to himself. "Perhaps you need a little less sustenance—you are becoming forgetful and careless!"

Satisfied that all was in order, he picked up his hoard and strode back out to the tabernacle. Double-checking that the door was securely locked, he returned to the sacristy, hung the keys and his mitre up in the cupboard, shut the door and left the room. As the candlelight faded from the room, I heard the door shut firmly behind me...and heard the unmistakeable sound of a key turning in the lock. Mai was imprisoned!

"Michael! What am I going to do? Mother will be worried; I said that I would be home before the bell strikes one!"

"Mai, we are here for the night. I will return to your mother and explain to her that you cannot return tonight."

"Michael, she cannot hear you, she can only see you!"

"I will find a way...wait, I will return."

With that, in the moment of a thought, I was in Mai's parents' bedroom. Her father was snoring but her mother was awake and restless. I stood before her and she looked towards me.

"Where is Mai?"

I beckoned to her to come outside and she quickly and quietly arose from the bed. Outside in the hall, she again asked the same question. I put my finger to my lips, managed a half-smile and nodded in a calm and relaxed manner. With my hands pressed together, I nestled my head to one side and rested this on top of the back of my hand.

"She is sleeping?"

I nodded in an approving way, with a kindly smile.

"Why is she not here?"

With an open mouth, I patted a yawn but retained a tranquil air.

"She was tired?"

I nodded approvingly.

"She will be back in the morning?"

Again, I nodded approvingly and decided that this was sufficient to satisfy her anxiety. With that, I returned to Mai. I lay next to her under the table and nestled her in my arms. She cuddled up to me and I really thought that I could almost feel her.

"Is Mother fine?"

"Yes, she is fine, Mai. Sleep now…we have a long night ahead."

Chapter 17

"Michael... Michael...speak to me...are you OK?"

I could hear Anna's voice and came to. The others had recovered but we were all in pain. The strain on our internal organs from Jupiter's intense gravitational pull had had a severe effect on our movement. Even Jamie was uncomfortable as I could tell from the grimace on his face.

"Are you our hero again, Captain Flash Gordon?"

"That...that was hard, Michael. I thought that I wouldn't survive and left my hand on the burners to give us a starboard manoeuvre. It worked, but the strain on all of us has taken its toll."

"Bad Boy behind us then?"

"Just a blip in the distant past."

"How long have we been out?"

"Eight minutes, give or take a minute."

"Petra, eradicate radiation shield, all communications, etc. to normal, transmit laser pulses, all electronic devices back on, please."

"Data report, Jamie?"

"Please."

"Speed...warp-drive factor zero-point-eight, trajectory coordinates programmed, Saturn encounter ninety-six minutes."

"Anna?"

"Got it, Jamie! Information processor is totally melted, though that may have been Jupiter as well. But now that I've got it identified, I should have it functioning within...the next thirty minutes."

"Hey, that's good...I feel good and...ouch!"

"Not as good as you should, huh?"

The main control room was back to its hive of activity. Though we were all a little tender, we felt comforted knowing that we had survived another risky tactic. Perhaps God really was on our side, after all.

"Petra, make sure Mission Control have current location and strategies performed."

"Sure."

"Jamie, if it's alright with you, would you mind if I do a little exploring? I feel like I'm getting a bit stiff here and my tender organs feel like a little light stretching would help. I think a little unwind floating around may help."

"Sure, go ahead; don't get lost, there's a lot of spacecraft here! Ha, ha. Hey Petra, do you think we should tag the little British guy so that he can find his way back!"

"I think I've got a collar with a long lead; will that do?"

"Michael, here, if you want to go exploring, this is a radio-controlled map of the ship. Just pump in the location that you want and follow the guide on your screen."

"Cheers, Jamie, I think I will."

I pulled myself out of the seat and floated towards the open hatch leading to the corridor outside. Using the grappling holds, I quickly found that I could propel myself with considerable speed along the various alleys that led off to a multitude of rooms. Though I had intended to explore, I found that I was getting a real buzz from just speeding along the spaceship. Overdoing the pulling on the holds, I found myself on several occasions bumping into the walls, which did cause some bruising, as I found out later. But at the moment, I felt like a kid alone for the first time in the playground, with all the rides at his command. Within a few minutes, I had become quite skilled at pulling myself from one side of the wall to another, using alternate hands. I arrived at a corridor with four passageways. Two were at ninety degrees to the other pair but in opposite directions. An arrow pointed to 'Levels 5 to 120', whilst the one opposite pointed to 'Levels 1, 2, 3'. By deduction, I calculated that I was on level 4. As this was my favourite number, getting back to this level would not present any problems. However, I had come a long way in the ten minutes that I had been floating along the ship. I looked at the radio map and typed in 'main control room'. Within seconds, the directions were on the screen, together with distance and estimated time. I looked at the values incredulously—two hundred and fifty metres! And this wasn't even halfway! This certainly was a 'big bird', as Jamie had put it. The umpteen rooms that I had passed as well began to put a truer perspective on the enormity of this spacecraft.

I searched down the index and found 'flight deck'. Now this I had to see; a flight deck on a spaceship! I quickly programmed this in and found I had to travel an estimated fifteen minutes with a distance of four hundred metres. Using my alternate-hands technique, I made the flight deck in twelve minutes. I pushed open the hatch and floated inside.

"My God! This is incredible…this is like something out of science fiction!"

This level was dedicated to an enormous runway with twenty planes secured to one side. The structure of these craft was interesting. All had stubby wings that had been folded in. Each one had a cone-shaped head with a hollow shaft. They looked like a mix between airplanes, helicopters and spacecraft. On the side was engraved 'Proxima Stargazer'. On the opposite side to the Proxima Stargazers were a series of maintenance and control rooms, almost like garages, but each one gleaming in the lights of the mothership. I pulled myself inside one of the maintenance rooms and there strapped to the walls were no less than thirty robotic workers. Each one had been shaped in human form and though gender was not an issue vital for the designers, they were divided into male and female forms. I pulled myself out and back into the main room. At the far end, I could just make out the massive hatches that opened out into the black beyond. However, what was most surprising was that the entire length of the runway—indeed the room itself—was circular. Looking upwards, I could see the ceiling, which was about sixty metres away. So, I was in a gigantic cylinder with an estimated length of three hundred metres and a diameter of sixty!

I pulled myself along the grappling holds and then, with a mighty push with my legs, propelled myself to the other side. As with my earlier experiences along the corridors, the force that I used was unnecessarily too strong and I found the other side coming at me far too quickly for comfort. I twisted my body so that my feet were the first to come in contact with the surface but the rebound action only gave further impetus to my cylinder-crossing antics. I needed to find a grappling hold and saw one coming towards me at some speed. Twisting my body around again so that my feet made the initial contact, I tried to cushion the force by bending my knees and twisting around at the grappling hold. My fingers found space behind the hold and as I curled my hand firmly around the bar, the force of my momentum nearly yanked my shoulder from its joint, but at least I was stationary. I could feel the internal bruising immediately, along with the bruises I had endured along the corridors and knew that if my plight became known to the others, I would be in for a lot of mickey-taking when I returned to the main control room.

I was now in some pain and felt that I had no choice but to go back to the others. As I tried to programme my path back to the main control, I realised that the bruising to my shoulder was more serious than I had initially thought—I could not move my arm. I lifted up my knee and rested the honing device on my thigh and with my other hand typed in my location. Twenty-one minutes! Still, I had no choice but to endure the pain-filled journey back, which was made even longer by the fact that I could only use my left arm. Much relieved, I pulled myself through the hatch and back beside Jamie.

"The prodigal son returns! Well, what did you think?"

"Ow!"

"You alright, Michael?"

"Jamie, I had a slight accident along the way and I have badly bruised my right arm. See, when I try to lift it—OW!"

"Dangerous things, spaceships! Ha, ha… Petra, we have an invalided astrophysicist! Can you spare a few moments?"

Then turning to me, with his thumb pointing towards her, he said:

"Trained medic, Petra; in safe hands there, Michael, but she does tend to be a bit heavy-handed. Just shout if you feel any pain, ha…ha…!"

"Yes, anything for a multi-linguist expert! But only a few minutes mind, Saturn is only thirty-five minutes away."

Petra moved over to me and with gentle manipulations uncovered an unpleasant truth.

"Michael, you've dislocated your shoulder! How the hell did you do that?"

"Erm…just a bit heavy-handed on the grappling holds, I guess."

"Heavy-handed! This is a real wrench! Michael, Jamie wants you."

I turned towards Jamie, who was looking straight into his screen.

"ARGH!"

"There, sorted!"

Jamie turned around.

"Seen Petra in action before—knew what she was going to do…can't bear the sight of a man in pain so had to look away! Ha, ha, ha."

"How's that feel?"

I gently raised my arm, then started to rotate the shoulder.

"Tender, but…yes, I guess that's good. Thanks, Petra"

"No worries, little man. Try and keep out of mischief for the rest of the solar system flight at least, ha, ha, ha."

I sat for a while gently rotating my arm around the shoulder. The bruising was tender, but it appeared that Petra had sorted it out. Every so often, Jamie looked my way and smiled—the sort of smile that said, 'You won't be doing that again in a hurry!' Anna was in the process of removing circuit boards from the Main and checking for faults. Simon had slipped out of the room and Charlie seemed to be intensely studying the monitor in front of him.

"Saturn encounter, ten minutes, Jamie."

"Petra… Anna, I am thinking of bypassing Saturn. I'm really worried about all the debris in those rings if we take an equatorial route. What are your opinions?"

"I have been wondering about that myself."

"Yeah, me too," replied Petra. "What about a pole skim?"

"Yeah? Possible. Any moon problems?"

"Just checking… The problem is that there are over one hundred and fifty moons and some like Phoebe are retrograde. I certainly wouldn't want an equatorial encounter!"

"Anna, what would be our speed gain?"

"Roughly, another zero-point-zero-five warp…giving us warp-drive factor zero point eight five."

"Is it worth the risk?"

"Would shorten our journey by over two months."

"Mr Astro?"

"An equatorial encounter would be calamitous. Petra is right, though; rings aside, moon retrogrades would be tantamount to celestial suicide. The pole skim is your only option, BUT Saturn's magnetic field could create other unforeseen problems. You will need all of Petra's skill in her engineering and electronics training to survive this."

"Petra, South or North Pole?"

"I'd go with South."

"Why?"

"I don't know…just a feeling."

"That's good enough for me… Michael?"

"Well, better the devil that you know than the devil that you don't."

"But we don't know this devil!"

"So, let's go with the devil that we do."

"Huh?"

"Haven't a clue, Jamie, but if we are going to go, I'd rather go with a woman's instincts. From a scientific perspective though, the justification for going with Petra's suggestion is that Saturn's magnetic field is the inverse of Earth's, so magnetic field lines travel from the South Pole. Also, the North Pole is far more extensively influenced by Saturn's magnetic field than the South."

"Jamie, decision now, please. We have eight minutes and you need to make flight path corrections; otherwise, we will find out just how much radiation Saturn's core gives off."

"South it is then! I shall aim for two hundred and thirty thousand kilometres from Saturn's South Pole—that will give us enough clearance from any rogue ring debris, but adequate pull from her gravity to pick up our speed to zero-point-eight-five. At least there won't be any radiation like we experienced from that Bad Boy Jupiter back there…I hope!"

Jamie nipped the plasma burners as he had done so many times before and we watched that brilliant cream planet come clearly into view.

"Just look at that glorious planet!"

We all sat and just stared as Saturn took on the air of majesty that she deserved. Though still one hundred and fifteen million kilometres from us, she looked immaculate, almost polished and ready for display. Those perfect symmetrical rings, which we now knew were far from flawless, to the unaided eye represented the solar system's most haunting of all the planets. Because of her composition and location, she was the most reflective of our other seven partners in this solar timepiece. 'Resplendent' would be an understatement—she was just in awe of everything we had so far come across. Jamie leaned forward and fumbled in front of him. He handed me something that I had not expected on a journey such as this—a pair of binoculars.

"Michael, you should know; anyway, look just south of the E-ring…"

I brought the lenses into focus and tried to ascertain what Jamie was referring to, then I spotted it.

"Enceladus!"

"Yes, stunning, or stunning?"

"I'd go with your first observation…stunning!"

We watched, fascinated, as the most lustrous of Saturn's moons came into view. Like a luminescent dot in a faint surrounding shell, she was not only enchanting, she was mesmerising. Saturn had normally been viewed from an acute angle, showing rings and some moons; now we were approaching from a pole direction and with the speed that we were travelling at, everything seemed to have frozen in time. The moons had stopped orbiting their parent planet; they were static in a spellbinding framework.

"Two minutes, Jamie."

"OK…no radiation problems, we're too far out, so leave anti-radiation shield down, Petra. Get a quick transmission to those guys back home, give them our latest strategy. Leave communication channel open and keep transmitting, so if anything untoward happens, Mission Control will be fully briefed first-hand of our fate."

"A bit negative, Jamie, not like you!"

"Not negative, Anna…realistic. Statistically, we have already used ten of our nine lives and one day, we may run out of luck…but *not* this time and *not* on my watch!"

Jamie looked at me and beamed his big smile. He knew he had just talked like James Dean, but his rhetoric was more out of bloody-mindedness and a determination to survive. He was a fighter and, at times like this, I was glad I was sitting alongside him.

"Alright…I liked James Dean!"

The three of us burst out laughing. Even at this crucial moment in our journey, there was an amity, an unspoken bond that, were it tangible would have enveloped us all in its web—an unbreakable chord.

"Here we go…twenty seconds!"

We were immediately back to the seriousness of our situation. Jamie's eyes were glued wide open with his hands on a multitude of controls, all spaced equidistantly between his fingers. Anna had stopped her repair on the Main and looked ahead, whereas Petra continued with transmissions and determining coordinates. Though still five and a half million kilometres away from the planet, we now were getting used to the enormous speed that we were travelling at. It made the back of my neck tingle somewhat to think that we were close to approaching the speed of light—an impossibility according to Einstein, but now within our reach.

"OK, Petra?"

"Speed increasing, Jamie… Warp-drive factor zero-point eight one…zero-point eight-one-five…zero-point eight-two…zero-point eight-two-five…zero-point eight-three…zero-point eight-three-five…zero-point eight-four."

"South Pole contact… NOW! What the—!"

"What's wrong, Jamie?"

"Controls aren't functioning! Nothing's working!"

Petra stared in front, her mouth agape.

"Jamie…are we circling Saturn?"

We all looked ahead and sure enough, all that we could see was a faceless cream planet beneath us.

"Yes! This is crazy! We are locked in orbit and…and…nothing's working! Michael?"

"Jamie, I think we came in too steep; not your fault. Everything would have been OK *if* the burners had worked. Then we would have blasted free. I think the controls aren't working because we are following the magnetic field lines and they are disrupting signal transmissions to all the controls. Everything that requires some kind of relay—magnetic device, flow of electrons—is out of action until we can break free of this magnetic field."

"But we can't break free!"

There was a dip in the brightness inside the room, followed by the emergency lighting coming on. Charlie shouted across to Jamie: "The nuclear reactor has gone into sleep mode to protect the system from overheating."

Anna looked up.

"Michael, what does this mean?"

"Well, as we can't get out and give the ship a push, then…"

"We will become a satellite of Saturn…for a long, long time!"

"I believe that Saturn now has one hundred and fifty-one moons!"

"Jamie, look at that!"

We looked through the canopy and watched a wondrous firework display. It was like the front of Proxima was a child's firework—a sparkler. Simon and Charlie were the first to realise.

"We are hitting ice crystals in the innermost rings. They are being totally destroyed and ionised by the shear impact speed."

"Oh no! Will the ship hold out, Jamie?"

"Well, frozen ice is the same as hitting granite rocks. Michael, input?"

"Simon is correct; we are striking small ice chunks. In the E-ring, most of the ice varies from a few microns to several centimetres…but then again, every so often, a rogue particle enters the fray."

"But every collision is bound to damage the shell?"

"Yeah, obviously impact damages both colliding parties; luckily, Proxima is much more massive, so far less damage."

"But for eternity?"

"Well, no; eventually, sufficient collisions will damage the hull to the point of fracture."

"So, not for eternity then?"

We suddenly all became very sullen. Five seconds ago, we were tense with excitement, twenty-five seconds ago, we were laughing at Jamie and James Dean and now we were contemplating a life expectancy far shorter than we had planned, or even hoped for. Without the use of any electronic devices, I had to resort to my training, knowledge and memory. In front of me was a writing pad and pencil. I leaned forward and withdrew the pair from their fastenings and drew out the plan of Saturn and its moons as best as I could remember. I knew that Titan would have an occasional pull on the magnetosphere of Saturn, but it was too far out to have any influence on us and our orbital position. My speciality was black holes and time but we really needed a Saturn specialist; not that he would have been any good in our current situation, but at least he would have first-hand information about our location. I sketched the ring system, especially the E-ring that every few seconds we were part of and those known moons within that locality, of which we were now one. I picked up the binoculars in front of me and scanned the cosmos.

"Jamie?"

"You've sorted it, Michael?"

"No, no, no. There's nothing that any of us can do…but…"

"But…?"

"But…but, without the use of calculating devices, and I am relying solely on my memory of Saturn and its inner moons…there is a faint…and I mean faint…slim…the absolute slimmest…"

"Michael, I have spent my entire career living on borrowed time with just the slenderest of hope that I'd live to see another day. What is this 'slimmest', which may give us some hope of survival?"

"We are orbiting Saturn every four and a half seconds…to the nearest half second. We are on the innermost tip of the E-ring and…look, there!"

"Look where?"

"You've missed it. Wait again, she'll be there in…four…three…two…one…there!"

"What?"

"Enceladus."

"Michael? Are you OK? We are in a bit of a dilemma here and you want to draw my attention to the most reflective moon in the entire solar system? Is this 'let's pass the time with Enceladus spotting'?"

"Ha, ha, ha. Oh, that's just tickled me! Ha, ha, ha…"

"Sorry, Michael. I know you a bit better than that. OK, so what is it about Enceladus?"

"Well, Enceladus and Dione—"

"Dione? As in Warwick?"

"Yeah, as in Warwick. Well, Enceladus and Dione…this pair are in orbital resonance."

"Which means?"

"Which means that every so often, the two are directly in line and their combined masses give an additional gravitational pull. Because of our location, this gentle 'nudge' may be just enough to pull us out of orbit."

"So, we are still in the hands of the gods, then?"

"By and large, yes. *But*, Titan, because of its position, every once in a while, draws off some of the magnetosphere from Saturn, which causes ionisation…this can be seen as a halo around the moon."

"Michael, I am gaining interest and you have my undivided attention."

As I did with Petra and Anna. I glanced towards them and they too, seemed transfixed by what I was saying. A chance of survival from this apparent inescapable situation, I guess that would have captivated anyone; even Simon and Charlie were listening intently to what I was saying.

"Well, I have just looked over towards Titan through these binoculars and unless I am seriously mistaken…"

"Yes?"

"She is wearing a halo right now."

"Are you saying that we can now escape?"

"There will be a slight reduction in the magnetic strength of Saturn's field right now, but I am not sure whether this will be adequate for our electronic equipment to function."

The words had barely left my lips and Jamie was switching at the burners.

"Damn it! Nothing!"

"Jamie! When you did that, I am sure I saw a twitch on the screen, a small reading, but…there was something!"

"Hang on, Jamie. Don't waste effort and energy on spontaneous reactions. This is why you need to spot Enceladus…there she is!"

"Yeah, I've got her, Michael!"

The cabin was alive with tense, nervous excitement. The energy alone in that room could have started a fireworks display, never mind about the one being performed by the hull of Proxima. Suddenly, there was a noticeable thud and slight judder. Simon turned around.

"A bit bigger than a few microns, I think!"

The front looked like the grand finale of a fireworks display when all the rockets go off at the same time. Fascinatingly, the atoms of the once existing lumps of ice had been ionised and the ions were flying with us in the direction of the magnetic field—it was as though we were flying through the length of a brightly lit sparkler and all the sparks were going in the same direction, just like iron filings on a bar magnet, except this was an aurora.

"OK, Jamie, make sure that you can identify her every time we pass, which is four…three…two…one…"

"Got her, Michael! OK, let me do this now. Four…three…two…one… Spot on!"

"Right! The time to fire will be JUST as you see Enceladus. On her own, probably the gravitational pull will not be enough, but in combination with Dione…well, we've come this far, it would be a shame if this is the terminus…"

"You want me to talk like James Dean again?"

"No…stick to what you're good at!"

"How much power have we got in our back-up batteries, Charlie?"

"Can't verify without up and running computer, but they should be close to fully charged. Obviously, with demand from life support, lighting, heating, etc, they should be good for a few more days."

"A few days! Then, after that…?"

"A few days, Jamie…let's just take one day at a time."

"How often do these two resonate?"

"I'm not exactly sure, you'd need a Saturn specialist, but if my memory serves me well, Enceladus orbits Saturn every thirty-two to thirty-three hours."

"So, every four and a half seconds for the next thirty-two hours, I have to try to energise plasma burners!"

"That about sums it up."

"And even then, they may not be in line?"

"Two out of two correct so far."

"And even when they do line up… Titan may have finished drawing off the magnetosphere from that bright boy to our left?"

"Takes you to the top of the class, Jamie. Perhaps it's better to start sooner rather than later; we could take shifts."

"Charlie, how much power do I draw off from the batteries every time I try to energise the burners?"

"About zero-point-zero-zero-three per cent."

"OK…so, that's not so bad, at least we've got about…"

"One and three-quarter Earth days!"

"Yup…that seems to sum it up nicely! Not exactly favourable statistics then?"

"OK, shifts everyone. I'll start and press the first eight hundred!"

"Hour shifts, then Jamie?"

"Yeah…that gives us a five-hour break before we are back on again. Everybody, I want you to practice observing Enceladus. If Michael is right, then it appears to be the only chance we have."

"At least we have hope, Jamie, without that, we might just as well curl up and give in."

"You're right, Simon, at least we have hope…"

The mood had changed from one of hopeful excitement to that of resigned doom. No one expected the plasma burners to fire; statistically, the cards were heavily stacked against us but it was the only chance that we had. By the time Jamie's shift had finished, all of us could spot Enceladus as we orbited Saturn. Simon took over next, followed by Petra, Charlie, Anna and finally, me. Jamie began his second shift and the others lolled around listlessly. There was nothing any of us could do; in fact, taking the shift at least gave us a motivation to work.

It was when Charlie took his second shift that Petra became aware of a change.

"Charlie! I saw a blip!"

"OK! Coming around a second time…now!"

"I swear that blip is stronger!"

We now all sat to attention! Was it possible that Dione and Enceladus were aligning? Was it possible that my hypothesis was correct? Was there more power in the gravitational pulls yet to come?

"Now!"

"YES! That is definitely stronger! Jamie, see what you think."

Jamie wasn't the only one huddled around Petra's screen. With the exception of Charlie, we all hovered by her.

"Now!"

"Yes…oh yes!"

"Charlie, let me take over now. Go back and calculate how much energy we will drain from the backups, using battery power alone to fire these burners."

Charlie floated over to his desk and started frantic calculations, all now based on theories and ideal situations, which we knew were mathematical hypotheses only. In the real world—the world we currently were in and aware of—nothing was ideal, nothing was pure, all was based on assumptions: assuming the exact alignment of two satellites to our right, assuming a constant flow of electrons in this bizarre magnetic field, assuming that Titan would continue to draw energy from this fascinating planet. Charlie looked up, but I could tell from his manner that these past few frenetic minutes had not produced the results that he had wanted.

"Jamie? Not terribly good news, I'm afraid."

Jamie did not look up towards Charlie immediately; I could tell that the strain of more bad news was beginning to take its toll—even on Captain Flash Gordon.

"OK, Charlie, what is it?"

"Well, bearing in mind that all calculations have been made manually, which has included a lot of rounding up, then we will draw off twenty-two per cent of the battery power."

"Why so pessimistic, Charlie? Twenty-two per cent—why, that's plenty, even enough left over to make the whole crew a cup of coffee."

"Yes, but that doesn't take into account how much power we can actually use, just how much power that will be required."

"Charlie, do we have enough power for a burn?"

"Yes."

"That's all I needed to know, don't look so glum!"

"If… Once you burn, we need to get the nuclear reactor up and running. That will require seventeen per cent of battery power and that does not take into account maintaining life support…"

"Charlie, do we have enough battery power for a burn AND restarting the nuclear reactor?"

"Give or take five per cent, yes, but I have had to round these calculations up; remember, they are not exact."

"Look, Charlie, the crucial thing is to break free of this orbit; if…once that has been achieved, then the nuclear reactor is our next priority. When that is back in action, all power can then be restored—life support, lighting, heating, battery regeneration, etc."

"Jamie! That blip almost lit up the whole screen!"

Jamie concentrated purely now on the plasma burner switch and Enceladus coming into view. Every four and a half seconds, he flicked the plasma burner switch; every four and a half seconds, Petra grew more vocal as the screen display grew in intensity, the whole crew waited for the next four and a half seconds.

I was looking at Jamie, but I noticed Petra's head slump and I heard her sniff as she tried to stifle away a tear.

"Jamie…the screen display…has gone."

He didn't look up but rested his hands on the desk before him. I could tell that the strain of the last eight hours had been too much. If there had been any gravity, Jamie would have just fallen back and slumped into his chair. Nobody spoke. It was Simon who broke the silence.

"JAMIE! Where is Saturn?"

We all looked up immediately! Saturn was nowhere to be seen. As if by magic, she had been erased from the canopy in front!

"What! But the burners didn't fire!"

117

"They didn't need to, Jamie! The resonance orbit and gravitational pull were just sufficient; nature did it all by herself!"

"The Hand of God, you mean!"

"I didn't know that you were religious!"

"Oh God! I've just been converted. Yeeha!"

The joy in that cabin was contagious. I hugged Anna as she sobbed on my shoulder—and Anna was a hardened fighter ace—Simon and Charlie were involved in a floating and rotating embrace, hugging and patting each other on the back and Jamie and Petra just let their heads entwine in quiet relief. As captain of the entire expedition, he had to bring logic and order back as quickly as possible.

"Right! Nuclear reactor—top priority! Charlie?"

"On it, Jamie. We have sufficient battery backup for a restart *if* the magnetic field hasn't damaged the circuitry on board!"

"Anna?"

"Sorry, Jamie; everything needs resetting and rebooting. You're looking at a couple of hours. BUT, the good news is that because Petra suggested that we should enter Saturn from the South Pole, the electron flow shouldn't have damaged the electronics!"

"I told you that I trusted a woman's instincts, Mr Fraser!"

"Michael, I want to thank you for your input over this crisis. Without your knowledge and idea, I don't know what we would have done…quite honestly."

"Jamie…at the end of the day, my input made no difference to the end result. The plasma burners would never have fired—the magnetic field had already defeated that concept. It was purely our location at the time and a lot, and I mean a *lot* of luck. In fact, if anyone's to thank, it's you and Petra; her idea of using the South Pole and your positioning of Proxima."

"Michael, you gave us hope and that was worth far more than any bit of 'luck'—positioning or no positioning. Throughout the entire ordeal, we all had hope, expectancy, a chance…albeit slim, that we could escape from this catastrophe. Mankind survives on hope—hope that tomorrow will be better than today, hope that your lifelong partner waits just around the corner, hope that you will find the answer to that unanswerable question…and you gave us that hope. Thank you."

Jamie stretched out his hand and squeezed mine firmly.

"Thank you. OK, I'm blind, folks! Where's Uranus?"

"No idea until Anna's fixed the software, Jamie; we're all blind at the moment."

"Jamie, I need to go down to the reactor room. It can't be restarted from here without electronics. I'll have to go down and reset the graphite rods manually from the reactor control room."

"We have enough power still, Charlie?"

"Yes…just enough."

"OK, Simon is priority. Minimum energy usage, folks, until the reactor is functioning again. Simon takes precedence now. How long?"

"If it goes as we have practised, about twenty minutes; plus, of course, fifteen minutes to get there—let's say forty minutes."

Simon disappeared through the hatch and left a buzzing and happy room behind him.

"Life support, Charlie?"

"All OK. We don't need to reduce any power supply there, but I will switch out all lighting and heating except for rooms in use."

"Leave Simon's path open."

"Yeah, that's done."

"Right… Uranus?"

"Jamie, we could be on the wrong side of the solar system right now. We will have no idea until Anna has rebooted all the software. If we are on the correct side, it will be about two to two and a half hours. If we are on the wrong side, then we must forget it."

"But without Uranus, we will not reach warp-drive factor-one!"

"There is one possibility…once more depending upon planetary alignment and may I say it again…luck."

"Shoot, Mr Astro. As far as I'm concerned, if you tell me black is white, I will believe you, without any question!"

"Anna reckons she can reboot within the next couple of hours. Uranus is…no, could be, two and a half hours away. That is too tight to make any burner adjustments. But Neptune is currently four and a half hours away, enough time to tweak us to our rendezvous."

"Yes, but we have missed Uranus."

"Not necessarily, Jamie. If we sling ourselves around Neptune *and*, and this is a BIG '*and*', Uranus happens to be in a complimentary orbit with Neptune, we can cut back inside to Uranus and complete your objective: warp-drive factor-one with only a slight detour."

"You know, Michael, you have such a calm, logical and simplistic way of putting these finer details in front of anybody you meet. You have a knack of discovering a problem and finding a solution."

"Not always, but this is where my forte comes in handy. So, what is it…the pretty way?"

"Yeah…let's go the pretty way!"

Chapter 18

Meanwhile, back at Mission Control, Karl Guttenberg had a mission of his own. After checking the laser probes and power supplies, he made his way to the library. Ensuring nobody else was present, he nimbly made his way to the back of the room. He thumbed along the lines of keyboards and settled down at the one furthest from the door. With head lowered, he signed on and traced his mouse to 'Proxima Mission'. With adroit precision, he honed into the capsule destined to be the downfall of everything he had worked for, everything that he loved. And Karl Guttenberg was capable of love, especially when that love was held under duress and far from his protection. He examined, in minute detail, every electronic receiving device on-board. With his 'override' authority status, he programmed unknown information into his computer—unknown, that is, to everyone but Karl Guttenberg. With all the data now set, he hesitated on the 'send' command as he searched for his communication headset.

"Danny, Karl here."

"Hi, Karl, what's up?"

"No problems this end…was just wondering whether there has been any communication from Proxima?"

"Had a signal seventeen minutes ago; laser blasts worked well. Currently at warp-drive factor zero-point-six but damaged memory chips. They've reverted to backup until Anna can correct the Main."

"Have they given an estimation for Saturn?"

"Not as yet but everything seems to be on target. We are still waiting on the Jupiter encounter. Why Saturn, in particular?"

"Oh, the Jupiter encounter is the one I fear the most. If they transmit post Jupiter, then they're likely to survive anything. So, Saturn is the one I was waiting for."

"At the moment, they appear to be smack on course and will be due to hit Saturn in…five minutes and ten seconds, if they have survived the Jupiter fly-by."

"Five minutes? Oh good, thanks, Danny…that's good news indeed."

Karl Guttenberg looked at the wall clock: 17:44. He then re-examined the data he had just programmed. Satisfied that all was in order, he lightly tapped his fingers on the desk in front of him. He pursed his lips together and allowed himself a self-gratifying whistle, which followed the rhythm of his strumming fingers. Though never a musician nor a soldier, he did have a certain tendency to the preference of militaristic music and the gusto of his whistling grew stronger as a tune of indiscernible origin and pitch left his lips. It was almost as though he was in an undecided and confused state, the whistling merely an alternative, a distraction to the task that he was about to perform. He looked up at the wall clock again: 17:47. Beside him was some paper and a pencil. He grabbed them and with an urgency that he had not yet displayed, started to scribble numbers and carry out some mathematical calculations that he had deduced with his computer. He looked at the numbers before him and in a frenzy scrawled away frantically with his pencil. In an almost manic way, Karl picked up the paper, scrunched it into a ball and with a cry of despair, threw it into the bin by the wall. It was 17:49. It was now or it was going to be never. It had to be now!

'Karl, you must do this, you must. The future of your beliefs, the lives of those you love, the future of the life you know, the destiny of Man is before you. Fail, and you fail with it.'

He examined the data before him again. Normally, he was self-assured to the point of being arrogant, but today...now he was, for the first time that he could remember, uncertain. With beads of perspiration welling up on his brow, he dashed to the waste bin, grabbed the paper he had seconds ago discarded in a frenetic fury and with shaking hands, undid the undecipherable contents. As though it were an alarm set to sound at the pre-set time, he thought that he could hear the clock strike the next number. He looked: 17:50; it was as if the clock could speak. He froze as the timepiece on the wall ticked out the numbers ten to six, ten to six... Karl took hold of the mouse again and sweating profusely, pressed on the right button with his middle finger. He waited and watched the screen in front of him. Nothing happened. Why! Why? He watched the second hand of the clock fall: 5...6...7... He surveyed the data before him again—all correct. Then why wouldn't the signal transmit? He pressed again on the mouse and again there was no response. Was this God's will...was he, in fact, wrong? Was there really a force, an entity, which had stopped this irreversible act? No! He did not believe in the infinite...the all-being deity who decided what was right and what was wrong! There was no ethereal force preventing this act of defiance, this deliberate sabotage of man's dream to go beyond the stars and to travel through time itself.

10...11...12... *Why will you not work*? Suddenly, Karl let out a cry of exasperation and relief...the right button, the right button... It should be the left button! He had already cleared his conscience that his action would have, as he had, of his own freewill, already depressed the button to destroy man's attempt at retribution; albeit the wrong button. 15...16...and with that, Karl sent the signal that would keep all that he, and all that mankind, had witnessed and experienced and indeed, would continue to do so. There would be no change now. It would be man who would determine the fate of Man, not a *persona non grata* who believed that all human history was the result of twisted minds of men of greed and power.

Relieved and calmer, Karl logged off from the computer in front of him. The task had been completed; at last he could relax, unwind. A bead of sweat ran down his cheek. With the back of his fingers, he brushed the irritating liquid away and realised as he did so that he was perspiring profusely—his shirt was drenched. He withdrew his handkerchief from his pocket and mopped his forehead. The cotton bandana was saturated. Still shaking, he got up, walked over to the window and with hands on the sill stared out at the manicured lawns and blue sky. Unexpectedly, the door opened.

"Karl…there you are! Have you not heard the intercom?"

"No…erm, I have been here working on some new coordinates and calculations…must have been too engrossed. What is it?"

"Phone call. Dial zero—phone over there on the wall."

"Thanks Ed. Will do."

Karl walked over to the phone and, dialling zero, waited with some hesitancy to discover who the voice would be on the other end. The female voice had a distinct oriental accent.

"Karl Guttenberg?"

"Yes?"

"I have the Chinese Ambassador…please hold."

"Karl!"

"Hello, Kim."

"How are you? How is everything going?"

"As discussed and agreed, mission has just been activated."

"That is splendid. Then I guess your stay in Florida is no longer necessary?"

"No, Kim; I have completed what I had to do. I am ready. I shall arrive at Beijing tomorrow on Air China flight CA 982, arriving twenty-three hundred. I have all the information for you to copy. Please confirm that my wife and son will be cared for?"

"Karl, your wife and son will remain the guests of the People's Republic of China. They will be treated with the respect that a Chinese hero's family would expect and will want for nothing. The state is indebted to you and its appreciation will remain in force for as long as they both shall live. Have a good trip."

With that, Karl replaced the receiver. He looked around the room and with a sigh of relief, made for the door.

"Danny!"

"Karl! Leaving already?"

"No, no…I was en route to the Main but just realised that I needed to check on the trajectory."

"Oh, that's OK, I'm coming into the library as well…keep you company."

"Ha, ha…I need a chaperone?"

"Ha, ha…you bet! You quiet ones always need a chaperone! Take a keyboard, I'll sit here."

The two men sat down at adjacent keyboards and logged on.

"Saturn?"

"On track. Jupiter information coming through in three minutes…provided nothing went amiss. What strategy you working on?"

"Flight path of Proxima from Mars…just want to verify that angle and speed meet with the predetermined calculations for Jupiter."

"You sure are thorough; I thought that you'd been through that a million times already!"

"A million and one!"

"Ha, ha."

The door opened and Donna poked her head in.

"Hi, guys. Danny, the chief wants a word as soon as you're free; conference room."

"Thanks, Donna, tell him…twenty-minutes."

"Will do!"

Karl could feel another bout of sweat building up on his forehead. He wanted…no, he needed to confirm that his signal was en route for its destined victim and this would be his last chance. Danny must not see what was on his screen at all costs; even a glimpse would create enough suspicion to possibly hinder his chance of success. It would certainly mean arrest and imprisonment—sabotage was a serious crime—and with the world as tense as it was now, it could well result in treason, and the punishment for that did not bear thinking about.

"Danny, coffee?"

"Sure, don't mind if I do."

"Actually, I was thinking perhaps you wouldn't mind getting them?"

"Oh, sure. Black, sugar?"

"Perfect…thanks."

Danny left and Karl logged on immediately. He brought up the data on Proxima and checked his signal path with the planned trajectory of the capsule.

"Extrapolate…come on, extrapolate."

The screen became a graph and with Proxima at the top, a rogue signal was spotted and plotted from the base, directly in line with the spaceship…its estimated time: 4.1 years.

Danny returned with two coffees from a door directly behind Karl and placed one down in front of his screen.

"Hey! What's that?"

It was the last thing that Danny ever said as he slumped onto the keyboard.

Chapter 19

I was ecstatic laying there with Mai enfolded in my arms. I could sense the gentle rhythm of her heavy breathing as she slept. As I lay with her, I deduced another plan to free her from her captivity; this was dependent upon my understanding of what I had observed in this church since arriving in this town. I saw a chink of light underneath the doorway and got up to check. As I walked through the door, I could see the first rays of dawn transmitting through the upper stained-glass windows. The craftsmen who created these colours were men of skill indeed. I gazed on, but suddenly was disturbed by the sound of movement at the far end of the cathedral; a heavy door opened, then closed. I returned immediately to Mai.

"Wake up…wake up, Mai."

"Hmm…"

"Time to wake up and prepare for your escape."

Bleary-eyed, this adorable creature before me gradually awoke. She looked at me, smiled and stretched out her hand to my face.

"Hello, Michael…"

"Mai, Matins will be very soon…usually, I believe, at first light. We must be ready; the priest will be here, possibly before the brothers assemble for Mass. Listen to my instructions and act immediately, OK?"

Mai nodded apprehensively. I heard the sound of footsteps coming towards the door and then the clunk of the lock as the key was inserted. With a noisy grating, the door was unlocked and the priest walked in. Going over to where Mai was hiding, he placed his candle on the table and went to the cupboard to retrieve his mitre and set of keys. I heard the harmonious voices of the friars as they chanted the Kyrie, filing towards the altar. The priest slipped on his robe, donned his mitre, picked up the keys and left the room.

"Mai! Now…quick!"

Mai quickly arose from underneath the table. I stood by the open door as the monks passed, making sure that I could not be seen by the clairvoyant friar amongst them. As the last monk passed the door, I beckoned to Mai and she swiftly came out of the room, hooded and robed and joined at the end of the queue. The monks lined up obediently, bowed and crossed themselves before the altar, settled in the pews and knelt in silence. As a Catholic, Mai knew the ritual for the public, but I could tell that she was a bit unsure how different it would be for the friars beside her. I could see that she had her head tilted slightly to the right so that she could observe the procedure and protocol to follow.

With the Mass over, it was, unfortunately, Mai who, having been at the back of the queue on arrival, now headed the monks off to their dormitories for silent prayer before beginning the day's tasks ahead. Though Mai knew the layout of the cathedral as a member of the congregation, she was totally ignorant of the format ahead of her or the passages to the dormitories. She knew the way that they had come in and started to lead the file slowly towards the sacristy. I sped on ahead to try to ascertain the location of the rooms that she was to lead them all to. I felt that I had enough confidence to show Mai the way and raced back.

"This way, Mai."

She looked up slightly at me and smiled but I could tell it was a nervous, 'thank you' smile that she wore. She continued along the cloister and was about to follow my directions when the friar behind her said: "Why have you come this way, Brother?"

Mai froze! She looked petrified. I knew that she dared not speak as her gentle, female voice would have revealed her to be a fraud.

"Brother, why have you brought us this way? This is not where we should be!"

Mai stopped, as did the monks and slowly turned around to face the friar directly behind her. She coughed, as deep as she could, and started to speak.

"ARGH! There he is again…the apparition!"

I revealed myself in a menacing form to the clairvoyant amongst them.

"Where? Where?"

Mai raised her hands in a manner demonstrating fear and the others followed suit. Chaos quickly took hold of the group. Fleeing in different directions, I beckoned to Mai to follow me. We ran along the cloister to the main cathedral. As we passed the sacristy, the priest, having heard the commotion, came out in front of Mai.

"What is it? What distresses you, my son?"

Knowing that she could not speak, Mai threw her arms into the air again and sped along the nave towards the large oak door. Outside, she paused for breath before following me into the shadows of the walls. Trembling, I held her as best as I could.

"Mai, I am so sorry, so very sorry."

"Michael, you could not have known. You did what you could and we survived."

"Not 'we', *you* survived."

I wanted to kiss her fear away, I wanted to hold her close to me, I wanted just to hold her and love her. I was uncontrollably in love with this sweet, innocent and adorable young girl before me.

"Mai…I cannot let you do this again. I must accept that this will not work…I must find another way."

She looked up at me and with the softest, most tender smile, stroked my phantom form.

"Michael, this is so important to you. You have risked all that we have been through and for what? No, don't speak. You have risked my welfare, perhaps my life, and knowing that you love me, as I do you, then this reason must be so important. We will continue…we must continue."

"Mai, Mai, my brave, brave girl…"

I was angry, angry with frustration that I could not caress this wonderful, selfless angel before me—I so desperately wanted to hold her.

"Mai, you must take off your cloak straight away before you are seen by any of the others."

We walked slowly back towards her house in the early morning mist. As disappointing as the night had been, I could not but feel inner serenity with having been with this young Indochinese girl beside me, and still being beside her as we walked along the street. If only I had a mortal frame, my life would have been complete. I cursed myself for thinking like this. I was dead and that was it! I needed to overcome all of these selfish and intense emotions, involving self-preservation and self-contentment.

"Mai, shall I come into your house and explain to your mother."

"Michael, I will be OK."

"No, Mai, you have done enough on your own for one night. You must be exhausted from the stress and fear. No, I shall come with you."

We walked in to see Mai's mother in a highly frantic state. She turned and saw Mai and threw her arms around her. Through sobs and hugs, she saw me and in an instant, her emotions changed to one of derision.

"Where has Mai been? Why did you not bring her back here at one o'clock as you promised? I have been out of my mind with worry. Father knows! I could not keep it from him; I was sick with fear—fear of what might have happened to her!"

"I am terribly sorry. Our plan…no, my plan was interrupted by events that could not be foreseen. Your daughter was in danger, that is true, but she showed bravery and courage far beyond her youthful years. I cannot even begin to explain just how much Mai means to me and I understand…I really understand how you were frightened not knowing what was happening. I feel your love for Mai—just as I feel my own…"

"What do you mean, you feel your own…your own what?"

"Love…"

"You love my daughter?"

"Yes, I truly and really do love your daughter."

"You fiend! You thing from the undead…leave my house and leave my daughter."

"Mother! Please, Mother! Michael is no fiend. He is the kindest, bravest, most selfless being I have ever come across. He has sacrificed himself…and as yet, I do not know how or why, but he has sacrificed himself for others. That purpose I mean to discover…and I believe it will be a justifiable purpose—even if it means risking me! Corporeal or incorporeal…I love him and wish to be with him until destiny deems otherwise."

"Is this true? How can you love something…something from another world…another dimension? Impossible!"

"Mother, you can only see Michael. You cannot sense him as I do. I feel his spirit, his emotions, his very soul. For all my life, I have known love for you and Father. You are the two people to whom I owe so much…there can never be a daughter who has been given as much love as you both have given to me. You are truly blessed parents and I pray, with all my heart, that the good spirit gives you the peace and rest you both so deserve when your mortal lives cease. But all children must grow up and when they do, they seek and need another love, the love of another person…a lover, a friend, a companion, with whom they can share their lives…eternally. Michael is that being, Mother…and I need him—just as I have needed Father and you. Mother, please, please, understand this."

The door burst open and a man, whom I assumed to be Mai's father, came in, grabbing his daughter as tightly as he could and with tears in his eyes, brushed her hair as he caressed her.

"Mai, my dearest, darling daughter…I was in the back room when you came in and, though initially angry, I heard every word spoken. I understand!"

Turning to his wife, he said with almost uncontrollable anger:

"Those savages invaded our villages and took us all away; they had no right! We were a peaceful people. We lived our lives the way our ancestors had taught us—in harmony with life around us. Everything that we needed was there, just for the asking, just for the reaching. We took lives of those poor creatures that we needed to keep us alive but we respected them, we prayed for them, we bore them no hate. We did not cause suffering, or beat, or bully; we took only what we needed. But these…these men of the West who came in their big ships with their big weapons of war. These barbarians who felt it was their right to take from others those things that they wanted—not needed—wanted, just because they were bigger, stronger, tougher and because they believed in a different god; these are the people who should be punished. I have never forgotten nor forgiven these swine of humanity who destroyed everything that we had and knew."

Turning towards the door, he then started to address me: "You…you being from—"

"Father, Michael is over there," Mai said, pointing to the fire.

"Michael, if you have come here to change the world for the better, then this is a good reason to fight. We were incapable of fighting back, our weapons…well, we had no weapons, just small spears and arrows with bows.

"We have been taken from our homeland, our friends either killed, abused or dispatched to other parts of this country to serve as slaves to these 'Christians'. I was fortunate; I can heal the sick so we have been 'accepted' as citizens here. But what I would give to be amongst my own people in my own country, living off the land, forest and the rivers, just like countless generations have done before. Here, this is not a life, it is an existence. We attempt to survive as best we can—and yes, we have a home but this is a home of mud, bricks and wood. In our land, we lived under the stars and with homes made of leaves, trees and love. If you are here to stop the men such as we have experienced continuing their loathsome trades, then the sacrifices that you have made—are making—and ours, will be worth it."

"Sir, you are too kind, too benevolent. But you realise the risk that you are taking is with the welfare and perhaps even the life of your daughter."

"You called me 'sir'. I have never been called that before, here. They allow me to live amongst them but that is all; there is no respect for our kind, we are subservient to the white masters. But you, you show me respect, you are no macabre being from the Underworld. Indeed, I believe that your true purpose is for the benefit of others. What is it that you seek?"

"I seek to discover my reason for being here. Without mortal form, I have no memory and do not know my purpose. With the help of the wizard, Nostredame, I hope to uncover the truth for my presence in your home, in your town, in your time. To that end, Mai, your beautiful, courageous and clever daughter, is my only means of finding that goal…and yes, I have fallen in love with her…is that so hard to understand?"

"No, not hard…impossible, maybe…but not hard."

Mai hugged her father, sobbing at the relief that the truth was now in the open with the two people most important in her life. I noticed, too, that her mother was now unhostile towards me; it seemed that she had realised in those few moments that my feelings towards her daughter bore no malice and that I was there not to frighten, harm or curse, but for a good reason, a humane reason. It was her father who continued.

"Like Mai, I too wish that you were mortal. As for 'love', Mai can seek that only amongst those people here, people who are cowards, bullies and do not have the moral virtues that she so deserves. These people are not worthy of Mai…but you, you have all the attributes that any father could wish for his daughter and I wish, and will pray to my spirit guides, that you be given the chance to find your true purpose…and your true love."

My emotions were in turmoil. If I had been able to, I would have shed many a tear. I could sense that it was from her father that Mai had inherited her goodness, kindness and wisdom; from her mother, she had inherited her beauty, protection and persistence. I suddenly felt that I was amongst friends, sharing a home with virtuous people, people who had suffered and knew hardship but people who would selflessly give love and help to those who needed it, even at the sacrifice to their own comfort and well-being. This was the aspect of human nature that outweighed any of the adverse sides of mankind. Despite all of Man's failings, it was this act of selfless sacrifice that put him amongst the realm of the gods.

"Thank you, sir. If at all possible I can find a way to be with this angel before me, I will move heaven and earth. I treasure your good wishes and will do my utmost to bring Mai safely home. Once she has rested, I will make preparations to procure my goal and, with the grace of God, succeed."

I caressed Mai's face and kissed her delicate lips. The sensation sent a tingling throughout my form and Mai shuddered slightly. With that, I departed for Michel's house.

Michel was in his library as I made my appearance. He wasn't as sensitive as he had previously been. In fact, he was totally unaware of my presence. He stood gazing into a roaring fire, completely lost in his thoughts. I heard footsteps descending the spiral staircase. Anne, his wife, walked in:

"Michel?"

"Anne…"

"You have missed breakfast. Is everything OK?"

"Breakfast! What time is it?"

"Why, just before nine. Michel? Did you come to bed last night?"

"Bed? Ah, no, my dear, I seem to have forgotten."

"Dearest, whatever is the matter?"

"We…I have a problem…a problem that I do not wish you to suffer."

"Michel, we have been through much together. I am Anne, your wife. This burden that you bear, it should be a burden that *we* should share. A trouble shared is a—"

"—Trouble halved, yes I know. But I am worried…so very worried. Worried for your…our safety, worried that once begun, it can never be undone, worried that the outcome will prove too momentous to undo once that evil has been unleashed."

"Evil! What evil?"

I moved nearer to Anne. As I did so, she turned and gave a slight gasp.

"Michel! Is that evil in this room right now?"

"Why no; what makes you think that?"

"I feel a presence nearby…not malignant, but a presence nevertheless…just like I felt before in the street on my way back from the apothecary. Strange…it does not mean us harm but it is present in this room."

"If there was evil here, my spirits would warn me as they have helped and presaged me for most of my life. It is for this reason and this reason alone that I feel that the path I am now treading is the right path. They showed me, they guided me, and surely, they have protected me to reach this cornerstone of my life but I am worried—nay, not worried—frightened! Terrified that evil beyond our control will walk this Earth unabashed as we defencelessly look on, helplessly and hopelessly entwined in its cadaverous filth!"

"Michel, tell me what is burdening you, tell me now."

"Very well; Anne. I have been contacted by a spirit—an entity, not of our time but of the future. He has been steered towards me by my guides. He is a good spirit; of this I am certain. He knows not why he is here but believes that he has a mission, a purpose for being here…now…and with me. Though he is unable to recall his motive, he believes that if he can possess a mortal body, then his experiences and emotions will reveal his thoughts and memories through the possessed. It is to this purpose that I am now committed."

"But Michel…you have never been possessed, have you?"

"No. I do not know how or wish to nor do I have the abilities to be taken from my dominion of consciousness by some unknown being. But I know someone who does…"

"Who?"

"The necromancer."

"Michel, no! I have heard of this man. He is dangerous… He is vile… He is—"

"—Our only hope."

Today, Michel Nostredame was unreceptive. For some reason, his guides were not able…perhaps not willing to communicate with him. Was it, then, that they wanted me to be privy to this conversation? To understand the enormity of the task, the danger, the very threat to Man himself. Could this possession be more than a momentary thing? Could it possibly be the irrevocable unleashing of the worst kind of demons throughout the world, spreading like this pestilence before us now?

The sound of shoes on the spiral staircase could be heard and we all turned our heads towards the library door. At the foot of the stairs, the sound changed as the noise of walking on wood altered to walking on stone. There was a knock at the door and the maid entered.

"Yes, Agnès?"

"Beg pardon, madame; there is a gentleman at the door with a sick boy. He is asking if the Master is at home."

"Well, I am a bit indisposed at the moment, Agnès."

"Michel, a father with a sick boy…"

"Sorry, my dear, yes, you are right. OK Agnès, show him into the scullery."

With that, the maid left and the sound of her shoes became fainter as she ascended the stairs. As Michel Nostredame left to go to attend to the boy, Anne took hold of his wrist and with an affectionate pull, whispered into his ear: "My darling, they will not let you down; they have always been with you and guided you, they will protect you."

"I know…"

He patted his wife's hand and left for the scullery.

I was intrigued by Nostradamus's wife; she was wise, caring and sensitive, to the point of almost being able to see me. She could certainly feel my presence and she sensed that I was not from the Underworld. Michel was lucky indeed to have such an understanding wife and, it would seem, a no-nonsense one at that. I wondered what Michel was doing with the boy and was immediately in the scullery. The lad was sweating profusely, had swellings around his neck and his breathing was laboured. He looked weak and was held in his father's arms. Michel pointed towards the table.

"Lay him down here."

"Will he be alright, sir? He's my only lad."

Nostradamus examined the lad before him. Using a goblet placed over the boy's chest, he listened intently to his rasping.

"Agnès, Agnès!"

There was the thumping of shoes on the floorboards as the maid came running in. She stood before Nostradamus and with a respectful curtsy, addressed him, "Sir?"

"Agnès, the medicines you brought from the apothecary the other day, where are they?"

"In the library, sir."

"Mandrake?"

"Yes sir."

"Please go down and ask your mistress for the mandrake potion and bring it here straightaway."

"Sir."

"Will the lad be alright? Is it the pestilence!"

"No, I think not. But I will bleed him and get him to drink a potion that I have prepared. This will make the lad sick, but that is to dispose of the ailment within him."

The maid returned with the potion and after bleeding, Michel lifted up the lad's head and managed to get the boy to swallow the contents. Laying him back down, he turned him over and called out to his maid again.

"Agnès, fetch a bowl from the sink…quickly, girl."

The maid dashed into the other room and returned with a ceramic basin.

"That's it…hold it there by his mouth and don't move."

Within a few seconds, the boy was retching into the vessel. After five minutes, sweating more profusely than ever, he stopped and his breathing pacified and became normal.

"He is cured, sir! He is cured! Oh, thank you, thank you, sir. You truly are a man of the good Lord. Bless you, sir…bless you."

Michel shook his head at the proffered payment, but the relieved father gave the maid a handful of coins and carried his weak, but cured son out into the street.

"Sir?"

"Give the money to your mistress, Agnès."

So, this was the man at his work. I was impressed with his ability to diagnose and heal a sick lad.

He left the scullery and made his way slowly and in deep thought back to his library. Anne had already left when he arrived back in the room. The fire had faded somewhat and he added another log. Within a few minutes, the fire was roaring again and he sat down in front of his crystal. I noticed that there was a glow within this orb but wasn't sure whether it was the candles, the reflection of the fire or something else. His concentration was diverted to this glass ball before him and he stared intently into it. Suddenly, he looked up.

"Ah, so you are here then?"

Not being sure whether he was talking to me or some contact within his crystal, I hesitated before replying, "Yes, I am here."

"What news?"

"Not good, I am sorry to say. We were nearly caught. But I will try again today. Michel, I was here earlier…your wife, she sensed me, but you did not know of my presence."

"No? My mind must be clear when I communicate and 'see'. I have been lost in troubled thoughts and I would have been unable to know of your presence. But if you were here, then you must have heard and seen everything!"

"Yes, I did. I saw you heal the lad too. That was good."

"Thank you. But you are now aware of the fear that I have!"

"Indeed, and I am also afraid that this man—this necromancer—may be too strong, perhaps too malevolent, too determined to unleash his terror on the world and that he will use the occasion to commence his despicable acts of evil."

"Yes, these were my very own thoughts, too. But and I do have some degree of confidence here, my spirits will protect me…us. If not, then why have they brought you to me?"

"But if he has the ability to unbridle this wickedness, why wait for me? Why not perform his deeds now? Surely, it is *me* that he should be afraid of. I am the one that can control his body!"

"Yes, but perhaps he does not care to return to his body? Perhaps he wishes to roam and spread his foulness around. After all, he will not be dead; his body will still be alive with you inside. He will become one of the undead!"

"Michel, at the moment I am here without fulfilling the purpose for which I believe I have come. I really do not see that I have any choice. Without this man, I will never know, and my death, if that's what it took, will have been pointless. We must use him…we have to use him and it is a risk for all of us…him included."

"I shall send Agnès tomorrow with a note to ask for a meeting between him and me. I suggest that you do not come for he may be able to see you and our plan will have been wasted. He absolutely must not know of your presence until he tries to raise you from the 'dead'."

"OK…what is his name?"

"His name is Jean LeMartre."

Chapter 20

Karl Guttenberg arrived back at his apartment and hurriedly prepared to pack his entire wardrobe. The current unforeseen drama had completely changed his planned departure. Realising that time may now not be on his side, Karl decided that he would take only two changes of clothes, together with appropriate underwear, jumpers, shoes, his laptop, some toiletries and those personal items that reminded him of his wife and son—a photograph, a pendant with a star and a mug that read, 'The World's Best Dad'. He quickly packed all that he needed into one small suitcase and a rucksack. The airport was an hour's drive away but Karl thought it would be better to take a taxi and leave his car on the drive. It would appear that he was at home and give him that bit more time that he needed to make good his escape as well as leaving his whereabouts unknown.

NASA was in turmoil. Danny hadn't been to see the chief after an hour and Donna had returned to find him as Karl had left him.

"Karl's not picking up, sir."

"Try him again! He must be able to shed some light on this! What time did you say, Donna?"

"Just before six."

"Then you were probably the last to see Danny alive, apart from Karl of course. No sign of a break-in?"

"Security has checked; no sign of forced entry."

"Doesn't make sense, Danny was well-liked, always positive and bubbly, no one could have held a grudge. Perhaps Karl is in danger, too. Well, he could be if it is more sinister than just a break-in. Anyone know where Karl lives?"

"Yeah, he has a condo somewhere in Winter Park."

"Donna ask Julie to call nine-one-one. Tell them that there's been a killing here and we have one other team member missing."

The taxi arrived to take Karl Guttenberg to Orlando airport. With the risk of being traced, Karl decided not to use his mobile phone. He had left his house neat and tidy as though everything was normal. He took a fleeting glance behind him as he climbed into the taxi; Karl was leaving his town, his job, his life and was sitting in the back of a cab taking him to his new home.

He hadn't wanted it this way. Danny was a nice guy; what a terrible shame he had to come in the back way with the coffees. *Ironic*, he thought, *Danny's life for a coffee!* But there were things that were far more important in the world than one man's life. Karl himself was sacrificing everything anyway and though he felt a tinge of regret, he had hardened himself to the outcome and the consequences that he may have to endure in pursuing his goal. He had a wife, son and an obligation to protect them in every way he could—even if that agreement had been made under coercion.

The police arrived at Karl's condo after having visited the crime scene. Receiving no reply after they knocked on the door, the forced entry was justified on the grounds of the serious nature of the investigation. What they saw did not make sense—a well-maintained house, neat and tidy and no signs of a struggle or rapid departure, food ready for his evening meal, even his car was out on the drive.

"Could be he's been abducted, you think, Chief?"

"Anything's possible at this moment in time! Have you tried his mobile?"

"Yeah, NASA tried, he's not picking up."

"Should we contact the airport and ports?"

"Yeah, notify them that if spotted, we want this man apprehended pending our investigation. You got a photo fit to send?"

"I'll get one sent from NASA directly."

At Orlando airport, Karl had checked in for his flight to Newark. Feeling tenser than he had when he had left home, he sat down on a bench in front of the flight departure screen, looking up every few minutes. The Orlando-Newark flight was due to depart in twenty minutes; he started to shake. Grabbing his arm firmly with his other hand, he held it stable but he could feel it twitch beneath his fingers. Was it his imagination or were people staring at him as they walked past? Did they really know that less than three hours ago, he had killed someone? Did he have *Murderer* written all over his face? He looked up at the screen again: *flight delayed 10 minutes*! The tension was overwhelming him now and it wasn't just his arm that was trembling, his legs started. He threw his small rucksack onto his lap and forced his wrists on top. The quivering abated somewhat but he needed to try and relax; the behavioural display that he was exhibiting right now would make any airport official wary. He had to act as normal as possible; he had to loosen up.

"Call for Karl Guttenberg. Please go to the information desk."

Karl's heart raced. He knew this wasn't a social call asking him if he was enjoying his visit to the airport. On the other hand, it may be the Chinese Ambassador. Had there been a change of travel arrangements? Perhaps the Chinese embassy was going to collect him and keep him concealed until the investigations had died down. Karl looked up at the screen again: *United Airlines flight EWR0020346 to Newark, go to Gate 27.*

At the information desk, he somewhat nervously strolled up.

"Can I help you, sir?"

"There's a call for me, I believe?"

"Are you Karl Guttenberg?"

"Yes."

"Please wait here, sir."

"What's it about? I have a plane to catch."

The girl behind the desk pressed the button on her microphone in front of her: "I have Mr Guttenberg at information."

He looked up and saw that his flight was displaying *last call.*

"I'm sorry, I cannot wait."

And with that, he hurriedly left for his boarding gate. The two burly security guards arrived as Karl Guttenberg was making his rapid departure through the main hall.

"Yes, that's him there," said the receptionist.

Armed with guns, the two men ran through the throng amidst worried looks from other passengers. One or two screamed at what they imagined may have been a terrorist attack. As he arrived at the boarding gate, the two security guards caught up with him and, pointing their guns directly at him, ordered him threateningly, "STOP! Put your hands behind your head!"

With trembling hands behind his head, he blurted out: "Why are you stopping me?"

"Your name is Mr Karl Guttenberg?"

"Yes."

"That's why we're stopping you. You need to come with us."

"Why?"

"Police will explain that."

"But I've done nothing wrong."

"Well, that's OK, then. The police will be relieved to hear that. This way, please!"

With that, the security guards took a worried and trembling Mr Guttenberg with them to the investigation room. Whilst one guard stood behind him with a gun pointed at his back, the other picked up the wall phone.

"We got him, sir."

"Who?"

"Mr Karl Guttenberg."

"Oh good. I'll let the police know, they're outside."

Within a few minutes, four heavily armed police officers arrived at the investigation room.

"You a Mr Karl Guttenberg?"

"Y…yes, I've already told these guys here. What's this about?"

"You are coming with us."

And with that, the man's arms were twisted behind his back as one of the officers handcuffed him.

"What's this about? I've a right to know!"

None of the police officers spoke as they marched their suspect from the airport and sat him in the back of the police car. Within thirty-five minutes, he was escorted into Orlando police station and taken immediately to the interrogation room. The detective sergeant behind the investigation screen telephoned NASA.

"We have a Mr Karl Guttenberg in custody."

"Thank you. I'll put you through to the Operations Director."

"Oh Sergeant, that's good. We all are still in a state of shock here. I'll come over immediately—should be with you within half an hour."

Having put down the phone, he walked into the room and nodded to the police guard to remove the handcuffs.

"Karl Guttenberg?"

"Yes."

"I guess you know why we've detained you then?"

"For the love of Mike, no! Nobody has told me anything. I get a call from the airport, harassed by their security, dragged into police custody...and for what?"

"Murder."

"Murder! I haven't murdered anybody...who am I supposed to have murdered?"

"Mr Danny DiMarco."

"Mr Danny DiMarco? I've never heard of Danny DiMarco!"

"Are you or are you not Mr Karl Guttenberg?"

"Yes, I am."

"Then you not only know...sorry, *knew* Danny DiMarco but, we believe, may either be responsible for his death or know the perpetrator."

"This is preposterous!"

A heavy hand slapped him from behind and forced his head on the table before him.

"Answer the good inspector's questions and don't be rude...it's not nice."

With blood pouring out of his nose, his head was jerked back as the officer pulled at his hair.

"Look, Mr Guttenberg, we can do this the nice, easy way...you know, the civilised, pleasant way—we ask you questions, then you give us nice, honest answers—or we can do it another way—we ask you questions and you keep having nosebleeds—but the end result is the same...you give us answers."

"I tell you, I have never heard of, or know of, a Mr Danny DiMarco!"

His head hit the table again.

"Constable, constable, be gentle with him. He is an innocent civilian that we have wrongfully apprehended."

"Sorry sir."

And with that, a Taser dart hit him in the back of the neck.

"AARGHH!"

"Sorry, inspector, I was just replacing the gun and it sort of...well, went off. At least it was on stun only...lucky that, eh, Mr Guttenberg?"

The questioning, based on guilty until proven otherwise, continued in this fashion for the following twenty minutes. The bloodied, battered and frightened suspect in front of the detective and his fellow officer was annoying both of them. They had dealt with common criminals and hardened criminals and knew that in the end, most would break, but initial encounters with the man before them suggested they may need to resort to more persuasive methods to get a confession out of this man.

There was a knock at the door.

"Sorry to interrupt, sergeant; the Director of Operations at NASA is here."

"Splendid. Dan, wipe the man's face, can't have police interrogation procedures brought into question. OK, show him in."

The Operations Director walked in and looked at the prisoner.

"Who's this?"

"This, sir, is Mr Karl Guttenberg."

"No, it isn't, at least not THE Karl Guttenberg."

"Hey, what's your name, fella?"

"Carl Guttenberg!"

Meanwhile, United Airlines flight EWR0020346 touched down at Newark and Karl Guttenberg walked out and climbed into an awaiting taxi.

"JFK, please."

Chapter 21

The emergency lighting suddenly brightened and warmth began to permeate around us. Though I hadn't realised it at the time, I had started to shiver and this feeling of comfort was a blessed relief.

Simon slipped back through the hatch.

"Reactor back on, Skip! Will need a few hours for full power to be restored, but everything's looking good!"

Jamie smiled his big, beaming grin and gave Simon the 'thumbs up'.

"Anna?"

"About thirty minutes, Jamie. Some units are fully operational but only a matter of time before we are back to one hundred per cent."

"Petra?"

"Onscreen data looking good. I have Neptune lined up for…four hours and twelve minutes. It's too early to say where exactly Uranus is; going to have to wait until Anna has finished."

"Charlie?"

"Looks like all units so far back online have not been affected. My only concern is the hull after those collisions; do you want me to get out and have a look?"

"Nah, Charlie; wait until after coffee!"

Jamie turned towards me, still smiling.

"Michael, to say I am relieved is an understatement. What we have been through has been beyond belief. Even sci-fi writers couldn't have created a better script with all the drama that we have experienced. What is your knowledge of Neptune like?"

"Well, not being a planetary scientist—"

"Not being a planetary scientist helped us out of a big mess a short while ago!"

"I'm not sure I'd agree with you, Jamie, but like the other gas giants, Neptune does have a strong magnetic field. Now, I have never been a gambling man and the chance of us being thrown out of orbit by that mystifying planet back there was pretty slim. The chance of it being replicated with a Neptune encounter is even slimmer! So, I would say that we do not attempt another pole skim if we can possibly avoid it."

"Rings?"

"Unfortunately, not much is known about Neptune's rings but yes, it does have some rings—all the gas giants do—but not on the same scale as Saturn. The rings will be far more tenuous than those of Saturn, so I would remain mildly confident that, like with Jupiter, the rings will not present a hazard to us and Proxima."

"Simon! Will the burners work yet?"

"Give it another twenty minutes."

"Petra…do we have twenty minutes?"

"Pushing it a bit, Jamie…the sooner the better. We need two to three hours for a plasma burn to effect a change of course at our current speed."

"Which is…exactly?"

"Warp-drive factor zero-point-eight-five."

"Simon, give plasma burners the next priority. We can possibly relax a bit once they have been activated and Anna will have all electronics up and running in five minutes!"

"Perhaps sooner, Jamie…if you are very nice to me!"

"Jamie, you must be exhausted after what we've been through; shouldn't you have a catnap before our next planet rendezvous?"

"The trouble is, Michael, I'm too tense from what we've just experienced…and yes, you're right, I should be fresh for the next phase. Anna, will you be OK to assume control after I've reset the Neptune angle—just perhaps one hour?"

"Yeah sure, I'm a bit tired myself though, Jamie. I've been working flat out on all the electronics for the past six hours and I may not be as alert as perhaps I should be for assuming command. I was thinking of taking some shut-eye myself once all this has been finished."

"Sorry, Anna, only thinking of myself. We have all been through hell and back and I guess we all need some 'me time' to unwind and recover. How about you, Petra?"

"Jamie, I think we *all* need some 'me time', but once you've redirected Proxima, I guess I can stay awake for the hour. What about Mr Astro?"

"Sure, if that's alright with you, Jamie. I am not one of the crew, though and I don't know how that will go with Mission Control if they learn that a 'civvy' is steering their multi-billion-dollar international starship towards another unknown hazard."

"Well, you're not actually steering…just keeping alert and keeping your eyes fixed on these screens. Anyway, there's no one better on board who can 'steer' us towards these planets and get the best out of them!"

"Sure, but my input remains purely mathematical—and hypothetical. I haven't got the skill of you three to direct this boyo anywhere."

"That's true, but your mathematical and theoretical knowledge is what we require right now."

"I need Uranus's position and trajectory before I can help on that score, Jamie. At least we are heading in the right direction and once Anna has the Main back on, we can determine the best course, if at all possible, for a Uranus encounter."

"Anna?"

"You haven't been nice enough to me yet, Jamie… Ten minutes perhaps?"

The atmosphere on board was very amiable and everyone continued with their respective tasks, professionally and efficiently. I reached forward for the pen and notepad and started to sketch the possible permutations of Uranus' current location based on how I remembered the planetary alignment back on Earth. I did not want to raise any false hopes and remained silent but felt that there was a possibility that both Neptune and Uranus were on complimentary sides of the sun right now. If that was the case and Jamie could get the Neptune approach at the correct angle, we might…just might be able to slingshot ourselves back—inwards and meet up with our seventh neighbour.

"OK, I am shutting down all electronics for a reboot. After that, we should be back in business. OK to go ahead, Jamie?"

"Simon?"

"Yup."

"Charlie?"

"Sure."

"Petra?"

"A second, please, Jamie. Just want to confirm Neptune coordinates…and contact time… Yeah, go ahead."

"Hit it, Anna."

Though the lighting remained on, there was a degree of uncanny silence as Anna turned off the heart of Proxima. We were now blind, totally blind. What was bizarre, nevertheless, was that we could clearly see ahead of us through the large canopy: the blackness of the void in front, perforated with a multitude of pinpricks of suns, galaxies and nebulae, and yet we were blind, unable to control or direct our future. We were purely in the hands of the gods, being sent to the stars beyond. As we sat in this eerie silence, lost in our own thoughts—thoughts of the infinite ahead—I realised just how insignificant and futile we were. In front—indeed, all around us—was the enormity of the cosmos and yet here, in this tiny capsule, compared to the vastness beyond, was the future of mankind…a grain of sand in the Universe ahead.

There was a bleep, then another, and another…and the silence was at last broken as the main computer came back to life. That beautiful sound of knowledge, direction, control and destiny was back at our fingertips.

"All stations are looking good, Captain Fraser!"

"Thanks, Anna. That's a huge relief. Our next priority is Uranus. Petra?"

"Give me a few seconds, Jamie. There she is. Well, Mr Astro, didn't you do well!"

"Don't tell me luck is on our side again, Petra?"

"It may well be…I have both Neptune and Uranus on the same side and would you believe it—Uranus is currently about three and a half billion kilometres ahead!"

"Michael, are you some kind of lucky charm?"

"I have to be honest, I did check the planet alignments before departure, I don't know why…interest, I guess. I remembered how the planet positions were configured and when we started to hit snags—"

"SNAGS! That's an understatement and a half. We were nearly annihilated and you call them 'snags'! Geez, how typically British!"

The cabin was again in uproar. Using our international idiosyncrasies, we kept the restricted working environment harmonious; we had—the six of us—an unbroken solidarity.

"How long until encounter, Petra?"

"Three hours and fifteen minutes."

"Anna, as soon as we are sorted here, I want you to take a one-hour sleeping break. When awake, I want you to take over, then I will do likewise before we approach Neptune."

"Michael, input?"

"Let me just have a quick check with Petra."

"Oh, she's fine; it's the trajectory I'm concerned with! Ha…ha…ha."

"Yeah, go on, Michael…check Petra out; make sure you're *only* checking though!"

"Thanks, Charlie!"

It was like we were all kids again; the banter was flying fast and furious. I have to admit, I did feel a tinge of embarrassment as I found Petra quite an attractive woman. We checked out the data that she had available and I floated back to my seat and quickly scribbled an amended diagram to the one that I had drawn earlier.

"Jamie, there is a reasonable chance of a successful slingshot bringing us in line with Uranus' orbit. The two planets are currently situated like this… OK?"

"Yeah."

"Well, if you approach on the Pluto-side of Neptune at about seventy-five degrees south of the equator, the gravitational pull will drag us and throw us in a north-westerly direction from Neptune towards the orbit of Uranus. But you must approach via its South Pole, which is inconveniently pointing away from us right now. However, if you aim for about 220,000 km from its outer atmosphere, we should spiral around and away from Neptune."

"Good, got it. So, almost a pole skim then?"

"Yeah; unfortunately, it has to be to get the trajectory correct. But that's not all."

"Oh?"

"No. Uranus, unlike all the other planets, has its poles facing the sun. It also has a tenuous ring system and a magnetic field…in fact, it has a complicated four-pole system—the magnetic field is simply bizarre. Now this really could screw up our navigational and electronic system."

"So, quite an easy encounter then! Routine, just like the rest!"

"For a start, you will need to disconnect all electronic devices and we will be travelling purely on manual control. You will need to divorce the plasma burners from computer control to manual only. The gravitational pull is less than the other giants, like Jupiter—more like Earth's. So, we can get closer than we did with Jupiter and Saturn. Now, Jamie, we will have about three hours and…seven minutes before our rendezvous with Uranus after Neptune. This should give you enough time to line up our trajectory whilst all electronics are correctly functioning. I suggest that you go the solar side of the planet AND if you get the pole angle right, together with firing the burners at precisely the right time, then you will sling us directly ahead and towards Proxima Centauri."

"At Warp-drive factor…one!"

"If you play your cards right!"

"Michael, once we are through the solar system…you and me—"

"—'I', Jamie…you and I."

"Yeah…you, I and me—all three of us are going to join Mr Jack Daniels and get rather wasted. It has been a bit more of a strain than I had thought back home."

"Just the boys, is it, Captain Fraser!"

"You think you can handle your liquor, Anna?"

"I'm from the West Indies…we were weaned on dark rum!"

"OK…I am going to enjoy this…watching my number two crawling to the sick-bowl."

"Competition time, is it, Captain?"

"I wasn't known as lieutenant 'Jack' back on base in the early years for nothing, lieutenant colonel Inniss."

"Jamie, Jamie…erm… Unless I am much mistaken, *Hanschell Inniss* distil Cockspur rum…sure you want to continue?"

"You sure about this, Michael?"

"Pretty certain."

"OK, Missy, you in any way related to THE 'Inniss'?"

"My great-granddaddy, Captain!"

"Right…well then, OK Anna, time for bed. See you in an hour."

I joined in the fun as Jamie found that he may have met his match, in more ways than one. I could not recall people of such ilk as I was with right now, creating such joy. Even drinking sessions back home as a student didn't really match what I was feeling with my fellow travellers. This was going to be a hard act to follow…and an even harder act to leave. Anna pulled the hood over her face, twisted a dial and, within twenty seconds, was asleep.

"Petra, we are going to need to burn away from Neptune and circle up underneath her so that we can approach from the South Pole; can you give me the new flight path, please?"

"Done, Jamie. New ETA…five hours and twenty-seven minutes. You need to burn starboard, zero-three-five degrees, then at sixteen forty-five, Earth time, you need to correct to port at five-minute intervals, three-three-zero degrees, for six activations."

"OK thanks."

"Jamie, I feel a bit groggy; I think I'll take an hour also…is that OK?"

"Sure. Charlie, Simon, perhaps you guys need to take an unwind too. Petra and me...sorry, Petra and 'I' will remain alert for the next hour, by which time you three will have come to, then Petra and 'I' will take an hour's shuteye."

"Will do, Jamie."

Chapter 22

Michel Nostredame walked up the dark and foreboding street, a reed basket over his shoulder. He held a lantern before him as he tried to decipher the name of the small winding lane leading away from the main part of town: *Rue du diable*—he just could make out the weathered writing on the plaque.

"Appropriate," he mumbled as he searched for number thirteen.

A dog started snarling at him as he walked up the street, barring his way. The growling grew in intensity and ferocity. Michel knew that it was going to be one of them that would regret this encounter and he made sure it wasn't going to be him. Speaking in Latin, he withdrew from his basket his means of defence and stared directly into the dog's eyes. With chanting and a swaying of the lantern in his hand, backwards and forwards, backwards and forwards, the dog's head moved with the light before him, still snarling. Suddenly, the dog let out a yelp as the viper bit him. Howling, the animal retreated, limping into the darkness. Michel lowered the basket onto the ground, still chanting in Latin and the snake slithered back inside. Picking up his package, he passed a small passageway and directing the lantern towards the gap, saw the dog lying, panting on the ground.

He arrived at number thirteen and climbed the stone steps that led to the front door. The wind had picked up and every so often, a gust would blow his lantern to and fro. He pulled up his hood around his head, but a strong gust blew it back down around his back. Looking at the heavy oak door, he hesitated before knocking loudly. Almost immediately, he saw a flickering light inside and knew that his banging had been heard. Not normally a nervous man, he could not but help feel somewhat apprehensive as he waited for the door to open. The light grew in intensity and then stabilised as the large door was slowly opened. A large Negroid with dashing white eyes stood before him.

"Sir?"

"I have come to see Monsieur Jean LeMartre, if you please."

"Is he expecting you?"

"Indeed, he is. We have a rendezvous arranged for eight o'clock."

"Would you care to come in, sir?"

"Thank you."

With that, Michel entered the hallway and handed the servant his reed basket and cloak. He was led into a large room near the front of the house, with a disturbing display of stuffed animals: dogs, cats, owls and a black panther.

"I shall let the Master know of your arrival, sir."

The servant left the room as Michel gazed around. He stood aghast as he saw, in a glass cabinet, a scorpion, mongoose and cobra in mortal combat. The snake was hooded and ready to strike, swaying like Michel had done but a few moments earlier in the street. The mongoose had already moved and held the neck of the serpent in its jaws, as the scorpion stung the reptile from behind. The commotion caused the glass frame to crack as the snake tried to throw the mongoose from its grip. The scorpion retreated to the back of the cabinet amongst some rocks and hid, well-camouflaged amongst the debris, sand and stones. With blood on its head from the force of the throw, the mongoose held on as the cobra's resistance weakened, until it finally lay inert on the sand floor.

"Fascinating creatures, mongooses, don't you think?"

Michel turned around and there before him stood the man he had been afraid of meeting. Dressed in a dark-brown cloak with a white laced shirt beneath, Michel eyed the man before him with caution. He had had no preconception of what he had expected to see but perhaps subconsciously, he had thought that the man would fly in on a broomstick. Somewhat smaller in stature than he had anticipated, he sensed a tension in the air.

"Indeed, they are. Has the cobra ever won?"

"Not against *this* mongoose, no!"

With that, LeMartre opened the top of the glass cabinet and dropped in a paralysed frog. The reptile had been twitching on the table beside the glass frame throughout the combat. Beside the frame were two jars containing lightly coloured liquids. Inside each, two metal rods were immersed and a silver wire from each was attached to the convulsing animal. The mongoose fell onto the frog immediately and started to tear at its flesh with the same sharp teeth that had just terminated the life of the dead snake. Nostradamus turned his attention away from the gruesome feast before him and addressed his host with a slight bow.

"Michel Nostredame…a pleasure to make your acquaintance."

"Jean LeMartre…and yours too. I have heard a great deal about you, Monsieur; your reputation precedes you."

"Likewise, Monsieur LeMartre."

"Your maid came around with a note that you would like a meeting and I am fascinated that such a distinguished man of the town would wish such a meeting. Pray, how may I be of service?"

"Are we alone? I would rather that our conversation not be overheard."

LeMartre rang a bell and his servant walked in.

"Jaafar, please bring in the burgundy and two glasses. After that, I don't wish to be disturbed."

"Yes sir."

Jean LeMartre directed Nostradamus to a chair in front of a welcoming fire. Settling himself opposite him, the two men surveyed one another as the servant brought in the wine and glasses.

"Shall I pour, sir?"

"No, no, that's fine; I shall do that myself, thank you."

The servant bowed and left as LeMartre poured out two generous helpings of wine. He displayed the label to Michel Nostredame.

"1546…it was a good year, what say you?"

"Ah yes…a good year indeed. A rather heavy wine, best with beef."

"A man who knows his wine…that is what I admire. Tell me, apart from the drinking of a good burgundy, why do you wish to see me?"

"It is a rather delicate matter and one which you, I believe, is the only person who can help."

"Intriguing…go on."

"I have…I had an acquaintance who was indebted to me for a considerable sum of money. I had helped him during financial hardship, for which he was extremely grateful. It saved both him and his family from poverty and in the end, he developed some means of his own. However, before he could complete his commitment to me, he sadly passed away. He, I know, had some hidden wealth with which he intended to settle his account and it is to this end I have come to you."

"You want me to find this wealth?"

"That is correct."

"Which would mean—"

"—That you raise him from the dead!"

"Oh, I see. You, of course, would have heard of my 'practices'. I am surprised that you yourself are unable to perform such a feat."

"It is not an area in which I feel comfortable. It takes a special gift, special methods, which I have never ventured to study. But you, you, I believe, are well-versed in the 'Black Arts'."

"Black Arts! Come, come, let's not call it by that name; it implies that I am some kind of devil worshipper."

"No, no, no, please, don't misunderstand me. I have used a wrong phrase. It is just that your practices differ from my own mystical procedures."

"Ah, yes, an unfortunate phrase indeed. What sum of wealth are we referring to…as I will need payment?"

"I am still outstanding thirty thousand francs."

"Of which, I will require half."

"Half!"

"The practice can be dangerous and there is no guarantee that I will survive unharmed. It is a generous fee, for the risks involved. Are we in agreement?"

"Well, half seems rather… Yes… As you say, the risks are great."

"Payment in advance."

"I cannot raise this amount. I am still waiting for what is owed to me, which is why I am here now. Let's say…half before and half upon retrieval of my dues?"

"That, my friend, justifies another burgundy. Your health, sir."

The two men sat discussing the finer merits of the '1546' and some radical experiments in the recent advances in astrology as well as the importance of the planets' alignment in prophesying the future of both the monarch and some of his nobles. Throughout, both men offered the other the respect worthy of gentlemen in this dark era of medieval France. Michel Nostredame sensed though, that his host had not only an air of haughtiness as he spoke but also an underlying secret. A secret that, if LeMartre had wished, could have overpowered and imprisoned him. He not only wished but he felt that he needed to leave his host and this house as quickly as polite protocol permitted. However, he needed LeMartre on his side without any suspicion that his purpose was not genuine and to this end, he felt compelled to stay.

The pleasantness continued, as did the wine. Michel, though, was not used to a wine of this potency in this quantity and he soon felt tired and struggled to maintain his concentration. As he gazed upon LeMartre, he felt sure that he could see his form change. Slowly at first, his host's face altered and seemed to take on the air of a fox…or was it a wolf? His cloak became enveloped in a brown fur and his teeth, which now became the most prominent feature in his sight, turned into pointed incisors, like daggers. The door opened and at the doorway stood the black servant. His dashing white eyes had now turned blood-red. In his hand, he held a knife. Nostradamus started to sway like a serpent about to strike. LeMartre let out a gurgling cry as he leapt forward in a frenzied attack and sunk his teeth into Michel's neck. As he did so, the servant, in one movement, stabbed the guest in the chest. He shook his head back and forth, trying to throw LeMartre from the grip on his throat but it was too much…LeMartre had won…his victory complete, Nostradamus fell back into the chair.

"Monsieur Nostredame… Monsieur Nostredame!"

"Jaafar, fetch the Hartshorn!"

Within a few seconds, the servant had returned and handed his master a vial, which LeMartre waved under Nostradamus's nose. With a repulsion at the contents, Michel jerked his head to one side and regained consciousness.

"What? What happened? Where am I?"

"In the land of burgundy 1546, I believe," LeMartre said with a sardonic smile.

Nostradamus tried to stand but fell back into the chair. He realised that he had re-enacted the very scene in the cabinet that he had witnessed upon his arrival. He indeed was, and perhaps still would be, the victim of a grisly masque. Never mind about the 1546, his host was indeed a malevolent perpetrator of the Black Arts and he needed to leave immediately.

"Jaafar, make up the guest bedroom. I think Monsieur Nostredame is in need of complete rest."

"No, no, thank you kindly, Monsieur LeMartre. I must away to my own bed. I confess the 1546 has claimed another victim but I will be better in the freshness of the night air. I shall despatch my maid with the agreed sum and await your instructions. Thank you again for your cordiality and I wish you a good night."

With that, Nostradamus regained his cloak and reed basket and stepped out into the night air. The freshness felt good, away from the malice that he had just left behind. Even the gusty wind made him feel free. The man, that necromancer, was a really powerful adversary and Michel knew that he needed the control and protection of his spirit guides ever more than before. Now that contact had been made, he knew he was now vulnerable to the man and he shuddered slightly. He paused as he passed the small alley and shining his lantern in the direction of that passageway, saw the dog, dead, with foam exuding from its cold lifeless mouth. As he arrived at the main path back to town, he sighed with relief and turning his head in the direction of *Rue du diable*, he was convinced that he could make out two red demon eyes staring at him from the darkness and he knew that he would have to make that journey again soon, and he was frightened…very frightened.

Chapter 23

When I awoke, Anna was at Proxima's controls and Jamie and Petra were taking their time out. Charlie and Simon had also recovered and Simon was floating back out of the hatch for some routine maintenance work.

"You here with your wife, Charlie?"

"Oh, no…unattached…oh, I guess you didn't know?"

"Know what?"

"None of the crew has Earth attachments; but as you're not crew, then you wouldn't have needed to know. But what about you; you surely can't have 'left a girl behind'."

"No, not lucky, or unlucky, on that score. Why can't the crew have attachments?"

"Well, as we won't be going back, then it would not only be pointless, it would be cruel to have family or loved ones back home who will never see you again."

"Oh yeah, that makes sense, but what about those families that I arrived with?"

"Those are complete families; they are not being parted from each other. There may be parents, brothers, sisters back home, but families are a complete unit—they have not been separated."

"Same with you, Anna?"

"I had a fella…we were going to be married but he had wandering eyes…and hands. So, I didn't think it was going to be a great success."

"Sorry to hear that, but you've got over it though."

"Actually, Michael, I have not got over it and this is the reason why I am here!"

"Oh! So it's recent then?"

"Last month."

"But if it's recent, how come you are here? You would have had to split up for this venture?"

"No, Darren was also a member of the crew. We were travelling together as husband and wife."

"So, they got a replacement for your fiancée then?"

"That's me, Michael."

"Oh, I had no idea, Charlie."

"Trained as backup. All crew had a backup just in case anything happened to the first choice. Mission Control took the decision that Anna would be more reliable and loyal to this project and dismissed Darren."

"Bet he was gutted!"

"Took it hard...but that's the payback you get for not behaving yourself."

"Sorry, Anna...I really had no intention of prying. It just seemed like harmless conversation when I asked; I certainly didn't mean to snoop."

"Michael, this venture, with what we have been through together so far, is the best thing that has ever happened to me. It has given a purpose to my life. I can devote one hundred per cent to this assignment without the emotional ties that being a couple may have brought. The bond that I feel with the four of you has given me a new trust in men; perhaps we could draw this conversation to a close now?"

"Sure, sorry..."

I felt somewhat uncomfortable with how I had, inadvertently, raked up emotional turmoil with Anna. Charlie didn't seem to have been too concerned and luckily, the other three were not present to hear our conversation. Like Petra, Anna was very attractive and I really wanted to hug her and try to squeeze away the hurt that she was obviously still feeling. But, having just put my foot in it, a hug would have been the last thing that I should have done, as much as I wanted to comfort her. I decided to busy myself with planet orbits for our next, and final, two encounters. Anna seemed to be concentrating on keeping Proxima on course and was regularly checking out the Main. I tried to bend the atmosphere away from the sadness of the past few minutes.

"Anna, are you really an 'Inniss'?"

Anna smiled, which was a relief.

"Yeah, but not *the* 'Inniss'! Don't tell Jamie that."

"I heard that!"

Jamie had just awoken and the laughter once again permeated the cabin. Petra also came around and after drawing on her oxygen mask, was fully alert and ready to continue with her analysis of the flight path.

"Update, please, Petra."

"Currently flying parallel with Neptune at one hundred and eighty degrees into her orbit. You will need to start corrective trajectory, three-three-zero degrees...still on schedule for sixteen forty-five, Earth time. ETA remains unchanged. I will notify you on countdown as we approach corrective changes. Six changes at five-minute intervals."

"Thanks, Petra."

"Oh, no!"

"What is it, Anna?"

"We have just received communication from Mission Control. It reads:

'*Today, at 0700 hours Eastern Time, North Korea, supported by China, invaded South Korea. Initial reports are sketchy but the attack began with a non-nuclear ballistic missile barrage on Seoul, followed by an aerial strike throughout the North. Satellite pictures show a build-up of military personnel along the border between North and South Korea.*

USA has condemned the unprovoked attack and threatened instant retaliatory action unless North Korea withdraws immediately and unconditionally from this act of aggression. An emergency meeting of the United Nations has been called, though it is expected that China will veto any military action against North Korea. NATO has been alerted and USA warships have been diverted to the war zone.'"

"Does it say how China supported... Militarily, strategically...?"

"No, it just says 'supported'."

"That's just what we feared."

"Mankind is on the brink of self-destruction so we must keep the hope...and the species of Man alive. That's why *we* are here."

"Actually, that's why *I* am here."

"You, Michael... What do you mean?"

"Jamie, as you said at the beginning, you and I need to have a long talk...perhaps with 'Mr Jack'."

"Yes! I am now intrigued, Michael."

And so were the rest of the crew around me.

Chapter 24

Karl Guttenberg arrived at JFK in the back of the yellow cab. He was in a tense frame of mind. He had managed one evasion of the police and security officials at Orlando airport and now had to face a second ordeal at New York's main airport. Walking as calmly as he could, he went straight into 'International departures' and searched along the digital screens to find the check-in desk for his flight to China. He caught sight of 'Air China' but couldn't believe the screen display before him: *All Air China flights cancelled until further notice.* Having kept a low profile, he had remained ignorant of the current situation in the Far East. He was reluctant to ask anyone as he specifically did not wish to arouse anybody's awareness of his presence. He decided to grab a coffee and mull over the drama developing before him. Sitting in the corner of one of the airport's numerous convenience food outlets, he faced a large flat-screened television, transmitting international news. *Why had all the flights to China been cancelled? How was he going to get to Beijing, whilst a fugitive on the run?* The monitor was showing a series of news bulletins and interviewers were displaying anxiety as they regurgitated what appeared to be serious global news. Karl had often wondered in the past, *Why show pixel images on a screen without any sound?* It seemed to be a pointless and unnecessary feature of airports; it was as though people could use ESP to understand the dialogue between groups of people discussing ground-breaking news by telepathy alone. This time, however, the images on the screen seemed to be more urgent than usual and he tried to understand what his limited comprehension of the events unfolding before him were saying. Suddenly he froze! One word passed across the screen as the broadcaster continued his silent presentation of the news: *China.* His focus on the screen was total now. Within ten minutes, he had seen enough to understand the tragic consequences that international disagreements had caused.

Recent events regarding the invasion of South Korea by North Korea had presented Karl Guttenberg with a major dilemma. His pre-booked flight to Beijing had been cancelled because of the current global crisis. He needed another escape route and realised that the Chinese embassy would be in no position to help him now. His contacts with the Chinese officials may well have been traced and he could possibly be regarded as a national security threat…a spy even. He had never wished his adopted country, or even Danny, any harm; his Chinese-born wife and their son lay at the mercy of the cruelty that a dictatorship invariably brought. But escape he must; for *their* safety, he must. He needed to find a route that would keep his whereabouts and himself concealed from American authorities—even the CIA may be on his trail. International air travel was now out of the question, yet he had to escape from USA. Risky as it was, his new idea probably presented the least visible means of his exit from America. Feeling somewhat more confident as his plan started to develop, Karl Guttenberg switched on his laptop and scoured the streets of Ottawa.

"Chambers street, please."

"Yes sir. What number?"

"Fourteen. Oh, the nearest ATM first."

"One just inside, sir."

Karl alighted from the cab he had just entered and nervously approached the machine in front of him. He needed the money and knew that it would only be a matter of time before his card would be frozen. Inserting his card and dialling in his PIN, he waited. 'Incorrect code' was displayed before him! He was certain that the four digits that he had punched in were correct. He repeated the exercise again, pressing the numbers very slowly in case he had pressed incorrectly in his haste. 'Incorrect code'. A warning gave him one final attempt; otherwise, his card would not be returned.

"Zero, four, eight, six…zero, four, eight, six…that is my code. Oh no!"

Suddenly, Karl remembered that he had mislaid his credit card a week previously and had applied for a replacement. The card had only been with him since Monday and it had not yet been used. It needed to be activated and equally importantly, Karl needed to punch in the correct code; there was no room for error this time. He had recorded his code on his mobile phone. Once turned on, his location would be uncovered. He now had to make a choice: turn on his phone and risk being discovered or risk losing his only means of obtaining his money…and freedom. He thumbed through his hidden texts and after removing his SIM card, he slid the phone under the nearest vending machine.

"Nine, seven, two, one…for God's sake, work!"

Sweating profusely, he waited for the machine to acknowledge his final PIN number. Had he been too agitated dialling in the numbers? Were they correct? Was his account frozen? Would a dozen armed CIA agents confront him where he stood?

'*Do you want a receipt?*'

"Do I want a *receipt*! Do I want a receipt! No, thank God, no!"

With that, the yellow cab pulled out of JFK airport and whisked Karl Guttenberg towards his next destination. The traffic, as usual, was particularly heavy and the trip by taxi took nearly as long as it would have, had Karl walked. But with one rucksack and a small suitcase packed with all he could fit inside, the walk would have pulled too much on both his humerus and his cervical vertebrae, both of which had been weakened in a skiing accident eight years previously. Karl settled up with the driver and, waiting for him to turn the corner, picked up his case and made for the next block to 27, Warren Street. Having used the ATM, Karl knew that both the police and CIA would be looking for him and the machine, more probably his phone, would give the location where he had drawn out his money. With what he had collected at home and his current withdrawal, he had enough to pay his way without the need to use his credit card again. He just hoped they would be confused into thinking that he had used the airport for his escape and would not be looking beyond the departure flights…for a while, at least.

"Yes sir?"

"Ottawa, return, please."

"Today?"

"Please."

"Return trip?"

"Friday, next."

"Address where you will be staying?"

"300, Lisgar Street, Ottawa."

"ID please."

"Driver's licence?"

"Sure…but Canadian Border Control will want your passport. Do you have a valid passport?"

"Yes, it's in my case…I'll get it out when I get to the border if that's OK?"

"Sure. That's two hundred and twenty dollars. Credit card?"

"No, I'll pay cash."

"Next bus will be in ninety minutes. Restroom to your right…snacks second left. Have a good trip."

A relieved Karl Guttenberg sat himself in the restroom, selecting neither a window seat nor any seat facing oncoming people. Keeping a watchful eye on the monitor above, he passed the longest ninety minutes in his life, nervously biting his fingers.

"Sir, we have a signal from Karl Guttenberg's phone—JFK!"

"OK. Contact airport security and send a call to New York City Police. Let them know we have our suspect in their location."

The throng of people in the bus terminus were oblivious to the additional security congregating around. Police and army were commonplace and had been for many years now. Even before 9/11, security had been tightened significantly, but the latest cataclysm developing in the Far East had increased this to fever-pitch level. Luckily for Karl, the current world crisis served as a double-edged sword. On the one hand, he was a suspect wanted for a very serious crime and couldn't make it to his place of sanctuary; on the other, the mounting predicament on the other side of the world presented a more serious priority for both the New York police and CIA. It may just be the break that Karl needed in order to escape into Canada. With his ticket in his hand, he boarded the Greyhound bus and settled down in the farthest seat from the driver. The bus remained stationary and vibrated to the gentle rhythm of the engine. After twenty minutes, Karl's patience was reaching breaking point. Fortunately, he had a seat to himself, even though the majority of the bus was full. The noise of the other passengers helped keep him calmer than he otherwise would have been. Karl's resolve suddenly weakened as he saw two armed police officers walk into the Greyhound bus terminal. His position at the back of the bus gave him a restricted view of the glass-fronted terminal, but he noticed that both officers, before disappearing from view, seemed to be taking a more than cursory interest in the passengers gathering around the ticket counter. One of the officers came out of the building and motioning to the driver to open the door, boarded the bus. Karl's heart raced! This was it; this was going to be the moment of him being discovered! The armed man walked very slowly up the aisle, stopping at every seat.

"ID please, sir."

Pulling out his passport, the apathetic old man gave a grudging nod as the police officer returned it to him. Moving nearer to Karl, the same scene opened up before him.

"Where's your destination?"

A mumbled reply seemed to have satisfied the tall man in dark grey. Karl felt that he could visibly see his heart pounding on his sternum. If it hadn't been for the hum of the bus's engine, he was convinced he would have sounded like a bass drum. After the couple to his left, it was his turn.

"ID please, sir."

Without raising his head, Karl fumbled in his rucksack for his driver's licence even though he knew it was in his wallet inside his jacket. His hands were shaking so violently that he couldn't undo the fastening straps. The officer regarded the shaking figure with suspicion.

"Are you alright, sir?"

"Parkinson's, Officer."

"Oh. I'm sorry, sir, but I need to see some ID. Can I help you with your bag, sir?"

"No, no, it's fine. Erm, I can't seem to find it. I was sure it was here…somewhere…"

"Jacket, perhaps, sir?"

"Pardon?"

"Jacket…perhaps it's in your jacket?"

"Oh… Why, yes…it must be in my jacket."

Karl knew exactly where it was but continued to delay the inevitable outcome of his detection by searching in every pocket except the one where it really was kept. Finally, realising that further delay would arouse even more suspicion, he pulled out his driver's licence and with shaking hand, passed it to the policeman, hoping he hadn't yet been briefed about Karl Guttenberg. The officer took the licence.

"Josh! Nine-eleven… JFK. Let's go!"

The other man in the dark-grey uniform had just saved Karl from certain identification as the examining police officer stuffed the licence back into Karl's hand, ran down the aisle and into the stationary patrol car in front of the bus. A bead of sweat stung Karl's eye as he saw the car accelerate into the distance.

With the satisfying sound of the changing of gears, the Greyhound slowly edged away from the bus station.

Chapter 25

I returned to Mai's house and found her sleeping peacefully and beautifully in the small chair near the fire. Curled up like a sleeping baby, with her lips slightly parted, I looked on, mesmerised by her youthful exquisiteness. Mai's mother was in the back, completing her tasks with the laundry. She stopped working at the sink and walked in to where Mai was sleeping. She turned and saw me, but though not addressing me with a smile of welcome, her look was not hostile. Though she could see me, she knew that without her daughter, communication was impossible and walked over to Mai and brushed back her fine black hair, uncovering her face completely. I felt my excitement quicken as I gazed into her closed, gently slanting eyes and moved forward, whispering into her ear: "Mai, I love you; I love you so much."

I saw her eyes twitch and her lips turn slightly upwards into a smile.

"Sweet dreams, my love, but we must soon away again to the cathedral."

Mai continued to sleep and purred gently like a kitten. *Perhaps*, I thought, *perhaps I can leave you resting for a while, you brave, sweet girl.* With that, I decided to return to Michel and, even as the thought entered my being, I was before him in his library. Anne was also with him and they were studying one of his volumes that he had removed from one of the shelves. Anne looked up towards where I had placed myself.

"Michel, I sense that Michael is here."

Michel Nostredame looked around the room and like Anne, sensed me too. He turned his attention to his orb and appeared to make out my form before him. Closing his eyes and concentrating, he addressed me, "What news, Michael?"

"I was going to ask you the same thing, Michel. Jean LeMartre...?"

"A fearful man indeed, make no mistake. His is a path that I would not wish to cross too often. Yet, I believe that he may genuinely be able to be possessed; the problem is that what the outcome will be? To that, I am none the wiser."

Anne looked towards me: "Michael, I am afraid for my husband. He has done much good for many people, and yet there are those who criticise him—"

"—In ignorance, if I may say, my dear."

"Ignorance or not, there are people who wish him harm—even without knowing anything about him and his works."

"The unknown," I replied, "is a fearful thing to many people. Tell or show them something that they do not understand and the human response is to condemn it. Because they cannot grasp its true significance or simply because it is an unknown and unorthodox article opening up before them, it is automatically and unjustifiably condemned."

"But in this case, Anne, it will not be I who will be practicing…it will be another—a formidable rival."

"Yes…yes, I know, but your mere association with the man, should it become known! And now that he knows you…"

"He knew me before, he said as much."

"But now that he has met you, perhaps his power over you will be so much stronger. Perhaps he can now influence your mind…possess you even!"

"Anne, I do not think that Jean LeMartre will harm or have influence over your husband. His practices seem to me to have one aim—delving into the occult, performing those rites that he feels will give him control of the unknown…the macabre. I am of the spirit world and though I have never met the man, I think it will be I, not Jean LeMartre, who will have the hegemony."

"Perhaps you could visit him then and see how he practises his art?"

"I cannot. Once he has seen me, then my plan to use his powers and indeed to have his cooperation will be terminated. The only time that he can see me…know of me, must be the moment when we use him."

"I understand… Michael! I have been talking to you! Communicating with you through my mind! I can…can…almost see you, and I feel your presence!"

"Oh! That is good, Anne! When I first saw you, you sensed me even then. You, like Michel, are sensitive to the world of spirits and your gift, perhaps, has always been there, but latent. Now, the recent events have triggered this to a higher level of perception and made you more aware, more sensitive to my world."

"My dear, this is indeed good news! I often have to rely on my orb but you…you have the 'gift' without the need for a psychic's crystal."

"Perhaps, Michel. It is only since Michael's arrival that I have sensed to this degree. Before, I'm not sure…the fear of a person, the apprehension of a place, these were, to me, just normal human senses—nothing exceptional. But recently, I seem to have become attuned to another level of feeling and I know that I am afraid of this Jean LeMartre…necromancer!"

"Have you met him, my dear?"

"No, but my sensing of him does not portend good."

"Because of his name…his practices?"

"Because of him!"

"Anne, I would like to say, 'do not worry', but it would be unfair and untrue for me to say that. Yes, I agree, Michel could be in danger but I think not. I will be in much more danger than your husband…and perhaps, Jean LeMartre…even more so. It is the unknown that we are now reaching into and, as I mentioned, it is the unknown that we are afraid of. Please, just trust me when I say that I believe that my purpose, my reason for being here, my contact with you, and now Jean LeMartre is part of a much bigger picture and we are all but mere pawns in this great game of chequers."

"Michael, did you have any luck with the 'finances'?"

"Not as yet, Michel. I will try again today once Mai has rested."

"Anne, my dear, Monsieur Jean LeMartre requires payment before he will provide his services to us. I have agreed on a half-payment now and half after the possession has been completed. Would you send Agnès with the sum, please?"

"How much, Michel?"

"A costly sum, my dear…"

"How much?"

"Seven and a half thousand francs."

"Seven—seven and a half thousand francs!"

"His services are expensive…"

"That's not expensive; that's extortionate! That is plain greed!"

"I…we have no choice, Anne; there is no one else."

"But then…we will have to pay another seven and a half thousand after the ceremony!"

"No, Anne; I am in the process of obtaining the remainder. You will not need to pay any more, in fact, you will not need to pay any…see this sum only as a loan, a temporary loan."

"How, Michael? How will you, a spirit, recover this money?"

"Perhaps it is best that you do not know, Anne. But it will be put to the use that God intended—good use. Michel, do not send your maid with the money, wait until tomorrow; perhaps I will have better luck today."

"As you wish…"

"In fact, I should return to Mai now. We have much to do."

And with that, I was caressing my little angel still curled in the chair.

"Mai, Mai, wake up, we must away."

She stirred and with an arm stretching towards my cheek, opened her eyes and smiled. I leant forward as she reached towards me and tried to kiss my ethereal lips. She shivered slightly as our mouths met.

"Michael, I can almost feel you…you are becoming more physical, more real…no, not more real; you are real to me! But every time we share a moment of intimacy, it is as though there is a fire inside me, a passion, a burning and a contentment, an overwhelming contentment."

"I feel that too, Mai. But I wish so much that we could touch, really, physically touch."

"In time, Michael, in time."

"Mai, we have to return to the cathedral. We need to try again to retrieve that chest inside the priest's tabernacle. Michel has contacted the necromancer and we must collect that blood money soon, very soon."

Mai arose from her chair and went into the back room.

"Mother, can you continue without me, please?"

"I can, Mai. You are off with Michael?"

"Yes, Mother. If anything happens to me, I will be at the cathedral."

"Mai, please be careful, very careful."

Mai kissed her mother on the cheek, a cheek that I wished I could have had, just to feel that soft touch. Her mother turned and threw her arms around her daughter and I noticed her eyes moist in the light from the small window.

"Mai, I would like to talk to Michael…"

"Michael?"

"Mai, I am here…I know what your mother said. Let her speak."

"Michael, I have had time now to understand a little about who you are and why you are here. I believe that your feelings for my daughter are sincere and honest. I know that you will do whatever it takes within your power to protect her and keep her from harm. I have never seen my daughter affected so emotionally before and I believe that she has found true love—even with a form from another dimension. We know so little of what lies beyond what we can see and touch and it may well be that the division twixt our worlds is but the tinniest hair's breadth. But that hair's breadth, be it but a whisper between us, must surely prevent any communion between you. I cannot envisage anything but pain and anguish for Mai once she finally has to accept that your union can never be. It is that anguish, that utter despair from her pained heart that I will find unbearable. A mother's love bends and sways with the breeze, as it has always done, but it is because it cannot break, that the bond a parent has for his child will forever be one of shared joy…and torment. When Mai's heart breaks—and it surely will— her angst will be mine…and that misery…that grief will break both our hearts. It will be a desolation that I am not sure I could live with."

"I do not know what to say. I feel such sorrow that should I now have a corporeal form, my tears would be falling, as are yours. If the choice were mine, I would stop now! I would stop, just to live for, and live with, Mai. But there is a force that I do not understand, a force that compels me to journey on, to continue, regardless of my feelings, my compassion, my love, for this wonderful creature before me. Believe me, I wish I could stop…I really do. But I also believe that there is a cause, a reason, that is greater than any personal emotions that I, Mai or indeed you feel right now. I do not know if there is a God, but if there is, then His motive for our turmoil MUST be so important that all other feelings have to be sacrificed."

"I will pray for you both…may God be with you."

Mai and her mother sobbed openly and I stood beside them looking on, feeling like I wished that I had never met this beautiful girl. How I could possibly endanger that which I loved beyond anything that I had ever known and, I now believed, that I could never have known from wherever I had come…never have known a love like this.

"Mai?"

"I'm coming, Michael."

With their arms outstretched as Mai parted from her mother, I led her outside into the freshness of the day. We walked together, slowly and sad. Mai quietly sobbed beside me as we worked our way through the streets; no words passed between us. For the first time—the first real time—I considered terminating this whole drama. Perhaps I was mistaken, perhaps there was no real purpose to my being here, other than by chance. I fought with these ideas and knew that it was my love for Mai and the hurt that she and her mother were feeling that made me question if the demand I was putting on myself, and this teenager beside me, could ever be justified. What cause could possibly be greater than the happiness, love and comfort of another soul? And yet I knew, deep down inside me, that I had no choice. The pain that we both were suffering was requisite, if my purpose here was to be fulfilled.

We arrived just outside the cathedral gates. I stopped and looked into Mai's eyes. Beads of sorrow still clung to her cheek and she could barely raise her head. The breeze blew her jet-black hair across her soft face and with it, took away that token of sadness on display but a moment before. She slowly raised her head and looked straight into my eyes. My whole being trembled as she gazed into my soul.

"I love you, Michael. You mean more to me than life itself."

"I love you, Mai, with everything that I am, I love you."

"But I also love my parents; I cannot bear the pain that they are suffering now because of me."

"I so dearly wish I could brush away the hurt that you feel. I so wish that I could stop the pain that your parents feel also. I find this burden almost too much to endure. This time that we have had together, I want it to last forever, and forever is where I am right now! Mai, I can say no more words of comfort; I am desolate…so terribly alone. I want to be with you every second, every moment of our lives, but the turmoil that you are facing now because of me is tearing me apart!"

Mai reached out her hand and stroked my face…and I swear I felt it! I turned my head and kissed that soft, gentle palm. Mai trembled.

"Come, Michael—we have work to do."

The door to the cathedral was open and we quietly went inside. I heard noises in the distance but I could see no person—as we entered. We traversed the length of the nave quickly and just before the altar, turned to our left and towards the sacristy. The door was shut.

"OK, Mai, as we planned…"

Mai knocked on the door and waited. There was no reply. She knocked again—silence. Somewhere in the background, I could hear noises, but it may have been the wind blowing through the arches and open doors throughout this vast house of worship.

"Here we go…"

Mai turned the handle of the arched oak door and lightly pushed forwards. Surprisingly, it moved inward at her touch. Furtively, she edged in, first her head, then her whole frame through the open doorway. The room was deserted. Over on the far wall, the priest's robes and flamboyant garments hung. Chasubles adorned with all the finery of a rich and corrupt order. Mai ran her fingers along the table as she made her way towards the small cupboard on the wall opposite.

I went back to the open door and looked out into the main cathedral. Despite hearing the same noises that I took to be the wind, there was no one.

"OK, Mai, carry on."

Mai quietly opened the cupboard. Hanging inside, as before, was the mitre. She carefully lifted it off the hook and laid it soundlessly on the table behind her. Turning her body towards the open cupboard, she reached out for the keys—

"Mai! The priest! He is making his way back. Quickly, put everything back! Make haste!"

Hurriedly, Mai returned the keys and the mitre and closed the cupboard. She made her way to the door, but this time, because of the brightness inside, there was no place for her to hide. She would have been in full view of the man striding towards them if she had attempted to leave the room. The priest was making his way swiftly back to the sacristy.

"Mai, close the door slowly!"

Gently pushing the door to, Mai stood back to await her fate. The priest put his hand to the latch, pressed down and started to open the door.

"Father!"

The priest turned around.

"Father, I wish to take confession."

It was Mai's mother!

"Come back later, I have other matters—important matters."

The priest continued to push the door open.

"More important than sin?"

"Sin? What sin?"

"My sin, Father. I cannot continue like this until I have made my confession before God Almighty."

The priest hesitated at the door, then closing it behind him, turned to the woman before him and led her off to the confessional.

With his back to the door, I called out to Mai: "Mai, quietly, quickly get out now."

"No, Michael. We have an important task that we must face. No more running away. Our lives are in torment and this must be faced! Let us end this misery now!"

I looked into her eyes again. Eyes that moments ago had been full of sorrow were now eyes of determination and courage. She was the one who was now in charge. Before, it had been me driving us forward, now it was this daring and feisty teenage girl. She strode over to the cupboard, removed the mitre, lifted up the keys from the hook and replaced the mitre before closing the cupboard door. I looked on at this young woman, not only in love, but in awe.

"OK Michael, let's do this."

I watched the priest enter the confessional, placing himself in the left-hand compartment facing away from the altar.

"Mai, the priest is taking a confession from your mother. Let's move quickly."

"My MOTHER!"

"Yes Mai. She is helping us; she is in no danger—let's use this opportunity wisely."

Mai tiptoed towards the tabernacle, holding onto the keys. At least she had escaped from the sacristy. As quietly as she could, she inserted the first key into the lock and tried to turn, but the key was not the right one. With a slight jangling of metals together as she removed the key, she tried the second one; again, the key did not fit. The third key turned easily in the lock and the lock mechanism turned with a dull thud. The priest pricked up his ears and started to turn around, Mai ducked behind the altar but Mai's mother continued:

"There's another sin, Father, the sin of theft."

The priest turned back towards the woman in the confessional.

"Theft?"

"Yes, theft, Father."

"From whom have you stolen?"

"From the Holy Church, Father."

"That is indeed serious… When God gave Moses the Ten Commandments, his eighth is written… *Thou shalt not steal…*"

"Yes, that is why I cannot continue without baring myself and my sins before my Lord."

"How could you possibly steal from the Holy Church?"

"It was desperate times, Father. The money was much needed…"

Mai's mother had totally absorbed the priest in her 'confessions' and this allowed Mai valuable time in opening the tabernacle door. She carefully removed the golden cross, paten and chalice and laid them on the ground behind the altar. Now she had to unlock the second door behind where they had been. This time the first key that she tried worked and the lock turned. With care, Mai pulled onto the key and the door opened, revealing the solid chest behind. She then tried to reach inside to retrieve the small chest containing the blood money of all those unfortunate enough to believe in the compassion and justness of the church. Though Mai had removed the hefty cross, she was just too small to remove the heavy chest behind.

"Michael, I…I cannot reach the chest, it is too far inside the tabernacle."

I looked around for a chair.

"Mai, use the hassock on the Bishop's chair…it is thick and should give you enough height."

Mai tiptoed to the large, opulent chair, magnificently carved from exotic wood and removed the hassock. Tiptoeing back, she placed it softly on the floor and stood up.

"Michael, I can reach it!"

With that, Mai pulled the chest slowly towards her, but the weight was too much and the chest scraped as she tried to drag it to the front.

"Michael, the noise will alert the priest; I cannot lift it!"

"Mai, use your shawl; lift up the chest and place your shawl underneath the base."

"I cannot lift up the whole of the chest, only the front."

"Even that will reduce some of the noise, Mai."

Mai raised the chest and placed a portion of her shawl underneath the front. Pulling at the shawl, the chest edged slowly forward but the grating was still audible, though far less than before. I turned and the priest seemed to be slightly aware of the noises that we were making by the altar. He seemed to have run out of patience also with Mai's mother.

"Repay to the church that which you have stolen and flagellate yourself before God twenty times for five days."

"But Father, I have also committed carnal sin."

The priest's ears picked up; this seemed to whet his appetite.

"What carnal sin?"

"I have looked upon another man with lust, Father."

Mai at last was able to lift the whole of the chest and remove it from the tabernacle.

"Place it under the altar, Mai; close and lock the door."

With dexterity, she quietly placed the heavy chest on the floor, locked the inner door, returned the cross, paten and chalice, closed the second door and returned the hassock to the chair. She needed no instructions from me now; she knew that she had to revert to the sacristy and return the keys. Placing the keys and mitre back on the hook, then closing the cupboard, she nimbly left the room and gently closed the door behind her. She looked at me and I could see that she was starting to panic. The shock-state that she had exposed herself to was beginning to tell. It was at this moment of realisation when we had almost completed our task that the real anxiety set in.

"Mai, quietly go to the pews and hide."

As Mai arrived by the pews, the priest stood up, giving Mai's mother further instructions that she had no intention of obeying and opened the confessional door. As though she had rehearsed this a thousand times before, Mai knelt down before the altar and recited the Ave Maria. Hurriedly, the priest passed her by and went straight into the sacristy. With the door now closed behind him, Mai leapt up and ran to the altar and picked up the heavy chest. Her mother helped her drag the chest from under the altar and they descended the stairs towards the nave. The latch of the sacristy echoed and both Mai and her mother spontaneously knelt down paying homage before the altar, with the chest between them. The priest turned, locked the door and adorned with his mitre and liturgical vestments, made his way towards them.

"Mai, the chest!"

Mai removed her shawl immediately and threw it over the chest, bowing low and keeping her body close to the ground, as did her mother. Bowing before the altar and making the sign of the cross, the priest ignored the two women prostrate before him and strode up to the Chancel. He walked up to the tabernacle and gazed at it, as though undecided what he should do, before turning back and making his way down the nave. The door at the far end closed and Mai and her mother arose, clutching the heavy chest between them.

Trembling from both fear and physical exhaustion, my teenage heroine let her mother put her arm around her and lead her out of the cathedral by the same door the priest had just used. Outside, the air felt good.

Chapter 26

The Greyhound pulled out of Watertown. They had been travelling now for over eight hours and Karl desperately wanted to stretch his legs. Just to walk, walk anywhere, anywhere that would lead to freedom. Tracking the route on his laptop, he knew that this was the last stop before reaching the Canadian border. He had about forty minutes to collect his thoughts and restore his self-control to normal. He had trained himself years ago, when practicing yoga, to allow his mind to relax. Then, it hadn't been too difficult; then, he wasn't a fugitive on the run having committed murder and attempted to annul his country's effort to change the course of mankind's history and future. He breathed as calmly as he could. He needed to prepare himself for the inevitable clash at the Canadian border. The placard displaying 'Route 81' passed by quickly as the bus picked up speed. Unlike the earlier confrontation with the New York City police, this time he knew what he had to face and felt more in control. He practiced again his preamble for that moment of deliberation with the border officials that would free him…or condemn him. Before he realised, the bus had started to slow down. To his left ran the St Lawrence River. That magnificent waterway that, even before man had set foot on Earth, had been flowing without interruption towards its final destination—the Atlantic Ocean. On the other side of this waterway lay Canada—freedom. Karl just caught a glimpse of the enormous bridge spanning his route to the border before the bus turned and kept his sight from the view. His heart started to quicken its pace, but Karl forced his mind into that state of calmness he had practiced following the teachings of Tirumalai Krishnamacharya and rehearsed again his planned dialogue with Border Control. The bus stopped and the engine became silent.

"Will everyone please leave the bus and follow the line to Border Control? Have passports and tickets ready. Leave all belongings on the bus. We will be leaving in twenty minutes."

All the passengers slowly filed off the bus and made their way to the Border Patrol guards sitting in a comfortable glass-fronted office, parallel to the bridge crossing the St Lawrence. Karl Guttenberg did not wish to be either the first or the last person checked. Without wishing to raise suspicion, he quickened his pace to overtake the last couple that had descended from the Greyhound and fell into line with the others. He looked up and saw to his left, a mere fifty yards away: 'Welcome to Canada'.

Calm, Karl, keep calm.

The USA border guards did not seem to be too interested and waved the people through to the adjacent Canadian Border Control. The queue shuffled quite quickly and Karl stood before the Canadian Border Control officer clearly wearing the Canadian emblem on his arm.

"Passport, please."

Immediately, Karl handed him his passport, together with his return ticket booked for a week later. The guard handed Karl back his ticket but kept his passport.

"What is the purpose of your visit to Canada, Mr... Guttenberg?"

"Family crisis."

"Family crisis?"

"Yes. Mother's dying and my sister has called me to visit her before the end."

"I'm sorry to hear of that, Mr... Guttenberg. Where will you be staying—with your sister?"

"No; she has only a small apartment and two children. I'll be staying nearby at the *SMR Residence Hotel.*"

"The address please."

"300, Lisgar Street, Ottawa."

The guard typed into his keyboard the information just given and hesitated while he examined the monitor before him. With a smile, he handed Karl back his passport.

"Yes, that's fine. Have a good stay in Canada and I'm sorry to hear about your mother."

Karl turned and almost staggered back to the bus. The relief overwhelmed him; he felt both delirious and weak. He could barely walk in a straight line, the tension of the past few days, and especially the last twelve hours, had proven almost too much. He needed to return to the bus but his legs were trembling so much, he stumbled.

"Are you OK, Mr Guttenberg?"

It was the Border guard who had just allowed him the sanctuary he had craved. He had left his seat in his comfortable glass-fronted office and was making his way towards Karl.

"Parkinson's—my mother has it too. I'll be fine; just need time, thank you."

The reply seemed to satisfy the guard who returned to his office. Karl made it to the Greyhound and started to climb the three steps up into the bus. He saw a USA patrol car arrive and drive up to the Border Control office. A heavily armed police officer got out and went inside. As he made his way down the aisle, the unmistakeable sound of a helicopter's rotors could be heard circling overhead. A second patrol car arrived and both officers got out and went inside the Border Control office. Karl trundled his way to his seat at the back of the bus and sat down. One of the patrol officers came out of the office and slowly and deliberately walked around the Greyhound, staring inside the windows of the bus. As he approached the back, Karl busied himself with a pretend examination of the contents of his rucksack so as not to make his face visible to the patrolman watching the faces of the people inside. After an unendurable seven minutes, the driver climbed the steps of his bus and started the engine. The comforting sound of that diesel engine once more gave hope to Karl, sitting fretfully in the back. No longer could he hear the drone of the helicopter's blades rotating above. The door hissed and the unmistakeable sound of gears engaging at last gave Karl Guttenberg that moment of euphoria he had been waiting for so long. The Greyhound edged away from its resting place and started to cross the bridge to liberty, to asylum. Again, Karl saw 'Welcome to Canada'; only this time he didn't just see it, he passed it and was now no longer an outlaw, a renegade—he was free!

Chapter 27

"Sixteen forty-five, Jamie."

Jamie viewed his flight path on the screen and, with a slight movement of his left hand, depressed the plasma burners' control. Petra left her seat and floated over the steps leading down to the main part of the control room, where Simon and Charlie were sat. With a mixture of giggling and eye exchange, I surmised that Petra and Charlie were more than just colleagues but, on the other hand, I had never been very good at judging relationships.

"Jamie, OK if I go for another 'float'? My arm is getting stiff from that dislocation and I would like to exercise it a bit."

"Go for it, Michael. We will be heading directly towards Neptune in…how long, Petra?"

"Thirty-seven minutes."

"Please be back by then; just in case, you know…"

"Will do…sixteen forty-nine, so that makes it…seventeen twenty-six."

I pulled myself up out of my seat with my good arm and floated back towards the door leading out into the corridor beyond. As I left the room, I heard Jamie's voice and pulled myself back in.

"Michael, here, you'll need this…"

And like a Frisbee, he flicked over the radio-controlled map of the ship. I smiled, grabbed the projected controller and pulled myself again through the door and floated down the corridor. As I got to the end, I heard Jamie call out again and launched myself back. As I entered, he looked at me and smiled that infectious, beaming smile.

"Bye, Michael."

With that, he let out a raucous laugh and turned his head back to the screen, waving his hand as he did so. *When we get to Mr Jack*, I thought, *it's going to be a blast*! With the deftness that I had learned from my first use of the handholds earlier in the flight, I was able to pull myself along with great speed, first the left hand, then cautiously with the right, making sure that I did not overdo the force, as I had done before. The sensation of whizzing along the corridors was very therapeutic and though I had no means of knowing my speed, I estimated that I was doing somewhere in the region of twelve miles per hour. Arriving at a crossroads, I saw the sign 'Pod area' and decided to investigate. Opening the door, the sight before me made me gasp. There, leading into the distance, lay row upon row of glass-topped pods. But on top of each pod, separated by a small ladder, lay another row of pods extending as far as the eye could see. It was as though I had just walked into the MRI examination room in a hospital. Everywhere was gleaming white and inside each pod was a living, sleeping person. The sensation was disturbing; it was as if I had entered a funeral parlour and before me was an endless line of corpses awaiting the crematorium. As much as I wanted to leave, I pulled lightly on the pod to my right and gazed inside. Slightly bearded, a youthful-looking man somewhere in his twenties, lay breathing shallowly, with eyes firmly closed. I thought that I could make out a very light mist inside and assumed this was the gaseous environment keeping everybody oblivious to the potential dangers that the six of us had recently faced...and maybe were going to face again. His name tag read: 'Mark Stevenson'. I pulled myself to the next pod, where I saw a ginger-haired woman, also somewhere in her twenties.

Pulling myself to the end, I looked and read her name tag: 'Kay Stevenson'. This appeared to be a husband and wife couple, though brother and sister was also a possibility. The deciding factor though was the next pod: 'Gail Stevenson'. Gail couldn't have been more than eight years old. So, this was a family dormitory, though the word *vault* went through my mind.

I hauled myself along this dazzling line of 'tombs' and left by a door at the far end. I turned around and estimated the length of this room to be over one hundred metres! But then, we were going to colonise another planet and the sheer enormity of everything I had so far witnessed made sense. Relieved to be out, I left the door behind me and was faced with another crossroads. Directly in front was written 'Gymnasium'. As a reasonably fit and sporty person, this I wanted to see and pulled open the door opposite. Neatly laid-out was a vast array of exercise machines of every imaginable variety: exercise bikes, weight machines, jogging tracks, mountain climbers; this was truly impressive. Next to the gymnasium was another door. I opened up the door and there before me were two full-sized tennis courts!

I closed the door and floated along the corridor until I came to another crossroads. A sign on the wall said, 'crop plantation'. Pulling myself along, I arrived at a small door and went in. I was dumbstruck! It was like being inside a giant greenhouse. The air inside was humid, almost like a tropical rainforest and the lighting was bright, causing me to squint. After a few seconds, my eyes adjusted to the light and I saw before me row upon row of lush vegetation. In varying shades of green, the rows extended into the distance as far as I could see. I noticed to my right rows of tomatoes and beside these, long lines of strawberries. To my left were ranks of aubergines and the unmistakeable foliage of carrots. In the distance, I saw another door and eagerly pulled myself along the grappling holds until I arrived at the entrance, which read 'cereal farm'. Opening up the door, I was immediately aware of the change in temperature and environment as I gazed in awe at the fields of barley, corn, malt and wheat. This really was an exodus! Irrespective of what we found on *Proxima b*, we were going to survive! The overwhelming urge took hold of me and with a gentle leap, I rose and drifted over those fields of cereals, allowing my hands to brush the sheaves of corn, wheat and barley as I floated on. Closing my eyes, I felt like I was back home on Earth in the beautiful dawn of a cloudless sky. I could sense the pinks and blues of the horizon as Earth turned and the sun came into view and its rays cast their long shadows on the endless meadows at the start of a summer's day. Nostalgia took hold and I found myself weeping, realising those times were never going to come again.

I looked at the time on the radio-controller: 17:19! Damn! I had forgotten about the time and needed to get back to the main control room. I dialled the location on the radio-controlled map and followed the directions. It took me nearly eight minutes to return and Jamie was preparing himself for the Neptune confrontation. Petra was back in her seat and the others seemed tense, though they continued working as normally as they could.

"Jamie, that was amazing! Those fields of cereals and the rich vegetation!"

"Yeah, pretty cool that. I just love that area. Whilst in Earth orbit a while back, when I could, I would just linger in the crop plantation section—it gave that feeling of still being back home. But NASA didn't just bring crops and vegetation on board for planting, they are balancing our ecosystem on board. The number of personnel has been exactly matched to the plant life that we have. We supply them with our waste products, on which they thrive and they supply us with their waste products—oxygen, on which we survive! Anyway, now we have to concentrate on the task at hand, I have set our trajectory towards the South Pole and we will feel the gravitational influence of Neptune in…"

"Two minutes and forty seconds, Jamie."

"Thanks, Petra. OK, two minutes and thirty-five…four…three…seconds."

"Have you set your line of approach to seventy-five degrees south of the equator?"

"Yes."

"Distance from that blue boy?"

"Two hundred and twenty thousand kilometres above cloud level."

"So, with a planet radius of about twenty-five thousand kilometres, that gives us a real radius of…two hundred and forty-five thousand kilometres and therefore, a circumference distance of…three hundred and eighty-five thousand kilometres around Neptune. What speed, Petra?"

"We are currently approaching at warp-drive factor zero-point-eight-five. If there are no mishaps, then we should leave at warp-drive factor zero-point-nine-three."

"Jamie, are the plasma burners separated from computer control?"

"Simon?"

"All yours, Jamie."

"Petra, what is the Neptune contact time?"

"One point four-five seconds."

"Look at that!"

We all gawped through the canopy in front as Neptune started to come into view. Small, perfectly blue, and from this distance a bit like Earth, but without the white wispiness of the clouds. Within seconds, she had doubled in size and the methane atmosphere became more obvious. We had faced Mars, Jupiter and

Saturn and by and large escaped unscathed. Now we had to face our third gas giant, though I felt much more confident with Neptune than the other two. Neptune's bizarre magnetic field bothered me slightly. Just like Uranus, Neptune did not have a fixed, regular magnetic field, though this one wasn't as whacky as the one that we were going to face in our final solar system battle.

"One minute and thirty-two seconds, Jamie."

"Michael?"

"As soon as Petra records our distance to be two and a half million kilometres, shut down all electronic gear; we will have just under nine seconds to contend with our next opponent and will be only on visual and manual again. From shutdown, Jamie, you will need to have Petra count you down to plasma burn—Petra, don't forget it will be a total of—"

"—Five point seven-five seconds."

"Hey, Jamie, she's good, isn't she…no wonder you employed her."

"Hey, Mr Astro, any more sexist talk from you and you can count yourself!"

"…Count yourself lucky to still be alive, Michael!"

Despite the solemnity of our immediate threat, the repartee was flowing again. Anna performed one final check on the computers and verified that everything was running well and turned to Jamie.

"When you're ready Jamie, I'll need three seconds notice for shutdown…no, make that five just to be safe; but you will be on manual and blind for fifteen minutes after rebooting the computers."

"Jamie, I'm on countdown; ready?"

"Let's go, Petra!"

"Petra, give me my marker too."

"Will do; Anna, you'll be the first."

"OK, thirty seconds…"

The tension took over again and we all became quiet. As though we were in a dream being jettisoned through a theme park ride, Neptune grew large and blue before our eyes. She was a truly glorious sight. Even Jamie was mesmerised. It was only Petra who failed to look ahead—she knew that all timings were based on her and she accepted her responsibility with total commitment. Momentarily, that blue king of sea and space beckoned to us, rising up like a monster from the depths of that inky blackness ahead, being watched by the multitude of sparkling eyes and misty tendrils of the infinity beyond.

"Jamie!"

"Oh! Sorry; I was totally transfixed!"

"Yes, I could see… Anna, three…two…one…now!"

With a nimble flick, Anna turned off both the main and then the backup computers. We now knew that we had nine seconds before we would be subjected to the influence of Neptune's gravitational pull. Nine seconds to discover whether Petra had calculated our speed, distance and angle of approach correctly. Nine seconds to discern if Jamie had lined up his flight path accurately, and more importantly, if Jamie had the ability and skill to direct and control both the trajectory of Proxima and the power of the plasma burners to project us towards our next, and final, goal—Uranus. Even at two million kilometres, Neptune covered the entire canopy in front. Charlie, Simon, Anna and I sat totally entranced with the oncoming view before us. Would the mythical king of the sea swallow us, like mariners of old, or would he let us pass safely by? It was only Petra and Jamie who were in total control now. Proxima's future depended upon these two professionals. Both were wide-eyed with concentration. Petra's calm and cool voice was the only audible sound.

"Five…four…three…two…one…mark."

"BANDIT!"

"NO! Triton!"

Coming around the surface of Neptune was the unmistakeable sight of a large rock of dazzling white. For the moment, it appeared directly in front of us approaching at enormous speed but within a fraction of a second, it had moved to two o'clock and then at right angles to us, before slipping out of view behind the canopy.

"Two…one…now!"

Jamie pushed hard on the plasma burners. Neptune was to our left and the haze below suggested to me that perhaps some form of electrical storm was taking place as the magnetic fields twisted and turned. Another burst from the burners sent Neptune behind us and out of view. Before us was, again, the star-speckled void.

"What was that?"

"That was, I believe, Triton."

"Triton?"

"Yes—the largest of Neptune's moons."

"Michael, you didn't think to tell us?"

"Look, folks. With your planned flight path and distance, I knew that we would be safe from Triton. So, I didn't mention it because I didn't want to put you all under more stress; especially as she has a retrograde orbit. Hence, we would be approaching head-on as we did. Triton was nearly another one hundred thousand kilometres from us—quite safe."

"All the same, I would have preferred to have been forewarned."

"Sorry, Anna, I am duly chastised."

"Duly chastised…duly chastised…surely only a Brit…"

And the laughter flowed again.

"Jamie, turning on computers…fifteen minutes to data supply."

With the ordeal of Neptune behind us, the control room became alive again. Without navigation aids, Jamie had to rely on sixth sense and trust in the pre-programmed data being correct. Though there was little that he could do, he remained in front of the controls, eyes glued ahead. Charlie and Simon floated up to the front and took a few minutes staring into the abyss ahead.

Petra left her seat and floated over to where I was drawing a sketch of our final encounter.

"Uranus?"

"Yes, just trying to get a feel for this baby; checking for moons, rings and our angle of approach. Did you know that the moons of Uranus are named after characters in Shakespeare plays? Miranda, Ariel, Umbriel, Titania, Oberon…"

"Makes a change from Greek and Roman mythology. What about its magnetic field?"

"I'm afraid no one has any idea about that, it's too whacky. The thing that worries me the most…"

"The magnetic field?"

"No…the unknown."

"Hmm?"

"Do you remember those pretty plasma lights—the ones where, as you placed your hand, plasma emissions would emanate around the globe?"

"Yeah, I remember those; we actually had one—pink."

"Well, the magnetic fields around Uranus are a bit like that. Not pretty and pink but sporadic and dangerous…well, dangerous to any projectile venturing within its influence, that is."

Petra continued to watch as the sketch started to include some data and numbers.

"What's your speciality, Petra?"

"Electronics and guidance systems."

"Masters?"

"Doctorate."

"A real whiz kid then!"

"No, not really. I found studying really hard…I don't just mean the long hours and self-sacrifice, but the understanding. Don't get me wrong, I really love what I do, and as a student I found it all fascinating, but the intricate, theoretical stuff…just so hard."

"Well, they don't give doctorates away for the sake of it. I think that you are belittling yourself—lack of self-confidence. I have observed you here and if nothing else, I can't think of anyone I would rather risk my life with than you."

"Michael, I am so flattered! Is this another 'chat-up' line, because if so, it's a bloody good one!"

"Oh, no, no! Sorry, I didn't mean it like that. What I meant was that I have watched you and your care, precision and calmness under such extreme conditions of stress is truly amazing. For me, with the risks involved here, I feel so confident in your professionalism that I trust you implicitly."

Petra kissed me on the cheek and I felt myself blush. She smiled and I looked into her eyes.

"And you have a pretty smile; that also helps!"

"Hey, Simon, Charlie! Mikey here's on a pull!"

Despite my slight embarrassment, the *craic* was in full swing and I loved it. If we took nothing else with us, the human ability to laugh—the emotion of humour and fun—must be one of the paramount virtues that mankind should, in my opinion, encourage in every civilisation that we should ever meet. It is priceless.

"Petra, how does this sleep process work? I mean, Jamie gives you a command to set yourself a specific time and, *boom*, you're out cold and wake up at exactly the correct time."

"The helmet that each of has contains several gas inlets—one for oxygen, one for air and one for knock-out gas."

"Nitrous oxide?"

"No, I don't think so, that's a bit archaic now. I'm not sure what the gas is, but as you have discovered, it leaves no headaches, nausea or tiredness afterwards. The headset contains some sensors detecting brain activity and distributes the correct amount of gas based on this. Active brain: gas, inactive brain: no gas, time out: oxygen. Simple."

"Jamie, lads, Petra…computers are coming online now."

Once again, the satisfying beeping echoed around the room giving us that feeling of comfort that something was guiding and steering us towards our goal. Petra returned to her seat and strapped herself in.

"Petra?"

"Hang on, Jamie…sorry, too early; give me another minute."

"Anna?"

"Everything seems to be coming back online without any mishaps. The idea of preventing damage through isolation seems to have worked. It's just whether our data before was accurate but currently all, so far, seems to be OK."

"Jamie, data's coming through now…speed, warp-factor drive zero-point-nine-two…"

"Damn…a bit short. Uranus?"

"On track…approaching towards the solar side of North Pole…or whatever Pole it happens to be at the time."

"Hmm…so we are going sunny-side up then! Distance and ETA?"

"Three billion two hundred thousand kilometres, with an ETA of three hours and three minutes."

"Simon, what's the situation with plasma supply, battery backups and reactor?"

"Batteries are fully charged and will supply on full-drain for twenty-five hours. Reactor functioning one hundred per cent with about twenty-three years' life remaining. Plasma down to ninety-one per cent but adequate for voyage completion."

"So, everything is on track except that we are slightly down on speed. Anna, will you compute time difference for warp-drive factor zero-point-zero-one, please?"

"Just under four months."

"Well, we have reserves and a reasonable food supply system, but it is not a delay I would really wish for. We need to get to *Proxima b* and use the resources there. It sets us a bit of a time limit on descent, cultivation and harvest, and that's if the conditions there meet the pre-assessments of our geologists and space biologists back home."

"Is it that critical, Jamie?"

"Well, I don't want to go scare-mongering, but the sooner we get there and settle down, the better. Why, any ideas, Michael?"

"There is one possibility but you need to be sure that those four months are vital; the risk is considerable."

"What do you suggest then?"

"Jamie, I am not going to suggest anything…it has to be up to you and the others to decide, but I will present one option that should give you the speed that you are after."

Despite the bleeping and everyone's individual workload, all heads looked in my direction; it was as if they had all downed tools and gone on strike.

"Jamie, we were fortunate with Neptune—nothing went wrong. But Saturn! That should have made us wary of playing dice with God. Let's look at what we have. Fact: we are all alive and well. Fact: unless anything unforeseen occurs, you…we will make *Proxima b*. Fact: personnel are virtually self-sufficient for several years aboard Proxima. Fact: risk-taking when the chances of success are good is foolhardy…what's the saying? 'If it ain't broke, don't fix it'!"

"Michael, we are all aware and from the moment of our training, *were* aware, of the high-risk factor of this venture not succeeding. This whole project has been based on taking risks. We are the pioneers and all decisions made have been, and *will* be, based upon the events and situations at the time. We are the ones writing the storybooks for those that venture after us; they need to be as fully informed as possible so that their chances of success will be more favourable than our own. So what's the plan?"

"We had originally planned to orbit around Uranus just inside its tenuous ring system; this should have slung us out to reach the speed of warp-drive factor one. If you feel that this is a fundamental requirement for getting to *Proxima b*, then I think that this can be achieved; but we will need to soar just above atmosphere level."

"What! If I'm not mistaken, you just mentioned 'foolhardy'. Now, forgive me if I'm wrong, but isn't what you're suggesting not only 'foolhardy', but suicidal?"

"Jamie, listen to Michael; so far he has got us out of all the mess that we've been in and I don't think he's likely to suggest something if it doesn't have some degree of credence."

"Yes, you're right; sorry, Michael. But you just hit me with such a weird suggestion, I thought that perhaps you may have lost your sanity for a second. Carry on…"

"No worries, Jamie. You had every reason to react the way you did. When I first considered the possibility of not reaching zero-nine-three, just after we passed Neptune, I doodled a bit before being molested by Petra—"

"—Molested! I'll show you molested!"

Petra smiled over to me and I felt a little twinge of shyness and warmth.

"Well, I could do with Anna to pull up the data on Uranus for confirmation but using my existing knowledge about her, her rings and her moons, I felt mildly confident that we could fly just above her clouds and atmosphere; let's say, two hundred kilometres above. We must be free of the friction of her atmosphere at all costs! But and here's where we will gain, the gravitational pull, together with the longer descent, will give you the additional zero-point-zero-one that you are after."

"But the gravity…it will crush us, surely!"

"No. Uranus has a weaker gravity than Earth—about ten to eleven per cent less pull. So, keep above the clouds and skim over the North Pole…*sunny side up*, as you said."

"But what about its magnetic field?"

"We will have to fly through her field, irrespective of whether we are at two hundred thousand kilometres or two hundred kilometres. But because it is so bizarre—currently the Pole is about fifty-nine degrees from her spin location—we will not know whether we will be totally bamboozled by her magnetic field or we will pass harmlessly through and on to *Proxima b*."

"Radiation?"

"Unknown, I'm afraid. Initial indications are that it does not have a strong field of radiation; we will be the first to find out!"

"So, how do you propose that we approach Uranus?"

"From the South Pole, which happens to be where we are headed now. If you approach at a shallow angle of twelve degrees to the equator, we will reach two hundred kilometres above cloud level at forty-five degrees from the North Pole. With maximum power on your burners and at that angle of approach, we will be whisked around and off to *Proxima Centauri*. Again, Jamie, you will need to fly blind—just as with Neptune. You will be on visual only and have about three and a half seconds to line up your flight path. The contact time with Uranus will be just over six-tenths of a second. After that, it's Mr Jack, I believe!"

"Moons? Rings?"

"All the Shakespearean actors in this play will be avoided—"

"—Shakespearean actors?"

"Oh, ask Petra. Because we will be approaching via a Pole region and at the distance that we will be above the surface of Uranus, there will be no lunar or ring encounters."

"Promise?"

"Promise."

"No surprises?"

"No surprises."

"OK, folks. As Michael said, it's our call… Petra?"

"I say, Go."

"Simon?"

"Go."

"Charlie?"

"I'll go with the majority vote."

"Anna?"

"Go."

"So, three in favour and one abstention means that Charlie's on board as well!"

"What about you, Jamie? Not that it makes any difference now."

"Will you be taking ice with Mr Jack, Michael?"

"Nah…that's only for girls and sissies…"

"Hey, watch it, you—"

The banter was back again!

Chapter 28

The knock at the door was answered by the large Negroid servant.

"Monsieur Nostredame?"

"Yes. Is your master, Jean LeMartre, in?"

"Indeed, he is, sir; would you care to come in?"

"Yes, thank you."

Michel entered into the same house he had a few days before. It was still daylight and the feeling of dread that he experienced before had abated somewhat. He disliked this place and a sense of repugnance came over him. He was led into the same waiting room as before but this time, the room was furnished in a more conventional fashion, without the glass-framed tank that had held such a hideous spectacle before. The servant took his cloak and hat, but Michel kept the package he had been holding at his side.

"Would you care to sit down, sir? I shall inform my master of your arrival."

With that, Nostradamus made himself as comfortable as his feelings would allow. He sniffed the air and noticed a somewhat sickly scent in the room—like one that was associated with the plague victims after fumigating the rooms where they had died. He arose and walked over to the large French windows at the back of the room. Looking outside, he noticed that there was no greenery; the earth looked scorched and dry and the trees were mere skeletons. No flowers bloomed—everything was black and sombre. At the far end in a corner, Michel saw the unmistakeable signs of several graves but without any crosses.

"Monsieur Nostredame! A pleasure, sir."

Michel turned around.

"Indeed, the pleasure is all mine, I assure you."

Jean LeMartre had entered the room without making a sound and walked over to the window where Michel had been gazing out.

"Nothing grows, I can't understand it—just dull and lifeless. To what do I owe the honour?"

"An agreement, I believe?"

"An agreement? Ah yes! You are here to settle your account?"

"No, not settle…more like open, wouldn't you say?"

"Yes, yes, of course…open your account."

"I have here the princely sum of seven thousand and five hundred francs—this being the agreed half-payment. I would, therefore, like to arrange a date that is suitable and convenient to complete our transaction."

"Indeed, indeed. Jaafar!"

As though he had been standing just outside, Jean LeMartre's servant walked into the room immediately. As his master had done a few moments before, Jaafar walked noiselessly across the room, making no sound on the floorboards as he moved.

"Sir?"

"Quill, ink and paper, please—and take them to my study, together with a 1546 burgundy."

"No, no…not for me, thank you."

"Too early? Make that a decanter of port and two glasses."

With the servant gone, Jean LeMartre bowed and, indicating with his right hand outstretched, led the way through the room and out into the corridor. A musty smell filled the air and Michel sensed the atmosphere to be one of decay and mould. After a few twists and turns, Jean LeMartre stood by an open doorway and with his left hand outstretched, indicated to Nostradamus to enter. As they walked in, Michel noticed on the walls a series of head mounts: a stag, wild boar, tiger and bear. Some framed paintings suggested a weird sense in the taste of art: a coven, a tiger with vampire teeth peering through the forest, a bat resting on top of a grave with blood running down from a mouse it had caught and an angel with black eyes. On his desk, however, was the disfigured and shrunken face of a black native. Michel shuddered; this, irrefutably, was an evil man.

"Monsieur Nostredame or may I say, Nostradamus?"

"Either, it matters not."

"Monsieur, the act for which you wish that I partake, whose name shall I evoke?"

"Michael."

"Michael? He is not French then?"

"No, English."

"Ah, so you lent money to an Englishman?"

"Yes, he was an acquaintance of mine. He came to France as a youth."

"And this 'acquaintance', he did not repay the money owed to you?"

"No…he had paid back some and was in the process of completing the loan, when he was struck down with the black death."

"You could not save him then?"

"No, he was too far gone when I became aware of his malady."

"And you know that he had the means to repay you in full?"

"Oh, yes; he had done well for himself and remained most grateful. I am sure he would wish, even now, to leave this Earth unindebted."

"Though perhaps his family would wish otherwise; hmm?"

"His wife has adequate means to care for her family and she, too, knew of his gratitude to me and his wish to repay."

"So why not ask her for the loan to be repaid?"

"She took on a second husband after his death; the scoundrel won't hear of her settling the account; just a money-grabbing, rich-widow hunter."

"Perhaps we should settle *his* account, then, hmm?"

"No…no need for that. I'm not after revenge, only what is owed to me."

The conversation seemed to satisfy Jean LeMartre as the servant came into the room with quill, paper, ink, a decanter and two port glasses. After he had left, Jean LeMartre poured out two generous servings of port, rested the paper on the desk before him and began to fill in the parchment. Perhaps it was his imagination, but Michel was sure that as he wrote, wisps of smoke billowed from the paper. A gush of air swirled around the room as the unmistakeable sounds of cries of anguish seemed to permeate the breeze. Upon completion, the necromancer opened up the drawer just below the desk and withdrew a knife. Trying to hide his fear, Nostradamus let out a faint gasp inaudible to the man beside him. Jean LeMartre looked Michel directly in the eyes and with a hint of malice, pushed the document before him.

"It is to be signed…with blood, Nostradamus."

"Blood!"

"Yes, blood. This is an undertaking between two worlds and the bond is to be made in blood."

"My blood?"

"Our blood."

"Our blood?"

"Yes, and from that moment, there can be no reversal. Any broken promises, or falsehoods, will be paid for in blood. This is my guarantee of safety from the world of the undead; for your life will be substituted for mine if your 'acquaintance' proves false."

Hesitatingly, Michel drew the knife from the table and with trembling fingers, held it in his hand.

"Before I complete the bond, may I read what is written?"

"Certainly…here."

I, Michel Nostredame, call upon the spirit of 'Michael' to come before me. I know of no evil purpose for the intent of calling him other than the repayment of that which is owed to me. His spirit will enter the body of Jean LeMartre, who demands, in blood, retribution should any mischief befall him whilst in the world of the undead. I, Michel Nostredame, willingly bequeath my body and soul to Jean LeMartre should any falsehoods harm him during his transition into the unseen world of spirits. To this, I pledge my honour and shall pay the sum of seven thousand five hundred francs.

I sign this testament with my blood.

Michel did not like what was before him, but he knew that he had no choice. He also implicitly trusted his friend, Michael, from the world of spirits and felt sure that his own spirit guides would protect him.

"Give me the quill, then."

No need…just sign with your blood."

Trembling, Michel sliced across his thumb and placed his bleeding digit onto the parchment. Jean LeMartre took the knife from Nostradamus and did the same. As he pushed his thumb onto the paper, a sizzling, as of pork roasting on a spit, erupted from the document. Michel looked down at the paper they had just both signed…it was blank!

"Written for eternity, Nostradamus, eternity!"

With that, the necromancer threw the parchment into the fire and watched the flames lick around the paper as it shrivelled, turned brown, then finally leapt into flames.

"Eternity."

"When can I ask for your services, Monsieur LeMartre?"

"I only work during a full moon; that is tomorrow night, I believe?"

"Yes, tomorrow night."

"Shall we say, eleven-thirty, so we can begin at midnight…it will be a midnight mass, no?"

A midnight black mass, Michel thought.

"Until tomorrow, then."

"Jaafar!"

As before, the servant was in the room even as the words left the lips of Jean LeMartre. And as before, the man made no noise as he walked across the floor.

"Jaafar, please show our guest out and expect him tomorrow, just before the hour of midnight."

Michel gratefully left the house and evil behind him. It was turning dusk and he was glad that he didn't have to make the journey in the dark as he had done previously. He now needed to contact Michael.

Returning to his house, Michel immediately descended the stairs to his study. He stoked the fire, placed another log on the glowing embers and lit a candle. Perspiring slightly, he sat down at his table. Beside him was a chest, somewhat less heavy than it had been yesterday. He stared into his crystal and speaking in Latin, he started to invoke his spirit guides.

"Michel! Thank God. I was so worried."

"Anne! You startled me. I did not hear you descend."

"Agnès told me that you had returned. I have been beside myself with worry. Tell me, what happened."

"Anne, I may have just sold my soul to the Fiend himself! Payment in blood, it was, payment in blood."

"Michel, you are frightening me; what do you mean, 'payment in blood'?"

"That man…that odious, evil, son of Satan…we have a bond—a blood bond…for eternity."

"Are you saying that you are in league with the devil—Betelgeuse himself?"

"If any falsehoods take place within the 'mass', yes; but not in league…no, only that I may not witness to see the Kingdom of the Highest."

"But there will be no falsehoods, will there?"

"Only inasmuch that the whole 'mass' will be based on fraud! Otherwise, no."

"Michel, what exactly are you using this wrongdoer for? Why is *he* so important?"

"Perhaps I can explain that?"

"Michael!"

"Michael…it is done…"

I could tell from the tone and quaking in his voice that Michel was a worried man. I had not dared be present at his meeting with the necromancer for fear of discovery, but now I wanted to know all. I needed to know what power I was up against.

"Michael, I am so worried for Michel!"

"My dear—"

"—Michel… Anne, do not speak, allow me to explain…may I?"

"P…please, I am feeling weak and my hand trembles so…see?"

Indeed, whatever Michel had faced a short while ago, I could sense it had been something formidable—it had shaken him to the core.

"Anne, please sit with your husband so that I may clarify, as best as I can. As best as I know how so that I may clarify why Michel…and now also you…why you have been involved with something to which you are both innocent parties.

"When I arrived at this level of consciousness, I was completely confused and knew neither my location nor purpose for being here. All my recollections—memories, as you call them—all these 'things' would have clarified for me why I am here, now, before you. But I have been unable to grasp the reason for my existence here. Occasionally, certain 'recollections' return to me; something sparks them off—for example, my name. When Michel told me his name translated into English—why, suddenly it was there as light as day. I also became aware that I am from the future—"

"—Yes, Michel said that you were from a time yet to come."

"It may well be that that is the reason why I am here. But this I do believe, that if I can occupy a mortal's body, I will be able to call on the functioning of that body and use it to recall all my memories. I must have experienced a life before this one and those experiences still live within me. That is why certain criteria, certain emotions trigger those experiences as memories. But in order to complete those memories as thoroughly and as quickly as possible, I need to possess a body."

"The necromancer?"

"Yes, the necromancer."

"Michael, I have a blood contract with the man; he owns my soul!"

"Michel, he owns nothing but his own self-importance and greed. His is a bloodthirsty soul that seeks vengeance, fear, lust and all the abominations that defile man. He serves but one master—the Devil. But as I understand it, there exists a higher deity than Beelzebub and you believe in him, as do you, Anne. This greater Being, He will not permit such atrocities to better His cause—the cause of the righteous. Michel, have no fear, he is one against so many."

"Be that as it may, I saw our contract burn in the fire before my eyes, signed with my blood…his blood. That is a contract that cannot be erased by any deity."

"Then, Michel, as you have signed the contract, it must be acted upon, for if you do not, then who knows what the recompense will be? The necromancer is now expecting to hold his 'mass' and has agreed—in blood too. His is as great a risk as yours, perhaps greater. Now you must trust in your guides and in me. I do not fear him; in fact, I am impatient to challenge him on my territory—the world of spirits."

"But his is the world of the undead…the Underworld."

"If I see his spirit, then he will be in my world and I have had longer than him to get customised to this new dimension. Your contract is to settle financially with him and, I assume, to ensure that no falsehoods occur?"

"Yes."

"For the purpose of recovering what is yours?"

"Yes."

"Can you recall the wording of the contract?"

"Oh, yes, it is written in my soul and burns in my mind."

"Recite it then."

…I know of no evil purpose for the intent of calling Michael, other than the repayment of that which is owed to me. His spirit will enter the body of Jean LeMartre, who demands, in blood, retribution should any mischief befall him whilst in the world of the undead. I, Michel Nostredame, willingly bequeath my body and soul to Jean LeMartre should any falsehoods harm him during his transition into the unseen world of spirits. To this, I pledge my honour…

I sign this testament with my blood.

"Michel!"

"As I said, Anne, he is truly evil; the Fiend could have no better an apprentice."

Michel slumped on the table, quaking. Anne leaned down and embraced him as I looked on. Then I heard thoughts whisper into my mind.

"Anne, please ask your maid to fetch a quill and paper. I shall return before the hour is up."

"Why, what is it you intend to do?"

Agnès entered a few minutes later with the quill and paper and gave it to Anne, who placed it on the table by Michel's crystal.

"Michael, it is here… Michael? Michael?"

"Mai, will you accompany me straight away to the house of Nostradamus, please?"

"Michael! Why? Is it so urgent?"

"Indeed, it is."

"I must ask my mother. It is to her that we owe the success of our mission to the cathedral; without her, we would not have achieved our goal. I think that she now fully believes in you and your cause."

Mai went into the back room and I followed her. As she walked in, for the first time, her mother smiled at me. My emotions were of elation; I had won

Mai's heart, though that never had been the intent of my reason for being here, but now, I had not only erased the hostility felt by Mai's mother, I could actually feel an affection. I smiled back.

"Hello, Michael, you have another mission for Mai, I suppose?"

"Yes, but this presents no danger to her at all. We must away to the home of Michel Nostredame and will return before the bell strikes twelve—I promise."

"Very well."

"Thank you."

"I must say that I felt good to take that chest and its contents from that 'holy' man. I have seen the burnings and many of those have been people that I know and were not evil. They were just people going about their daily routines. The pandemonium created by these clerics of the church to further their cause…and their coffers is a sin against man and his God."

"Yes, I agree and I find it abhorrent, too. But for now, your daughter is no longer at risk; she has completed the task that I set her. It is to her I shall return and remain with as soon as my part has been completed. For now, I need her but a short while…"

"Godspeed—be prudent, Mai…and by midnight!"
"Yes, Mother!"
Mai and I sped through the streets that were now thoroughly black. Within twenty minutes, we were outside the home of Anne and Michel.
"Michel! Michael is here with a rather pretty young girl."
"Ah, that will be Mai."
"Mai?"
"Yes, I have already had reason to meet this charming young girl."
Michel seemed to have somewhat recovered from when I had seen him a short while earlier. Mai and I went down to the library and were followed by Nostradamus and Anne.
"Mai, please take the quill and write on the paper:

I, Michael, owe to Michel Nostredame an explanation of my purpose and for involving him in the pursuit of my existence here. I have, therefore, summoned the necromancer known as Jean LeMartre and will use his body to discover that purpose. To this end, I shall repay him in this knowledge.
I sign this testament with my blood."

"Michel, a knife, please."
This time, Michel Nostredame felt no purge of fear. Returning from the kitchen, he brandished a large kitchen knife.

"Mai, this will hurt just a little bit…would you do it willingly?"

"Oh indeed, Michael!"

Mai nicked the top of her finger and a few drops of blood oozed from the cut.

"Mai, take my hand and press it down with your cut finger onto the paper."

"Michel, do the same, please."

Michel willingly reopened the wound he had made previously and placed this, likewise, on the paper.

"Now, throw the paper into the fire!"

The four of us watched it burn as the flames licked around the paper. Michel Nostredame felt good!

"Tomorrow night awaits!"

Chapter 29

The journey into Ottawa was considerably less traumatic than the one he had experienced eight hours ago. Nevertheless, he knew that he could not drop his guard until he was safely on Chinese soil. Even his arrival in Russia, though less harrowing than Canada and indeed, USA, could still present problems, especially in a country with a one-party government. Karl Guttenberg arrived at the bus terminus and soon found a taxi that took him to his destined hotel.

"I believe that you have a room for me?"

"Mr...?"

"Guttenberg... Karl Guttenberg."

"Ah, yes. You have booked in for six nights...is that correct?"

"Yes and if it's alright with you, I would like to pay in advance—cash."

"Well, that's not normally our procedure but if that is your wish, then certainly."

"US dollars OK?"

"No problem. Please just sign here and I will get the porter to show you to your room."

Once inside, without unpacking, Karl attached the 'Please do not disturb' sign outside his room, fell onto the bed and lost consciousness. It had been a very demanding thirty-six hours.

Karl awoke sometime in the afternoon of the next day. Unshaven, unwashed and hungry, he needed to recover. His clothes were no longer wearable in their present state and underneath his shirt and trousers, his underwear smelled of stale body odour. He stood under the shower and savoured the fresh odour of sandalwood and vanilla. Despite the extravagance, Karl remained under the running water for over twenty minutes, relishing in his newfound freedom and the freshness of the oils that his body had now absorbed. After shaving and dressing in some fresh clothes—jeans seemed appropriate, as did a T-shirt and loose-fitting jumper—he made his way to reception and requested that his dirty laundry be cleaned. After eating heartily and consuming more red wine than was sensible, he made his way back to his room and with his laptop, searched for flights to Vladivostok. Though he knew that he could get a quicker flight with 'Air Canada', he felt it more prudent to use the Russian 'Aeroflot' carrier. He could lie low for a day and fully charge all his batteries for the remaining part of his journey. He also knew that there would be an extradition arrangement between Canada and USA and unlike other countries throughout the globe, his presence in Canada wasn't as guaranteed as it would have been in, say, Mexico or Asia. Searching for small B&Bs in the city, he easily found a small family-run two-bedroom house near the railway station that would take him quickly and surreptitiously to the Macdonald-Cartier airport.

Collecting his laundry the next morning, Karl went up to his room and neatly packed his suitcase and rucksack. Descending the stairwell, he arrived at the ground floor and keeping close to the wall, walked slowly towards the reception desk. Leaving his suitcase by the desk, hidden from the staff, he asked for a taxi to be called to take him to the World Exchange Plaza. Within minutes, the taxi arrived and Karl got into the back, heaving his rucksack onto the seat beside him.

"World Exchange Plaza?"

"Please… Oh, I've left my suitcase by reception—would you be so good as to collect it for me, please?"

"Certainly, sir."

With that, the driver walked into reception, picked up the suitcase and walked out. No one even noticed. Upon arrival at the Plaza, Karl got out, paid the driver and walked into the building. He searched for a phone booth and dialled the number for another taxi.

"Yes, sir."

"16 Spartan Avenue, please."

He had done his best to disappear and now apart from security and customs at the airport, Karl Guttenberg was as good as home.

Karl arose early the next day and having breakfasted, made his way by foot to the railway station. The trains were frequent to the airport and within thirty minutes, he had entered through the terminal door and made his way to the Aeroflot booking desk. Paying cash, he now had a ticket for the next day's flight to Russia.

Ottawa was an intriguing city and as he had never been here before, Karl decided to pass the day as a conventional tourist. The eruptions in the Far East were not as intensely felt here as they had been four hundred miles away. But then, America had taken unilateral steps to intervene in this conflict and seemed determined to prevent the further advance of a secretive dictatorial state imposing its will over another—especially one that was democratic and a close ally of the West. The most worrying of all, though, was the backing and support that China had given to this outbreak of violence. Not renowned for its charitable and democratic processes, China was a world power to be reckoned with and USA knew that. Also, the value on life in this vast and beautiful country was not viewed with the same degree of welfare as in the West. In most cases in the West, governments and processes were in place to prevent a clandestine and spontaneous act of aggression against another sovereign state. There was a level of nervousness whether the same rules applied in China. China, however, needed trade to survive and with the world on the brink of a global and terminal war, negotiations were going to proceed before the ultimate decision to end Man's short-lived domination of Earth was taken…it was hoped.

With eager anticipation of his pending freedom, Karl got out of bed the next day and having breakfasted and settled his bill, saying that he was returning to USA, again made his way by foot to the railway station.

At SMR Hotel, 300, Lisgar Street, Ottawa, two smartly dressed men, one in a grey suit, the other in blue, walked in and approached the reception desk.

"I believe that you have a Mr Karl Guttenberg staying with you?"

"I'm sorry, sir, we do not discuss our guests with anyone!"

"You may change your mind with this, son."

And with that, the smaller of the two men displayed a wallet clearly displaying *CIA*.

"You realise that this is Canada, sir—not the US."

"Be that as it may, son, I have here a warrant for the apprehension of a Mr Karl Guttenberg and may I remind you that the cooperation between USA and Canada has been unimpeded since the end of hostilities in 1945."

"Hostilities?"

"WW II, son World War two! However, if you wish to remain uncooperative, we will wait here while we contact the Ottawa police department, together with the American embassy and mention that a Mr...what's your name, son?"

"Very well. Mr Guttenberg is currently residing in room two hundred and thirty-seven and is due to check out on Friday."

"You have a spare key, I presume?"

The two men made their way upstairs and withdrew their guns as they stood outside room 237. The taller of the two quietly inserted the electronic tag and the door unlocked with an audible click. With his gun held at the ready, the blue-suited agent nodded to his partner as he quietly pressed on the handle and slowly opened the door. Cautiously stepping inside, the sight that greeted them wasn't the one they had been hoping for.

"Son, why didn't you tell me that Mr Guttenberg had checked out?"

"He hasn't checked out...I told you, he checks out on Friday. Besides, he has already paid for his room so even if he did leave early—"

"Already paid for his room?"

"Yes...cash."

"Son, didn't you find it just a bit strange that a guest walks into your hotel, pays IN CASH, IN ADVANCE, for a room? Didn't that ring any alarm bells?"

"Well, it was a bit unusual, but that was his choice—he had paid and that was sufficient."

"OK... When did you last see Mr Guttenberg?"

"Yesterday. He took a taxi to World Exchange Plaza."

"Did he have his baggage...suitcase...with him?"

"No, just a rucksack...no other luggage."

"Then how come his room is empty? How could he take his belongings with him then? He must have come back?"

"No. I saw him being driven in the back of the taxi...and I was on duty all day. He did not return."

Without a by-your-leave, the two agents left the reception and returned to their black Buick.

"This guy is a pro. I tell you, he's planned to disappear into the mass and leave his trail cold."

"Call Central and tell them what we've found so far. From here, he has train, bus, plane, boat…or just gone into hiding somewhere."

"What d'ya think…still here or moved on?"

"What's your gut telling you, Gus?"

"He's moving on."

"Think it's time we involved City Police?"

"Yup, it's time."

At Macdonald-Cartier airport, Karl Guttenberg stood in the queue at the Aeroflot check-in counter. He noticed the armed security milling around the airport. The Canadian Police presence was noticeable and Karl wondered whether this was routine or if they had an ulterior motive for being out in such numbers. It seemed that every time he managed to slip through the net, another one was waiting to catch him. Orlando, New York and now Ottawa. The thing was that this time, he really would evade capture once on the plane. Though there was cooperation and collaboration between Canada and USA, no such alliance existed with Russia.

"Sir?"

"Oh, sorry…I was in a bit of a daydream."

"Ticket and passport, please."

This was it! Had she a list of US fugitives on her screen before her? Without batting an eyelid, would she press a button informing every security guard in the building that the most wanted man in US history was standing before her, booking his flight to freedom?

"Mr Karl Guttenberg?"

"Yes, that's correct."

She studied his passport and looked directly at him with no hint of emotion, certainly no hint of affability. Judging by the few words that she had spoken, Karl judged her to be a non-Canadian, possibly even Russian. He tried to remain calm and gave her a warming smile. He had always seemed to be able to charm the women and his mixed Asian, German and American accent seemed to give him that edge; just sufficient to arouse more than a cursory acknowledgment of his presence in a room. She appeared to be taking more time than Karl thought necessary, especially when the family of four in front of him had just passed through with hardly any dialogue passing between them.

"I'm sorry for the delay, there seems to be a glitch…"

"What appears to be the problem?"

"I'm sorry, sir; for some reason, your flight details don't appear to conform with…"

Karl watched her hands carefully. Were they going under the desk to press the button to condemn him and his family to a life of imprisonment? Was she merely delaying because before her right now on her monitor was a picture of

Karl ending Danny's life in front of a similar monitor? Was she really looking at a range of passport names and numbers that read 'Wanted'?

Trying to remain as relaxed as he could by leaning on the counter before her, Karl watched her hand go into a drawer beside her and as quick as he had ever seen anyone, she pulled out a small handgun and held it before him.

"I believe, Mr Karl Guttenberg, that you are wanted back in USA. Remain here with your hands behind your head. Security has been summoned and they will deal with you."

"Are you alright, sir?"

He looked ahead and the check-in girl was holding out his passport and boarding card before him.

"Wha...what?"

"The glitch has been resolved; a small technical problem. Your boarding gate is thirty-four. Have a good flight."

"Yes...thanks."

In a trance, Karl retrieved his passport and boarding card and left the check-in desk. His legs were like jelly and he wove unsteadily through the mass of people around him towards the departure lounge. He needed to sit and recover from this hallucination. He realised that his mind was no longer as much in control as it had been just a few days ago. He slouched on a seat and rested his head in his hands as two smartly dressed men, one in a grey suit, the other in blue, walked into *Departures*. Approaching *Information*, the two men were directed by a finger pointing towards where Karl was sitting. Walking up towards him, they hesitated and then turned into a door that read *Airport Security-Authorised personnel only* beside a slumped man on a seat. Feeling that he had to move on, Karl Guttenberg adjusted his posture, reached for his rucksack and strode towards Gates 21-40. Placing his rucksack on the conveyor belt, he allowed himself to be frisked after having set off the metal detector gate alarm. He retrieved his belongings and watched the screen monitor showing that Aeroflot SU 5436 had not yet started boarding. He needed to remain concealed and meandered through the various boutiques and shops, keeping his face towards the merchandise on display. As desperately as he needed a coffee right now, he denied himself even this basic prerequisite for fear of being exposed.

The monitor flickered and all the characters changed: *Aeroflot SU 5436 to Vladivostok, go to gate 34*. Karl's heart skipped a beat as he saw this wonderful display on the screen. As much as he wanted to pick up his rucksack and run to gate 34, he put into place the mind-soothing practices he had developed all those years ago following the teachings of Tirumalai Krishnamacharya. He picked up another book full of medieval caricatures depicting scenes of the black death, the Inquisition, carnage and the four horsemen of the Apocalypse and browsed through the descriptive prose and well-imagined designs. He knew that it would be at least another twenty minutes before *Boarding* would be displayed and he did not wish to expose himself in an open-plan glass partitioned room.

The grey-suited and blue-suited men completed their briefing in Airport Security and with half a dozen armed airport officials, came out into the main departure area. Dividing up, each carried a photofit picture of their wanted man and pushed their way to the various check-in counters, asking the same question to each member of the check-in staff. The check-in agent at *Aeroflot* signed off, turned off her computer and rose to go for her well-earned break as the photofit was being shown to her colleague with *Air Canada*. She crossed through *Departures*, went outside and drew heavily on her cigarette. It had started to rain and as much as she needed her cigarette, she also needed a coffee. The rain helped her decide and stamping out the unfinished cigarette on the pavement beneath her foot, she went back inside. She made her way to her favourite coffee shop, walking passed the expectant mass of people: some excited, some sad, some just plain bored—businessmen mainly—who had to endure another trek across the skies to some far distant destination. Sitting herself down with her *Americano*, she took out her Sudoku and studied the next pattern of numbers.

The monitor displayed: *Aeroflot SU 5436-boarding.* Karl put down the book and thumbed through others with a similar theme. The Bruce Pennington designs caught his eye, as did the monitor outside the bookstore. *Not yet, Karl, not yet.*

Outside gate 34, two armed security guards walked in and surveyed the passengers queueing up with their passports and tickets, waiting to be let onto the awaiting Aeroflot plane outside. They scrutinised the milling crowd, then ambled outside and onto the next boarding gate. Security officials were having another bad day as computers once again crashed and had to be rebooted. The screen monitors went blank and electronic communication was momentarily lost. *Display, come on, display*, but with nothing showing, Karl now knew that he had no choice but to make his way to gate 34. Outside gate 36, the two security guards continued to study the people inside but made no attempt to step to the other side of the dividing screen. Karl saw Gate 34 in the distance but had not yet noticed the two men with their carbines outside Gate 36. Having seen the last remaining passengers passing through the barrier at Gate 34, Karl noticed the two armed men now turning and slowly making their way back towards him. He slowed his pace, as his heart picked up its own, so as not to look too anxious. His assessment of the distance that both parties had to make left him in no doubt that he would arrive at the entrance to Gate 34—and freedom—before them. Suddenly, the monitors displayed all the information that had been missing for the past ten minutes. *Aeroflot SU 5436-last call.* Timed to perfection, he wondered whether God was really on his side, but then, would God condone murder? Passing to the other side of the glass screen that separated him from the two passing security guards, he quickened his pace and approached the boarding counter in front of the corridor leading to his Aeroflot flight to freedom. With a cursory glance at the documents held before him, the ticket agent tore the slip of his ticket and handed his seat number back to Karl Guttenberg. He was free! Well, almost.

Outside the coffee shop, the smartly dressed man in the grey suit noticed the Aeroflot uniform and walked inside. Handing her a photofit of the man they had been trying to detain, she studied the picture closely.

"Yes, I think that is him."

The agent's heartbeat quickened.

"You sure, Miss?"

"Yes. He acted somewhat strange when I handed him back his ticket. I thought that he was ill or going to faint…he seemed to almost stagger away after I handed him his ticket."

Noticing her slightly foreign accent, possibly Russian, the CIA agent withdrew his mobile phone from his pocket and dialled his partner in the blue suit.

"What flight, Miss?"

"Aeroflot SU 5436."

He looked up and saw the monitor just outside the coffee shop: *Aeroflot SU 5436-gate closed.*

The two CIA agents, together with the six airport security guards, made their way to gate 34. Running through the scattering crowds before them, they arrived at the glass-fronted screen divider and dashing inside, found the corridor empty and the security door at the end closed. Dashing back to the large window overlooking the runway, they saw an Aeroflot plane taxiing in the distance.

"Quick! The Airport Traffic Control Tower—which way?"

The security guards started running along the moving walkway corridor, giving them additional speed, with the two smartly dressed men hotly behind them. Luckily, all previous passengers had long departed and the corridor was clear, giving them unimpeded use of the fastest means possible of getting to their next destination.

The Aeroflot plane circled on the blast pad as the Air Canada flight roared into the distance. Karl watched through the small circular window as the airplane accelerated away from him and then, like a graceful bird, left the ground and soared into the air. Aeroflot SU 5436 completed its turn and now faced directly onto the runway, its engines roaring, but not yet at full throttle. Karl felt the plane vibrating, wondering how the metallic structures survived these extreme forces without rupturing. Unable to see ahead, he could only surmise, with what he had just seen, the picture in front of him. Now his heart was really beating fast; surely nothing could prevent him escaping now. The plane continued to thunder but remained stationary. *Come on, come on, let those engines roar!*

"Aeroflot SU five, four, three, six, you are clear for take-off. Godspeed and have a good flight."

"Roger, Ottawa—thanks."

"STOP!"

The security guards followed by the two CIA agents rushed into the Control Tower, shouting out their instructions to Air Traffic Control.

The plane's engines roared into life and Karl felt that beautiful sensation of acceleration sending his adrenaline into hyper-mode.

"Stop that Aeroflot take-off… National security!"

"Aeroflot SU five, four, three, six, please abort take-off! I repeat, please abort take-off!"

But the plane had just accelerated beyond the point of no return and had to continue its majestic journey skywards. Karl Guttenberg bit his bottom lip in a euphoric manner as the rumble of the wheels became silent and the plane left the ground.

Chapter 30

The clock struck eleven. Michel had spent the past hour gazing into his crystal and concentrating. As though in a trance, like the first time that I had met him and I now realised that he was tuned into the world of spirits.

"My guides are with me, Michael, and you are as clear as day!"

"Michel, please take care. Do not underestimate the power of this demon!"

"Anne, have no fear; my guides have fully charged my strength and resolve! They are with me now—I feel them by my side. I walk with confidence and, if I may say, with joy; such blessed joy!"

I had noticed earlier that Michel had been busy in his library. Using a pestle and mortar, he had been grinding a mixture of ingredients including, I noticed, nutmeg and some strange-looking mushrooms. Something in my senses recognised this, but I could not recall exactly what it was. Nevertheless, it had given him newfound strength and extrasensory awareness. Kissing Anne on the cheek, he mounted the stairs and reached for his cloak. Beside his cloak, on the floor, was a chest. He picked it up.

"My future awaits!"

"Our future awaits!"

"Ah, yes, *our* future awaits!"

Out into the winter's night air, Michel Nostredame and I strode with a gait full of expectation and exuberance. This time, he did not seem to be afraid as I had seen him the day before. Was it his concoction, was it because I was by his side, was it because he felt that he had superiority over the man he had feared before, was it because he felt vindicated now that he and I had a blood-bond contract? It mattered not; just that he was confident was sufficient.

We arrived at the necromancer's house and though Michel was full of gaiety, I began to feel somewhat apprehensive. Michel was now safe; no harm would come to him as the result of any denigrated parchment, signed in blood and offered to the god of the Underworld. Now, it was my turn. I was entering the true unknown; it was I who would have to battle with these monsters of the night…and I didn't know how. All I understood was that I had no choice. It had to be. Michel had demonstrated bravery, Mai—my precious Mai—had displayed the ultimate courage, Mai's mother had gone above and beyond any call of duty to ensure that tonight…*tonight*, my destiny would be revealed. It was now up to me and I think that it was because of the sacrifices of these mortals, risking their lives for someone they did not know but believed in, that had made me worried. Could I possibly live up to their expectations, could I possibly find the strength and courage that they had shown to see this through? Would I crumble before that foul ghoul and let him take control of me? I had to believe that I, Michael…whoever I was, had a resolve to be here—in this time, in this place, at this moment. I had to believe in me.

The door was opened by the tall Negroid servant. He opened the door wide and with a polite bow, indicated with his hand to enter.

"Monsieur Nostredame, good evening, sir."

He took Michel's cloak and hung it on a hook beside the door. He had not seen me!

"My master is expecting you; please follow me."

The servant led us down the same corridor that Nostradamus had been down yesterday and though I felt no foreboding, I didn't feel that this was a particularly nice house. As we approached the study, I began to sense a feeling of malevolence. Bowing and indicating with his hand, the servant gestured to Michel to enter the room; I stayed outside.

"Monsieur Nostredame, welcome."

"Monsieur LeMartre, good evening."

I peered in from the doorway. The scene was slightly disturbing. On the desk, where he was sitting, burned two large candles, each at either end of the desk. At one of the ends was a thurible; at the other end, a bell. In the middle of the desk was a large, leather-bound grimoire, open at the page that read 'Summoning the dead'. The paintings on the wall, though artistically perfect, represented the occult and I knew that the man before me was a practicing sorcerer. But more than just a sorcerer, he was foul. His cloak was not as I had imagined—grey and dark—but a quilt patchwork of scenes depicting earth, fire, water and, in the centre, a familiar…the horned goat. On the floor, in the middle of the room, was laid out a circle of candles and in the middle, the fascinating and mystic symbol of the Pentacle. Across the Pentacle, lay a walnut staff.

"You have the remaining payment?"

"Indeed, sir, I do. I was able to find the means, though now I need my dues even more to reimburse the fee paid to you."

Michel placed the chest on the table before them beside the grimoire. The necromancer opened the lid and gazed at the contents. With a sardonic smile, he placed his hand inside and allowed the coins to fall through his fingers, enjoying the tinkling sound as they fell back on top of each other.

"Seven and a half thousand?"

"As agreed in our bond."

"A port? It will be another fifteen minutes before the hour is upon us."

"Thank you, yes. That indeed will be most warming, especially on such a cold night."

Though the fire was burning brightly, there was a chill in the air. I noticed Nostradamus shiver slightly and sensed that he would have preferred to have kept his cloak. Above the fire hung a mirror. The mirror was directly in front of me, yet I displayed no image. LeMartre poured out the port from his decanter into a silver chalice and offered it to Michel. Cupping his hands around the goblet, LeMartre did the same but his goblet had the insignia of a goat.

"Your good health, sir."

"And yours, too."

"And to a successful evening!"

Michel looked around. He had already witnessed the art on the walls, but the shrivelled head had been removed. However, he felt it more judicious to omit this observation from the conversation.

"An interesting room indeed. Mine is not so elaborately adorned."

"Come, come, you humble yourself too much. Yours is a reputation, known even to the king himself."

"Well, yes, that is true, but splendour can often conceal hidden depravities."

"You are referring to the Court, I presume?"

"Why, of course, what else could I possibly denote to?"

The two men laughed, but the laugh was a polite, hollow laugh. I sensed that the port had removed some of the inhibitions that Nostradamus had felt as he had walked into the room, but that LeMartre had no need of such sustenance.

"Of course, you have witnessed possession before?"

"Of course," Michel lied.

"Then you will be aware that as I am taken, my form will be transformed, my voice will not be my own. The transition period will be one hour. At the stroke of one, I shall return and you will no longer have communication with your departed friend and it will be I who will possess my body again. That is understood, I presume?"

"Oh, indeed."

"You will need to profit during this hour; ask the questions that you seek answers to but do not be vague. The questions must be specific. Will you need quill and paper?"

"Yes, I have them here…but ink, I do not have ink."

"Here, my friend, here is your ink…"

LeMartre opened up an inkwell and the contents appeared to be more of blood than ink. He arose from the chair and walked over to the fire. Taking a small strip of wood, he lit the splint and walked back to the desk. He opened the thurible and placed the flame inside. Closing the cover, a sweet, but at the same time, repugnant smell arose as the smoke swilled around the room. Though I could not smell, I sensed this through Michel; his was the brain and mind into which I was currently attuned. I began to feel somewhat nauseous and wondered whether it was the burning incense or the preparation for my transition that was making me feel this way. I was soon to find out.

He poured a second glass and as the decanter was placed on the table, the clock struck the midnight hour. The bell started to rise and rang, first gently, then violently. The mirror over the mantelpiece quivered and with a noise like a whip, cracked from one corner to the next. Split in two, I noticed a faint reflection…my refection? But it was fuzzy and I couldn't make out any clear details. The alarming thing was that only the right side of the cracked mirror reflected my wispy image, the other side did not!

"Our summons!"

Taking out some runes from within the desk drawer, he threw these into the circle of candles and watched the pattern that was to dictate the form of the séance. With that, he picked up his staff and stepped into the pentacle. Muttering chants in Latin and with arms stretched out like a 'Y', he summoned the spirits to obey his commands, but nothing stirred. I sensed the room becoming colder, even though the fire was now a roaring blaze. I stared into the flames, mesmerised by the patterns that danced and licked around the hearth. He called out again, summoning those phantoms from Hell to obey his words. Suddenly, I felt drawn towards him. This was a powerful magus indeed and though I still had the strength to refute his calls, I wanted to be part of him—I was being inexorably drawn to him. With a violent thud of his staff, he called out with all his strength: "MICHAEL! Come forth!"

I stood before him and saw the fire in his eyes. Like embers in a blazing furnace, his stare was hypnotic. As though he was talking through water, I heard his voice as his eyes pierced through me like a knife.

"Are you Michael?"
"I am."
"But you are not—you are false."
"I am not false—I am Michael."
"But you are not of the Underworld—your soul is transparent."
"I am the Michel that Nostradamus seeks; pass by, that I may use your body."
"You will not use my body. He has deceived me; you shall not pass!"

A sentinel stood before me protecting this man from Hell. His disfigured form, putrid and rotting, bore pure malice. With a sword that shimmered like a mirage, he raised his weapon to cut my soul and send it to purgatory. I felt the piercing heat of that instrument of torture and it was like none I had experienced before. Then, I felt the icy wind of the North ravage inside me. I saw a light in the distance, but it was beyond my reach. I heard the marching of a multitude of empathies pass before me. Then, I witnessed this filth from Hades blaspheme as the sword descended.

"STOP! You will destroy yourself and that vermin beside you! If that sword touches my soul, you will be damned forever!"

I heard the necromancer shout:

"Halt!"
"There are no falsehoods; it is you on whom this soldier of Satan will turn if that fire touches even a breath of me."

"Oh, no…we have a blood contract—I have that man's soul…and yours too, written, signed and sent to the court of Hell for eternity!"

"Yes, that is true, if there were any falsehoods! But there are none!"

"You are not the Michael of whom I was told!"

"But I am."

"You do not owe recompense to this Michel Nostredame!"

"Oh…but I do! It is written, signed in blood—my blood and his and despatched in the furnace to the Master of the Dark for eternity! It is you…you who has a blood contract with the Devil. It is you who will suffer these ogres from the abyss if you break that contract. It is written in the flames of Hell! And you have been fully paid, as agreed."

I turned towards the light that now shone as bright as the morning sun and commanded the marching empathies:

"Bring forth my contract!"

Raining down before us and incandescent in the air, the necromancer read:

I, Michael, owe to Michel Nostredame an explanation of my purpose and for involving him in the pursuit of my existence here. I have, therefore, summoned the necromancer known as Jean LeMartre and will use his body to discover that purpose. To this end, I shall repay him in this knowledge.

I sign this testament with my blood.

"Read, digest and obey, man from Hell!"

The ogre before me raised his iridescent sword and turned towards the necromancer. Facing him, as he had done with me, he raised his weapon that blazed before him and I could tell that it was now *he* who suffered the heat of the fires before him.

"I honour my contract."

The beast lowered his sword, still glaring at LeMartre. Hesitatingly, the necromancer left his body and I watched his phantom form glimmer and disappear like foggy dew. I closed my eyes, drew on my consciousness to help and protect me and disappeared from view. I opened my eyes and there, in front of me stood Nostradamus. He looked frightened. The bell was back on the desk, stationary and silent. I looked towards the mirror and saw the left side reflected the man I now possessed; the right side reflected nothing but the wall behind me.

"You have summoned me?"

"Are you…are you Michael?"

"I am."

"Yes, your voice is different…and your mien changes; you are no longer Jean LeMartre?"

"Until the clock strikes one, I remain Michael. You must make haste and record our discourse."

"But it is already a quarter past the hour! Can you volunteer the information for which you seek?"

"Your questions must be specific; this necromancer has deemed his body fit for use only as a tool for communication."

"Right! Well then, why are you here?"

"For my purpose."

"What is your purpose?"

"To impart to you the future."

"The future? But I can already see the future."

"You think you can, but your quatrains and prophesies are vague and can be misinterpreted. They are undecipherable verses that make no sense but appeal to those fantasists who wish to create sensations by their explanations. It does not display the true future, the future that people will accept and believe."

"So, you have knowledge of the real future, the future that does happen; you can be explicit and give me that information?"

"I can."

"Why is this so important to you, why have you come to me?"

"Your divination of the future, as a cautioning to Man, is believed by some but not many. If your prophesies can be precise, then yours will become the warnings that Man will heed."

"That is an onerous task indeed. To think that what I say will determine the future of mankind."

"Indeed, it is an arduous task but you are losing time; ask your questions that Man may be saved—saved from himself."

"How can I ask questions; how can I be specific if I don't know the questions that will be so fundamental to Man that he will believe!"

"Ask for dates and I will answer."

"1605…"

"There will be a plot against the English king, James I of England. The plot will be foiled."

"1805."

"A great sea battle between France and England will take place. It will be known as the Battle of Trafalgar."

"Who will win?"

"The English will win under the command of Lord Nelson. But you need to have vision; look further into the future."

"OK. What century are you from?"

"I am from the twenty-first century."

"Twenty-first?"

"Yes."

"What will happen in the twenty-first century?"

"Mankind will be annihilated."

"How?"

"By his own hand. He will action his own self-destruction."

"Ye gods! Can this be avoided?"

"It can."

"How?"

"Man must choose his own path—a path of free will and free choice. Others, seeking power and dominion over his fellow man by selfish, autocratic and clandestine means, will hide from Man the truth. That truth will allow Man to choose freely, with full knowledge of the consequences, so that if he chooses to destroy himself, it will be because he has decided to, not because some despot has decreed it for him."

"Can you give me names of these tyrants?"

"I can."

"So, I should start at the twenty-first century?"

"No, before."

The clock chimed the half-hour. Michel became agitated. Here, for the first time, he had real proof of the future. His spirit guides had always been good at helping him 'feel' for the future, but now he had a source that could give irrefutable proof for his predictions.

"The twentieth century."

"What date?"

"1903."

"Man will take to the sky and fly."

"He will grow wings?"

"No, he will build machines that will fly."

Nostradamus sat busily at the desk and scribbled as fast as the quill would permit. He was convinced now that he saw the writing that it was blood, not ink, in the inkwell.

"1912."

"The greatest boat that man has built will sink."

"What is the name of this boat?"

"The Titanic."

"1924."

"Josef Stalin becomes leader of Russia."

"Is he a tyrant?"

"He is."

"1933."

"Adolf Hitler becomes chancellor of Germany."

"Germany?"

"It is known as Prussia but becomes 'Germany' during the nineteenth century."

"Is his appointment important for the destruction of Man?"

"It is."

"Is he a tyrant?"

"He is."

"1940."

"The greatest war that Man has witnessed is underway."

"Does this German tyrant have anything to do with it?"

"He does."

"1945."

"The greatest war that Man has seen ends. The people of China have a new leader—Zedong Mao. In Korea, Kim Il-sung seeks power and wins the support of Russia. Armageddon strikes the people of Japan."

"Are these people tyrants?"

"They are."

"If Man takes heed of these people, won't the history of Man change?"

"It may. If the future remains unaltered, it will be because Man has decided. It will be his choice. It is not the individual's decision to choose for others; a man can choose only for himself."

"Give me time, I must write these things down."

Michel looked up at the clock; he had three minutes left.

"1963."

"The American President, John Fitzgerald Kennedy is shot dead."

"Is he a tyrant?"

"No."

The clock chimed the hour.

"Do not forget what you have been told…the destiny of Man is in your hands. My time is at an end…"

LeMartre thumped his staff inside the pentacle and fell on the floor. Michel's natural instinct was to rush to the man's side and help him, but he needed to complete writing all that he had been told by the necromancer whilst in trance. The man lay on the floor twitching as Nostradamus completed his record of all that he had been told. He felt no sympathy for the man prostrate on the floor— loathing was nearer to the emotion that he felt. However, he was a fellow human and as much as Michel despised the obscenity on the floor at his feet, he felt compelled to assist him from his anguish. He stooped down to pick him up.

"He will recover—he is not harmed."

"Michael! The gods be praised!"

"He is foulness itself, Michel, make no mistake. He works with and for Lucifer."

"Michael, I was afraid! I cannot recall fear as I experienced it here, in this house, in this hour."

"Michel, did you find out why I am here? Did I recount the future? Did you discover my purpose?"

"Indeed! Oh, indeed! But I have only recorded a tip of the iceberg that is still floating. But surely, you have now recalled all your past?"

"No! I was entranced throughout the whole experience. I recall nothing more than I knew before."

"Then, perhaps if I relate to you all that you have told me, this may jog some memories…some past experiences?"

"Let's hope so."

I looked at the necromancer convulsing in the pentacle before us. This quivering filth drew no compassion from me, only repugnance. I looked up and the mirror was now complete, as it had been when we arrived. It reflected only Nostradamus and the wall behind him.

"Jaafar!"

The servant was in the room in an instant. He looked slightly dishevelled and seeing the scene before him, appeared to show fear in his mannerism as he approached the man sprawled in front of the fire.

"He has been with the Dark Lord?"

"I believe so but I think he will recover."

"Yes, he always recovers after seeing the Dark Lord but it will take time."

"Do you need help with him?"

"No, he must raise himself. Have you been inside the pentacle?"

"No."

"No one must go inside the pentacle…it could harm him."

"Then, perhaps you would show us out, please, Jaafar."

"We?"

"Sorry, 'me', perhaps you would show me out, please?"

I knew that the servant could not see me and felt confident to walk out alongside Nostradamus. The air outside was decidedly chilly as I could tell from the way Michel pulled the collar up around his neck. As he spoke, the air filled with vapour, highlighted by the full moon. Around us, I swear I could hear the unmistakeable sound of the patter of tiny feet and the cries of children at play. Like Nostradamus, I was also glad to be out of this house—it reeked of abhorrence.

Chapter 31

"Uranus…five minutes."

"Thanks, Petra."

Though we were still over eighty million kilometres from the planet, out here time appeared to be more significant than distance. In the past, on Earth, distance was the criteria that we used to assess how far something was. Now it was time. We measured distance in time and *time* was exactly why I was here.

"Final checks please! Charles?"

"All good, Captain."

"Simon?"

"Here too, Skip."

"Anna?"

"Ready to shut down on command."

"Petra?"

"We are lining up Uranus approach now, coming in via South Pole…angle to equator, twelve degrees; estimated contact height…two hundred and fifty kilometres above atmosphere."

"OK with that, Michael?"

"Yeah, I can live with that."

"Current speed, unaltered at warp-drive factor zero-point-nine-two."

"Petra, please send all information to date back to NASA. This will be our final opportunity—after that…well, I am not sure. Nobody's sure if radio signals will travel without distortion at the speed of light. Or whether there will be any Proxima left to despatch signals."

"I don't think the radio signals will be altered, Jamie. And as for Proxima, think of Chuck Yeager."

"Yeah, and like him, we will be delving into the unknown. Michael, what's your intuition telling you about signal distortion?"

"Possibly, yes."

"Really?"

"No one knows, Jamie. It is all speculative but, just like the sound barrier, theorists may well cogitate about what they believe could happen, only to find out that they were wrong all along."

"What do you really think?"

"I think that there may be an influence beyond our understanding and I would err on the side of caution."

"In other words…"

"In other words, I believe that as long as we are travelling at the speed of light, no transmissions will be possible. We certainly won't be able to receive any, so why should we be able to transmit any."

"Sure, I can understand that but once we are below the speed of light, then we will be able to receive those signals, albeit out of context with when they were sent?"

"Yes, and likewise, we will be able to transmit BUT whilst we are travelling at the speed of light, then—"

"Who knows?"

"Yes, who knows?"

"Get all data sent to NASA as a priority, Petra. As we are all lined up for our birthday surprise with Misty up ahead, then you may as well use your time wisely!"

"I'll give you *wisely*, Captain James Fraser!"

"Touchy, isn't she, Jamie?"

"Sure is, Michael. Why, I don't understand these women at all…you know, give 'em a bit of responsibility and they go all to pieces…and, ouch!"

A well-aimed pencil hit Jamie on the ear.

"What was that for?"

"I'm sure I don't know, Captain Fraser; I guess I must have gone all to pieces with this responsibility. Goodness alone knows what will happen next!"

Though she turned her head away from us, I caught a glimpse of Petra's face and could see a broad smile on her face.

"Met your match there, Jamie—but I'm sure glad that she's riding shotgun with us!"

"Yeah, me too…but don't tell her that, she'll think I like her next!"

Jamie turned his head towards Petra, who was already blowing a kiss towards him.

"Michael, I forgot to ask, after Uranus, what about the Keiper belt?"

"We are going in the wrong trajectory for the Keiper belt to affect us. As we are going via the polar region, there will be no debris floating our way—quite safe."

"Quite sure?"

"Quite sure."

"Jamie, thirty seconds."

"OK, everyone…strap in. Transmissions, Petra?"

"They have everything to date. Anna forwarded all data so far recorded, including all conversations, which have been stored in the voice bank. Despatch was confirmed twenty seconds ago."

There, just before us at some mere eight million kilometres, lay the mysterious misty-blue planet. By now, we should have been used to the sudden appearance from nothing to a clear view of a celestial body, but it still captivated us. Jamie seemed much tenser than with Neptune. So far, every planet had presented us with a different problem and here was *Misty* in the throes of challenging us once again. But I knew that this time, Jamie had to use his flying skills to the ultimate. At two hundred and fifty kilometres above cloud level at this speed, it was effectively like trying to hit a bull's eye on the Sea of Tranquillity from Florida.

"Petra...confirm data again, please... Anna, ready!"

"Twelve degrees to equator...one hundred and seventy-five kilometres above atmosphere—South Pole distance—three million six hundred thousand kilometres. Speed, warp-drive factor zero-point-nine-two."

"Anna?"

"Ready...give me a mark, Petra..."

"Ten...nine...eight..."

What lies beneath you, Misty? What lies beneath the depths of all you beautiful watchmen of our solar system? What are your secrets that you have hidden from us since we first gazed to the heavens? Will you let us pass or will you jealously keep us to yourself?

Jamie's concentration was total. He had trusted in my knowledge, he had trusted in Petra's guidance, he had trusted in all of us. Now it was our turn to trust in him. The planet was now enormous, occupying every part of the canopy in front. Though not as blue as Neptune, it was still a wondrous sight.

"Three...two...one...mark, Anna!"

All bleeping ceased. Jamie now had just over three seconds to manually line up his approach. I felt the hum and vibration of the burners as the angle of approach was altered slightly...then quiet. The South Pole was immediately in front and slightly to the right. Jamie fired the burners again as we rapidly closed the distance between Proxima and Uranus. I wanted to close my eyes and throw my hands in front of my face, but I was fascinated as well as frightened with our impending fate. I could almost feel the wisps of hydrogen surrounding us as Proxima started to butt. Jamie had been given all my knowledge and had based his flight path on that information. I now panicked! Was it correct; was it true? Jamie, I knew, would pull us through, if all that I had told him was accurate...but was it? Just as with the moon encounter, I could feel again a force...gravity; but if it was gravity, we were too far out to feel its effect surely? As light bends around a star, we were bending towards Uranus. But we had mass—light did not! Were we rewriting the laws of physics? Mass and the speed of light...impossible! We were at the point of unchartered mathematics and known mathematics was what determined our flight path now! I felt the burners fire again, but not momentarily—they were vibrating constantly and the shuddering was frightening. I tried to look to Jamie, but my head would not move. I could just see his hand twitch on the plasma burners' control, but it wasn't a hand that I recognised—it was flat and wrinkled, as though it had been made from plasticine and squashed. I wanted to scream, but even the sound from my voice was trapped. The only sound was the deafening roar of the engines, fighting to keep us from the grips of that giant beneath us. But surely, no sound was possible in space? Were we within the atmosphere of that monster beneath us? Had I miscalculated?

An unbearable noise now reached my ears…silence! From roar to silence, the effect was cataclysmic. My mind could not adapt to such extremes as I watched Charlie rise before me. He floated over and embraced Anna. In a swirl of limbs entwined around each other, like ivy around a tree, they rose and rotated in a kiss of death. Neither mouth left the other and with eyes closed, they rose above the room, turning and twisting, spiralling towards their doom. Petra arose, floating over to me and with a hand outstretched, stroked my face as she spoke my name.

"Michael… Michael…it's all over, well done."

"Over? Well done?"

"Yes! We've made it!"

"Made what? Where's Charlie and Anna? They were up there…"

"I'm still here, Michael."

"Yeah, me too. Are you alright, Michael?"

"Geez! I must have just hallucinated! Where are we? Where's Uranus?"

A male hand reached out and shook mine warmly. It was Jamie and he was beaming from ear to ear.

"My friend, you have just channelled us through the day of reckoning! Uranus passed us by forty seconds ago! Thank you."

I felt Petra kiss my cheek and return to her seat. I still felt as though I was dreaming.

"I don't think I am cut out for these extreme physical sensations, Jamie. How you managed it…well, I just do not know."

"We were selected on our physical as well as our psychosomatic fitness, Michael. We have been trained and yes, I admit that was the most extreme situation that I…we have faced, but we have been trained to endure hardships that your everyday Mr Joe Average would not be able to endure."

"Did you remain conscious, then, Jamie? I mean the moon encounter was bad enough…"

"This was harder but something just kept me alert. With the moon confrontation, I knew what to expect, but with this one…I guess my mind forced me to stay alert."

"Anyway, it's not 'well done' to me. No, Jamie, it's 'well done' to you. I couldn't have guided us through what you have just achieved! That was amazing flying skill!"

"Anna, had I been unable, would have guided us through as well. It's what we have been taught to do."

"Well, have we done it?"

"You'll have to wait fifteen more minutes, but if we haven't, then we gave it a damn good try…our best shot!"

"Whatever, Michael, we have no more opportunities for acceleration…we've run out of bullets. It is what it is."

The entire cockpit was slowly adapting to accepting that the tensions of the past few days were finally at an end. However, there was tautness in the air, not that of fear or worry, but that of apprehension—apprehension as to whether the target had been reached: had we achieved the speed of light? It was akin, I guess, to the arrival of the final exam results; yes, I suppose it was a fear of sorts but not in the true sense of the word, it was more, perhaps, like the arrival of a birthday or Christmas Eve with all the expectation and anticipation these moments brought. Though I had no role to play in the organisation and running of the ship, I could tell that the others were not functionally one hundred per cent either. Even Jamie seemed fidgety as we waited for the bleeps to return. No small talk passed between us. It was that Christmas Eve expectancy for everyone. I tried to break the ice.

"I've never drunk Mr Jack through a straw before, that'll be a first. I have heard, though, that by drinking cider through a straw, you become more inebriated than drinking in a glass—maybe this'll have the same effect?"

"Can't say that I've ever tried, Michael, I'm not really a cider drinker—never have been. After a day's training, it has always been down to the bar for a few beers, never cider. But why are you talking about drinking Mr Jack through a straw?"

"Well, I can't see how we can possibly drink normally in a glass. Though it would be fun to pour some into the room and chase around trying to drink it."

"Ha…ha…ha…I don't somehow think that'll be necessary."

"Oh! Why not?"

"Little surprise!"

Jamie, normally boisterous and flamboyant, was still skittish. On Earth, I had seen him take the most innocuous remark and turn it into a real prank, joking around with those of a similar disposition. If we knew what the data was, we could have got on with our lives in a normal fashion; it was this unknown that was putting us all on edge. I wanted to talk to Jamie, long and hard. NASA had briefed me that I had to let him know of my true mission and the purpose for being on Proxima with the rest of the crew and the New World pioneers, but this really was not the right time. Also, it had to be just me and him. Anna would have needed a long and justifiable rest so that she could assume command. And if I was going to be totally honest, Mr Jack Daniels was certainly going to be consumed…in large quantities.

Though we had been waiting for the moment, when it first arrived it was hardly noticed, but by the second beep, everyone was acutely tuned into that melodic sound.

"Wait everyone! I need to reboot slowly. We've waited this long; another ten minutes won't change anything; better to wait than rush and ruin."

I looked over at the main console and lights had started flashing as more beeps sounded. If everyone had been edgy before, then that was nothing compared to what we were feeling now; it really was that Christmas morning sentiment. After what seemed like an eternity, Petra finally let out a gasp.

"What is it, babe?"

"I'm online!"

"And you'll be the first to know!"

Petra started pressing various buttons in front of her, then stared at her monitor. She waited, as we all did, then sighed in frustration as she repeated the exercise again. I watched her eyes and mouth for that give-away sign but was sadly deceived. Though she smiled initially, it turned into a pout.

"Sorry, Jamie..."

"We didn't make it then?"

"No...I'm so sorry..."

"What have you got then, Petra?"

"Current speed warp-drive factor...one-point-zero-five!"

"Ah well, we gave it our best—What! One-point—!"

"—Zero-five! We are travelling *faster* than the speed of light!"

"Faster! *Faster*! Michael, do you know what you have done?"

"Yes, confused the laws of physics! Even I don't understand this one."

"Faster than the speed of light...that means—"

"We will arrive before we are seen!"

"Like a bump in the night!"

"Except that bump will be obliteration!"

"But we can't even tell NASA! We can't tell them what we have achieved! Why, this changes the whole ballpark of physics!"

"And mathematics!"

"Yes, and mathematics. Why, all that we have been taught could actually be—"

"—Wrong?"

"No... Why, yes... Wrong!"

Chapter 32

Aeroflot SU 5436 began its descent towards Vladivostok. Though he had travelled by plane many times, it wasn't his favourite mode of transport. With rather long legs, he suffered quite easily from cramp with them scrunched underneath the seat in front. And his ears always popped as the plane rapidly lost height. It was night-time and he could just make out the sodium and neon lights below. He knew that he would have to face immigration upon arrival and without a local destination or a reason to be on Russian soil, he felt that his transfer to China should help him pass easily through without being detained in custody and sent back to Canada.

The plane landed, circled around the runway and finally taxied to a halt outside the *Arrivals* gate. After disembarking with the other passengers, Karl Guttenberg strode, upon being summoned, up to the immigration desk and handed over his passport. The Russian Immigration Officer looked fierce as she had been trained to do. Hers was not a job to make friends with the passing public. She hated her job but with two children and a railway worker for a husband, she had little choice but to help with the family income. She looked at him as though he was the sole reason for her having this detestable job and returned his passport. Picking up his rucksack, he made his way to baggage reclaim and, from there, to the Air China booking desk. Noticing that the next flight to Beijing was a mere three hours away, he hoped that his late arrival would not impede his connection to his new homeland.

"Ural Airlines Flight, U 6881 will be departing in three hours, Mr Guttenberg and there are three seats available."

With the briefest of delays, he made his way to *Departures* and completed the necessary procedures to allow him to pass into the departure lounge.

"Please make your way to gates ten to fifty."

Feeling like a normal human being instead of the outlaw that he was, at last he could make his way in the normal leisurely way that passengers did when awaiting their departure to distant locations. Feeling unflustered, but drowsy, he observed the monitor indicating that Ural Airlines Flight U 6881 to Beijing had been delayed; another reason why he disliked flying, there were always delays. Luckily, US dollars were accepted everywhere and so he was able to buy himself a coffee and something that resembled pastry, though it left his mouth rather dry. Finally, being able to relax, unless the cooperation between USA and Russia had suddenly improved to the point of returning immediately upon arrival any suspects wanted for murder on American soil, Karl fell into a fitful sleep in the departure lounge. Even if he missed his flight, he no longer felt like the fugitive that he had just twelve hours ago. He could catch another, though that would be inconvenient and he so much wanted to be with his wife and son again. As he dropped off, he shook himself back to consciousness again. The monitor still gave no indication of his flight to Beijing being ready for boarding, so he decided to stretch out onto the three seats and sleep.

Just by chance—or was it a sixth sense?—he opened his eyes. On the screen above him was the display he had been waiting for: *U 6881, go to gate 42.* He roused himself and made his way to gate 42. Handing over his passport and boarding pass, he felt apprehensive for the first time since leaving Canada. The ticket agent seemed unsure and talking to her colleague, asked him to stand to one side. Not understanding Russian, Karl was at a complete loss as to the reason for this and tried using his most charismatic charm to understand why.

"Is there a problem?"

"We have been told that you must stay here."

"Why?"

"We have been told…that is all."

If this had been Canada, Karl would have known the reason why. But this was Russia and if he *was* a fugitive, which he was, this should work to his benefit, not the other way around. He noticed just the other side of the screen two armed Russian guards. They had not been summoned to him nor did there seem to be a security infringement. He felt mildly confident that this was simply a misunderstanding and waited for the other passengers to pass through.

"Excuse me?"

"Please wait…"

Knowing what he had done and been through during the past four days, Karl began to wonder whether there really was an international warrant for his apprehension…and deportation. He started to feel uncomfortable.

"Karl!"

"Kim?"

"So good to see you!"

"And you. I didn't expect to see you here!"

"The Chinese Embassy in USA has been closed, as you may not have been aware, but probably not surprised?"

"I am totally ignorant of the recent global situation; I have not been privy to world news since I was at JFK and then it was only unspoken videos and screenshots."

"Our comrades in North Korea have taken on the mighty imperialists of the West."

"Yes, I had heard that tensions were running high whilst still at NASA. Indeed, that was the main reason for the rapid research and launch of Proxima."

"Yes, we are aware of Proxima—thanks to you. Which is another reason for your detention here, Karl."

"Detention! Well, I was hoping to board this flight to Beijing and then I was going to contact you after seeing my wife and son."

"The problem is, Karl, you are wanted by the CIA and now by the FBI for murder and espionage."

"Well, I assumed by now that they would have pieced together my movements but not my motives."

The ticket agent came over into the empty departure lounge and spoke to Kim in Russian. Kim replied in Russian and she left, looking slightly anxious.

"It could help international relations between our two countries, which at the moment are the lowest they have been since 1949, if we were to cooperate and return you to Canada. But that could put a strain on our close ties with North Korea and our friends there. North Korea would welcome you with open arms."

"Kim, I am totally exhausted. I have been on the run now for nearly a week; I have killed an innocent man to keep my wife and son safe; I have endured emotional stress to breaking point; I have no more money—my account in USA would have been frozen; and I have no home…tell me what you want in simple, plain English."

"Well, flight U 6881 to Beijing is waiting for your decision."

"What decision, Mr Ambassador?"

"We want to be certain that history cannot be rewritten. We want…no, we *need* to ensure that there will be no change to the outcome of your, my, our existence. You and I should be having this meeting, as we are now…there *must* be no alternative. Should the course of history change, the outcome could…no, *would* be catastrophic."

"I have done everything I can to ensure the failure of this mission. I have betrayed my country and those people close to me. I have done everything—"

"—Not quite everything…"

The ticket agent came over to Kim and spoke again. This time Kim became angry and she left, knowing that the next time they spoke, it would be Kim who would do the approaching.

"Not quite everything?"

"Your wife is enjoying the home comforts of a grateful state. Your son attends the most exclusive school in Beijing. They want for nothing and can continue to do so for the remainder of their lives, if things remain unaltered."

"So, what is there left to do that I have not already done?"

"Karl, you have given much, for which the East is most grateful, but there is one other sacrifice that you will need to consider. It will be the ultimate sacrifice to guarantee that I will still be here tomorrow and that our friends in…well, will be Korea, not just North Korea…that they will be left unharmed and able to spread the word and will of the People. And flight U 6881 is awaiting that decision."

"What is this 'ultimate' sacrifice?"

"You need to follow him."

"Follow him!"

"Yes, Karl, follow him."

"But that is a one-way ticket. There will be no coming back; my wife, my son—"

"—Will become heroes of the state. They will be honoured and remembered for the sacrifice that they gave—the loss of husband and father—for the good of the People."

"But how…?"

"The People of China have been very industrious. We have made a copy of Proxima—with improvements. We have monitored Proxima's voyage through our solar system and have been impressed with the adaptability and innovations of the crew; though we think that your astrophysicist friend may have been responsible for much of what has happened."

"He is not my friend…"

"Then you will have no compunction about preventing his success—even if it means another death?"

"But it took over fourteen years to build Proxima; you couldn't have built a copy in a few days!"

"No, of course not. We started at the same time, with the same points of view as the Americans. In fact, we were ready to launch over a year ago but decided to wait and observe the pitfalls…and successes of your prototype. With data that you have fed us plus, of course, our own means of codebreaking and signal interception, we have improved our model significantly."

"You mean there are other conspirators in the NASA team?"

"Oh, yes, but not just NASA—higher up in the realms of government and military. We have not been idle. So decision time…I cannot hold this flight up indefinitely."

"Will I have time with my wife and son…to say goodbye and have some final moments together?"

"Oh, yes, of course…we are not a cruel people."

"I don't see that I have any choice then…"

"An excellent decision! And, I believe, we have a first-class seat awaiting you."

Without addressing the ticket agent, Kim took Karl Guttenberg by the arm and led him down the corridor to board U 6881 to Beijing.

Chapter 33

I let Nostradamus sleep before we were to work together. He had been through much and I was bitterly disappointed. I thought that once able to use and function with a mortal brain, I would remember everything: about who I was, my life, my purpose, but this was not how I had hoped it would be. I impatiently waited for Michel to finish sleeping; I desperately needed to know as much as I could about myself and, hopefully, revive some of the dormant memories of my past.

I wanted also, frenetically, to be with the girl of my dreams and as the thought entered my head, I was there. It was dawn and my sweet teenager lay blissfully asleep. Her hand hung out of the bed and I saw the small wound on her finger that she had used to make the blood-bond. I knelt and kissed it. As before, when I had tried to embrace this young enchantress, her lips turned upwards into a warm, loving smile. *How much longer until we can totally and properly embrace*, I thought. *Once my mission has been completed*, I decided, *I will endeavour every way I can to physically hold you.*

"My beloved, I pray with all the strength that I have that we will be in the same dimension—to hold, love, laugh and be together for eternity."

A tender hand pushed towards my arm and stroked it gently. Sleepily, she opened her eyes.

"One day, my love…"

"Mai…"

"Michael, when I am in the land of dreams and you talk to me, I am sure I can feel you, really, physically feel you."

"Mai?"

"You hesitate…what is it?"

"Mai, I…would you…?"

"Lay with you?"

"Yes, oh, yes, if only one day that could be possible."

"I have thought much about it since you first mentioned it. I said that it was forbidden until we can be married. I know that will always remain impossible but I yearn for you so much that if it were possible, then yes, I would lay with you. I would want nothing more than to lay with you."

"Oh, my love…my sweet, sweet love…"

Downstairs, I could hear the sound of Mai's mother working in the kitchen: the scraping of buckets and the thud of washing being scrubbed. Mai arose, stood before me and allowed her nightclothes to fall around her ankles, as she had done before. With an excitement pounding inside of me, I walked over to her perfect body and, stroking her hair, her shoulders and then her arms, put my arms around her. She raised her head and with her eyes closed, inhaled sharply.

"Yes, my love, I will lay with you…"

"Mai, you need to help your mother."

"Yes, I will prepare Father's breakfast, then work with her."

Mai dressed and I followed her downstairs. Her mother had completed one set of laundry that was already hanging on some twine hung between the two longer walls. As she walked into the kitchen, Mai's mother saw the two of us.

"Good morning, Mother."

"Good morning Mai. Good morning, Michael."

"Good morning…"

"Wan. My name is Wan."

"Good morning, Wan. When Mai has finished her work with you, can she come with me to the house of Michel Nostredame, please?"

"Is it for another task?"

"No, her tasks have been completed. I have to hear Michel Nostredame relate my experiences last night and it may be interesting for Mai. Besides, even if there was no other purpose, I would wish to be with her…just to be with her."

"Michael, you do realise this…love…this love can never be, don't you?"

"As long as I have a consciousness, I will use every fibre of my being to find a way to be with your daughter; that is how strong my love is for her."

"I feel it will end in sorrow for both of you, but yes, Mai can accompany you to his house—don't be late!"

"Thank you, Wan, we will not be late, I promise!"

I spent the day watching Mai work with her mother and tried to keep my thoughts only on her, for I knew if I thought about anything else, I would be there. I wondered, as I watched them working together, just what I had told Nostradamus during the séance and whether he would be open to my suggestion. It was too late…I was in his study, where I saw him browsing through some books.

"Michel?"

"Ah, you have returned."

"You are sensitive to me again?"

"Yes, yes. Last night was an experience that I do not wish to pursue again, though."

"Me, neither!"

"You have come to work through what you told me last night, then?"

"Not yet, no. I wish to bring Mai with me if that is alright with you?"

"Yes, yes, that will be fine. So, what have you come to me for?"

"Well, two things. First to ask if I could bring Mai, so that has been sorted. But the second is of a very delicate, sensitive nature…"

Michel Nostredame closed his book and stared at me for what seemed like perpetuity. He arose, walked over to the fire and taking a splint, let the flames ignite it and lit his pipe, which had been resting on the mantelpiece above.

"Michael, I think that I know what you are going to ask and it is impossible, absolutely impossible."

"Have you tried it before?"

"No, never. But I know that I am not that person; I cannot."

"Michel, we have been through more together in the past few days than you probably have been with anyone before; perhaps even Anne?"

"That is for sure! Yes, we are almost like two soldier comrades together—"

"—Bound by a bond…"

"A blood-bond!"

"No, I was thinking more of a brotherly bond…the bond of comradeship."

"Yes, now I think about it; why yes, like two brothers!"

"Then, would you permit me to try?"

"I…I am not sure. I am afraid and I do not think that I have the skill."

"Perhaps you could consult with your spirit guides—they would not permit any hurt to come to you. They could advise you whether they have the power to help you achieve what you had never dreamed possible. Besides, you trust in all of us, in me…and in them to keep you from harm."

"I…I do not know. Let me ponder on it for a while."

"Ponder what?"

"Ah, Anne, my dear—I did not hear you descend."

"No, I think you were too engrossed in conversation with Michael."

"Hello, Anne."

"Hello, Michael. What does my husband need to ponder about this time?"

"Well, my dear…"

"'Well, my dear' usually implies that you need to be tactful about something or that I may scold you…yes?"

"Anne, may I explain? Michel has nothing to do with my request—"

"—Apart from the fact that you are requesting something from him, that is!"

"Yes, I am requesting something from Michel…"

"Which is?"

"That I permit him to use my body…to be possessed."

"Possessed! Correct me if I am wrong but haven't you used the necromancer for 'possession'? Do you need further information?"

"No Anne…I need love."

"Love! What are you talking about! You need to love Michel?"

"No…I wish to…long to—"

"—He wishes to use me to love Mai."

"WHAT!"

"Anne, would you be without Michel's love?"

"Why, no!"

"Can you imagine what it would be like to be without his love, not to embrace, not to talk and feel the comfort of each other?"

"Well, no, that is not something that I would care to consider or imagine."

"When you were first lovers, would you have sold your very soul if you could not be together?"

"That was a lifetime ago…"

"But do you not remember that passion, that desire, that love? Have you forgotten so quickly those moments of tenderness when the world was yours just because you were together and no one else existed…just you two?"

"Mai?"

"Yes, Mai."

"But you are from another dimension—Mai is mortal."

"And that is why I am asking Michel if I can use his body for just one night."

"My husband…with another woman!"

"Anne, it will be Michel's body…but it won't be Michel; it will be me."

"And you have agreed, Michel?"

"I merely said that I would—"

"—'Ponder'! That's where I came in!"

"Hmm, precisely."

"Michael, I know how much this means to you, I really do. Believe me, I remember, even now, how much I loved Anne and how I would have moved heaven and earth to hold her, caress her, love her—"

"—You do! You really remember!"

"How could I forget? That passion of young love, when the world could be yours or taken from you in an instant! When all that your body and heart desired was but just a breath away, but you dared not take it for fear of losing the one you loved or because this was a forbidden love."

"Yes! Yes, I remember too. I remember when all I wanted was to be with you, talk with you, lay with you. Oh, I understand too well those moments of true and tender love, and love like that comes but once in a lifetime; in an instant, it is there and then it is…gone…gone."

I saw such sorrow in Anne's eyes and I was not mistaken when I saw the moistness of that sorrow revealed.

"I…I am sorry, Anne…I did not mean to put you through such anguish. Please forgive me for being so selfish."

"Hush, Michael! You have brought back to me those precious moments that have forged my love for this man before me. And if you agree and will try, Michel, how can we deny this poor soul that moment of love, forbidden or not."

"Anne! I…I don't know what to say…thank you…thank you from the bottom of my—"

"—You don't have one, Michael, but I can see that the emotion you feel does not need a heart; you feel with your very soul."

"Michel?"

"We will try but I can promise nothing. I will consult my orb and ask my spirit guides, but please, don't hold out hope…I feel that it cannot to be…"

Elated, I was back with Mai in an instant. She was upstairs hanging linen on the line that hung between her house and the house opposite. Her father had attached a pulley and Mai could pull dried washing in and let fresh washing out. I tried to throw my arms around her but they held nothing. Mai shivered.

"Is that you, Michael, or was there a breeze?"

"It is me, Mai!"

"You have been gone such a short while, yet it feels like a lifetime ago!"

"Mai, I have something to ask of you."

"Speak, my beautiful spirit."

"Tonight, I will work with Michel to unravel the mysteries of the future and my part in it."

"That is wonderful. That is what you asked permission from Mother for…so that I can be there."

"Of course. But there is another reason why I have returned so quickly…"

"When my day's work is done, we shall walk together. It means so much to me that Mother sees you differently now and has agreed."

"There is something else, Mai…something I am not so sure that she will agree to…"

"Michael? What would she not agree to?"

"Mai, would you lay with me, as you said that you would, really lay with me?"

"With all my heart, YES! Oh, I see…yes, you are right. She would not agree to that but we know that never can be—"

"—But there is a slight possibility that it could be—"

"—TRULY! But how? I can almost feel you when our lips meet and when our hands entwine, I feel a shiver, a sensation, a feeling of warmth and undying love. But how can we truly touch and embrace as mortals?"

"With possession, Mai."

"Possession! But possession by whom? No, no, no, not the necromancer…never, never!"

"No, not the necromancer; we will never indulge with that evil son of sin again. With Michel."

"Michel Nostredame! But he is an old man!"

"He will be the body, but I will be the person, the spirit within that vessel."

"Michael… Michael, I had never considered, never thought that for a moment it would be with anyone but you."

"But it will be, Mai. You and I together for one unforgettable, one magical, wonderful night…"

"Oh Michael!"

Mai fell on the floor and started to cry uncontrollably. I had never seen her so upset and it was breaking my very soul. As much as I tried to comfort her, she was inconsolable. I heard the stairs take the weight of someone ascending and I knew it would be Wan.

"Mai! Whatever is the matter, child?"

"Oh Mother! My heart is breaking! My one true love and we can never be."

"Mai, my darling daughter, it leaves me wretched to see you so. As much as I admire that spirit who has stolen your heart, this love cannot happen. You have given to an emotion of unselfish and pure love, that I know; but he is from another place, another time. It is almost a forbidden love—it can never be."

Mai's mother had not seen me; was it perhaps because I was so distraught that she could not see my being before her? When Mai had seen me angry, she said that my countenance had changed; perhaps this was also the case now? At this moment, I did not want her to see me. I was distraught beyond words and my presence, had it been known, would have been a humiliation.

"Mother, how can love hurt so?"

"My darling, most people do not get to love as you do. The more you love, the more it hurts. That is the nature of love. For love is caring, caring deeply and sincerely and when that love is threatened, the pain is almost unendurable. So many have given their lives for love, but you must be strong. The only thing that is perhaps stronger than love is an emotion we don't have at all..."

"What is that?"

"Time."

"Time?"

"Time overcomes love, eventually, but you must give *time*, time."

"Time really overcomes love?"

"No, no, that is wrong. Time overcomes hurt...no, nothing overcomes love."

Mai rested her head in her mother's lap as she stroked Mai's raven-black hair. I watched the two of them, almost like sisters. But here, before me, was another love-bond and this was also a bond that was unbreakable. The love a parent has for its child...and the child for its parent was perhaps a truer love than the demanding love of a man for a woman. This love was totally selfless and undemanding; it did not say, 'love me if I love you', it simply said, 'I love you'—no conditions. I felt humble. I had placed upon Mai my selfish love. No different perhaps to the world's lovers, but that was not an excuse—it was a selfish love. How could I rid myself of all these thoughts and emotions that were tormenting the two of us?

"Mother?"

"Yes, my darling?"

"If I had a chance to lay with Michael, would that be so wrong?"

"Mai! I had not expected such a question! Why do you ask; how could you possibly lay with Michael?"

"He has asked Nostradamus if he would be allowed to possess him."

"WHAT! But that...that is obscene...you with an old man."

219

"Mother, Michel Nostredame is an old man who wears an old man's body, but if Michael possesses him, it would be a younger man in an old man's body—you must see beyond the physical."

"Even young women marry old men, I suppose, but without marriage?"

"Mother, have you never ached so much for something that is just beyond reach, but just fleetingly it is within your grasp? By stretching out your hand, you can grab it and hold it. Would you bypass that moment? Would you let your heart's desires go, just on an ethic? Or would you hold on, as if your very life depended upon it? Would you hold it to your bosom and swear to die before letting your grasp loosen that which you had yearned for, for so long?"

It was Mai's mother's turn to sob.

"When we were taken as slaves, I was young and loved your father with the same passion that you feel now. I thought that my world had ended. I did not believe that I would see your father again…ever. I prayed to the spirits and swore an oath that if they would permit us to be together, I would honour the memory of them. They answered my prayer and I honour them every day; even when I attend Mass, I think and serve only them. The candles, spices and flower petals that your father lays out every day—that is the ceremony to them. It was at that time, when our lives were uncertain, when I believed that I would never again be free to lay with your father, that I realised nothing was more important than love. Before, I had simply accepted it, but then I became aware of it; I was conscious of it. And you, my little angel, you were part of that love as well. How can I deny you that moment? How can I deny that, knowing what I had to endure myself?"

"Mother?"

"Even for an ephemeral instant, Mai, you must grasp that moment…for it will pass you by to a lifetime of regret."

"I have your approval?"

"You have my blessing. My dearest, darling daughter."

"Oh, Mother!"

What emotion was greater than what I saw before me, as both women hugged and wept. Here, before me, was the truest love that I had ever witnessed and it made me realise how insignificant my passions were compared to this undemanding, selfless and committed bond—this *was* true love.

Chapter 34

In a state of euphoria, we soared through the heavens. Looking behind, though moments ago we had faced that colossal planet, there was nothing but specks. Specks that were giant planets of almost unimaginable size. The whole cabin was a hive of activity as each member of the crew performed the duties that they had been trained for.

"Well, we have one more final manoeuvre before we can wake up our 'guests'."

"Oh? There are no more planets, Jamie, and as I said, the Keiper belt will not be a hazard for us."

"Do you remember that I said there will be a little *surprise*, Michael?"

I saw the gleam in his eyes; it was a wicked, mischievous gleam and a grin to match. The others knew what was about to happen but were equally awaiting the effect.

"OK, Jamie, yes I remember. What is it, then? What is it that you are so desperate to show me?"

He turned his head to the others, with a grin stretching almost from ear to ear.

"Ready?"

"Ready."

It was a universal reply, all speaking at the same time.

"OK… Strap in."

Jamie leaned forward and stretching his hand to a control just beyond his screen, gave a lever a gentle push. There was a whirr, then a rumbling sound as the gyratory system kicked into action. Though I felt nothing at first, slowly, I became aware of a force acting on my body. It was a force that I had been familiar with on Earth, a satisfying, comforting feeling, but it was also a force that I had experienced in space, the memories of which were far less pleasurable.

"Recognise the effect, Michael?"

"Gravity? Gravity! You have gravity!"

"Hey, he's smart; he'll go far, this kid!"

"How did you do this?"

"Me, personally, I have to be honest with you, Michael…I didn't. Well, not initially. It was considered by some of the gurus back at base. After that, it developed into what we have now, which took close to eighteen months to complete."

"So, what's the secret?"

"We are in a giant centrifuge. Proxima is rotating and causing us to be centrifuged against the surface of whatever we are in contact with. Look ahead."

I looked in front and there, before us, was the cosmos, slowly turning right before our eyes. I stared, mesmerised.

"Wow! I never even considered for a moment that we would have such luxury. Mind you, I never gave the design any thought anyway; I was just going to turn up and off we would go! This is fantastic!"

"Now, what is really weird with this one—and I absolutely love it—well, you can walk on the ceiling!"

"No way!"

"Yes way! Just like a fly!"

"Wow!"

"Makes sense, you know. On Earth, we are on top of a giant centrifuge; here, we are inside one. So, wherever you are in Proxima, the gravitational pull...sorry, the centrifugal push is the same."

"Except, Jamie..."

"Except?"

"Well, if you are almost in the middle of the room and the pull is equal from both sides...so—and I'm thinking out loud here—so...your head receives less pull than your feet or if your feet were in the middle of the room, then your head would receive more pull!"

"Yes, that is true but these rooms are so large, you won't experience that, unless you needed to do some maintenance work in the middle of the room. Then I guess you could be standing on your head!"

The crew burst out laughing as Jamie said this and I, with a mixture of elation and relief, joined in the fun.

"Shouldn't we say it is, in fact, the centrifugal force, not gravity?"

"Oh, you damn Brits, you always have to be so exact, just like your Saxon descendants and spoil the fun! Alright, Michael, yes, the centrifugal force...but do you mind if the rest of us call it gravity!"

The cabin was in uproar as the banter flew from one to the other. It was as though we were back in school again. At times like this, it was difficult to accept that this was a serious mission with far-reaching consequences. Here we were like schoolchildren, simply larking about and having fun.

Jamie studied his screen and with his hand on the 'centrifugal' switch, pushed up slightly as the dial registered 0.5G.

"We need to bring this up to 1G, but it needs to be done in stages—a bit like divers underwater coming slowly to the surface. The organs don't take kindly to too much sudden exertion."

"Hey! I must try this! Walking in an artificial gravitational field!"

"Forgive me if I'm wrong, but didn't you just call it 'gravitational', young Anglo-Saxon! Take it slowly though, Michael. Just like when we were in that training pool, slow and easy. It will feel very strange even though it's been only a few days. Let the muscles adjust gradually."

I pushed myself up and for the first time in space, I was actually balancing under the force of gravity, albeit far less than back home.

"God, this is good! But then, so was floating around; that was good, too. Do you know, I whizzed down those corridors…must have been doing twelve miles per hour!"

"Thirteen, Michael, you were doing thirteen."

"How do you know that?"

"Every part of this ship has a sensor. We watched you disappear along the ship; we even took bets on what speed you could achieve. Anna won; she got it on the nail."

"And what about you, Jamie, what did you go for?"

"I said sixteen, but then I forgot, you're not as fast as me!"

"Cheeky!"

As I moved, I felt my legs start to wobble; my muscles needed time to customise themselves again to the force of gravity. My sense of balance, which for all my life had been certain and secure, was for once unsure. I pushed my right leg forward and my left crumpled under me and I toppled over falling onto Jamie. With his hand still outstretched, he pushed the centrifugal lever forward as I knocked him onto the floor.

"Sorry, Jamie; I lost my balance—I'll be better in a few moments."

Both Jamie and I lay on the floor laughing, but then I saw a hint of panic in his eyes. It took a few seconds but then Anna realised too. She tried to get up from her seat immediately but was strapped in! Desperately pulling at the securing straps, the buckle at last undid, but it was too late. She was forced back into her seat. I was on top of Jamie and Anna was locked firmly in her seat as were the others. I looked up but could only just turn my head. Petra's pretty face was a hideous distortion as Proxima rotated faster and faster. We were locked in a giant centrifuge and powerless to move. I could just see the screen…7.7…7.8…7.9…8.0G! At this force, not only were we unable to move, but our internal organs were under the most extreme pressure and could even rupture.

I tried to come to terms with what had just happened. We had survived the most cataclysmic events possible, beyond imagination. We had survived because of man's ingenuity, skill and, I suppose, to a certain degree of luck—albeit created by natural forces. But here, due to a simple accident, we were now in a situation from which there was no escape. We were powerless to save ourselves. *How paradoxical*, I thought; thinking was all any of us could do now. If Proxima continued to increase her centrifugal force, we would have about one minute at 10G, before the pressure would stop the flow of oxygen to the brain and we would simply die! Crushed! And I was also on top of Jamie—his body surely wouldn't survive. I tried to rotate and managed to slowly roll my frame from his chest. Now I could not see the screen and had no idea what G-forces were acting on us, but it made no difference whether we were to be crushed to death as Proxima increased her grip on us or whether we simply waited to die as we were—the outcome was going to be the same—we were condemned! I gave up any thoughts now of survival. This was it, and the fifteen hundred people asleep below would die with us. At least theirs would be an unconscious death, dying in their sleep—the lucky ones!

Proxima hurtled towards her destination, spinning ever faster. In less than four years, she would deliver her cargo of human corpses, which would probably be unrecognisable to any other civilisation that came across her. Immediately in front of her was a signal—a transmission from Earth, despatched a few days ago to ensure that the history of Man remained unaltered. A signal to override electronic commands and send a capsule speeding to oblivion. A signal that bypassed Proxima during her enslavement with Saturn and Proxima was catching up with this transmission…fast.

All went dark; it was pitch-black everywhere. I was dead! But the pain endured. This wasn't how death was supposed to be, was it? Surely, when you died, all pain desisted, didn't it? But I was still conscious, in pain, under pressure, but conscious! The complete ship was as silent as the grave—no bleeps, no lights, no sound. I listened intently; I could hear breathing—rasped but audible. So, the others were also still alive? All of them? Though I had tried already, I attempted to move my head and look upwards. Surprisingly, with difficulty, I found that I could! The pain had started slowly to abate. I heard Jamie groan. I found that I had a voice.

"Aaaannnaaa…?"

"Y… Yesssss…?"

"You…are…alive?"

"J… Just…"

"C…can…you…move?"

"N… Not…yet, but…the…pressure…is…less."

"What…has happened?"

"Something has…isolated all the…electronic communications!"

"Can you move?"

"I…think so. It is getting…easier; the pain on my chest…is less."

"Jamie?"

"Is Jamie…alright?"

"I can hear him…breathing…but he is…unconscious."

"Petra?"

"Recovering, Anna. What…was that?"

"Michael fell on… Jamie and he pushed the…centrifuge to maximum."

"Yes…I saw that…but why aren't we…dead?"

"I have no idea. But something…has cut out all the electronic…commands. The centrifuge engines have been switched off."

"But how?"

"I have no idea! Oh, I can move!"

"Me too!"

"Michael?"

"Yes, I think I can get up now. But I can't see my hand in front of my face."

"Simon… Charlie?"

224

"OK, Anna. Like you, we are recovering; but God, that was torturous—I've never known such pain."

"Anna?"

"Yes, Michael?"

"Anna, I can't feel the floor…I can't feel anything!"

"Michael! You are floating; we have lost all centrifugal force! Everyone, strap in!"

"Right, we need to get our bearings. Everyone, hum softly. That's good. Now we can picture where we are from the sounds. Picture the cabin everyone, as you hum. Nobody move yet. We need a light. Can anyone remember where the flashlights were?"

"Simon!"

"No, Simon won't know, Petra, he hasn't been involved with storage."

"No, Anna; Simon was wearing a headtorch when he went to investigate the reactor!"

"Simon?"

"Hey! That's right! Now where did I put it? Charlie, search around with your hands; it has to be here somewhere."

Despite shuffling and scraping, no headtorch could be located.

"Simon?"

"Yes, Michael? Michael? Michael…where are you?"

"No idea, Simon. I can hear your voice below me, but that's all. Simon, I don't remember you taking the torch off. Is it still banded around your head?"

"Of course! Yes! Hang on, the switch is just here!"

Though small, it was not insignificant. Those few photons of light were now our lifesaver. In the gloom and shadows, we could at last make out a small trace of the control room. I had nothing to pull on and remained suspended in the air, but I saw Anna, Petra and the others get their bearings.

"OK, everyone, whilst Jamie is unconscious, I am assuming command of Proxima. We all need to wear headtorches, which are located… Charlie?"

"In the strong-box with the other emergency gear. There! Simon, turn your head over to your left…a bit more…stop! There!"

"Keys for the strong-box?"

"Not needed, only sensitive issues were kept secured."

"I'll fetch."

"Thanks, Simon. Give one to all of us. Right, we now need emergency lighting and backup. Charlie, you and Simon go to the reactor room. Switch on emergency power. Batteries were fully charged and should give us twenty-five hours service, by which time we should be up and running."

"Anna, should we try and lift Jamie into his seat?"

"That was next on my list, Petra. Shouldn't be difficult with no gravity, his mass should be weightless. Just gently lift his shoulders with me and place him in his seat…good. Petra, please strap him in and check if he's OK."

Jamie remained unconscious as I hovered above. I tried to flail my arms and legs, but I had no surface to work off and remained hopelessly suspended in the middle of the room. I could just make out Jamie with Petra examining him below. It was difficult to make out with the cabin mainly in the dark, but there appeared to be a spattering of blood on his chest. I hoped that it was just a shadow. Suddenly, the entire cabin became alive as the emergency lighting was restored. A few minutes later, Charlie and Simon returned. Jamie's head was turned to one side, but I could see that his chest rose and fell as he breathed. It was Charlie's idea how to get me down—simple and effective.

"Michael, keep still and hold your arms by your sides. I shall leap up and push you towards the ceiling. Once you have the momentum, use your legs to push yourself down here, but don't overdo the push!"

"I think I've learned my lesson with that one, Charlie."

With barely a leap, Charlie came towards me and pushed me firmly towards the ceiling. The force caused Charlie to fall back to the ground, whilst I continued upwards. As the ceiling approached, I put my left leg forward, gave a gentle push and descended. I managed to grab hold of my seat and immediately pulled over to Jamie. He looked groggy, but unhurt. The 'blood' proved to have been a shadow after all.

"Jamie? Petra?"

"I think Jamie's alright. He was obviously crushed under your weight as well as his own. Even in the centrifuge tests back at NASA, Jamie usually flaked out before the rest of us, but he has the constitution of an ox. I am confident he will recover."

We now all waited for Anna's commands. Compared to Jamie, Anna was equally as efficient but she lacked Jamie's charismatic manner, his humour and his laid-back way of working. In fact, sometimes I felt that if he became any more laidback, he would fall over.

"Right! We need to first recover all electronic communications and devices, that is the number one priority. Second, we need to discover what the hell changed the course of our fate! Third, we need to ensure that the G-force on the centrifuge cannot repeat the disaster of the past few minutes—we really are lucky to all be alive!"

"What do you want me to do, Anna?"

"Petra, I shall remain here keeping control of Proxima. I want you to take over my role and recover all electronics and devices. Simon, I want you reset the principle circuitry and check—and if necessary—restart the reactor and then scout and verify that everything that could have been affected is in order. Charlie, would you keep an eye on Petra's area; let me know if and when communication returns."

The cabin was alive again and Jamie started to regain consciousness. With a sudden increase in the brightness, all the lighting returned to normal and we knew that Simon had recovered and reset the principle circuitry attached to the reactor. Warmth returned, even though with the tension of the previous hour, the onset of the cold had remained unnoticed.

"Anna, the Main is rebooting. I…I can't make out whether there has been any permanent damage yet…but everything appears to be in order. About fifteen minutes for complete restoral. What caused all the electronics to cut out…that's what I want to know! But even more…how come we could recover Proxima? We should still be revolving forever!"

"What the hell…? What happened…?"

"Oh, thank God, Jamie!"

"Oh…my shoulder…and chest…"

"Sorry, my friend. I think you may have taken a blow when I knocked you over. I'm so, so sorry. I think you may have passed out before I rolled off you."

"Proxima…?"

"Waiting for reboot to take effect, Jamie. We are still flying, but we will know in…eleven minutes."

"How did we recover from the centrifuge?"

"That, Jamie, is the sixty-four million dollar question that we are all asking. All I can say is that whatever it was, thank God. By rights, we should all be dead!"

"Anna, you need to take command…"

"A bit late, Commander! She already has!"

Jamie appeared to be recovering from his ordeal slowly. His breathing was a bit grated, but otherwise, he seemed to be in reasonable spirits. I was impressed by the no-fuss manner in which Anna had taken command and everything had simply flowed without fuss or confusion. But then I suppose this scenario must have been rehearsed many times before in case of such an eventuality.

"Anna, activity in front; screen coming online."

"Me, too…"

Bleeps were again being heard around the cabin and together with flashing lights, this suggested that everything was becoming normal again.

"Charlie, have you got a plotted course on the monitor?"

"Just coming on now, but I think Petra will be better to assess what this data means."

"Petra?"

"Your data bank is loading now, Anna. When complete, shall I put Proxima onto 'Auto'?"

"Yes, then we can all resume our normal roles. But before we centrifuge again, can you set the centrifuge control to 3G max?"

"You've been reading my very thoughts, Anna."

"As all electronics and communications were cut, I guess we'll never know what stopped Proxima rotating?"

"It's a shot in the dark but maybe Mother Nature has given us another helping hand?"

"You have an idea then?"

"It's weak, I know…but in deep space, there are nebulae, gases, dust…all kinds of debris, and it may have just so happened that we passed through a film of this…even Dark Matter. And because of the speed we are travelling at, we passed through the entire volume of this material and the friction we encountered slowed down the rotation just enough…well, exactly in fact, to stop Proxima turning. After all, all communications and commands had been cut so the centrifuge engines stopped? Just a suggestion… Either that, or the Almighty lent a hand."

"And a plausible one, too."

"What, the debris and Dark Matter?"

"No…the Almighty!"

The banter was back; Jamie had recovered!

Chapter 35

I left Mai's house in despair and meandered, lost in my thoughts and the hopelessness of what was before me. If there was hell or purgatory, where you were held in limbo as the very fabric of your being was torn to shreds and all you could do was look on helpless, then this was surely it. How could Mai and I be in the same dimension? I would need to be reborn as a mortal or permanently possess another being! Neither choice was an option. But with the light beginning to fade, I made my way sadly back to Mai. There, before me, was my beloved! She saw me and almost ran towards me.

"Michael! Oh, my darling…I have such good news."

"Mai, I know what you are going to say… I was there…"

"But did you know, Michael, did you really know how you have made Mother and me realise how precious this time is that we have together. Tomorrow, you may be gone forever! Tomorrow, I may be gone forever; but what we really have and what cannot be taken from us, what we really have is now!"

"Mai—"

"Shush, you beautiful spirit; that I may gaze upon you, again."

I held out my arms and Mai rested within my grasp. I could feel her heart beating, like a call to war. As we stood there, Wan walked in and smiled warmly at me; this time, I guessed, my spirit was visible to her mind.

"Michael, I know what has been arranged. You have my approval; Mai has my blessing. Take care of her and protect her with all the love that you have."

I let Mai go and walked over to this wonderful woman who had given so much. I stretched out my arms to her and she walked towards me and, as though she could feel me, let her head fall into my embrace.

"Thank you, Wan, thank you so much, from all my being, thank you."

"Go, the pair of you…go! Enough tears shed for one day—go!"

I smiled at her and noticed that perhaps there were still a few more tears to fall as her lips trembled and she raised her apron to her eyes.

"Goodbye, Wan, may your God be with you and bless you."

Mai and I set off to Nostradamus' house. A few minutes ago, I had been in misery and now I felt as though all the cares of the world had been lifted from my shoulders, if I'd had any, that is. We arrived at Michel's house and Agnès let Mai in. With a curtsy before this young teenager, who was not much younger than herself, she showed her into the drawing room immediately on the right. The room had not been altered and Mai sat down on one of the sofas. Like me, she seemed to be fascinated by the picture hanging on the wall, though the demon eyes in the background appeared to be fainter than I remembered them to have been. Anne walked in. Mai stood up, smiled and curtsied politely. I decided to see Michel.

"Mai, there is no need for that…I am not Queen Catherine."

"Sorry, madame."

"It's 'Anne', please, Mai."

"Yes, madame… Anne."

"Mai, before you and… Michael, are you here?"

"I think he has gone to the library to see your husband… Anne."

"So much the better. Mai, I want to talk to you before we go downstairs, that's why I asked Agnès to show you in here."

Mai could not look up at Anne and kept her eyes fixed to the floor. Her gentle hands fidgeted nervously before her. She had a secret, a terrible secret, and this charming woman before her was unaware of the unfaithful act she was about to perform in this very house.

"Mai, I am aware and I totally endorse the union that will take place tonight, in this house and in our bed."

Mai looked up.

"W… What! You know?"

"I do. I know. Though it will be my husband's body that you will use, it will not be him that you will be laying with."

"B… But how did you know?"

"Well, Michael was here earlier today and asked my husband. I was privy to that conversation and I admit, I do not feel totally comfortable with what will happen, but I understand; and it is because of that understanding, I have accepted and will not stand in your way."

"Oh, madame… Anne! What can I say? Oh, bless you…thank you."

"However, be prepared to be disappointed; my husband has already told Michael that he holds out very little hope for the possession to be successful. He has never done this before and feels that he does not have the 'gift'. Of course, you do realise that you can only lay with my husband's body—not with my husband?"

"Madame… Anne, I do not want to lie with anyone else but Michael…your husband included; no offence meant."

"And none taken. You are so pretty, Mai, it is no wonder that Michael has fallen for you."

Anne stood up and beckoned to Mai to stand. As she did, she held her in a tender embrace as Mai slipped her arms around Anne's waist.

"Let us go and see what the future holds, eh?"

In the library, Nostradamus and Michael had already started to study the predictions given during the possession. Anne and Mai walked in as the third date was underway.

...1903...
Man will take to the sky and fly.

"Yes! I remember. Two Americans…"

"Americans?"

"Yes, this is the New World that Christopher Columbus discovered in—"

"1492."

"Why yes, that's right…I think? Well, they built a machine that had wings."

"Like a bird?"

"Yes, just like a bird; but they didn't flap; they remained stationary."

"How did the machine move, then?"

"The wings were attached to an engine…a machine that propelled the plane forward and then, by adjusting the angle of the wings and propeller, the plane could fly just like a bird."

"Can you recall the names of these 'Americans'?"

"They were brothers… Right… Dwight…Wright! Orville and Wilbur Wright."

"So, I need to write a quatrain about this?"

"Actually, Michel, I was thinking that perhaps each prediction should be sealed and held somewhere secure. Then, during the year before that prediction, the prophecy should be opened and revealed?"

"Why?"

"Because this way, there can be no vagaries, no ambiguities, and because the prophecies will be found to be exact, then the people—the masses—will take heed and act. But at least they can make their choices based on presented facts, especially if written four to five hundred years before the events!"

"Good point. I have sometimes wondered whether what I have 'seen' has been simply inspirational or really as my spirit guides have shown me. The pressure to write another quatrain for another inquisitive noble does make me question whether I really can see the future or whether I am just good at holding people's attention with fantastic vagaries. Has this helped you discover who you are?"

"I think so, a bit. Let us continue and see if further memories can be recalled."

...1912...
The greatest boat that Man has built will sink.

"You called this boat 'Titanic'."

"The Titanic was the largest boat built up until this time. It sailed from Southampton—"

"—Southampton?"

"In England, sometime in April, to the New World—America. She hit an iceberg and sank."

...1924...
Josef Stalin becomes leader of Russia.

"Now you said that this, Josef Stalin, was a tyrant?"
"Yes, he murdered thousands of his own people."
"Why?"
"Because he wanted power and had some ideological belief that what he did was for the good of the people—except for the ones he murdered, of course."
"But this just applies to the people of Russia?"
"Well, yes and no... At the time, it only affected his own people but the consequences of his actions and the development of his cruel regime had a global effect upon humanity. An artful politician with a ruthless attitude, he occupied and controlled vast areas of Eastern Europe, imposing his will on the populations of those lands that he occupied. He is a tyrant who must be stopped."

...1933...
Adolf Hitler becomes chancellor of Germany.

"You said that this man was also a tyrant."
"Oh, yes, probably the worst of them all; not so much because he was any more evil than the rest, but the consequences of his position in power had the greatest effect on the entire world for countless generations."
"Why was he so bad compared to Josef Stalin?"
"Well, he wasn't just an ideologist, he was also anti-Semitic—"
"—Anti-Semitic?"
"He was a racist—he hated Jews and held them entirely responsible for the defeat of Germany in a previous war in which he had fought. He believed that only pure-blooded Germans, who he referred to as the 'Aryan race', should rule and wished this race to dominate the world. He regarded the Jewish people as sub-human and murdered over six million of them. His ideology and his belief in his divine appointment resulted in a war that engulfed the entire world."
"Six million! Why, that's more than the population of Paris, Avignon and Aix combined!"

...1940...
The greatest war that man has witnessed is underway.

"Is this the war that you mentioned above?"
"It is."

...1945...

The greatest war that man has seen ends. The people of China have a new leader—Zedong Mao. In Korea, Kim Il-sung seeks power and wins the support of Russia. Armageddon strikes the people of Japan.

"Then this war comes to an end."

"It does."

"And this Adolf Hitler... He won?"

"No, he lost and committed suicide."

"So, if he was beaten, surely he becomes unimportant?"

"No, on the contrary, it was the outcome of this war that effected so many global changes. Without this war, other tyrants may never have come to power the world would have been different and I may not have been here!"

"Zedong Mao...?"

"He was also known as Mao Tse-tung. He became a tyrannical leader of the Chinese people and his ideology matched that of Josef Stalin. In 1949, he created a secretive country that had global consequences."

"This leader of Korea...?"

"Kim Il-sung..."

"Why is he so important?"

"He began a dynasty that led to his grandson, Kim Jong-un, becoming leader of a brutal and tyrannical regime. It was this regime that began the road to the annihilation of mankind."

"Shouldn't we mention his name, *Kim Jong-un*, then?"

"It didn't occur in the possession?"

"No, we stopped at 1963."

"Then I have remembered more than just what I had been asked! My memory is returning!"

"Then, who are you, Michael?"

Mai held her breath expectantly. Who was this man who she had fallen so completely in love with?

"I'm...I...flew up in a spaceship..."

"Spaceship! What, a boat?"

"No...a spaceship is a rocket that flies into the sky above the Earth into space."

"What space? Do you mean up into the sky?"

"Further. You see, this planet Earth is one of thousands, perhaps millions, of other planets—homes to countless other civilisations..."

"No, I do not understand! This world of ours, it is God's footstool. It is He who is in the sky above, in His Heaven. It is to this place we shall go if, and when, He deems it fit. Why, He sends the sun around in the morning and the moon around at night. He gives us the stars to twinkle and shine—some say that these are his angels looking down upon us."

"Michel, you may find this very hard to believe and accept but the Earth is not at the centre of this Universe. The sun doesn't rise nor the moon. It is us on our planet Earth that travel as it turns around. Why, Earth is a huge ball—it is not flat."

"Impossible! How can we not fall off if the Earth is a ball?"

"Imagine a small ball and hold it up to your eye; you can see that it is round. Now imagine a ball as big as this room; climb to the top, lay down and look ahead. You know it is still a ball but you can start to see a horizon—the top of the ball is taking on the appearance of being flat. As the ball becomes bigger and bigger, the appearance of flatness becomes more predominant until, finally, you can't imagine anything else, as you are witness to now."

"But how do we hold on—why do the seas not fall off at the bottom?"

"There is an unseen force called gravity. It holds everything in place: you, me, the oceans—everything."

"Perhaps I should mention this, as further proof?"

"Certainly. The force of gravity was determined by…by… Isaac Newton in…1686, I think."

"And this *Armageddon strikes the people of Japan*; the country was obliterated?"

"It was devastated by a bomb of enormous power. One bomb annihilated an entire city."

"This bomb must have been incredibly large, then? How did they manage to carry such a large explosive device without being detected?"

"The bomb was quite small. It was the power it contained that was large; it was the beginning of the 'atomic age'."

"Atomic—as in the Latin, 'Atomos'?"

"Yes."

…1963…
The American President, John Fitzgerald Kennedy is shot dead.

"Kennedy was a young charismatic president of America—the New World. He averted a global war, which was brought about indirectly through Josef Stalin. It involved another Russian statesman—Nikita Khrushchev; the confrontation was known as the Cuba crisis. You see, it is not necessarily the person in power at the time, at which stage it becomes too late anyway, it is the foundation: how it all started—and that start was with Josef Stalin and Adolf Hitler. Stop these tyrants and the whole course of the world would change."

"Yes, I see. Then I need to begin fresh quatrains about all these events?"

"Yes, and give them to someone in authority—someone who you can trust. Have them sealed and dated, only to be opened, as I suggested, in the year for their prophecy. Then it will be for the people of Earth to decide on the fate of man, not these dictators!"

"I know who I can trust—Queen Catherine. She holds me in high regard. I have completed almanacs for her children, including her son, the young Dauphin, Charles. She will trust in me and she will find a refuge for these prophecies."

"My love, tell me more about yourself… I want to know so much more."

"The trouble is, Mai, I seem to be able to recall only transient events brought about by some incident that sparks another experience. But this I do know: I came here to help prevent the destruction of Man by his own hand. It is this man before us, Michel Nostredame, who will save mankind through his predictions of the future; I was merely the messenger."

"But who are *you*?"

"That may come in time, Mai. But I have come from my time—your future—to your time—my past—to bring these predictions for Michel. I can see me with others in this spaceship travelling to one of these other worlds. But…but I didn't complete the journey…we parted…we parted because of…time? Then, I can only see blackness, a void before me…"

"Michael, do I need to remind you of another reason that you have come here?"

"Anne, it has been on my mind constantly. Indeed, it was difficult to concentrate on these predictions, except that I needed to know more about me, which I have! But yes and thank you. Thank you so much for your understanding and concern."

"Michel, do you think that it is possible…?"

"We can but try; here, help me draw the pentacle. Anne, please would you fetch the two silver goblets from the drawing room? Mai, my staff is by the door in the hallway; would you, please?

"I have studied my crystal and listened to my attendants. They enlightened me and guided me to this book that I have before me. There may be a way but…well, I have already said that I do not feel that I have the 'gift'. But if I do, then until the morrow."

Michel walked over to a drawer and removed a thurible, just as I had witnessed at LeMartre's house. Walking back to the table, he set it down and withdrew some incense from within his cloak. Unlike the necromancer's coat, this was not a multicoloured quilt with a horned goat in the middle. Indeed, it was quite a sober and dull cape, without the startling and macabre designs that I had witnessed the day before. We completed the pentacle, by which time Anne and Mai had returned with their wares. Muttering in Latin, Michel poured two portions of wine into the goblets.

"Michael, we need to make a blood-bond."

"Mai, would you do what we did before, my love, please?"

"But, Michael, you must drip the blood into the chalice before you and you must not spill a drop."

He withdrew a dagger from beneath his robe and laid it on the table. Mai picked up the dagger and stared at me. In her eyes, I saw the fire and determination of that same brave girl who had risked her life, everything, for us to be together, and now was that moment. She closed her eyes, reached out to find my hand and, holding our hands together over the vessel, sliced the top of her finger, allowing the blood to fall into the wine. Nostradamus did the same. He then gave us his chalice and picked up ours.

"Drink, drink all of it…and close your eyes."

235

With one gulp, Michel emptied his goblet. As with the spilling of blood, Mai's mouth and mine joined in a spectral and mortal union as Mai swallowed the contents of the chalice. We closed our eyes and I became cognisant of the sounds around me. My senses took on a new dimension of awareness. I could hear the fire crackle loudly in the grate, I could hear Mai breathing heavily beside me, I could hear Michel chanting his 'mass' in Latin, but it was the smell that I became aware of and it was having a reverie effect on me. At first, the smell of the incense seemed purely medicinal, then its potency grew and I felt as though I would faint…but I could not smell…it had to be that I was sensitive to those others in the room and smelled through their senses. Then, as he thumped the floor with his staff, the last sound that I remembered: "MICHAEL, COME FORTH!"

I opened my eyes and there, before me, stood the blessed white spirit of my friend. He looked at me, smiled and spoke to my mind: "I really didn't think I could do it…until morning…"

"'You are to become what I am'! As you said when we met. Bless you, Michel…until morning…"

I turned and gazed at Mai.

"Mai…"

"Michel? It did not work then?"

"Mai, that is not Michel. I know my husband; that is Michael."

The countenance of the great wizard changed visibly before the two women's eyes and the visage of the old man altered into the face of a younger man.

"Michael! Michael! Is that you?"

"Mai, my dear, dear Mai! Let me hold you, touch you, embrace you now!"

Anne looked on, knowing that the man embracing this young girl before her was not her husband. She smiled, held open the door and said gently: "I believe the bed has been warmed for you—it is upstairs. Agnès will show you the way."

I gazed into Anne's eyes; those emerald eyes infusing sincerity and selflessness that had captivated me at the start of this momentous journey. I embraced her and kissed her on the cheek.

"Thank you, Anne. This means so much to me, and you—"

"—Hush. Michael, your time is limited. Go and give this young girl all the love that you have."

The maid entered, bowing before her mistress and, with a gasp, followed her commands and led the couple up to the bedroom.

Naked, for the first and only time, Mai and Michael held, stroked and stared. Without moving his gaze from her, Michael caressed her hair—that raven-black hair that had enthralled him so since the first time that he had seen her. It felt like silk, soft and tender. Mai reached out and with the palm of her hand, stroked the face that a few moments ago, had belonged to another man. With trembling fingers, Michael allowed his hand to fall, stroking the neck, then the shoulders of this goddess before him. Mai took his hand and pushing it gently away, leaned up and put her mouth to his. This kiss, this first and lasting kiss, was the moment that both had yearned for since they had met. The clock struck one, but though the night had barely begun, both knew that there would be no sleeping this night. This night would never be forgotten and would forever be held dearly in their hearts.

"Your eyes, Michael! They *are* blue! They are the deepest, purest blue I have ever seen."

Mai held Michael's face and kissed each eyelid in turn. Gently, she brushed her lips across his cheeks and again found the lips of the man beside her. With tongues entwined, those ebony and blue eyes closed to all but the sensation of this most ardent and tender of moments—and time had, for these two lovers, stopped.

Michael tenderly pushed Mai back and slowly withdrew the covers that shielded their nakedness. There, before his eyes, was the most perfect female form. Mai sighed as he let his hand descend from her shoulder to her arm. Taking his hand, Mai pressed it to her breast and gasped again. With his mouth, Michael kissed that olive skin, that skin that had been denied to him for so long. With a rousing desire, Mai pressed her lips onto the male form before her: the neck, the shoulder, the arm and then the chest. Then, with a passion that only true lovers know, the union was complete. The lovers gazed into each other's eyes, not uttering a sound; love needed no words. The world was theirs.

As Mai rested her head on Michael's chest, caressing the face before her, the clock struck the half-hour! Through the shuttered window, the first rays of the day seeped through the gaps. Mai held Michael tightly, as though he would break. Michael hugged Mai too, holding firmly that tender body that had a few moments ago, yielded to his final loving caresses.

"Mai?"

"No, no, not yet, please!"

"Michel gave us this time…in love, the love of friendship and kindness. I…we…cannot betray that friendship."

"Michael, kiss me one last time. Let that kiss endure on my lips forever. Never let me go."

"I will never let you go, my darling Mai. I will always be with you. At least I can make that promise—I will love you for eternity. And one day, we will be together for eternity."

Mai let her tears fall freely on that chest, which a few hours ago, she had supported willingly and with longing. Michael took her hand and kissing it for the last time, placed it beside her. Pulling the covers back, he looked down at her angelic form and again kissed her soft, olive skin before finally pressing his lips onto the trembling lips of this perfect young woman beside him. Standing up, he held out his hand to Mai.

"Come, my love…dawn awaits."

In their naked forms, the two lovers walked downstairs and into the library. Michael held out his arm to Mai as he walked into the pentacle. Gazing at her for that final moment, he hesitated as though his heart was breaking and without turning his eyes away, spoke quietly: "Michel, come forth."

Nothing changed! He was still there. Mai was trembling before him, weeping unashamedly as she held her hand in his. The clock chimed the hour! Turning towards the fire and then back again to Mai, he uttered these final words: "Michel… MICHEL, COME FORTH!"

"NO!"

Chapter 36

Normal life—well, as normal as deep-space travel permitted—was abundant on Proxima. The gravitational field had now been running without flaws for nearly four years and several women had even given birth during the voyage. The first deep-space baby had been a girl and in celebration of the event had been named Petra Anna Nicola; whether this had been chosen by design or by chance was irrelevant, but she was known as PAN by everyone on board and the mythological god of the wild and nature became female in this domain of the cosmos.

The robotics had been a godsend performing tasks that were either too arduous, too monotonous, or just too dangerous for the human company to perform. On several occasions, they had been despatched outside to check around the hull for any damage and report on sections needing attention. The only disconcerting thing about these machines was their resemblance to human form, with eyes that were soulless. It was as though we were sharing our journey with an army of zombies.

Still a dot, albeit a brighter dot, *Proxima Centauri* was getting ever closer and though still insignificant amongst the other milliards of specks in its background, was becoming more predominant. The six of us had become so close that we were like a family. Despite our propinquity, none of us had become romantically attached; though I felt that Anna had a certain appeal to Jamie and Petra was fond of being near Simon. I knew that my time to leave Proxima and her crew was getting increasingly close and it was starting to tear at my emotions. I had a task, the fifteen hundred people on board each had a task, but our tasks were different and I was not going to be able to share my task with anyone—and that was sad…really sad. I wiped my cheek and unsurprisingly, found a tear running down to my lip. Jamie had become like a brother and we had shared many joyful times together in the company of Mr Jack.

Though I had been briefed by NASA to fully inform Jamie of my real reason for being on-board, the dramatic events at the outset as we tried to leave the solar system had pushed the disclosure of my intent into the background. After that, well, a mixture of forgetfulness and a feeling of the time not being quite right had kept my motive concealed—not intentionally, but concealed, nevertheless. We were approaching part of the cosmos that had been of much interest to the astronomers back on Earth. Not just *Proxima b*, also regions nearby—nearby in astronomical terms, that is. One area of particular interest was the triple-star system of *Proxima Centauri*. Not only was the triple-star system fascinating, somewhere in the region was also believed to be a stellar-mass black hole. Distortions in space, as measured back at NASA, had uncovered an anomaly that was believed could be attributable to the environment created by a black hole. Also, the speed and change in orbits of these three stars suggested that perhaps there was a force present that couldn't be explained by any conventional means. My mission was to confirm what was causing this anomaly and, unfortunately, with my one-way ticket, attempt to address the problem of the self-destruction that we were witnessing on Earth as we left. Indeed, right now, there may not be an Earth to return to; not that that was ever an option for me, anyway.

"Jamie, I'm getting some strange signals coming from somewhere in the region of Cygnus X-1!"

"What kind of 'strange', Petra?"

"Well, as you know, we've been transmitting our presence to the entire sky at fourteen-twenty megahertz?"

"Oh…the…the…"

"Hydrogen line…yes, that's right. Well, we seem to be receiving some kind of interference from that area, at fourteen-twenty megahertz."

"When you say 'interference', exactly what do you mean?"

"Pulses."

"Pulses?"

"Hmm, pulses. Unfortunately, this is not my area of expertise—we'd need the boffins back at base—but there really does seem to be something out there transmitting…at fourteen-twenty megahertz."

"Michael?"

"Cygnus is a well-known X-ray source and other radiation wavelengths are also highly likely. However, the hydrogen line is being used from Earth as an attempt at intelligent life communication. Interference suggests…"

"Suggests?"

"Suggests that we should keep an open mind. For my part, the existence of extra-terrestrial civilisations goes without question. Intelligent civilisations, almost certainly; however, the time gap between our existence as an 'intelligent species', in *modern* terms, that is, only goes back about two hundred years. Even if we had started our fourteen-twenty megahertz searching then, we would still possibly be waiting for a reply even now. So, your signals being replied to is most unlikely, Petra. However, that doesn't mean to say that those strange signals are not due to an intelligent life form, just not one that's replying to us."

"What would you attribute these 'pulses' to, then?"

"Are they regular?"

"Yes, they were—"

"—Were?"

"Exactly. I may not be an astronomer but I do understand the regularity of a pulsar… These 'interferences' could have been…could be from a natural source, such as a quasar; perhaps even overlapping the original signal that I was picking up. But somehow…well, it's the irregularity that I cannot understand."

"Well, if we were back on Earth, with what you are saying, every telescope in the sky would be pointing towards CygnusX-1 right now! Have you tried another frequency?"

"I have been scanning through the infrared, radio and microwave frequencies most commonly used but…nothing. The hydrogen line, though…regular, and then spasmodic pulses."

"You know, if there is any Earth left, something like this could pull the entire human race together—something to deviate away from this mindless self-destruction. Something that says: 'stick together and discover something wonderful'. All you can do, Petra, is to log everything, keep recording the data and when we are able to transmit again, send everything that you have back to NASA."

"I agree with Michael. As thrilling and challenging as this is, our goal is to safely arrive at *Proxima b*, land and colonise; we are not equipped to perform more than a cursory glance and report back."

"Will do. Enthralling though. Enough to make me want to take up serious astronomy!"

"Jamie, are you busy?"

"Busy, busy, busy; always busy. Why, Michael?"

"Jamie, since we left the solar system, I've wanted to talk to you about my mission and the reason why I am on board Proxima."

"You mean there's more than your scheduled observations and research on *Proxima Centauri* and the triple-star complex?"

"Yes, there's more…much more, in fact."

"Spread the word, Brother Michael, I'm all ears! Shame really, I was hoping to be better looking than that! Ha, ha, ha…"

"I sure am going to miss your humour, Jamie, that's for sure!"

"What do you mean, 'miss my humour'? You talk as if you are going away somewhere."

"Jamie, when you are free to talk for half an hour, can we go somewhere private?"

"Michael, you've really got me worried now! Anna, would you take over please? Michael and I have a meeting with Mr Jack."

"It didn't sound like a Mr Jack meeting to me, Jamie!"

Anna looked at me with a serious and slightly worried face. I had always believed in female intuition and maybe she had an inkling of what I was going to say to Jamie. As I passed her, she took hold of my arm, pulled me down and kissed me on the cheek.

"What's that for, Anna?"

"That's for being Michael."

She stared at me, looking at me fully in the eyes as though searching for some hidden truth. This was the first time that I had ever been really close to her and her piercing look was as captivating as her prettiness. She continued to gaze into my eyes, to the point that I began to feel self-conscious.

"Anna…?"

She kissed me on the cheek again and I swear I saw her eyes moisten.

"I believe you have a rendezvous with Mr Jack."

I bent down and kissed her on the cheek, as I followed Jamie out of the door.

"I believe I do…"

Jamie's office was a lavish affair, suited for the captain of the first starship, but it did not suit his character. Jamie came from a working-class family, the roots of which he had never forgotten and his down-to-earth approach did not fit in with what had been bequeathed to him for this project. Jamie and I had passed many happy and intoxicating times together in this room over the forty-four months that we had been on board. He had really started to warm to my British sense of humour, though *his* happy-go-lucky manner was addictive from the outset. He went over to his cupboard, took out two tumblers and poured some Jack Daniels into each.

"Carry on, Michael, what happened when Barry arrived?"

"Well, Jamie, he was a nice enough guy but he just talked about himself all the time—you know, real boring; he never really listened to what you said, he was just ready with another anecdote about himself. I remember once we were having a drink outside a pub and a dog came along and defecated on the grass nearby. He looked appalled and started to berate the animal, and ended up saying:

'What use is dog mess! It stinks, it's filthy and contains diseases.'

"To which I replied, expecting some kind of amusing follow-through:

'Well, the flies seem to like it!'

"Instead, he allowed the open-ended humour to fall to waste and related some boring dialogue about the time he had walked in some, sometime previously…"

"Come on… 'When Barry arrived'…"

"Oh, yes. Well, we were parked up by some railings outside a church—"

"—We?"

"Oh, a girlfriend and some student friends. Anyway, we were just about to leave when a car approached and started to park next to us and someone said: 'It's Barry! Quick, hide, don't let him see us, we'll be here for hours listening to him talk about himself!' I was the driver and we all ducked—me included—so that he could not see us. 'Go, Michael, go!' So, I threw the car into gear and accelerated away, only to discover as the car started to move that I was in reverse. We carted into the railings behind us with a crunch as I desperately changed into first and drove off!"

"Ha, ha, ha, did he see you? Ha, ha."

"I don't know. We still had our heads ducked down; he must have thought, 'What the…! There's no one driving that car!'"

"Ha…ha…ha…"

"Yeah, I still laugh about that even now!"

"So, serious time…"

"Yeah, I guess…I'm not sure exactly where to start."

"Well, if it will make life any easier, Michael, NASA did brief me that your inclusion was nothing to do with colonising *Proxima b*. They told me that you would let me know in your own good time, but I must admit, I had totally forgotten!"

"So had I! Well, not entirely forgotten, but it slipped my mind on many occasions and when I did remember, it just wasn't appropriate. OK! Let me start at the very beginning.

"I went to a spiritualist meeting during my first year at university. The building was in the city but in an area that was rather run-down. I remember that there was street after street of terraced houses and it didn't have a feeling of wealth. For some reason, I was quite excited yet apprehensive at the same time. I couldn't understand this mixture of emotions, but probably thought that it was pre-exam nerves. After all, I had been studying intensively and needed a lighter outlet. Anyway, after the service had finished, there was a demonstration of clairvoyance. As always, everyone was hoping that the medium was going to address them and I was no exception. Suddenly though, in hindsight, I feel it had been happening slowly for several minutes—I began to feel distant. The room became a haze and I started to lose awareness of my body. It was as though I was about to faint—and I've never fainted; I can only surmise this feeling I had at the time. As I started to lose full awareness, the medium addressed me:

'I'm drawn to you...yes, you, young man.'

"I acknowledged him speaking to me, even though I was not fully in control of my actions and felt sleepy.

'I believe you can feel a presence that is starting to take control of you. Do not worry; let what will be, happen. I can see by your side a large man, with very dark skin...I would say he appears like what I imagine a Zulu warrior to look like. He wants you to allow him to get closer to you and he says:

'Relax, we will do great things together. When you are prepared, I will show myself to you. Be patient, you have much to give to the world. Indeed, you are a vital part of the destiny of Man.'

'Take this with you when you leave here and don't be afraid. God bless you, son.'

"I tell you; this experience took my breath away, it really did. I went home on an absolute high; I couldn't sleep. Yet, at the same time, I was scared. This world of the unknown; did it exist, didn't it? I prayed out loud for this to happen, to at last experience the proof I had longed for. Indisputable, substantiated, absolute. As I lay in bed in the dark, the mattress suddenly depressed as though someone, or something, had sat down! Then a breeze blew across my face! My heart was racing...racing, I tell you. I opened my eyes but there was nothing.

"Well, the next time that I went to this spiritualist church, as before, I started to feel faint. The medium approached me with a message. The séance went along these lines:

'*I have a man in a service uniform. He is wiping his brow; he is in a hot country.*'

"I immediately thought of my brother, Derek. He had been called up to complete his National Service. He decided to go into the RAF and had served in Singapore as an apprentice electrical engineer, servicing the aircraft.

'*This man is young and he is wearing wings on his uniform…it is the RAF.*'

"Well, at this stage, I started to get goose bumps because the mediums usually referred to the deceased for messages, not the living. I asked the medium whether my brother had died! It really was an uncomfortable moment. The conversation continued like this:

'*Is this man living or on the other side?*'
'*He is on the other side.*'
'*This message cannot be for me—I know of only one person in a service uniform and he is not on the other side.*'
'*I'm sorry, but this message is definitely for you. This man passed over before his time; it was tragic. He wishes to be remembered to someone down south.*'

"Now I really did get goose bumps! My brother lived down south but the worst was still to come.

'*Please take this memory with you… I want to go to Dunstable. The man wishes to go to Dunstable… He says*: "Brian wants to be remembered to you".'

"Jamie, I nearly passed out! My heart was beating like a military drum. My brother lived just outside Dunstable! But the thing is, Dunstable isn't a romantic, historic, touristic town…or any place of interest. It is just a nothing place except for the people that live there. I mean, if he had said, *Nottingham* or *Edinburgh*…or *London*, you could have thought that the guy was guessing…but *Dunstable*! Ye gods!"

"Is that it?"

"No! This was October. I went to stay with my brother for Christmas…oh, by the way, I telephoned him the next day to confirm that he was still alive! Now, Derek knew that I was interested in the paranormal and that I was investigating spiritualism. He was an unshakeable non-believer and I was a bit reluctant to ask him about this incident, for fear of ridicule—"

"—He knew him, didn't he?"

"YES! He was his bunkmate in Singapore! He drowned in a yachting accident; my brother was very upset as they had been good friends."

"Wow!"

"The thing is, Jamie, it couldn't have been telepathy—I knew nothing of this man or his connection at all. It was nothing to do with me and that's what made it so incredible. If it had been for me, then people could have done some research. You know, found out a few things and made up a pretend story to make me believe, but they didn't. And I have never forgotten. Oh, and at the same time, he told me that I had mediumistic powers."

"Do you?"

"I don't know...I've never tried. Anyway, after this event, something else happened. I became ill with very severe back pains and the doctors failed to identify the cause; basically, they dismissed me as a malingerer, I suppose. The pain was very intense and very real. As a last resort, my parents had some friends, who gave their unpaid services as spiritual healers—some called it *faith healing*—but these people were adamant that they were spiritual healers. As I was being 'healed', it was dark in the room. I saw in a glass-fronted cupboard, which was reflecting the 'healer' behind me, I saw the whole of his head start to glow a hazy yellowy-orange. It wasn't as if it was a show—'look at me glow orange'. I had my back to the man while he worked...I just saw this light emanating from his head!"

"Michael, I'm beginning to get goose bumps now!"

"Yes, well, you can understand that, with experiences like that, my interest in the occult—in this case, spiritualism—grew. I was never a 'who goes there?' person; I examined and researched with diligence as well as curiosity.

"Perhaps it was ingrained; perhaps it was because of these unaccountable experiences; perhaps it was because the entire human race was fascinated by the subject; but whatever the reason, I became fascinated by ghost encounters. I must have read every known book about unexplained mysteries from Erich von Däniken and his *Chariots of the Gods?* to Arthur C Clarke's *World of Strange Powers* and lesser-known authors concerning spiritualism, the occult and hauntings. I ended up with one conclusion—there were too many accounts of the unexplained to dismiss it all as fantasy. There had to be...no, there *was* an explanation for everything! The problem was we were barely scratching at the surface.

"In terms of hauntings, there is the classic one of Anne Boleyn's ghost being witnessed by soldiers in the Dean's Cloister at Windsor Castle. This can be so easily dismissed as pure fantasy—a good ghost story from the times of medieval England. Taken in isolation, yes; but during the 1970s, the Enfield Poltergeist at 284, Green Street, took the nation by storm. Caught on camera, Janet Hodgson was filmed levitating in her bedroom; a no-nonsense policewoman witnessed a chair move across a room; but the most intriguing part for me was her possession by Bill Wilkins who had died in the house years before. Her voice changed to that of an old man and she related events that were later confirmed to be true.

During her possession, she was totally in a trance. Now, I realise that during my very first experience in that séance, I was in the process of being possessed, too!"

"Michael, I'm shaking here! I…no…*we* need another Jack Daniels!"

There was a knock at the door; it was Simon.

"Chief, Petra's got some more data on the hydrogen line…it really is looking quite strange! Will you be coming back soon?"

"Tell Petra I may be another half an hour and to keep logging the data. At the moment, I would rather not be disturbed."

"OK, will do…sorry for the interruption."

"Michael, don't stop now!"

"There are two other incidents that I would also like to mention. I lived in France for a while and to make ends meet, I looked after a house used as a holiday home. During the short time that I was there, two separate guests, who were not at all acquainted, reported at different times that they had seen an apparition at a bedroom window. It was a young girl looking out into the street. Both reports were identical and at the same spot—the bedroom window.

"The other incident involved me directly. I was on holiday, believe it or not, also in France. I was staying somewhere in Brittany. There was nothing unusual about the house, but every night when I was lying in bed, I heard footsteps on the floorboards above. The thing is that upstairs was a bare loft—there was nothing there and no one else was in the house. Twice, as I lay in the bed, I felt a presence creep up to where I was sleeping; the air was electric! Then it pushed down upon me! First, I pulled the covers over my head, but then I leapt up…"

"But there was no one there?"

"Exactly."

"Michael, is this why you are here, because of your paranormal experiences?"

"In part…but I need to explain more. Jamie, am I losing your interest and credulity?"

"On the contrary, this is fascinating; carry on."

"Well, after years of investigations, I have come to a conclusion—supernatural experiences are as valid as are the existences of extra-terrestrial civilisations. The extra-terrestrials can now be accepted; Drake's equation proved this theoretically even though there has been no solid proof. But the paranormal, well, science is still more reluctant to accept this, despite the plethora of reports. For me, there are two kinds of supernatural occurrences: the intelligent type and the non-intelligent type. The intelligent type are those that are current—you can communicate, like the Enfield Poltergeist and the message I received for my brother. The non-intelligent type are the non-communicators—the reruns, the repeats, with an ethereal being replaying some event, like Anne Boleyn or the phantom at the window. The fascination for me here is because these involve time. The events have travelled through time! And 'time' is why I am here—it is my area of expertise."

I looked down at our tumblers; Jamie was right, he really was fascinated, he hadn't touched a drop of Mr Jack during my whole recitation.

"Michael, enthralling as the past ten minutes have been, you still haven't told me your real purpose for being here. I mean, your experiences and fascination with the occult are truly captivating, but what is it that you will be doing when we arrive at *Proxima b*?"

"Jamie, I'm getting there, but what I have told you *is* the reason for me being here."

"I still don't understand. I have seen your expertise and guidance see us through some amazingly difficult times—the Saturn encounter, when we were being pulled by Saturn's gravitational field—"

"—Pushed."

"Pushed?"

"Jamie, I was born with a questioning mind. If you say something is 'red', I believe you because you told me that it was 'red'. But sometimes someone says something is 'red', but someone else says 'green', and then we have a dilemma: is it red or green? Or is it neither?"

"Michael, don't go off at a tangent! I merely questioned your implication that Saturn's gravity is a pushing force?"

"Well, the *tangent* you mentioned is exactly what I am getting at. Every scientist in the world accepts that gravity is a pulling force—a force of attraction—that every particle exerts a gravitational force on another particle; that within each particle there is a force that cannot be identified but attracts other particles towards it."

"Yeah, standard classroom physics…"

"But what if *gravity*, as we understand it, is a repelling force?"

"Impossible! Michael, are you for real?"

"For very real, Jamie. Physics states that gravity is a weak force. Even as a student, I could not accept this concept. Why, the sun holds us—all the planets—in orbit. We do not feel the strong bonds that hold the sun together—the nuclear reactions…well, yes, as light, heat and other radiation…but we do feel the force of gravity. Black holes, the ultimate gravitational force. This small entity holds an entire galaxy within its grip! Now if that is a weak force, then I am on the wrong planet."

"Was…"

"Was?"

"Yes, Michael, sorry to be facetious; *was* on the wrong planet. I was merely throwing in a light remark; do you remember Barry?"

"Barry? Ha, ha, ha! Well, at least I'm not talking about myself!"

"No, that's true. But what about your purpose?"

"Now, at the moment of creation—"

"—Let there be light and—"

"—And there was light, eventually; some three hundred thousand years after the Universe began. But at the moment of creation, the Universe was thrown apart with unimaginable force. That force was imparted to every item of energy in existence. That energy has always been and always will be. The edge of space…the very limit of our Universe was created by these energetic forces, as they still are; space is constantly being created by 'inflation'. But the energy within every force included one of motion. Motion was, and remains part of, the energy that existed at the beginning of time. This force slowly transformed into a physical Universe as we see and experience…so we can now talk about 'matter'—physical, solid, observable matter. As matter was created, protons, electrons, neutrons, the original forces pushed these together to form mass…and mass has gravity. But it is held together because the rest of the Universe is pushing on it from all directions. It is matter in combination with these forces of motion that creates gravity. In other words, it is *momentum*; this is how we experience gravity. Matter gets in the way of a balanced Universe. The more the matter, the greater the force acting against it; hence, greater the momentum and, therefore, the gravity. But matter does not possess gravity; it is the momentum of the Universe that is the gravity. Matter, in fact, resists the pressure of gravity being forced upon it."

"Hell, Michael, that's a bit deep. Have you discussed this idea of yours with other scientists?"

"We debated but it was a foregone conclusion that radical ideas like this would not be accepted. As I said to an old friend many years ago, 'science is arrogant'. Science likes to think it has an exclusive right—a monopoly—on original ideas but once these original ideas become accepted…well, it's almost like it becomes apathetic, it clings onto these concepts, these dogmas, of convention and cannot, or is reluctant, to think out beyond the box."

"But that is not true. Look how scientists and astronomers have discovered some amazing and startling events, inconceivable, but just a few generations ago."

"Yes, that is true. Scientists have made many truly wonderful discoveries, all based on the acceptance of conventional theories and laws. But have they really thought outside of the accepted convention?"

"What do you mean, accepted convention? They have used the world of mathematics—"

"—That is the convention that I am referring to."

"The world of mathematics?"

"Yes!"

"Are you saying that it is the world of mathematics that needs revision?"

"Exactly!"

"But the world of mathematics—"

"—Is a truly beautiful world! I love mathematics! Mathematics is *my* world! But we have relied on it and accepted it for too long. This is the convention that I was referring to."

"And mathematics has got it wrong?"

"Well, both yes and no. For a start, what we are doing contravenes the principles of currently accepted mathematics; we are travelling *faster* than the speed of light *and* we have mass! Also, take general relativity and quantum mechanics…"

"OK, OK, you've got a point, I guess."

"Well, it's more than a point, Jamie. The two do not agree and yet these two hypotheses were developed using conventional and accepted mathematics. Now, if the two do not agree, then either one is wrong…or both are wrong! Mathematics is mathematics, period. If the mathematics developed by man is exact, absolute and correct, then ALL formulae would agree…but they don't! Man observes, Man deduces and Man manipulates what he has seen with numbers, but that doesn't mean to say he has correctly calculated what he has seen into formulae; it just fits nicely for that moment, for that occasion.

"Mathematics, as developed by Man, is several thousand years old. It was based on concepts by brilliant men of their time. Their brilliance was that they had nothing but formulated this new world of mathematics that is still used to this day. In fact, without these original thinkers, we would not be here flying to *Proxima b*. Man could possibly still be a 'hunter/gatherer'. He would have no means to translate the worth of something in his possession for something else that he wanted. But the creation of mathematics was for the needs of the time— it suited then as it suits now—but science and man have moved on and so…"

"Mathematics needs to move on as well?"

"Precisely."

"How does it need to move on? What more can we do?"

"The world of the theoretical and the world of reality overlap but are definitively different. Maths was developed and has been based on the acceptance of linearity; but linearity doesn't exist!"

"What do you mean doesn't exist; of course linearity exists! You simply have to draw a straight line to prove that it does."

"But there is no such thing as a straight line."

Jamie reached for a ruler in a drawer. Then he took a paper and pencil and, placing the ruler on the paper, drew a line and pushed it in front of me.

"I'm sorry, Michael, but I think your hypothesis may be slightly incorrect."

"Jamie, what you have done you assume is straight…but it isn't. It is, in fact, curved. You see, Earth…any planet come to that, like the cosmos, is a sphere. If you continued your line for, say, 100 kilometres, then you would start to see a curving of the line that you have drawn. Albeit infinitesimally small, one side of the line is lower than the other. Linearity and, therefore, 2D works over short distances, but over the vastness of the cosmos, linearity-and, hence, the mathematics that we know, breaks down. The same with pi, one side of the circle is at a different height to the other, so pi does not have the value it is recognised with; it could possibly even have a finite number. It may be that dark energy would be understood if the mathematics we use was changed. Linearity is unreal and imaginary. As I said, Jamie, mathematics now needs to move on."

"But the world of the theoretical has created all the wonders of the real world."

"Yes, to a point. Jamie, I love mathematics, I really do. From the age of thirteen, I developed a passion for this science. The world of numbers, of formulae, of calculations, the beauty of digits fitting together, of plotting and extrapolations—this was the world where I belonged. I didn't realise then; it was much later that I had a gift for this subject.

"If the concept of gravity, as I believe, is correct, then the cosmos is all moving in direct proportion to the focal point at the centre, like the spokes in a big wheel; unlike local solar systems that rotate by a formula concocted by the brilliant Kepler. He determined that distance and speed from the parent star were governed by the equation that the distance cubed is proportional to the orbital speed squared. In other words, local systems operate by gravitational forces based on the mathematics known at the time. In fact, it was this third law of Kepler that inspired Newton to develop his theory of gravitation. After that, it was commonly assumed that the Universe would follow the same empirical formula, but it doesn't! The entire cosmos is held together by that original energetic force, now called 'dark energy', and that, to me, makes sense."

"But isn't that 'dark energy' pushing us away, not holding us together, if your theory holds true?"

"Yes! But we are all being governed by the laws of motion at the same time. On every side of us, there are unseen forces—dark energy. These forces are equally balanced, so we feel no effect and remain 'glued' together. But every so often, there is a cataclysmic implosion of localised energy and the super massive black hole is born. The concentrated mass unsettles the balance of dark energy and that pushes towards the black hole and the galaxy is born!"

"But shouldn't we then implode?"

"Not necessarily. The power at the time of creation has been pushing, yet holding the cosmos in energetic equilibrium, and if it weren't for the creation of black holes, we would be still expanding. Do not forget motion; it is this energetic force that is responsible for the sensation of gravity."

"Does this explain how we feel gravity on Earth then?"

"Perfectly. Earth spins, just like Proxima; it is a giant centrifuge. In theory, everything should be thrown off and into space. But the dark energy forces become unbalanced and we only feel them at our point of terrestrial contact and we get pushed down by the force of momentum of the cosmos. Once up beyond the protection of Earth's mass, we become subjected to the equally balanced forces of the Universe and hence feel no gravitational force—everywhere the forces balance out and we become weightless."

"But the force of the entire cosmos pushing on you…surely that would crush you to death?"

"Yes, if it was all focused on you, but it isn't. It is dissipated throughout the entire Universe. It is only the forces, equally balanced all around you pushing in every direction *and* exactly equal to your mass, that are at play.

"Also, consider, for example, Earth…though it could be any body of considerable mass. If, as scientists have advocated, mass possesses gravity, then as you descend into the depths of that mass, the influence of gravity should become less. At the centre of Earth, therefore, there should be no gravitational effect…but it is the opposite—it becomes greater. However, if the momentum of the Universe is the true cause of gravity, then the pushing above Earth in combination with the mass of Earth being forced together would account for the effects of increased gravity. What is fascinating, though—"

"—*Fascinating* isn't exactly a word that comes to mind right now…mind-boggling may be more descriptive…"

"Yes, delving into the realms of the imagination can be a bit daunting, I guess."

"*Fascinating, daunting*, sheesh, Michael, you have no idea!"

"—But what is *mind-boggling*, if you like, is that as you descend into a black hole, the pressures and energetic forces will become so great that all matter—protons, neutrons, electrons, quarks, charms, light, even time itself—will start to be broken into their original forms, becoming just energy. Therefore, at the centre of a black hole—it may take a super massive black hole to achieve this—but at the centre, mass no longer exists and if there is no mass, then there is no—"

"—Gravity!"

"Precisely."

"Hell, Michael! I think I'm going mad! So, if there is no gravity at the centre of a black hole—?"

"Then the Universe will eventually disappear into…nothing!"

"Ye gods! I fully understand now why you didn't want to share this information with the scientific world. It may well have put the cat amongst the pigeons!"

"Worse! I think that I would have been laughed out of court with such a 'ridiculous' notion. I believe that my career in the world of astrophysics and cosmology would have been very short-lived."

"But surely, with this idea…"

"With this idea…?"

"Surely, with this idea, the Universe would not still be expanding; in fact, it is accepted that it is accelerating?"

"But is it?"

"Is it? The Universe not expanding! The evidence is irrefutable!"

"Tell me Jamie, how do the astronomers of the day show that the Universe is expanding?"

"They use the concept of the *Doppler* effect."

"Yes, that's right. Edwin Hubble himself…he was also a radical thinker, a genius and recognised as such in his own lifetime. He was prepared to risk controversy with his inconceivable notion that the Universe was actually expanding. But let's take the analysis that he used. He showed, indisputably, that the wavelength of the light from distant galaxies was lengthening and that the further the galaxy, the greater the increase in that wavelength."

"Red-shift…"

"Yes, red-shift. Unquestionable. And hence, not only was the Universe expanding, it has, as you mentioned, been found to be accelerating. However—"

"—I was waiting for that 'however'; I just knew that it was coming…"

Jamie had his broad grin and I realised that my friend was beginning to warm to my own ideas and this was a comfort. I had been so worried, afraid even, to speak my mind. But the frustration had now got the better of me and, in combination with Mr Jack Daniels, I was telling someone my own controversial ideas and the relief was overwhelming. I smiled back.

"However, at the time, there was no concept of dark matter and, more importantly, dark energy. It is now strongly accepted that both exist, though they could be synonymous. Now if dark energy is real—if it is there making up most of the Universe—then one has to question the effect that this energy will have on, for example—"

"—The Doppler effect?"

"Yes, the Doppler effect."

"So, dark energy absorbs the energy of the transmitted light and gives an artificial reading for observers here!"

"Correct! So there is not, and never was, a red shift; they are false readings but not registered as false, it's just that the dark energy effect was not taken into account. And on top of that, the more distant the galaxy, the more the dark energy effect, and hence the illusion of expansion!"

"But if the Universe is not expanding, then is it—?"

"—Steady state, deflating even—or really expanding? I have no idea. After all, the density of the Universe remains constant and if it were expanding, then energy…matter would be being created from nothing…and the laws of physics state that that is impossible.

"But imagine a photon of light from a distant star. It has travelled millions of light years across the vastness of the Universe, only to have its existence extinguished by your eye, and the person next to you has another photon of light from the same star, also extinguished at that same moment. In your brain, the photoreceptors will use that infinitesimally small amount of energy and react in some bio-functional way—perhaps merely create an emotion, for example; but that energy, albeit so small, that energy will be dispersed within you—it cannot be destroyed. Now imagine the vastness of the Universe containing all those zillions of photons from zillions of stars transmitting not only light but every conceivable miniscule amount of radiation. If you can picture that, then you have a cosmos that is no longer a void; it is transplendent, complete, saturated even, awash with energy—dark energy."

"But an accelerating Universe isn't based on red-shift."

"Correct, but if the Universe is curved, then light from supernovae will not travel directly in a straight line, it will rise and fall within both the curvature of the Universe and via dense objects. In fact, this inconsistency could determine the curvature of the cosmos, perhaps?"

Jamie got up and went over to his intercom.

"Anna, unless Proxima is on fire or we are under threat from an advanced civilisation, I don't wish to be interrupted."

"Mr Jack that good then, Jamie?"

"Ha, ha, ha… Better!"

He came back, sat down and poured a further measure of the whiskey into both glasses. I was beginning to lose my concentration and the radical ideas were starting to confuse me. I needed to keep a clear head and pushed the glass to one side. Jamie took a good swig and placed the tumbler rather heavily on the desk. I could tell that he and Mr Jack were getting quite close.

"But this brings me to another aspect of theoretical mathematics and the world of reality and where they no longer overlap."

"OK, the world of reality and the world of mathematics…"

"Now, either the Universe was created from nothing or the Universe has always been here, albeit in a microscopic form. Which do you opt for, Jamie?"

"It could not have been created from nothing; it had to be created from something, but this 'something' changed, as has been suggested."

"Right! And that is also my belief and that is where the theoretical world of mathematics and the real world no longer overlap—at the very beginning!"

"Michael, I believe you have about another two minutes before Mr Jack takes priority, or at least takes over!"

"When mathematics was first conceived, there was an almighty flaw…well, a flaw in terms of its relevance to the real world. If I had one of something, it doesn't matter what, but if I had one and you took it away, what would I have left?"

"Nothing, my friend, absolutely nothing."

"Hmm, nice fit in the world of mathematics, that is…absolutely correct. But in the world of reality, zero does not exist."

"Hang on, look, if I had, say, one dollar and you took it away, I would have no dollar. Correct?"

"Correct. But you would still have something."

"I would have no dollar—period!"

"You would have no dollar but you would still have something; after all, you stated that the Universe must have been created from something…yes?"

"No, no, no, Michael…you are missing the point. One dollar taken away means I have *no* dollar!"

"Yes, I have already agreed. But we are not talking about dollar. I take your last remaining dollar, have you anything left?"

"Well, of course, I have…my house, my car, my—! Wait a minute…you are changing the subject!"

"No, I'm not, Jamie! I am trying to show you where the world of mathematics and the world of reality no longer overlap. Mathematics is fundamental to our world; it is a beautiful science, but it does not necessarily tell the truth. If the world of nothing *only* exists in the theoretical world of mathematics, then the world of mathematics needs to be rewritten to fit into the real world—our world."

"But that makes your argument about maths being wrong…is wrong! You have already said that *nothing* exists! The black hole disappears into nothing, remember!"

"Yes, but on the other hand, at that moment of *nothing* being created, the entire super massive black hole disappears into itself in an instant and spews out its entire existence into pure energy. *Nothing* is not zero…*nothing* is a positive force. In mathematics, zero is nothing, but the two are not the same.

"Following on from the idea that zero cannot exist, that, unfortunately, brings us to another frightening aspect—"

"—Michael, *frightening* is an understatement…"

"The inverse of zero is?"

"Infinity…"

"Yes, infinity; so, if zero cannot exist, then neither can…"

"Infinity!"

"Hmm… Since time began, man has searched for answers, always towards the unknown. The greatest scientist of his day, Nicolaus Copernicus, was brave and original enough to suggest that the planets revolved around the sun, including our own planet, and at the time this was a heretical idea. Then another brilliant scientist showed how this was all possible by the force of gravity.

"Newtonian theory held fast…well, mainly fast, for several centuries before another genius, Einstein, gave us what we currently believe to be the ultimate evidence for our Universe's existence involving space-time, and it is this theory that we hold onto now. You see, every few centuries someone brave and pervasive enough to challenge the establishment, changes the well-held beliefs of the time—Copernicus, Galileo, Newton, Darwin, Einstein, Hawking, to name a few—but there have been countless others, just less well-known. You asked me what my purpose is when we reach *Proxima b* and what I have told you is the reason why I am here."

"To present to the world your theory of a repulsing gravity and that the world of mathematics is wrong?"

"No. Science is too arrogant to accept such radical ideas. I wouldn't be prepared to risk such notorious concepts becoming known to the world; I am not brave enough. This is purely between you and me."

"Then why are you here?"

"Because I believe that time-travel may be possible…"

"M… Michael… Michael, have you gone insane!"

"Well, I certainly hope not."

"You… You… You talk about ghosts, the erroneous world of mathematics, the inconceivable idea that all the scientists in the world haven't a clue about the infinite Universe…which will eventually disappear up its own bottom…and now you talk about travelling through time…if that's what I think that you are getting at?"

"Yes, that is exactly what I am getting at and as I mentioned before, *that* is why I am here."

Chapter 37

Mai was inconsolable as we walked dejectedly back home. It had been several weeks since Michel and I had used LeMartre's body to resolve my mission. Michel had written his quatrains, dated and sealed them and was on his way to Paris to see Queen Catherine.

"Mai, we have had a beautiful moment together—one never to be forgotten; please don't be so sad."

"Oh, Michael! Such a moment as that? Such a wonderful moment together as we had. Yes, yes…but now I know what is to be missed. Now I know what can never be. I want so much for that time to be forever. Oh, the sensation of your tender touch, of your caress, of your kiss… Such rapture as that, I will never know again. That is what makes me so, so sad."

"Mai, unlike mortals that make lover's oaths, only to break them because they have not realised that they are incapable of keeping them…unlike mortals, Mai, my oath to you is true, it is sincere, it is forever; truly, really, forever."

"Michael, you do not need to comfort me with words. I love you and only you…passionately. I cannot even begin to explain the pain that I feel, knowing how we have loved and knowing that can never be again."

"Not even knowing that I will always be by your side now…and until the day that you step across to this dimension of life? Mai, lovers promise, lovers part; but ours is the truest, rarest love that there can ever…and has ever been, for my promise, unlike mortals…my promise, I can and will keep. I will be with you in your joy, in your pain, in your every moment. I will weep with you, laugh with you, sing with you, love with you; I will never leave you—even during your transition to the realm of eternity. Mai, I love *you*."

Without further words, we walked silently along. Even though the birds were singing and the day was bright, nothing could shake Mai from her misery. As we approached her house, she held out her hand to find mine. That tingling sensation was as strong as ever, but not a modicum on the sensation that we had felt during that one unforgettable night together, as mortals.

"Michael, I am sorry, so very sorry. You are right; we have been blessed with one perfect night together, and for that I will remain ever grateful. I know that I am being selfish, but wanting you so badly…is that so wrong? Should I perhaps seek another—one of my dimensions—who can fulfil my life as much as you?"

"Mai! Mai, if I had a heart, that would be breaking right now to hear such words! But how can I see you suffer so? It is I, I who should apologise for entering your life, for using you to fulfil my purpose. And yes, perhaps this love is doomed to fail…both of us loving too much? A mortal and a spirit! Mai, say the word, and I will leave your side. I will leave you and remain tormented—just as you are now—so that you may love freely and happily. My eternity will become my purgatory; but perhaps, I will be comforted knowing that you will be happy."

"Michael, no, no, no…never, never leave me! I was speaking foolishly! No one…no mortal, no other spirit, no other soul, could ever replace my only love. Forgive me…please, forgive me…"

I lifted up Mai's head with my hand to gaze into her ebony eyes. Eyes so full of sorrow, yet so full of love. And then I realised what I had done…what we had done…

"Mai! Did you feel that?"

"Feel what?"

"I raised your head with my hand! You felt it?"

"Michael, I felt a sensation…then, I felt that you wanted me to lift my head and so I did…"

"It's getting stronger, Mai…I know it…I just know it! Come, my love, let us give peace to your parents that you are safe and home."

Chapter 38

"Your Majesty, Michel Nostredame."

"Michel! What an unexpected pleasure."

"Queen Catherine, the pleasure is all mine."

"The day is good. Come walk with me in the garden and tell me the purpose for your visit—unless, of course, it is of a serious nature!"

Dismissing the guard by her side, the Queen led Nostradamus through the main hall and out into the landscaped gardens. The view was magnificent, befitting the monarch of the time, with adorned flower gardens and neatly pruned hedges and trees. A cascade of water flowed effortlessly into a small fountain and babbled pleasantly in the morning light.

"Charles is doing well, Your Majesty?"

"Very much so and so much thanks to you. Indeed, I feel somewhat indebted to you for what you have done for him and his siblings, of course."

"You are too kind, Your Majesty."

"Michel, come speak your mind. Have you travelled all the way from Salon-de-Provence, just to ask me about my family?"

"No, indeed not. Unfortunately, I am here on 'serious' business."

"Oh?"

"As you know, I have been blessed with the gift of a seer."

"That is why you are so precious to us, Michel. The soothsayer of France, as some have referred to you."

"Your Majesty, I have recently been inspired to write fresh almanacs and prophecies. But these prophecies are not for any of the nobles here but are for the future of mankind. These are crucial for the very survival of our species."

"Then come, share them with us."

"That is the dilemma, Your Majesty…I cannot."

"Cannot!"

"Their very credibility relies on them remaining unseen and unknown until the dates immediately preceding the events of these prognostications."

"Why is that, may I ask?"

"Because our species…the very nature of Man is to aspire to destroy himself by his own hand. It is foretold in these divinations I lay before you now."

"I see. So if that is the case, why have you brought them to me now?"

"I need them to be safeguarded. I need someone that I can trust to ensure that they remain sealed until the day of their openings."

"And you are entrusting me with the future of mankind?"

"I believe that you, amongst the nobles of France, are the sincerest and most honourable of them all. I would trust no other."

"Not even the king himself?"

"I do not know the king as I do you. I believe that if it suited to benefit France, he may be tempted to glance into the future himself. But the future here is not his future, it is the future of Man and is beyond the lifespan of every person living in France; it is the far future."

"Then, Michel, as a man of honour, your confidence in me will be justified. I shall stamp my royal seal alongside your own and place these parchments in the hands of my Chancellor. He will be sworn to guard them with his life and hand these down to his successors; to be opened only at the time written by the seals."

"Your Majesty, thank you."

"Was that your 'serious' news, Michel? If so, I could do with more serious news like this and less other 'serious' news—the news of war, espionage and ambition! Serious news such as this would indeed make the world a less dangerous place! Now, let us return to the palace and indulge in the delights of 'lapin aux truffes'—a speciality of my new *Maître de Cuisine*!"

The prophecies were stamped with the royal seal and given in confidence to the Chancellor, Michel de l'Hôpital. Nostradamus was unsure of this man but trusted in the diligence of Queen Catherine and believed that these were now in safe keeping. Having sampled the delicacies of the French court, he made his leave of the monarch and Queen Catherine. She arose and accompanied him to the gate as he bade his farewell.

"1565! A good year, Michel, don't you think?"

"Indeed, Your Majesty, but I fear it may be my final one."

"Your final year, Michel? Surely not!"

"My good fortune is passing me by and I have foreseen my demise. I will not see another Christmas after this one, Your Majesty."

"No! That cannot be so!"

"It is written—and by a greater author than you or me…"

With a courteous bow, he entered the carriage and started his long journey back home. His body was telling him that journeys like this were to be things of the past.

Chapter 39

"Michael, are seriously telling me that you believe in time travel?"

"'Believe' is too strong a word. I think that time travel *may be* possible, and if Einstein was correct about space-time, which I believe he was, then travelling back in time should also be an inherent part of this theory. In fact, it will be an area where the world of theory and the world of reality do actually agree and exist together."

"What about the future, then? Can we travel into the future?"

"No, that won't be possible…unless the future has already happened and we are actually living in the past."

"But to others from the future, we *are* the past!"

"*If* there was a future already in existence, then yes. But we couldn't travel forwards, we can only travel back."

"Why?"

"Two reasons. First, we cannot create a time that has not yet existed—the future. I believe that we are in the only time there has been. We live the present and that then becomes the past. There is no future, it has not been written; only the present and the results of that existence are written. But the past has happened; it is real."

"Or was real?"

"It *was* real if it cannot be experienced again; but if it can be experienced again, then it *is* real."

"And the second reason…?"

"The second reason is that black holes take *time* and 'swallow' it along with everything else; they do not create time."

"What have black holes got do with time? Are you saying that you believe that time travel through a black hole is possible?"

"As I said, *believe* is too strong a word. I think that time travel *may* be possible and yes, if it is, then it would be through an object that swallows and digests *time*. I suspect that black holes do that—and perhaps, so did Einstein!"

"But you wouldn't survive a passage through a black hole! Not even close! Now you are living in the land of the fairies! Michael, you *are* insane!"

"Jamie, I don't expect to survive…"

"WHAT!"

"I don't expect to survive. In fact, it is a physical impossibility."

"Then what the hell are you doing?"

"I have a one-way ticket…here."

I handed over to Jamie my official authorisation from the Director of Operations at Mission Control. With some incredulity, Jamie slowly read through the letter:

To: Captain James Fraser,

Due to serious global confrontations, the Board at NASA has unanimously agreed that Michael Grinshall is authorised to travel in the shuttle, 'Proxima Venture', to the destination of his choice.

We have discussed with Michael over several weeks his theories, as well as some of his unproven hypotheses and have decided that, in the absence of a satisfactory relaxation of hostilities between the current warring factions and due to the shortage of time for verification of his suppositions, he be permitted to travel without hindrance and with your full cooperation.

It is understood that his thinking may be unconventional, but we believe that for the benefit of the survival of the human species, he be given the opportunity for validation of these ideas. Michael himself realises fully that such an undertaking is a one hundred per cent, full-risk venture and does not expect to return. His theories concerning black holes and time have been fully studied and whereas his ideas concerning the paranormal remain an enigma, we have total confidence that at the time of this undertaking, his time/blackhole proposals appear to be flawless. We just pray that his paranormal suggestions will prove equally so.

We wish you all Godspeed and trust that in His own good time, we may benefit from the trust and confidence that we place in each and every one of you for the continuation and survival of the human race.

Sincerely,
Thomas Peterson
Mission Director

He put the letter down and reached out for his tumbler; it was empty.
"Look, Grunge-Futtock—"
"—Grinshall, Jamie."
"What's this crazy stuff?"
"Jamie, haven't you listened to a word that I have said?"
"Yeah, I've listened to every word…every one goddamn word. It's just that…you're for real…aren't you?"
"Yes, afraid so. It has been difficult, as I said, finding the right time to talk to you—I mean, you're like a brother to me now, Jamie…"
"And you me, you little English toe rag…"
Jamie and I threw our arms around each other and hugged as only two brothers could. I kissed Jamie on the head and saw that his eyes were redder than they had been a few minutes ago.
"When do you plan on leaving?"

"As you approach *Proxima Centauri*."

"Why there?"

"*Proxima Centauri* is one of three stars orbiting together and that would be fascinating in its own right, living in a triple-star system. But other astronomers, together with my own independent research, have almost certainly discovered that within that triple-star system, there lurks a small...well, small in cosmic terms, that is—a small, stellar black hole. Recent discoveries and observations have shown changes in orbits and speeds of these stars; the evidence is there."

"So, you're just going to up and fly directly into that beast, then...have I understood right?"

"Yeah, that's the gist of it, Jamie. But I won't be able to fly directly into it; the orbiting forces will be too great. The vortices—as I approach the Event Horizon—will drag me inexorably inwards, spiralling towards the centre. I mean, the friction alone will have frizzled *Proxima Venture* long before."

"But how do you expect to time travel, frizzled?"

"This is where my stories and suspicions of the paranormal come into play. Remember, there are two sorts of supernatural occurrences—intelligent and non-intelligent? Well, non-intelligent—the replays—are to me an indication, of sorts, that these are re-enactments of events that actually happened; these show that they have travelled through time to recreate their own event. The intelligent...well, these show, irrefutably, that the spirit lives on after death. In other words, life, in the incorporeal form, continues."

"So, you will enter a black hole dead..."

"In incorporeal form, Jamie."

"OK, you will travel into a blackhole in a non-physical form...and then...what!"

"I believe...no, I hope that the spirit lives on after death. I will have passed into the realm of the next dimension long before I enter the blackhole. As I approach those unbearable forces, I will perform euthanasia and pass peacefully into the next realm. BUT whilst I approach this moment of passing, I will be listening continuously to my objective played through my earpiece telling me of my mission, which, I hope, will be retained by my consciousness in the next dimension..."

"Which is...?"

"To seek out the prophet, Nostradamus, and forewarn him of the future."

"What the *hell* will that do?"

"Well, I hope his factual account of Man's future will warn the people sufficiently and that they will take heed and not allow those self-important dictators to control and rule them. That mankind...the populations of the world will decide their own fate and not leave it to these megalomaniacs. That is what I hope to achieve—that is my mission. Also, by being in a non-material form, I will not be able to inadvertently change the future by physical intervention; the future will continue unchanged until the moment the *people* decide their fate."

"I'm lost for words, Michael...I really am. I had absolutely no inkling of your real motive for being with us; but now it all makes sense...those comments that you made about *this* being your purpose…for the benefit of mankind. God, I am truly stunned. But you have volunteered for a suicide mission! Shit!"

"Shit, indeed, Jamie…but shit is what Earth was facing when we left. Let's hope there's still enough left and that mankind hasn't ended up wiping its own bottom!"

"Can I tell Anna and Petra?"

"You are going to have to. Part of my mission, whilst in this dimension anyway, is to continue relaying data as I approach that bad boy out there. NASA will want to know every morsel of information that I can obtain as I get closer. Physics and mathematics will probably be rewritten once they have had a chance to examine the forces at play—though the forces *inside* that beast will still remain an enigma. As long as we are both travelling at the same speed, I should be able to relay that information to you, but once you begin to reduce your speed… How are you going to reduce your speed, Jamie…apply the brakes?"

"Ah! Those bright sparks back at base have worked that one out, I hope. As we approach *Proxima b*, we will set ourselves in orbit at approximately fifty thousand kilometres above its atmosphere. We will then deploy those laser shields that we used for our acceleration. Every minute, Proxima will drop by one hundred metres. Initially, there will be no friction, but slowly as we go lower, we will start to meet the molecules in the outer layers of its atmosphere and the friction, together with reversal from the burners, will slow us down to more traditional speeds. At our current speed, we would be frizzled, like you, if we adopted a conventual re-entry."

"But that will take…?"

"Over eleven months; yeah, we know. But we are the pioneers and this is the process felt most likely to succeed. We will feed NASA our data and probably, next time, they will have discovered a better, more efficient way of slowing down and landing; if there is a next time."

"What, like applying the brakes!"

"Yeah, like applying the brakes!"

Jamie went over to the intercom. He turned and looked at me. His expression was no longer that of a jovial, macho commander running the renegades out of town. His eyes expressed deep sorrow, as of one in bereavement.

"Anna?"

"Done with Mr Jack, Captain Fraser, or do you want me to send down another crate?"

"Anna, I'd like you and Petra to come down to my office, please."

"What? Jamie, this sounds serious; I'm not sure I want to hear this."

"Ask Simon to look after things for the next twenty minutes or so."

"Is this anything to do with Michael?"

"Anna, please, just come down."

Jamie's voice cracked as he spoke to Anna. He turned and with sad eyes, sat back down. He pushed the bottle of whiskey away, but I felt that perhaps it may be more comforting with it back in arm's reach. I leaned over the table, took the bottle and poured a measure into Jamie's glass. He swigged it back in one gulp. There was a knock at the door.

"Come in, girls."

As they entered, I could tell by the expression on their faces that they had a suspicion of what was going on; though the exact details were still obviously unknown—just that what they were about to hear was not going to be good news. Jamie briefed them and I could not even raise my head to face them. Petra gasped and Anna, for the first time that I could remember, wept.

"Michael, how could you? I thought you were here for the duration, like the rest of us."

"Sorry, Anna, I wish there was another way…"

"But we need you! You have seen us through so much; we wouldn't have made it beyond the solar system without you."

"Yes; you gave us that confidence. Just you being with us was like…like nothing could go wrong. You were our lucky charm and your knowledge has seen us to the brink of colonising another planet, another world. Can't you stay until we have landed, at least?"

"Sorry, Petra. I need the speed that we are travelling at for this mission to stand any chance of success. Your mission is for the survival of the human species on another world; mine is for the survival of the human species back home."

Anna could hold back no more. She burst into tears and threw her arms around me. I felt her body tremble as she wept on my shoulder and her tears mingled with my own as our cheeks brushed together.

"You… You… You are all like a family to me. I could not have wished for dearer sisters…or…or…"

"Brother…?"

But the words would not come. It was Jamie who had to complete my unfinished avowal. Petra joined Anna and the three of us held each other in a consoling embrace. I noticed Petra's eyes were now red, just as Jamie's had been. This assistant commander was first and foremost a woman, with all the weaknesses as well as strengths of the emotions that her gender possessed; her role in supporting Jamie and Anna with the command of this starship now took second place.

The intercom buzzed. Jamie got up and walked over.

"Yes, Simon?"

"Something here I think you are going to want to see, Jamie."

"What is it?"

"A small habitable planet, revolving around a red dwarf star—well, three stars actually!"

"Hey, that's…that's…that's terrific news. We'll be up straightaway."

Jamie stayed facing against the wall. I saw his body shake and I heard him openly weep.

"Well, that's it, then. Our goal is in sight. We had better go back up on deck and start making plans for our approach and orbital line-up. Petra, Anna, would you mind going ahead? I just have something to do here first…"

The women both knew that Jamie had nothing to do. He was needed upstairs, but he needed a few minutes to recover from his emotional state and perhaps have a few quiet moments more with me. Jamie and I sat at the desk but did not speak. I stretched out my hand and laid it on top of Jamie's. He grasped it and kissed the top, not as a lover, but as a comrade and friend.

"Come on, Jamie; we still have work to do…"

We arose and hugged, just as I had done with Anna and Petra. He pushed me away slightly and looked at me with reddened eyes and a face that held all the troubles of the world on its shoulders.

"Michael, I love you! I love you as only a brother can. I have never known another that I would want to share my time with—"

"—Apart from Anna!" I joked.

"Yes, damn it! Apart from Anna. But what I feel for you goes beyond the physical love of a man for a woman. It is a deep, spiritual love, the love of a true friend, someone you would run into battle with and pull him out even to the sacrifice of your own life."

"That is true love, Jamie. And God, if ever I had had a brother, I would have wanted it to be you…no mistake!"

We embraced one more time and went back to the main control room. As we walked in, Anna and Petra looked at both of us and knew that we, too, were being torn apart by the future in front. Without any hint to Charlie or Simon, they continued their tasks as they had been trained to do. It was Jamie who broke the ice.

"Charlie!"

"Capn', sir. What'll you be a'wantin' then?"

At least Charlie managed to make Jamie smile.

"Charlie, we need to start crop planning and planting for the next four years ahead. Would you organise the agriculturists on board to submit their planned crops and cereals rotation programme?"

"We've got a meeting due Wednesday, but we can bring that forward, if you wish."

"Wednesday will be fine. Right, arrange with construction their planned schedule for housing, hospital, school, roads and infrastructure. Then, after the initial appraisals, perhaps you could include me in the follow-up."

"What about excavations and surveying?"

"Get your guys briefed about our current understanding of *Proxima b* and ask them to submit their assessments and schedules. Petra, what is our current trajectory and ETA for orbit?"

"*Proxima b* at three hundred billion kilometres; ETA at warp-drive factor one point-zero-five, eleven days and two hours. Setting up countdown in hours…now."

In front, on a red LED display, the digits 266.68 were glowing down upon us. That gave me eleven days and two hours to prepare myself for my departure. I needed to work with Simon to ensure that the shuttle that had been assigned to me was fully functional and with Charlie to ensure that I could survive another, possibly, twelve months before I would no longer have any need of nutrition and sustenance. Though initially, this had seemed more than sufficient time, once we had started to work together, I realised that I had cut it a bit fine. I also needed Simon to work with me on the simulator so that I could perform the basic manoeuvres needed to guide me to my destiny.

The next day, I looked up and there, before us, I saw the digits 241.35. The despair of the day before had subsided somewhat, with the others having had time to digest what my mission really involved. Though there was still a certain degree of sadness, the ongoing preparations for the pending arrival at their destination had occupied every one of the crew and whatever they really thought, they remained silent.

"Michael, I have a meeting with the judiciary and the people's representative now. Do you want to sit in? I thought that with the strength of your commitment to democracy and fair-play, you may be interested?"

"Yes, I would like that, Jamie. What's the meeting about?"

"It's about setting up our legal system: law enforcement, punishments, crime, policing, representatives—all in all, it is a start-from-scratch approach to how we run and organise ourselves down below. We want a society that is diligent, conscientious, hardworking, innovative and prepared to abide by the rules and laws that we shall decree over the next few months."

"Won't you be responsible for that, as commander of this expedition?"

"Oh no! Michael, isn't that exactly the system that's causing the conflict back at home? No more dictators! This will be a democratic society. Whilst on board, I am captain; I set the rules and make the judgements. On *Proxima b*, my jurisdiction ends. That is why we need to start the process of democracy here and now."

"Sorry, Jamie, I hadn't given any of that a thought. I have been totally mission-orientated, but yeah, you're right, we need an uncorrupted, democratic society—let's do it!"

I was pleasantly surprised at the attitude of the people sitting around the table. There was a positive buzz in the air and everyone appeared to be singing from the same hymn sheet. It was difficult to imagine with the people that I had met on board that we should be discussing 'murder' and 'rape', but eventually—perhaps not with this generation on board—but eventually, human nature being what it was, it would need to be addressed. I was again very pleased how they discussed these serious issues, not from a revenge perspective, but in a conciliatory and constructive way. At the end of the meeting, I felt that this was going to be a society that was going to build on the finer aspect of humanity and felt sad that I would not be part of it.

Working with both Charlie and Simon, together with keeping myself as trim as possible while I could still enjoy the luxury of gravity, time passed incredibly quickly. I attempted to use the running wheel as often as I could and absolutely loved the sensation of running upside down. With it being perfectly and strategically placed at the centre of the ship, the centrifugal force created by Proxima's rotation acted evenly on the whole wheel. But it wasn't so much the exercise that was rewarding, it was the sensation of running around the inside of the ship that became mesmerising; and running counter-clockwise gave the sensation of running twice as fast as I really was!

Without realising, I walked into the main control room and, as I did every day, looked up at the monitor. I could not believe what was in front of me! A red display reading 2.61! This was it! These were going to be my last moments with the people who had become like the family I never really had back on Earth. In a few moments, I was going to lose all visual and physical contact with any human being—ever. It frightened me and I deeply regretted persuading NASA to back my wild notion of travelling through time. But if I had not persuaded the Operations Director and his colleagues, I would never have had the opportunity to meet these three wonderful people. I did not want to leave but at least I had been blessed with four years of us being together and that I would never forget. As I walked in, all three looked my way and we all attempted a half-smile; a hollow, half-smile. It was Petra who was first to speak.

"*Proxima b*, three hundred million kilometres. ETA: two hours and thirty-six minutes."

"When do you plan on departure, Michael?"

"Two hours and thirty-six minutes, I guess…give or take a few minutes. I want to see this planet first and know that you are locked in orbit. When will you deploy the sails?"

"As soon as we have stabilised our orbit, I guess…give or take a few minutes."

I appreciated Jamie's humour; God, I was going to miss this…and him. We both smiled. It was Simon who called out.

"Michael, you'd better get your suit on—you'll need at least ninety minutes. Kathy is waiting for you in the Pod room. When do you plan on returning?"

"Oh, I have quite a bit to do first, Simon. Closer study of that red dwarf in front; Jamie will keep you briefed; let's hope nothing goes wrong!"

We had decided that my mission was going to the grave with the four of us; though my grave would, undoubtedly, be the first one. Trying to explain irrational behaviour to a population full of the promise of a new era and a new life seemed a bit pointless. It would remain, as far as the others were concerned, an experiment that went wrong. Simon and Charlie knew me well enough, but we were not close like I was with the other three. So, sensation seemed unwarranted and unnecessary.

I went down to the Pod room and Kathy was waiting to help me get dressed into my life-support protective clothing. As she was finishing, the intercom came to life:

'All personnel, Proxima b is directly ahead. Those wishing to view, please go to the observation points situated at the bow on all decks.'

"Michael, let's just get your helmet fitted and we're done."

"Kathy, would you mind if we left that until I enter *Venture*, please? I want to go and say farewell to Jamie and the others."

"Michael! You sound as if you're not coming back!"

"Well, you never know, Kathy; things sometimes go wrong…"

"Oh, don't be so pessimistic! It is only an observation, after all."

"Just in case, Kathy, if you wouldn't mind…"

"Very well, Michael. You pop along now—I'm going to get a glimpse of our new home!"

I returned to the main control room. The air was tense with excitement. There, in front was *Proxima b*! Forty trillion kilometres from the place we had all known as home. Four years, one month and five days, as light would have it. But we had made it in three years, ten months and twenty-two days ahead of schedule! Nearly three months early. I looked up at the LED. The time was no longer in hours—there, in red, were the digits, 02:43. I looked in front at the bright speck still forty-three million kilometres away; the LED read 02:35. Jamie, as with every encounter we had faced, was tense. Petra and Anna were totally focussed on their monitors; I'm not even sure they were aware that I had returned to be beside them.

"Two minutes to orbit, Jamie."

"Got it, Petra. Anna?"

"All systems good; readouts and feedback fully functional."

"Angle, Petra?"

"Prograde or retrograde?"

"Which is it to be, Michael? Oh, I forgot, no Michael…"

"I'm here, Jamie."

I saw both women quickly glance towards me; their expressions were those that I had seen eleven days ago. Here I was, kitted up in my final suit and now we all knew it was for real; this was the evidence.

"Well, which would you advise?"

"If you go retrograde, you run a far greater risk of increased friction and possibly ship damage. If you go prograde, then slowdown time will take longer, but you will have a much improved chance of a successful manoeuvre…and survival. But, Jamie, that decision must always rest with you—I can only offer my suggestions."

"As you always have done, my friend, as you always have…done."

I heard Jamie's voice crack with emotion, knowing that this would probably the final time that he would ask my advice about anything.

"Jamie, retrograde or prograde?"

"Prograde, Petra."

"OK…zero-one-six degrees, latitude, zero-one-two…"

"Jamie, are you planning on a polar orbit or equatorial orbit?"

"I had planned on a polar orbit; that way, we will be able to survey and plot the landscape and pick our best place to land when we send down our first expeditionary force. Why, Michael?"

"I personally feel that an equatorial orbit would be more prudent; this way, you will get a break from the solar glare and radiation bursts. Basically, you will reduce your solar contact time by one-half. Polar orbit may cause the ship to overheat from that red-eyed baby out there."

"Jamie?"

"Equatorial orbit, Petra."

"OK…zero-one-six degrees, latitude, zero-two-seven degrees, longitude."

"Anna, data on gravitational pull?"

"1.05G."

"Anna, ask all personnel to secure to the nearest grappling hold; I don't think it will be needed, but just as a security measure."

"Will all personnel please use the nearest grappling hold? This is for safety measures only. All children under ten years old to be hook-secured."

The screen displayed 00:35. I had probably less than thirty minutes in the company of my friends. The euphoria of seeing the voyage of Proxima finally reach its destination, mixed with my despair at leaving, left me in a confused state of mind. I couldn't fully enjoy this moment of elation with them, I was too upset. Jamie held his hands on the plasma burners and I watched his eyes widen with concentration and anticipation.

Proxima b was now visual. A somewhat strange planet to exchange for our own Earth. Looking like Earth with a Mohican haircut, its Goldilocks zone possessed a strip of fertile regions that stretched completely around the circumference, top to bottom. With the planet rotating like our moon and tidally locked, the sun-facing side was parched and barren. The nocturnal side was permanently frozen—hopefully with water. In the middle was a red sun and *Proxima b* was only seven million kilometres from its surface, orbiting every eleven days. At this incredible distance, back in our own solar system, this planet would have not only been burnt to a cinder, it probably would have been part of its solar companion, anyway.

"Jamie…ten…nine…eight…seven…"

With the confidence and calmness he had shown throughout, I watched Jamie's eyes glue onto his monitor, with just a brief glance through the canopy in front; his fingers had already called into action the plasma burners, as I felt them start to hum.

"Three…two…one…contact!"

Jamie knew that if *he* had the angle or the burner power wrong or if Petra had misaligned the coordinates or if Anna had overestimated the G-force of the planet below, then in the blink of an eye, we would be off into the realms of an unknown and hostile cosmos. Worse still, if my assessment had been incorrect, Proxima and the rest of us were headed directly for the red-eyed beast before us. I felt that having come this far, it would have been the ultimate irony to fall at this final hurdle. I looked below as I watched the planet beneath us change from light to dark every half-second. All in the main control room held their breath.

"Planet distance closing in, Jamie! We are spiralling towards *Proxima b*!"

Jamie activated the port side of the starship. At two-second intervals, there was a hum and then silence.

"Planet distance…holding! We are in orbit!"

The roar in the cabin was deafening. Unlike our escape from the solar system, now we were held down by Proxima's centrifuge; this time, we couldn't float around in celebration. These wonderful, wonderful people had created the miracle of the age. They had taken an idea, a hope, a dream, and had created a reality! Only Jamie remained at his post, ensuring that the guidance of our starship remained in a stable orbit; every few seconds turning on the plasma burners to hold us on our course around the planet. Simon, Charlie, Petra and Anna hugged and yelped in unison.

"Folks, don't you think that we should let the rest of the people on board join in?"

Anna came running across, kissing Jamie on the cheek and then looking at me, she stroked my face, kissed me gently on the lips, smiled and whispered:

"*Thank you…*"

Without breaking eye contact, she strolled over to the intercom, looking at me as she reached for the switch:

"Personnel, all personnel, we are in orbit around our new home. You may continue your normal routine…"

She strolled slowly over to me and put her arms around my waist, then gently rested her head on my chest.

"Don't go, Michael—we need you…*I* need you!"

"Anna, I feel the same. The only thing that stopped me making you aware of my feelings was knowing that my time was limited and that would have been unfair…and selfish. Jamie needs a companion—and it would warm my heart to think of you two dear friends being together."

I kissed Anna's hair as it brushed against my lips and held her head where it rested.

"Michael, I have an anomaly in the direction: longitude zero-three-five degrees."

"What kind of 'anomaly', Petra?"

"Starlight in the direction of Centaurus has changed position…one star, HD 117440, has…disappeared!"

"My fate! This must be the blackhole I have come to find!"

My heart was beating so violently. It was a mixture of elation and fear. My apocalypse was in sight! Six years ago, when I had first approached NASA, the idea of finding a blackhole was purely academic; it had not presented me with the palpitations that I was feeling now. An idea, a plan, a strategy, and now…my eternity. I could still choose! But what a choice! My life, for that of the eight billion or so people back home? My life, with a woman that I could love and grow old with. A betrayed friendship? No, I had no choice, and it was that decision, at that moment, that kept me calm.

"Petra, please log in those coordinates into the *Venture*. Any idea of distance?"

"A very wild guess…between two months to one year."

I looked down at Anna and brushed the tear from her eye. I released my hold, but Anna held on tight.

"I have to go, Anna."

Gradually, she let her grip slacken and returned to her seat.

"Jamie?"

"Already, Michael?"

"Almost. One last question though; what is your intention if you find civilisations down there?"

"It never has sensibly been approached. The concept was not seriously discussed at Mission HQ. The priority was the logistics and technology; philanthropy was not too high on the agenda."

"You realise, that if there are civilisations down there, then we are the aliens! It is their home and that home is their birth right; it is not ours to take."

"We will not go down there with guns blazing, Michael, I promise you that. We will need to negotiate, live in harmony, learn from each other—even inter-marry if that is at all possible. But we have not come to destroy or dictate; we have learned that from those last few years on Earth. I will raise that issue when I have my next meeting with the judiciary and people's representative."

I held my hand out to Jamie.

"Godspeed, my friend. May Providence remain with you all."

Anna wept openly and Petra continuously wiped her cheek, as she stifled away the tears welling in her eyes. Jamie got up.

"Simon! Please take over for five minutes. Starboard burners, five per cent, six-second intervals."

"Will do, Jamie."

"Charlie, Simon…bye."

"See you in a bit, Michael. Have a good trip."

"Yeah, see you in a bit, lads…"

We walked down to the airlock. The other side: my waiting transport, *Venture*. Kathy was already there with my helmet. I hugged and kissed Petra and, as with Anna, she did not let go. My heart was pounding…pounding with grief. She relaxed and I reached out to Anna. Even through the suit, I could feel her heart beating, as her body shivered in my grasp.

"Goodbye, my little West Indian companion…"

"Take this with you—and remember me…"

She removed a medallion from around her neck; one that I now remembered that she had worn since we started out four years ago. I had never seen her without it! With shaking hands, I put it around my neck.

"I will wear this and always remember you as long as I live…"

The two women stood to one side, as Jamie and I faced each other.

"There's only two things that I've never liked about you, Jamie."

"Oh? What's that?"

"Your face."

"My face? Oh, my face! Ha, ha, ha…"

I threw my arms around him and we both wept openly and unashamedly.

"Hey! Don't blub on this suit; it'll go rusty!"

"I will never forget you, Michael. You brave, brave, man."

I kept my gaze fixed steadily towards Jamie as Kathy lowered the helmet over my head. As she secured it down around my neck, I looked for the final time at my companions, the last humans ever and gave them a thumbs-up. I walked towards the hatch, which opened with a swish and then closed. I was alone.

Chapter 40

In the early-morning dew, Mai and I had strolled up to 'our' tree. Knowing that her mother had another heavy day with the laundry, we made our way back to start the day's work with her. We went inside, but something seemed wrong. Mai's mother was not at home and things seemed to have been left somewhat haphazardly.

"Mother? Mother?"

We searched around the house, but neither of her parents was at home.

"Michael! I think something is wrong! Mother is always at home, or if she isn't, then she would have told me."

"Perhaps something happened that your mother needed to attend to. Perhaps she has had to go and fetch or deliver some laundry?"

"Yes, yes, you are probably right. I just can't help worrying…"

When Mai's mother had not returned by lunch, Mai could contain herself no longer.

"Michael! There is something definitely wrong. Father isn't here either… I know he has to work, but something is wrong—I sense it!"

I sensed it too; in fact, I had sensed it from the outset, just like Mai, but we had lied to each other just to keep the hurt and panic away.

"Mai, wait here. I shall find Michel and if he cannot help, I shall search around the town; but please, wait here. Promise?"

"Promise."

Within a thought, I was beside Michel. He was in his library sat at his desk with quill, ink and paper.

"Michel!"

"Michael! What have you done to this old body of mine, eh? You're not back to borrow it again—I don't think it could cope. Ha, ha… You seem a bit troubled, what ails you?"

"The reason that I am here is because Mai's mother has not returned home and Mai is very worried that some ill has come to her. I wondered whether you may know or have heard of some incident around town that may have caused her to be delayed?"

"No, none! But it did occur to me at the time…and now that you mention this incident, it does occur to me again… I suppose the church will not have taken kindly to the fiscal loss that they may have just discovered."

"No, certainly not, but how could they possibly—Oh! Mai and her mother were present when the chest was removed from the tabernacle! Mai's mother distracted the priest with a pretend confession! Surely not…"

Without even thinking, I had left Nostradamus and was in the cathedral. Wan was bound by her wrists and was on her knees before the priest.

"Tell me, woman, why did you steal the property of the church?"

"I have stolen no property of the church, Father."

"But I know that you did! You came in here and confessed to me that you stole from the church, did you not?"

"That is true, but you gave me absolution. Surely, once given, it cannot be retracted?"

"Yes, that sin has been forgiven, but now you have stolen more church property! You were here when His house was violated by your lust for wealth. *Thou shalt not steal; thou shall bear no false witness*; you have broken His commandments and I demand retribution in His name!"

"If that original sin has been forgiven, Father, then I repeat—I have stolen no church property."

"Liar! Take her to the magistrate immediately! He will see justice done!"

Within a thought, I was back beside Mai. She had busied herself with the laundry that Mai's mother had left, but I could tell from her countenance that she was worried.

"Mai?"

"Oh Michael! What news?"

"Mai, please sit—"

"No! Michael, tell me what has become of my mother?"

"She has been taken by the priest to the magistrate. He accuses her of stealing the chest, though your mother denies it."

"No! Mother is no liar, Michael. She has always told the truth. She helped *me* steal the chest. It was *me* that stole from the church. It is *me* that should stand accused!"

"Mai, your mother did tell the truth!"

"But you told me that she denied stealing the chest—that is not the truth!"

"The priest accused her of stealing church property. Don't you see, she didn't steal church property, it was not the church's property! It was the people's! She has told no lie!"

At that moment, Mai's father walked in.

"Wan! Wan? I'm back. Mai! Why the tears?"

"Father! Mother has been taken by the priest to the magistrate for stealing the money that Michael needed!"

"What! No! Tell me this is not true?"

"Michael has just witnessed it, Father. It was he who just told me…"

"Where is he?"

"I am here. It is true, she has been taken. She denies stealing the property of the church, which is true. But the priest will not hear of testimonies contradicting

what he accuses her of. He is sinful, he is dishonest, he is hypocritical, but he is a man of the cloth and no magistrate will find against him. She will be convicted, but I know not what the sentence shall be."

"Mai, I must away to the magistrate now!"

"And I too, Father!"

Though I could have travelled in an instant, I stayed with Mai and her father as they rushed through the streets to the courthouse. As they entered, the crowd that had gathered inside gave vent to their detest of the man of the cloth, who was once again demanding 'justice' of another innocent victim of his greed and corruption.

"This court finds the accused guilty as charged. Theft from the house of God demands the maximum penalty. For violation of His Holy place of worship, you will burn forever in the fires of Hell—those fires start here and will continue into your damnation—"

"NO! SHE DID NOT STEAL… IT WAS ME!"

"Mai! No! No!"

"I took from the church the property that was never theirs! Property that they took from the innocent people of this town in His name! It is that man there—that hypocritical, sinful man who preaches the word of God but practices the deeds of the devil! It is he who should be burning at the stake, not us, the guiltless victims of your obscene faith—!"

"Guards! Arrest that girl!"

Mai was immediately held firmly by two armed guards and led into the dungeon. She did not struggle; in fact, I felt that she somehow seemed content. My whole being was in turmoil; what could I do?

"Father?"

"Well, the girl confessed… You all heard her! It will be she who will carry the sins of the unrighteous into Hell. You can let this woman go—"

"—No…no…no… Leave my daughter, you fiends; take me if you need someone to punish…do you hear, TAKE ME!"

But the court paid no heed to her pleas. They needed a culprit, that's all they needed and they had one. Mai's mother was in shock and lay trembling and weeping on the floor. Slowly, she staggered to her feet. She had been beaten and the welts on her back were visible evidence of the cruel practices of the church when wishing to obtain confessions of guilt. So many before, and so many still to come, had the 'truth' extracted from them by such means. Wan's husband ran to her side and held her firmly, as she found neither the strength nor the will to continue. Her daughter, her beautiful and only child, was going to be inhumanly and barbarically destroyed by the most unholy of syndicates that had ever walked on the face of this Earth. I couldn't even communicate with them and, though psychic, Wan would not have been receptive to me now anyway.

In despair, I made my way to the dungeon. Barely a few hours ago, we had been in one another's embrace, talking of love eternal, and now I found Mai sprawled on the floor in the filth of this cess pit. Her sobbing was audible, but yet there was a stoicism about her.

"Mai!"

"Michael?"

"Mai, I am so sorry. Will you ever be able to forgive me? I have brought this on you and your family. I have dragged you into the abyss and only ever brought you misery and hopelessness."

She looked up at me with those mesmeric, ebony eyes. In the filth that she had just been thrown, her beauty stood out like a beacon. A ray of sun shone through the narrow slit in the wall and radiated on her wonderful face. Tears stained her face, which I had once caressed and kissed with the lips of a mortal. And yet that fortitude, that bravery, that resoluteness of this courageous girl was shining brighter than any sunlight ever could. She held out her trembling hand towards my face. I moved closer and felt that sensation of her touch on my spirit. She smiled!

"Michael, don't you see? We have been blessed. The spirits have taken us and blessed us. Our lives could not have carried on in this way. We were given a time to feel like mortals in love just once, and that was an exquisiteness I will always hold dear to me. But, even more than this, we have now been allowed to be together...for eternity. Our sacrifices must have been great enough for them to have granted us this final time to be as one. I am frightened of the pain, but I am so wanting to be with you, forever."

"Oh Mai, my sweet, darling Mai. I cannot believe how you can be so brave and yet, kind and beautiful...and...and...and I just do not know what I have done to deserve you; adorable, wonderful, you! Yes, yes, you are right, we have been blessed...I have been blessed! Perhaps our purpose in life has been achieved, our mission accomplished, and now we can have everlasting peace, joy, happiness— until the Great Spirit judges otherwise."

"Michael, will you stay with me, please? I am frightened of the pain that I will suffer."

"I'm going nowhere. I shall burn with you in those flames; that fire will be our flames of love; Mai, we are to be together! I will shield you from the pain of that transition, just as I—Mai! I also *died* for love! I have remembered! I died for the love of mankind! I died for my fellow man! I was facing a formidable force that was to take me...? Take me...through time and to here... I was destined to come here, to you, to Nostradamus. And my mission has been completed! You are my reward; you are my blessing...it had to be...it just had to be...!"

"You died for your love of Man? You travelled through time to be here...with me? I was part of this plan?"

"Mai, I don't know whether you were intended to be part of this plan—I don't think so, it was a coincidence...a very lucky coincidence—but the pivotal part of this plan was Nostradamus. I now know that I came here to try and stop Man destroying himself...of that I am certain. My life during my mortal existence is still very patchy, but the snippets that I can recall have directed me

275

to this conclusion. During my trance, when I possessed LeMartre's body, I heard the voice of Michel and for every question that he asked I was able to reply with preciseness. I was unable to delve further into my past and myself; I could only respond directly to the information that he sought. I was able to guide him but the real me, the reason for my travelling through time to be here, that was withheld; and *that* was the main reason that I wanted to possess him—I wanted to discover me."

"But you have discovered me!"

"Yes! Oh, yes! Perhaps 'me' is not as important after all! Upon reflection, Mai, given the choice between the two of us, the answer is simple. I would choose you every time!"

Mai nestled up close to me by the wall and I embraced her. Her fear seemed now to have abated and she closed her eyes. Laying there in the sparse light of the dungeon, we comforted each other knowing that this would be the last time we would never be able to hold and touch. Tomorrow would bring the new light of day—a new dawn and a new life for us. As I rested there, I surmised that Wan and Mai's father would be distraught. Their lives would now be in tatters as their cherished daughter was to be so cruelly taken from them. I wanted to go and comfort them too, but I could not leave Mai—hers was a punishment that I would not allow her to face alone. I looked down and saw my love asleep. She only had to face a few moments of anguish and then eternity awaited us. I saw her dreams as she lay before me. Dreams of peace and love and joy; of us together, riding a never-ending rainbow where the colours of light were interspersed with the colours of the spectrum, in a joyous sunrise. I could feel her dreams and it brought joy to my very soul. How mundane, I thought, the life of mortality is, when we only had to imagine and it was so. I remembered how Mai had seen me visibly change into a form of horror when my thoughts became dark. I understood now that I only had to think and there I was. When Mai would be with me forever, we would live in our world of thoughts! We would create our own heaven, together! Every colour conceivable would be ours to create and twist and turn in every tangible and intangible form. We would raise children of colour and forms filled with laughter and joy…this was eternity…this was our paradise!

Chapter 41

"Michael, the airlock has been sealed and the main hatch now opened. You are clear to leave."

"Thanks, Simon. Here we go…"

I depressed the burners' control slowly and effortlessly, *Venture* rose up.

"Middle of the room, Michael…good…hold!"

The space shuttle hovered exactly in the middle of the room, some thirty metres from the floor.

"OK, front and port burner together…slowly…wait until you are almost facing the open hatch at the end of the runway… Stop! Starboard burner five per cent… Stop!"

Venture faced the black void before me. The only discomforting sensation was Proxima rotating to hold on to her gravity and I was rotating with her. In front, the abyss was turning, but it was just a mass of blurred light intermingled with the black beyond.

"OK, Michael. You now need to stabilise *Venture*. Do not look down or at the frame of the ship. Look directly ahead."

"Simon, that's difficult! Everything is turning; it's like I am drunk…and I think I want to be sick!"

"OK, look at the floor of the ship. Good…nausea passed?"

"Yes, just."

"Right, now which way was Proxima turning?"

"Anti-clockwise."

"OK, you are laterally stable, so you don't need to touch those controls. Now, you need to activate the port base and starboard top burners together…but slowly. As you do so, Proxima will start to rotate as you counteract her rotation; you are, and will remain, independent of her gravity at your current lateral position. As you rotate, wait until the sensation becomes too great and *then* look straight ahead. In front, the cosmos will still be rotating, but much slower. As you continue to activate those top and base burners, your rotation will eventually stop; keep looking straight ahead! Do not look down!"

"OK, Simon, here we go!"

"Keep listening to my voice, Michael. Port base and starboard top burners…gently, gently…good. You are speeding up. As you see the cosmos stabilise, you must reverse the process, otherwise you will turn the other way. How do you feel?"

"OK, but Proxima is starting to turn too fast now!"

"OK, look ahead…focus on the cosmos before you! Is it turning as fast?"

"No, it's almost bearable…getting better… Yes, I can cope with this."

"Right, reverse starboard and port burners…gently…stop…gently…stop. It's now up to you to finalise your stability."

The void in front was turning very, very slowly, but within ten minutes, I had mastered the port and starboard controls. I was still aware of Proxima rotating, but by focusing ahead, I could concentrate without feeling nauseous. The temptation to look down became overwhelming—like a moth attracted to the light and I knew that I had to escape through the opening at the far end.

"Michael, you now need to edge forward. Use your forward thrusters and ignore the rotating frame of the ship."

Venture was a pleasure to manipulate. I inched her out of the main hatch exactly as Simon instructed me. As I eased her into the blurry blackness of space, I used the backward thrusters to hold me at a constant distance from Proxima.

"Simon, thank you. I think that I'm OK now."

"Godspeed, Michael, see you later."

"Yeah, see you, Simon."

"Michael, we have started our descent. Speed is still warp-drive factor one-point zero-five. You will see us drop slowly beneath you."

"OK, Petra, thanks. Look, I don't think that I will be in contact with you as long as I thought. We are still travelling in unison, but as soon as I leave this orbit, we will no longer be able to communicate. So, I need you to keep this channel and this frequency open well into the next two years. Hopefully, my transmitted signals will reach you…eventually."

"OK."

"I will transmit once every day during my wakening time and record speed, light distortion and any other anomalies to get an idea of the blackhole location and effect. *Venture* will continue to despatch all technical information. I trust you to do the rest. I mean, NASA won't get this information for nearly five years if that greedy black monster is as far as you think it might be."

"Will do. God bless, Michael."

"God bless, Petra."

I watched Proxima drop slowly. Knowing the size of her, I began to appreciate the distance that now separated us. Even after ten minutes, she was still clearly visible, silhouetted before *Proxima b* below. Though we were still travelling at the same speed, her shorter trajectory around the planet had edged her forward slightly. I didn't want to press the orbital escape burners, but I knew that I had to.

'Goodbye, my friends' was the last message Proxima heard from me.

That difficult decision and the manoeuvre finally made, I looked back but there was nothing to be seen but a speck of bright red light. Petra had programmed the coordinates of the space-time warp and the shuttle was running on automatic pilot. Away from orbit, stars again took on the sharpness that we had been used to during the past four years. Carbon dioxide and oxygen levels were kept perfectly in balance and I programmed my sleep schedule for eighteen hours per day. Just in front, on the floor, was my euthanasia package. I was no longer frightened or upset, those moments were behind me. I was getting excited, though, at the prospect to witness a blackhole as close as it would permit me to do.

I had asked Simon to set me up an exercise machine and allotted myself a daily one-hour isometric routine. Perhaps it was because there was nothing else to do, but I extended my exercising up to two hours per day and logged my observations and data recordings into a shorter time agenda. I felt as though I was being steered by the hand of God at times; as though this vast emptiness was His playground and He was directing me onwards, like He had done with Moses. And, like with Moses, He was toying with me, testing me, finding the limit of my mettle. But I, like Moses, was determined to endure any test He placed before me. Then I realised I was pitting myself against God! In this vastness, emptiness, loneliness, if there was an omnipotent Being, I was considering myself His equal—someone to do battle with Him! I needed to combat this sense of isolation and the effect that it was inevitably having on my sanity.

I found I had started to talk to myself; telling myself out loud what I needed to do next and then having dialogue about whether I should exercise again, or if I hadn't yet exercised, or whether I should exercise at all. I knew at this stage— though it had obviously been latent weeks before—that all that I was experiencing had to be despatched back to Petra. They needed the psychological and physiological effects of my loneliness as well as the technical data I was sending back. I needed action; I needed something to occupy my mind. Luckily, the hand of God at last intervened. The mettle was forged.

"Venture to Proxima. Two months and fifteen days from separation. Speed has, to current date, remained constant at warp-drive factor one-point-zero-five. Today, directing towards constellation Centaurus within location of triple-star system, speed has increased to warp-drive factor one-point-zero-six…and is rising. Outside temperature was at negative two-seven-one degrees but has risen to negative two-six-five degrees; inside temperature remains constant at two-zero degrees. External visual observations indicate starlight is distorting and star HD 117440 has reappeared. This suggests that there could be a blackhole immediately to port as I can now receive light from this star. I am applying starboard burners to direct me to port."

I held onto the burner switch for five seconds and repeated this three times. I now felt that I needed to return to sleep mode as although I had to record the data as it happened, I also needed to be alert for the more crucial moments as I got closer. I awoke eighteen hours later and was immediately sensitive to some significant changes.

"Venture to Proxima. Two months and sixteen days from separation. Speed has increased to warp-drive factor one-point-one-two. Outside temperature is now at negative one-five-one degrees, inside temperature remains constant at two-zero degrees. External visual observations indicate starlight is distorting more intensely and starlight colours are becoming rainbow in appearance. I am leaving Venture on current course but I have a feeling that I may be too late to change anyway, even if I wanted to."

I was now getting really excited. I had to force myself to settle down to sleep but set a warning alarm based on internal temperature. I now placed on my head the ear-set, reminding me who I was, my motive, my contact and the year I wanted to travel to. I just prayed that this repeated information would be fed into and held in my consciousness once I had passed beyond this dimension of life. I fell into a restless sleep and kept seeing images of an old man stooping over a crystal ball. I was awoken before my allotted time to the sound of the temperature sensor. I looked up and saw that it was now reading twenty-nine degrees.

"Venture to Proxima. Two months and seventeen days from separation. Speed has increased to warp-drive factor one-point-three-five. Outside temperature is now at positive one-two-one degrees; inside temperature has now risen to two-nine degrees. External observations now show a distinctive hazy vortex. All starlight appearances are merging into one giant light source of varying shades and colours. Slight turbulence is now being felt. I have decided to reduce sleep pattern to two-hour intervals. Will contact now every awakening moment, leaving transmission open."

"Venture to Proxima. Speed is now warp-drive factor one-point-eight-three. Outside temperature is two-zero-three degrees; inside temperature is now recording three-eight degrees. I shall not be requiring any more sleep mode. Data change is now constant. Outside visual is amazing. All the starlights are converging into one. It is as if I am under a giant coloured magnifying glass. The brightness has become too much and I feel that I will damage my cornea if I look directly into the combined light. At home, I used to wonder what it would be like standing in a rainbow and looking up and this is exactly what I imagined. But the brightness I had imagined was a passive, gentle affair; this is turbulent and intense. I hope I can make warp-drive factor two before I decide to reach for my sleeping pack. On the far horizon, the electric, or perhaps even ionic, discharge is continuous and appears to be crescent-shaped. I am now feeling gravitational pull and it has started to become uncomfortable. I need to have everything ready by my side in case I cannot soon move. I also need to allow time for the information in my headset to be fed to my mind, so I must not evaporate too early. If I can see warp-drive factor two, I shall start euthanasia procedure. Proxima! Please note…I have just witnessed expulsion of intense radiation from the distance! Is this the Hawking radiation? But surely, that only occurs when two blackholes combine, or does it! Readings on board Venture have registered extreme outbursts from that location with temperatures exceeding one hundred billion degrees. X-rays and gamma rays are being detected, *but* their energies are being increased and altered beyond anything ever recorded…or known! These are not in the electromagnetic spectrum as we understand it! In fact, it appears as though all electromagnetic transmissions are being drawn together: radio, infrared, light, ultraviolet, X-rays, gamma rays—everything! Am I witnessing anti-matter before me? Or am I witnessing pure energy being created…as must have happened at the beginning of time? It is like a giant energetic torch radiating across the cosmos. Is it possible that a blackhole can only take so much material before it, too, has to defecate!

"My speech has started to slur, the frequency of my voice is rising, like breathing…helium. If it wasn't painful, it would make me la…laugh. I can feel a turbulence—a violent turbulence! Am I now … now with…in a storm … of gravitational…waves? Warp-drive factor two-point-zero-one! Twice th…the speed o…f light! Headset o…n. Introducing triplicate dri…p feed. Have set th…e phials to … No! I will only t…ake two phials—thio…pental and the …n-pavu…lon. Have dec…id…ed not to com…plete card…ia…c arrest—will le…t that m… onst… er in fro… nt… do… tha… t. Goo… d… bye… my… fr… ie… nds…"

Chapter 42

The rays of the new day pierced through the narrow slit in the wall. Mai lay with her head resting against me, our fingers interlocked.

'Be brave, my love, be brave.'

She stirred and slowly opened her eyes. Looking at me, she smiled.

"Is it time?"

"Soon, Mai…not yet. They still need to fill their bellies!"

"If only I could see Mother and Father one last time."

"They will be there, Mai; you can say what you want from there. That vile man cannot stop you speaking, even as he takes your life, he will not take your spirit."

"Michael, what shall we do tomorrow?"

"Tomorrow! Why, the world is ours tomorrow! Have you ever ridden a rainbow?"

"A rainbow! No, never!"

"Have you ever soared into the sky, like an eagle?"

Mai laughed. "No, never!"

"Then that's what we shall do tomorrow. Tomorrow, Mai, we shall do whatever you want to do! Shall we haunt that vile priest?"

"Yes, yes, that will be fun, to make him run from us! I would like that…but that would be revenge, not justice…"

"He will get his comeuppance, Mai, of that I am sure. No God of mercy will allow his foulness to continue."

"But, Michael, I must contact Mother and Father—they will be devastated!"

"What is it to be first, Mai—Mother and Father or rainbow riding?"

"Mother and Father… And we must stay with them as long as they need and want me, promise me that?"

"Mai, the choice and the world will be yours. We will stay with your parents, but perhaps in between, we can soar with the eagles?"

"Oh, darling, I am so looking forward to us being together. I just can't wait! I could never believe that such a heaven was waiting for me and it is just around the corner."

Outside, I could sense the preparation of the pyre as I heard sticks and bundles of wood being dragged across the rough ground. I think Mai heard it, but she showed no sign of fear. Who would be that Master Executioner? It wouldn't be the priest—he needed others to perform his profane deeds. He would stand with his head erect and declare from the scaffold that this young innocent victim before the people was a sorceress in league with the devil, who stole from the house of God to practice her evil and heretical Arts. He would fabricate all manner of lies just to justify his satisfaction, his craving, for controlling the lives of those too afraid to speak out. Most knew that his were false accusations but it was fear that kept them in obedience.

"Mai, can you hear the birds?"

Mai strained her ears, then smiled. "Just…they are very faint, but just."

"Tomorrow, we shall sing with them. We will join in the dawn chorus and sing! We will watch the sun rise and—"

"—But what if it is raining?"

"Mai, it will rain only if you want it to rain! You will create your own dawn every day! The sun will rise, the sun will set. We shall watch all the glorious colours of dawn spread across the sky and at dusk, we will watch the sun disappear in an array of colours—the reds and blues and greens—all the colours—"

"—Of the rainbow!"

"Yes, of the rainbow."

"And *then* go riding!"

"And *then* go riding!"

Keys rattled in the heavy wooden door keeping Mai from her fate. Two burly dishevelled soldiers came across to her, lifting her roughly off the floor. Force was unnecessary, Mai was a willing martyr, but they still dragged her out of her cage. Outside, the priest was standing. He spat in her face.

"You will burn, witch! Burn in the fires of Hell!"

The soldiers pulled her outside and up to the waiting pyre. There was no shouting and jeering from the crowd. Instead, the mood was that of resignation and they looked on with elegiac eyes to this brave young girl who had stood up to the corrupt establishment. The priest mounted the scaffold and faced the crowd, as Mai was bound by the post pinnacling the staves beneath her.

"This witch has confessed to the most abominable crime—theft from the house of God—taking gold and money that she was going to use for her Black Arts. The church has no place for these servants of Satan…and they will be vanquished and sent to that fiery pit. This witch, as beautiful as she seems, is an artful sorceress; beneath this façade of beauty lies a hideous goblin, most foul. She will no longer share the air we breathe nor steal the food from our plates nor poison our minds with her debauchery and lies. Frogs, toads and serpents have been seen paying homage to her as she cast her spells of pestilence and ills. Witnesses have heard her summoning that black death to our city…but no more, I say! This witch will burn…and her soul shall perish in these fires of God!"

The priest was greeted with total silence. There was unrest amongst the people; a quiet, but growing anger against the institution and its representative standing before them. The priest descended from the scaffold and nodded to the hooded executioner. Lighting his torch, he walked up to the staves before him. Looking up at Mai, ragged and dirty from the harsh treatment during her confinement, he saw, as had the others present, an innocent victim of the cruel and unjust times of the era. He hesitated, unsure what was to be his fate in the eyes of God, before pushing the lit torch into the woodpile before him.

"MAI!"

"Mother… Father… Where are you?"

"Here, Mai!"

Looking on at the back of the crowd, Mai saw her parents through the rising smoke, openly weeping.

"Mother, Father, do not weep, please! I have only a few seconds of pain and then I will be with Michael—forever. He is here; he is giving me strength and love…and oh, I so wish that I could share him with you."

"Mai, I see him; he is smiling back and comforting us, as only he can."

The smoke rose higher and Mai started to choke. Her appearance was filthy, unkempt, sooty, and her hair—that beautiful, raven-black hair was knotted with the dirt and excrement of the dungeon floor. But as I looked into her eyes, those God-made ebony eyes, I only saw beauty—her beauty, her wonderful, shining spirit. This courageous young woman before me should have been standing in a royal palace, not here on a burning pyre. The flames started to penetrate through to her skirt.

"Mother… Father… Michael has promised… We…will…we…will…be with…you. Watch…for…us. We…might be…riding…a…rainbow… AHHHHH!"

Her scream of pain echoed throughout the courtyard as the flames seared her flesh.

I took hold of Mai and looked into her eyes. These eyes of love, now filled with pain.

"Mai, I love you…look into my eyes."

I held her as she gazed towards me and placed my mouth over hers. Our lips met. The open scream was silent as she pushed her lips to mine. The burnt rope dropped into the flames and with free hands, she wrapped them around my waiting and eager form. It was a kiss that would last a lifetime, for a lifetime is what we now had.

"Michael! I can feel you…I can touch you…I feel no pain! Michael, I love you…thank you…thank you."

Some people in the crowd fainted. Many swore that they could see two people enveloped in the flames, embracing like two lovers in a myriad of colours with their arms entwined around each other. The priest only saw the charred form of a young girl on a burning pyre.

Chapter 43

"Father, I need to make a confession before you and God."

"I have a few moments; come, I will hear your confession."

The priest led the man to the confessional and drew the curtain across the entrance.

"Father, forgive me, for I have sinned."

"What is your sin, my son?"

"I have thoughts of killing a man, Father."

"Killing a man…that is a serious confession to make before God. Why do you want to kill a man?"

"He took my child and murdered her, Father."

"Children are the innocent and any man who takes the life of a child deserves to be punished."

"Then I am forgiven, Father?"

"If, as you say, the victim was a child…an innocent child…and this man brutally took her life, then in the eyes of God, you may be forgiven for your *thoughts* of revenge. But forget not, it is written: 'vengeance is mine, sayeth the Lord.'"

"And mine…!"

The priest looked on wide-eyed as the dagger plunged into his neck. The last thing he saw was the man with the olive skin leave the confessional.

In the palace, Queen Catherine handed to her trusted Chancellor a chest containing parchments stamped with the royal seal alongside another seal, less well-known. Her trusted official accepted the documents and with a respectful bow, left the court and made his way back to the chancellery. A recent addition to the office was a young man of impeccable character and references. It was he who was given charge of the 'quatrains of the future of Man'.

"These are from Her Majesty, Queen Catherine, and are to be guarded with your life!"

"Yes sir."

"They must be secured, sealed and no one, not even the king himself, must have access to them."

"Then who is to open them; who has the authority?"

"That is not for you to know. See the dates stamped upon each parchment?"

"Yes sir."

"The first date is when…?"

"1605."

"Right. You will secure that parchment in a strongbox in the chancellery. Into that box you will lay underneath the date, place and key for the opening of the second box. Likewise, for the next box and so on; it will be like a treasure hunt. When you have completed your task, bring to me the plan of the location of the first box."

"Yes sir."

The assistant took the chest containing all the parchments to the basement in the chancellery. The room itself was like a fortress, with solid walls, two heavy oak doors and a grill through two openings in the wall, allowing light to penetrate the room. Placing the parchments down on the heavy solid walnut table, the assistant went over to the fireplace and placed a couple of logs on a fading fire. Blowing into the embers, the dried wood soon took and brought both light and warmth to the room. Standing up, he turned and there, before him, was a man in a cloak that he had not seen enter the room.

"Can I help you?"

"Yes, I have come from Queen Catherine. She would like you to return the parchments to the palace. She has decided on another secure location for those testaments."

"You have her sealed authority?"

"Yes, here it is..."

The assistant felt the cold steel enter his abdomen as he looked with shock and pain at his assailant before him.

"Why? Who...are...you...?"

"I have come a long way for those papers...the name is Karl Guttenberg."

The name meant nothing to the dying man on the floor; it meant more to the future of mankind, though.

Karl Guttenberg lifted the chest containing the prophecies and poured them out onto the floor in front of the now roaring fire. With hand outstretched, he sneered: "To the destiny of Man!"

"Take that man!"

The red guards rushed into the room and seized LeMartre's body from the fireplace, dragging him up to his feet.

"What is your name?"

"Karl Guttenberg..."

But somehow, the eyes looked absent, distant...as though he were in a trance.

"Take him to the Queen; he has some answering to do before he is executed."

LeMartre would never use his body again.

Flames licked precariously close to the parchments scattered in front of the fire. Outside, the wind had picked up in ferocity. A blazing log started to fall as its centre of gravity changed. As it burned, the flames blew this way, then that way, then...